Providence Pond

A Novel by
Beresford McLean

Providence Pond
A novel by Beresford McLean
Anancybooks

Further Information:
For additional information about the author Beresford McLean or his books, please make contact at the following:

Anancybooks.com
PO Box 28677
San Jose, CA 95159-8677
Phone: 408-286-0726
Fax: 408-947-0668
Email: info@anancybooks.com
URL: www.anancybooks.com

ISBN: 0-9753297-1-5
Library of Congress Control Number: 2005933526

    1. Author 2. Title 3. Inspirational Folklore
    4. Magical Realism 5. Historical Fiction

Providence Pond is dedicated to my parents and to all the ancestors who left pieces of this story everywhere, guiding me to find them, so that we could tell this tale together.

Contents

Part 1: The Engagement

(1880 to 1899)

A Simple Dare

Love brought the women together again, bonding them forever in life as it would in death. Yet, as they sat at supper in the tavern that evening, they didn't know. How could they have known? Another meal was finished, but the real substance of their lives was just set to unfold.

With her open palms pressed firmly against the edge of the table, Nweka – or more correctly, Afia, for so her parents named her – pushed her chair backwards and sat upright, signifying that, for her, supper was over. As she raised her head, her long, plaited braids swung delicately, framing her dainty, black face.

Esi, her dearest friend, remained arched over the table, announcing that once again she had been deeply engaged in thought. She raised her eyes sufficiently to meet Afia's and, with a quaint smile, reestablished rapport with her. Afia, Friday's child, looked at her friend's light complexion and her soft, gentle eyes beneath wide-arching brows. She smiled once more in appreciation of Esi's kindness, her support, and enduring friendship.

The last rays of the aging sun cascaded over the rugged greenery of the Jamaican hilltops, gilding Afia's curly hair and a side of her face, reminding Esi just how beautiful her friend was.

Afia, avoiding the glare of sunlight, looked around the room, admiring the things that were so familiar to her. Where an old pulpit once stood, men and women sang old, sad slave-songs, alternating with more joyous, richly harmonized folk music. Their instruments were all homemade: the bass, funde and akate drums, banjos, bamboo-fifes, conch-shell horns, whistles, tambourines and scrapers. The musicians played and sang above the heavy chatter of the smoke-filled tavern.

That bucolic tavern had recently become a second home for Afia; and it held her sympathy, if not her sadness. It knew her plight – her loneliness and frustration – that her husband had mysteriously vanished not only from her but also from Providence. Afia looked around at the faces she knew. They seemed to reach out to her, signaling that her solitude – her loss and grief – was theirs as well. Afia acknowledged the empathic gestures with a wry smile as her tears flowed. Knowing her sorrow might grow to despair and anger, Afia stiffened her spine. She lifted her head once more, as if raising herself up, and focused her eyes on the dais. The lead drummer, Byah, nodding at her as he smiled, increased the tempo of his drumming and brought more dancing and merriment to the house.

Esi, imitating Afia, looked around, to see the belly of the ancient, rustic building and an aged, wood-carved Jamaica wafting in the air like an island. Wires held it suspended from the rafters. Esi scanned the artistic relief, searching for Providence Pond in western St. Mary where they sat. Satisfied that she had found their location, Esi changed her focus, observing the bodies of the other patrons unknowingly absorb the music's rhythm. She found the melody relaxing and hoped that it had so touched her friend, calming her unsettled soul.

Esi had chosen the supper that Afia liked best: dukunu, a spiced corn cake served with a steaming portion of the stewed spinach-like vegetable, callalou, and flavored sour-sop juice. That, Afia's first meal of the day, brought solace and hope to Esi.

She soon found Afia's eyes, this time searching for hers. Esi asked, "How do you think things really happen, Afia?"

"I wouldn't presume to know, Esi. Some say it's by chance. Others say it's by destiny."

"Maybe they are both right, Afia. But I would feel so much better knowing that things happen by a plan, in a determined way."

"Yes. But I wonder, what would be the plan in my case, Esi? No one seems to know. Or if they know, they are not telling. But I need to know, Esi! Bem is my husband. I want to understand what happened to him," Afia said, shaking her raised, open arms as if pleading for help.

"You are right, Afia. Bem could have said something. He could have at least said good-bye. Or, now that he is gone, write a letter, take a horse or pram and return home. Anything!"

"So frustrating . . . just meaningless!" Afia said with a bitter grimace.

"Ah, Afia!" Esi sighed, "I just wish I could have been here for you . . . it's all so strange."

"Yes, it's such a strange, vexing thing to have happened, Esi. I feel so sad!" Her eyes welled almost to tears again as she listlessly threw herself on the table.

"Oh Afia, Afia. I feel worried for you, too," Esi said, reaching out for her friend's hand. "We have been talking about this all day, and we came here thinking that this outing would enliven you."

"You have done a lot for me, Esi. And you know, I will not let this get me down. Since no one will tell me, I will find Bem myself!" Afia said, bringing her resolute fist down on the table. "I will find him!" she repeated with a determined grimace.

The women were referring to Bem Covey's bizarre disappearance on his wedding night. On that day two weeks before, Bem and Afia had said their vows; then Bem left the ceremonial hall and had not been seen since. From that time, Afia had taken comfort from Esi, her best friend.

Afia's recent marriage to Bem had moved her from her small farming town of Oxford where she lived with her parents, Mr. and Mrs. Edward McCracam, to Providence, Bem's domicile. Esi's hometown, Free Hill, and the village of Oxford were adjacent to each other. Both were large farming estates in the fertile foothills of western St. Mary. Even though these communities were only about nine miles from Providence, this fateful time was Esi's first trip. It was Afia's move there that gave Esi her initial reason for visiting Providence. Until then, Afia and, to a lesser extent, Bem were the only ones Esi knew in Providence.

The women had spent the earlier part of the day at Afia's home where Mr. Covey, Bem's father, had graciously taken Afia and seen to her comfort soon after Bem had vanished. This he did without leaving any indications of his son's whereabouts, even though Bem had asked him to and did receive his father's ardent promise that he would. Mr. Covey never intended to keep that promise. Rather, the elder Covey seemed so distraught about his son's disappearance and Afia's grief that Afia's attention was drawn more to his sorrow than to her own. Afia, however, did manage to extract from Mr. Covey his promise of letting her know of Bem's whereabouts as soon as he knew. His pledge, regardless of Afia's later pleadings, remained unfulfilled.

As she sat in the tavern, Esi remembered the story of Mr. Covey's pain just as Afia had recounted it and, looking up at her friend's troubled face, said, "Yes, Afia. This is indeed strange. It's stranger still that not even Mr. Covey knows about his own son! Bem could have found a way to contact you. He certainly could have! But you know what?"

"Just tell me, Esi!"

"Maybe it's chance, maybe it's fate. Anyway, life has to go on." Esi sighed and sat up, looking askance at the billows of night-clouds shading the valley. "It's beginning to get a little dark outside, and we have a long walk home. Don't you think it's time for us to leave?"

"Yes, Esi. It is. I know you do not like the dark," Afia teased her friend.

Having spent the day in Bem Covey's — or rather, Afia's — house, the young women had planned to have supper at the *Any Questions* tavern, then walk back to Afia's and there pass the night playing cards and swapping stories of times past.

Afia beckoned to the proprietor to make her payment. He saw and acknowledged her call. The proprietor, Puncus St. John, also the head and only waiter, however, replaced the food that was intended for yet another table in the kitchen and mounted the podium to join Byah, his mute and lead drummer, and his other musicians. The music had so enticed him that Puncus could not resist dancing a few steps of his favorite quadrille while shaking maracas in his wide, outstretched arms. The broad, open smile on his bobbing, sweaty face told of his deep pleasure. Byah drummed harder and faster, sweating as he did. With his eyes closed and his entire body pulsing, he seemed lost to the place where he played, whispering only to the Great Spirit. When St. John was quite sure he had not lost his timing, he danced his way back into the kitchen and restarted the delayed service.

In the meantime, either out of habit or duty, Esi scraped the banana leaves in which the dukunu had been steamed and served, onto a dish. She then stacked the crockery at the end of the table. With her bare hands, Esi began brushing away crumbs and straightening out the tablecloth.

"Leave the tie-a-leaf alone, Esi!" Afia said as she motioned again for the bill. "He makes me so mad, sometimes. I just feel like pulling him over here by the collar," Afia continued as she demonstrated by tugging her own collar and bearing her incisors.

"Why, Afia? It's nothing! And how can you still be so agitated?" Esi asked, sharing the laughter.

"This thing with Bem is really gnawing my insides out, Esi," Afia said, throwing her arms up, then letting them fall lifelessly on her lap.

"Yes, where could he be?" Esi asked as they both fell into silent contemplation.

St. John hesitated at the table he was serving and, as he always had, involved himself in a conversation that was not really his. But he was at home, in his element, some would say. When he had first stumbled into Providence, Puncus was just out of high school and his parents's house, seeking a life. Providence was where he landed, maybe too weary for further travel or perhaps merely where night bounded his first day's sojourn. Not having more strength and unburdened by further ambition, he remained. The building into which he broke and first slept – if entering an open, abandoned building may be regarded as breaking in – was an old god-forsaken church. Not only God, but also the penniless preacher and his wife who had long before died without kin had left it to vermin. The town's folk feared the building – that failed church – which they interpreted as the devil's home. They would not even pull weeds from its façade, let alone from the graves in its lonely burial plot.

After his first few weeks, it became clear to the adventurous young man – seemingly with either the mind of a sage or a silly – that nobody cared, not even to enquire about him. He started to cook and care for himself there. Slowly, Puncus transformed the old church into his home.

When, in the evenings, he started playing drums or his guitar, folk gathered. Then he shared his food, entertaining his first customers, though at first no one saw it that way. From those austere beginnings, the *Any Questions* arose and never stopped growing.

"First, it's by listening to the gods that we become beguiled by them . . . I mean, it's by agreeing to follow their plan. In that way we become their agents and things happen," said their bearded attendant, with a full self-assured smile, as he finally delivered the bill to the women.

"What?" asked Esi. "What? What did you say, and who are you talking to?"

"Well, you asked, didn't you?" responded Puncus.

"What did I ask?" questioned Esi, placing her hand over her heart.

St. John, because of his rugged, heavy beard and long unkempt hair, looked much older than he really was. He kept a respectable distance from the women so they could see his tall, erect frame, broad shoulders and the look of gentle youth in his eyes.

"You didn't ask me, that I agree," said Puncus. "Nevertheless, Miss, you asked, 'How do things happen?' Do you remember?"

"Yes. I did ask that of Afia in our private conversation," Esi replied.

"So, there's your answer, Miss. Whether or not we want to . . . we are servants of the gods . . . that's how things happen. The question was asked, but no one gave an answer. That will not happen here, at the *Any Questions* tavern," Puncus explained.

"But, did I ask you?" Esi protested. She began to lose that soporific feeling derived from the warm, rustic atmosphere of the tavern and Afia's company.

What Esi, a visitor to Providence, didn't know, since Afia hadn't yet explained it to her, was that the proprietor was obliged, by the mission of his enterprise, to respond to any questions posed therein.

"Yes, I agree. But at the *Any Questions*, Miss, it is only sufficient that you ask."

"Why do I still sit here listening to this?"

"It's all right, Esi," said Afia, holding Esi's hand. Afia knew St. John quite well. In fact, everyone in Providence knew him. They were not particularly fond of him since he remained mystical or unfathomable, no matter the extent of their efforts to decipher him. Yet they trusted him and gave him their loyal patronage. "It's all right," Afia affirmed.

"You still have to pay," said the proprietor gently, presenting the bill to the women.

"What? Pay for you to frighten us with your strange remarks and appearance, or for your cold, insipid food?" Esi questioned.

Afia reached down in her bankra, one her mother had made as a wedding present. The handbag was sewn from sisal, a pliable plant fabric that had been dried and dyed tan. Its clam-like design had been adorned with red and yellow crocheted patterns of doctor birds seeking nectar from the flowers of the Wood-of-Life tree. Afia retrieved the money – a guinea composed of four five-shilling notes and two six-pence pieces – but delayed payment.

"Either is free, miss. You pay only to congregate here. That's why there is a flat charge, and you pay only when you leave. Food or no food, drink or no drink, fright or no fright, the price is the same. This is a very simple policy, Miss."

"Isn't it time we leave, Afia?"

"It's okay, Esi. He likes you."

"So, will you please pay now, Miss?"

"Well, here is your quattie," Esi said, laughing, as she held out a penny and a half to him.

"I set the charge, Miss, and it's not a quattie nor a jill, either. And tonight I even threw in a small brata with my little jig," he laughed.

Finally, Afia placed the money on his tray. Puncus acknowledged the payment with a childish smile and a gleeful nod, seeming surprised to be paid.

"You should meet him, Esi. This is Puncus St. John, otherwise known as Divine. He owns the tavern. He came here all the way from Fellowship in Portland."

"Why is he so fool-fool?" Esi mumbled.

"Sorry to break in on you like that, Miss," Puncus said. "Are you visiting Providence?"

"Her name is Esi. She is my best friend, Puncus. And yes, this is her first visit to Providence."

"Glad to have you here, and welcome to Providence, Esi. You will love it. And sorry it took me so long to get your answer. I had to meditate on it for a while. Then, when the answer finally came, I gave thanks for it with the little caper you saw there. "

"Thank you, Puncus," Afia said. "I see you learned to dance the quadrille at last."

"Is everyone from Portland just like you?" Esi asked, smiling.

"Oh, no, Esi. Some of us observe some even stranger customs!" replied Puncus. "Please come here any time you want and ask anything you like, Esi."

"Yes, thank you," said Esi. They left the table and walked outside. The music gradually faded as the door closed behind them, but the smell of smoke from the burning pimento logs still lingered.

The dome of the sky was a shimmering silver-gray. To the west, the hills towered up to meet the firmament. These shaded the vast fertile valley that tapered out to the east, casting it prematurely into night. The women walked in the darkness, listening to the sounds of dusk until they approached a rigid, wooden turnstile at the entrance of an easement.

Suddenly, Afia stopped. It was as if she had been struck by an idea so stupendous she could not let it go.

Seeing the change in Afia's face, Esi asked, "What is it, Afia?"

Afia searched for a reply, not wanting to alarm Esi with the novelty of her emotions. Esi thought of her home in Free Hill. There, the two young women had met and become friends in the school and church that served their adjoining villages. The McCracans, Afia's parents, lived in Oxford while Esi's worked on the large estates in Free Hill where Esi still lived. Love and later engagement to Bem Covey had moved Afia from Oxford to Providence.

To quiet the longing she felt for her missing husband, Afia spent much of her time roaming the countryside and meeting her new neighbors. Afia decided to impress Esi with her superior knowledge of Providence.

Rather as a boast, Afia said, "You know, Esi. This shortcut leads to my house."

"Is that so, Afia? The path seems to lead backwards . . . I mean, away from where you live."

"It might look that way, but I can prove that it will take me home."

"How?"

"With this bet. You go along the road," Afia said, pointing the way to Esi. "I'll take this shortcut, and I will bet you that I can get home before you!"

"I dare you, Afia!"

"Then bet me."

"Okay! I take the bet!"

"Well, you will see. I'll take that dare and I will win you, Esi!"

"Okay, Afia, but why are you taking off your clothes?"

"Because I want to run free and win!" Afia replied, handing Esi her embroidered silk blouse, long pleated cotton skirt, and bloomers.

"You are so wild, Afia! Are you taking off your clothes just to win a bet?" Esi asked as she took the clothes. She tried on Afia's bracelet of decorative beads and seashells along with her snake-headed silver bangles.

"Not only that, Esi. But to run with the night!"

"Ah! Are you still that undomesticated girl you have always been, Afia? "

Before Esi got her response, Afia was on the other side of the stile, preparing to run.

"You look like a Saturday morning higgler-woman selling ol-bruck . . . or, should I say, her wares?" Afia laughed. She eyed Esi in her plain, ankle-length, floral dress that buttoned in the back from neck to hem, tying at the waist with a narrow, twisted, leather belt.

"But I have something to tell you, Afia."

"When we get home!"

"It's very romantic, Afia, about someone I've had my eye on for sometime now."

"See who gets home first," she shouted and started running down the hill. "And remember to tell me about it when we get home."

"What a dare!" Esi yelled.

"A simple dare," Afia shouted back.

Esi, feeling a trifle disappointed, had to face the darkness by herself. She had just turned nineteen. Being of humble stock, she had recently secured the position of apprentice in the Boydells' household, an affluent farming family. The kind woman of the English household was understanding enough to teach Esi the skills of running a house. In time, Esi would move on and gain employment as a maid or be an efficient and highly prized wife.

To comfort herself after Afia had parted from her, Esi recollected how they met. It had never been clear to her how it began. Her childhood memory told her that it was with her clothes, which on the first day of school had been muddied. On that nervous day with everything complete: the pleats in her navy blue skirt, the starched, stiff white collar, the cleaned slate and sharpened pencil – everything, to the last kiss on the cheek and the "Run to school now, mi love" admonition of her mother. Everything was perfect until Esi fell. It was not her fall that was the problem, for she soon sprang unaided to her feet. It was her bellowing! For, on seeing the mud covering her clothes, she knew she had destroyed her mother's dream. Esi refused to go home despite the gentleness, the reassurances of her teachers and their promise to explain the accident to her mother. Esi couldn't go home, for she would be the news, and it wouldn't be well delivered. Afia, like an angel – she must have been an angel then – and right before the astonished teachers, dropped her clothes and exchanged them, the same color and style, for Esi's.

At home, Afia's mother fussed, but Esi's rejoiced. Her daughter was successful at school! Afia's mother, however, on learning the facts, washed and pressed the dirty dress, making it good again, and returned it to the rightful owner. There, she gushed her dissatisfaction with Afia's behavior, vowing to spank her daughter as soon as she got back home. That didn't happen, though. The women, after discussing the entire matter, saw the depth of Afia's passion. That was what they pondered as the mothers sat, sipped tea, and became friends.

So it was, over mud, that Esi remembered how she and Afia were brought together, connected. Esi even remembered how, long after she had outgrown those very clothes, Afia took them from her, folding them with her own and keeping them as their special souvenir. That recollection now comforted Esi even as she walked into Afia's house, winning the bet. Then she had to wait: wait to know if Afia had now fallen in mud.

Afia's Run

The vast green slopes down which Afia ran were owned by three of the wealthiest landowners of Providence, a village of less than a hundred residents. Cattle grazed the sun-drenched hills, and acres of fruit orchards filled the flat lands. The slopes of Providence fed a pond of almost seven acres that lay at the bottom of the hills. The borders of the properties were so set that each landowner had access to the pond.

Providence Pond itself was a thing of beauty and mystery. Some say it had always been there. Others, that it started suddenly but slowly grew after an earthquake of ancient times had ruptured the rocks, sending tiny rivulets from the earth and feeding the deep cavern separating the hills. The topography of Providence Pond and the surrounding terrain, it was widely known, was reminiscent of a great woman in repose, facing the heavens. Yet all stood in awe of it, for the pond brought life and death to Providence.

Two of the men, far apart in age, were joined in mutual interest in their adjacent properties. The older and more experienced, Aren Tyler, mentored Vijay Boydell who, in his mid-twenties, was about half Tyler's age. They differed in temperament, too. Aren was the wiser for his age and, a descendant of a local slave family, was considered a true gentleman, highly regarded in Providence for his good nature and genteel mannerisms.

Vijay, the son of a wealthy British plantation owner and an Indian peasant, Bessie Bukergy, lived a rebellious if not dangerous life. He was handsome, well provided for, and, having more time than he could wisely use, set about doing whatever pleased him. Vijay Boydell lived in his father's house, or, really, the family home, which he shared with his uncle and aunts.

The third estate, belonging to Covey, bordered the properties owned by Boydell and Tyler. It was Covey's illegitimate son, Bem, who had wedded Afia and vanished just after the end of the ceremony, leaving her in confusion and despair.

Rampant reports of stealing prompted Aren Tyler and Vijay Boydell to take up watch on their property from time to time. They were friends and found the hours spent outdoors more helpful in discussing their future than in doing their self-imposed police work.

Until recently their haunt had been the *Any Questions* tavern. Puncus St. John and, to no less an extent, the *Any Questions* tavern had a curious history which perhaps gave them a greater draw than the naïve inventiveness of the beverages or food served.

"When is Bem Covey coming back?" Vijay Boydell asked.

"Oh, about four months from now, Vijay. Why?"

"Why? He just got married. Pretty little Miss Afia McCracam must be dying of loneliness," Vijay responded, not wanting to accept her marriage to Bem Covey.

"Yes, that's true. Not only that, she must really be worried about Bem's disappearance. Can you imagine what it must be like for her?"

"As wild as Afia is, I doubt anything bothers her, Aren."

"Well, she does have a free spirit, but Afia has feelings like us, Vijay. She must be lonely and worried."

"You must be right. You know, I often feel like visiting her at night."

"Whatever for, Vijay?"

"To provide her with what her husband isn't."

"She must be lonely, but you needn't think that way, Vijay."

"And why not?"

"First of all, it would be wrong for you to interfere that way. And, moreover, you could destroy whatever is left of their marriage."

"It would be wrong only if Bem knows. But if he does not, and if Afia goes along with it, where is the wrong?"

"You may have a point, but there is the question of your conscience, Vijay."

"Listen, Aren. Bem Covey filched her from me."

"What exactly do you mean, Vijay?"

"Don't be coy with me, Aren. You know quite well that before the beauty pageant, Afia was set to marry me. Don't you remember that?"

"Yes, Vijay, quite well."

"Okay! But, after she won the pageant, every man wanted her. Do you remember that?"

"All right, Vijay, I see what you mean. You think Afia McCracam jilted you and married Bem instead. Is that it?"

"Yes! That's my point. And the way I see it, Aren, someone owes me!"

"Well, she is Mrs. Afia *Covey*, now, Vijay, and that's a big difference."

"Not to me, Aren. Someone owes me!"

"For goodness sake, Vijay, let it go!" Aren said. "Bem's made the deal. Bem was not really responsible for his own disappearance and Afia's misery."

"Mr. Covey paid for her, all right. But what about my feelings, Aren? I loved Afia!"

"Not paid, Vijay. Mr. Covey didn't pay for her. He gave Mr. McCracam an ample, quiet dowry. And what's more, Mr. Covey wanted Bem's situation off his hands."

"That is true."

"Yes, and to keep Bem, whom he still considers a bastard – his little shame – away from the family estate in Oxford. Mr. Covey gave Bem this adjoining property, on the condition that he marry Afia. You can't blame Bem for that, Vijay. And, moreover, Mr. Covey forced Bem into attending the seminary."

"That's some story! And imagine, he forced Bem to leave Providence just after he said, 'I do.' I didn't even think the dirty buzzard kissed his bride," Vijay said, laughing.

"Yes, Vijay. That's a difficult situation. It must have been hard on Bem, too!" Aren responded. "But think of it this way. In four months Bem will be like one of us, a landowner. He and Afia need to live a respectable life here in Providence. So, Vijay, for everyone's happiness, please let it all go."

"Wait! Did you hear something?" Vijay asked, holding his cupped hand to his ear.

The men were sitting on either side of the fence separating their properties. Another turnstile along the easement connected the estates.

"Yes. Quiet. Maybe, it's the thief!"

"Remember, we trap him from each side as he goes through the stile."

"Yes, quiet!"

"It sounds like a horse."

"Quiet! Here he comes."

The men hid in the darkness and waited until the running slowed in the stile.

"Goodness!" Aren gasped.

"Look what I trapped!" yelled Vijay, as he gawked at the naked female form they had trapped in the darkness.

"What are you doing here!" cried Afia, frightened.

"You are as naked as a babe!" shouted Vijay. "We are watching for thieves and trespassers, and we caught you!"

"Here," said Aren, handing Afia the sheet on which he was sitting. "Cover yourself."

"No," said Afia, flashing her head from side to side, "I will soon be home."

"Not so fast," said Vijay, taking the sheet from Aren and tossing it on the ground. "You will have to pay me first! You were trespassing."

"Pay you for what? Walking home?" Afia asked.

"Leave her alone, Vijay," Aren said.

"Stay out of this, Aren. The only thing you can do for me is lock her up in your Barton House jail until Bem Covey returns."

"No. Not Afia!" Aren protested.

"I decide, Aren. The offence is against me."

"It is against me, too, Vijay. We are all neighbors. But I am willing to let her go."

"Not me. She owes me!"

"Well, whatever I owe, Bem will pay when he comes home. You did say he is returning? Right, Vijay?"

"Keep Bem out of this, girl. This is between you and me. We have something to settle. And furthermore, since your husband is not at home, you certainly don't want this incident discussed at the *Any Questions*, do you, Afia?"

Afia saw the implication of his question. The exposure and embarrassment could complete the destruction of her marriage, hurting Bem irreversibly. Moreover, Vijay spoke as if he knew of Bem's mysterious whereabouts. He was alive, he was returning! Afia's thoughts ran. She wanted to encourage Vijay to talk. Maybe he would say more about Bem's disappearance.

"Tell me where Bem is and let me go, just like Aren said."

"Not so easy for you, Afia. You owe me!"

"What is your charge?" Afia asked. "And what do you know about Bem?"

"Well," said Vijay Boydell. "You visited my land. What if I visit your house for payback?"

"All right," agreed Afia, "if you will tell me about Bem."

"Okay, then. One of us will visit you," said Aren. He wanted to let Afia go and forget the whole incident.

"Then one week from now, all right?" Afia asked.

"Yes, Afia, that's okay," Vijay said with some hesitation.

"Since you are between our two properties," Aren interjected, scratching his chin, "We will have to toss a coin to decide which of us will visit you," he continued. Aren wished to win the coin toss and set Afia free.

"All right then. Toss your coin. But hurry. I must get home now," Afia said, as if putting an inconsequential matter to rest. The idea of foiling Vijay's plan by visiting Esi's played in her mind.

"Heads, it's Aren. Tails, it's me," Vijay said.

"Agreed."

Aren tossed the coin and allowed it to fall to the ground where it rolled and came to rest.

"Amazing!" said Aren, shining his light on the coin. "We both win." The coin was standing on its rim, but slightly tilted, exposing the tail side.

"But since the tail faces up, I get to visit Afia. Revenge! " Vijay said with the jubilance of a schoolboy at recess.

"Agreed," said Afia, sharpening her plan to thwart his efforts.

"Agreed," said Vijay.

And with that, Afia left the men at Providence Pond and ran up the hill to her home, thinking always of Esi.

It was still early in the night when Afia got home. Esi was already at the house. She had won the bet. Afia wanted to tell Esi what had happened to her but instead listened to Esi as she had promised. Esi had much to say. It was all about Vijay.

The Boydell family had taken Esi as an apprentice. Vijay, seeing her youth and beauty, was not slow in making his approach to her. Esi had been caught in a whirlwind ever since. The thought of having Vijay Boydell as her friend, her lover, or husband filled Esi with delight. But was it too much for her? Esi found Afia's ears and spent the rest of the night filling them with her confusion, her delight and excitement. In silence Afia listened.

The Honeymoon

About four months went by. One night as she lay in bed, Afia heard footsteps coming up the gravel path to her house. They were the rapid, heavy steps of a man. "Bem!" she thought. "Bem?" his name quivered in her mind, "Bem? It must be him!" This was her hope. The person didn't linger. He simply opened the door and entered the bedroom where she lay.

Afia knew it was Bem. She was sure. She didn't jump to greet him, nor did she show any joy at his presence. Nervousness, maybe, but no joy filled her. Bem didn't speak. For him this was the beginning of their marriage. It really should have been the midst of their honeymoon. His father, however, saw things differently.

Bem Covey undressed himself, got in bed and started kissing his wife. Afia tried to resist him at first, turning away. She gradually relented, however, behaving as she had when they were courting. Afia accepted him, first as a friend, then as a man, and finally as her husband, yet with mixed feelings of anxiety and joy at their first sexual union.

Bem Covey remained in bed late the following morning. His long trip home made him tired. He was weary, being unable to resist Afia's repeated enticement of love. He was simply exhausted.

Afia didn't quite know how to approach her husband. She knew she had to, but was afraid. She sat on the bed beside him, leaning against the headboard. Despite the affection he had shown her, Afia's anger – her disappointment and despair from Bem's unexplained absence – had not been hushed. Yet they did not diminish her joy of having him home. So she remained, thinking, with her fingers gently stroking his head and face until he opened his eyes.

"I love you, Afia," he whispered, gradually coming alive.

"You love me, Bem! You love me, you say, and left me alone right after our marriage!"

Bem, unprepared for Afia's outburst, sat up, wiping his eyes. Afia did not realize until then just how angry she still was with Bem.

"Do you know what I have been through because you were gone? Where did you go, after all? What on earth happened to you?" Afia asked with tears rolling down her face.

"I went to the seminary, Afia. My father sent me there."

"And you didn't even tell me! I stood helpless in the church not know-ing what to do. Your father had to bring me here. It should have been you, Bem. You should have taken me home!"

"I owe him for that, Afia," Bem said. "But I did ask him to tell you about his plan for me. I mean – about us, I should have said."

"He certainly did not! And here I am in this strange town with my husband missing, and no one even to talk to. Do you know how hurtful that was? Do you? And what did you expect me to do, Bem?"

"That was not my plan for us, Afia."

"Your plan or not, this was horrible! If not for Esi, I would not know what to do. She was the one who comforted me. And where was my hus-band? I just hope that some day I can pay her back and be her companion if she should be lonely!"

"I do share your disgust, your anguish, Afia. Believe me," He looked up at her and their eyes met, creating a lull in the conversation. Bem continued, "I don't know why my father brought you here without telling you where I was. But you know something, Afia?"

"What, Bem?"

"Knowing my father as I do, this is certainly understandable!"

Afia looked at Bem, sensing his honesty. "You know," she said, "If it were not for Esi's company, I would have gone back home for good!"

"I would have done the same if I were in your position, Afia – except quicker," Bem said, smiling.

"Were you all right, Bem? I missed you very much." Afia started to sob.

"I am sorry, Afia," Bem said, stroking her face. "I didn't know I would be going."

After a pause, one tinged with guilt and shame, Bem did what he had never believed he would ever have the courage to. Bem started to reveal more of his concealed, earlier life to Afia. He told her how his English father had treated him, recounting his early childhood. Bem told of his father's kindness that was often tempered with neglect and scorn . . . that his mother, a servant-girl of Nigerian extraction, had died soon after his birth and that his aunt – another of the Covey's house-girls – subsequently cared for him.

Bem, for the first time, made it clear to Afia that even though he was the Covey heir, he had been disallowed from living in the family house and relegated to mere servitude. The fact of his parentage – an English landlord and an African peasant – made it so.

Bem recounted that at eighteen his father installed him as headman for the property in Providence where he would live independently. His abode in Providence solved his father's dual problems: first, to find trustworthy management for his remote holdings, and then to permanently keep Bem's embarrassing presence from the family estate in Free Hill.

For as long as Bem had been courting Afia, he had never before disclosed to her that depth of both himself and the turmoil within his family. On the one hand, Afia was unhappy to hear of her husband's plight. Yet, it aroused in her much deeper feelings of love and attachment than she had felt before. Afia's grief, caused by the mistaken feelings that Bem had forsaken her, soon gave rise to a stronger sense of forgiveness. Her love for him was slowly returning. Bem's poignant recounting of his earlier life stirred similar sentiments of her own past.

She had just turned sixteen when the elementary schools and the churches in and around Oxford planned a beauty contest. The winning prize consisted of a few acres of land in Providence and, hopefully, an independent start in life.

Afia, who had been quite an ordinary looking girl until a few years before, began sprouting beauty like a rose in bloom. She was petite, carrying her well-proportioned frame with confidence and graceful composure. It was her large, alluring eyes set under heavy brows on a narrow face of velvety, black skin that showed her quaintness. She wore her dense, curly hair in plaits that dangled down about her face and neck, defining yet concealing something of extraordinary inner beauty and pride.

With urbane looks and well-honed talents, Afia easily won against girls from seven other schools.

Afia's promotion to her high state of charm and seduction vastly increased her desirability. Mr. Boydell, a successful British gentleman, saw Afia then for the first time. He would have her, though not for himself. He imagined her to be the perfect partner for his son, and an addition of inestimable worth to his estate.

Before his father even noticed her, Vijay Boydell had already seen what Afia could become. He had made an offer of marriage to her. It didn't start with his proposal, and neither would it end there. Vijay wanted Afia's love; but when she rebuffed him, Vijay's second plea came through the door of marriage as the entrance to her affection. That didn't work either.

At first Afia tossed his offer about as a sea otter would a shellfish before rejecting it. She wondered why he had never tried the sure key of true love. Vijay, devastated but undaunted, had never accepted her rejection of him. He had never been refused and he was still sure to have her. Why Afia changed her mind was never adequately explained, especially not to Vijay. His pride and bravado kept him believing that she belonged to him.

Vijay, young and attractive, was from both wealthy British and poor Indian stock. He was unmarried and seeking a wife. Maybe it was because he was looking in so many different households at once that his offer appeared lacking. Or was it because of his intolerable hubris? True, he had behaved in a gentle and respectable manner to her, but Afia's lineage was poor. Her ancestors had worked on the elder Boydell estate, generation after generation. Why was the landlord's oldest son so suddenly interested in marrying her? That was Afia's query, and it formed the basis for her conclusion that Vijay wanted her for nothing but sensual pleasure. Perhaps, also, his belated love songs were out of tune.

It was not because Bem was a social castaway that Afia loved him. It was not because of sympathy either, nor was it out of a passion to rescue him. It was, rather, because Bem seemed to know himself. He understood how to think things through with her, and he cared for others. But more, it was simply because Bem genuinely loved and respected Afia. That was the quality that distinguished Bem from Vijay Boydell and her countless other suitors; it endeared him irrevocably to her. She reciprocated, fully trusting him. Finally she married him.

Bem had rejected his father's class doctrine in every aspect of his life. He found it particularly disgusting that it excluded him from the family proper. As soon as his mother's pregnancy had been announced, the indigent girl was given a small cottage at the back of the plantation – the very one in which Bem now lived – where her promise of silence guaranteed her free abode and her safety. After she died, Bem's aunt moved into the cottage and cared for him. As Bem grew old enough to be graced with the appearance of manhood, Mr. Covey gave the cottage and a few acres to Bem on the condition that he relinquish all future claims or relationship to the Covey estate. With that, Bem was cast aside and permanently separated from the Covey family, except by name. That, by his innate loyalty and self-respect, Bem was bound to uphold.

Their similarity in parentage but difference in upbringing, worth, and vision had soon brought Bem and Vijay into childhood rivalry. They went to different schools, lived different lives, but were joined as landowners at Providence Pond. Later, in their mutual interest in Afia, Vijay still imagined he had a life that would claim her. Vijay couldn't bear to know that Bem, a lad of lower esteem, as he saw it, gained the woman who, in his calculations, belonged to him. After all, hadn't Vijay known and wanted Afia before she had value? Wasn't her value based on his attention to her in the first place? He thought so. He also believed that it was his continual interest in Afia that upheld her worth.

Afia, however, had made her choice, and so had Vijay. He was going to get her! More than anyone else, he was especially worthy of her affection. Despite her rejection, Vijay didn't abhor Afia. For what he knew of love and lust, he concluded that he loved her. He was still sure she loved him. Vijay, therefore, saw Bem as a rival, a thief, and a barrier to his belongings. If he couldn't have Afia, then Vijay would make Bem own her in pain. If nothing else, he wanted to announce to Bem that he had taken his wife's maidenhood.

As soon as Bem reached eighteen, Mr. Covey arranged his marriage. He presented the offer to Afia's father and it was accepted, provided that, according to the elder McCracan, Bem attended the seminary so he could learn how to tame his wife. Bem was to profit from this also.

As his father-in-law saw it, Bem's hitherto unmanageable temper must also be checked. Afia's father knew of Bem's acid temper and feared for her life as well as Bem's. Mr. Covey finally concluded that Bem's attendance at the seminary could only help him and, consequently, his marriage. With the offer accepted, and monies passing silently downstream, Afia was offered in marriage to Bem.

Bem had fulfilled his entire obligation, the last and secretive part of which was to attend seminary school starting on the night of his marriage. He had to stay there, and Afia would remain virginal for an additional four months. Vijay Boydell learned of the arrangement from Aren Tyler.

That plan for Bem was disclosed to Aren Tyler because he ruled the jail at Barton House. Fines and possibly jail-time would result if either side broke the contract. It was Aren's responsibility to prevent any such forfeiture.

Barton House was the mansion belonging to the Barton family during their tenure in Providence as slavers owners. The Tylers worked as house slaves and then as butlers and maids for the Bartons. During a long period of sickness, the Bartons, without kin, sold the property to the Tylers at an extremely low price with the understanding that the Tylers would continue to provide for them until death. Following the demise of the Bartons, the Tylers would come into possession of the estate after rendering honorable and decorous burials, which the Boydells, who held the sale agreement, had to approve. The other stipulation was that the estate would keep the Barton name.

The Tylers kept their part of the bargain. On the death of their bene-factor and former employer, the Tylers, without hesitation or strife, took possession of the Barton estate.

Beneath Barton House, in its dark, sad cellar groaned the notorious jail. It was a leftover from slavery, the place where attempted runaways, the lazy or the unruly were housed until their repentance, sale, or death.

In more recent times, though, the jail had served to increase revenue to the Barton estate. Lawbreakers, at the consent of the honorable judge, Mr. Aren Tyler, would be locked away until the family paid restitution. This recompense was hastened since the jail didn't allow visitors of any kind, nor did it feed the inmates. The institution, being necessary and the only one of its kind for more than twenty miles around, prospered even though it was hated as much as it was respected.

This was what Aren Tyler inherited from his father. With the jail came ready income, respect, and hate. Aren Tyler was a quiet, gentle and honest man. He learned the rudiments of the business from his father, and now he had a young son. His wife had recently died. Aren was determined to transform the jail into a place of respect and honor and let it serve to add to, rather than detract from, the worth and reputation of Barton House. Bem had his eye on Aren and unknowingly had taken him for his model of genteel living.

That morning, after his overdue attention from Afia, Bem finally rose. He sat at the side of the bed with one leg dangling above the floor. He reached across the bed for his wife's hand.

Without looking at her, he said, "I love you, Afia, and I want us to remain in love, forever."

Afia squeezed his hand so hard that Bem looked across the bed at her. The mounting dawn sun still shone brightly through the window, highlighting her naked body. He really looked at her for the first time – the neck and shoulders which he liked so much to kiss and caress. Then he looked up to her face again and saw tears in her eyes, for she had been quietly sobbing.

"What's . . . what's the matter, Afia?"

Afia didn't reply. Her weeping increased and she pointed to her stomach. At first Bem didn't understand. He looked up again, and again she pointed downward as her sniveling turned to a loud cry. Bem's eyes following, her hands soon started to rub her stomach. Thinking she was in pain, he asked, "Where does it hurt?"

"There is no pain, Bem."

"What then, Afia?"

"I am expecting, Bem."

Bem immediately pulled from her and stood up. "What did you say? Pregnant?"

"Yes."

"How? I mean, who?"

"Vijay Boydell."

Bem grimaced. At once he thought of revenge, murder! And his mind found his guns right where he had left them. "Vijay Boydell?"

"Yes. Vijay Boydell." Then Afia reported the incident at the pond and what followed. "I didn't intend to cause you any harm or disgrace. Vijay insisted that Aren put me in jail unless I agreed to go to bed with him."

"That was low of him. But you didn't have to agree to that, either, Afia."

"I didn't."

"But you said you did, Afia."

"Yes, but I intended something else." She paused.

"What on earth!"

"What I wanted to do was to get away from Vijay at the pond. I would have told him anything so he would let me go. I told him one week from that day he could visit me. I had no intentions of going to bed with him."

"But you did."

"It was at night when I spoke to Vijay. I expected him to visit me the following Wednesday. My intention was to spend that night with Esi, in Free Hill. We had it all planned."

"So?"

"So! Boydell showed up the night before, on Tuesday. I was here. The lights were off. He came in the house and forced me. He held me down and forced me, Bem!"

Bem seethed with anger. For Afia it turned into confusion. Something was going to happen.

"Let's leave it where it is, Afia."

"Not in silence, Bem. I am afraid of that."

"I am going to do something about this, Afia!"

"That would be better."

"Tell me, Afia. Who except us knows you are pregnant?"

"No one. I have kept it a secret, even from Esi."

"Are you sure?"

"Yes, Bem."

"Good then. Tyler and Boydell know I should be returning this weekend."

"Yes, I could have a welcoming party for you at Providence Pond on the weekend. We could talk about it then."

"No, Afia. Not next week. Tomorrow. See if Puncus can cater a small party for us, and only Vijay, Aren, you, and I need to be there."

"And Esi too, Bem. You know, she could not get the day off from the Boydells to attend our wedding. But this time she can be with us. She is my best friend. She must be there!"

"Okay, Afia. Esi, too."

Immediately, Afia readied herself and set out to solicit culinary assistance from Puncus St. John and then invite the guests to the party. The last on her list was Esi. Afia rode to Free Hill and brought back Esi with her for the picnic on the following day.

Bem rested for the remainder of the day and night while he finessed a plan to force Vijay into a public confession of raping and impregnating his wife. Once Vijay confessed, Aren Tyler would have no choice but to throw Vijay into his infamous Barton House jail and, besides, have him pay restitutions.

If that plan failed, or even if it didn't, with Afia's accusations and swelling proof of Vijay's guilt, Bem's raging anger and open display of hurt would have justifiable cause to force Vijay into a fight. He would then shoot Vijay in self-defense. That was Bem's true intention. Everything else was his pretext.

As for Afia's pregnancy, Bem would attend to that later.

Puncus St. John

Puncus St. John, or Divine, as he was sometimes called, was just turning twenty when he first arrived in Providence. He came there from the coastal town of Galina about fifteen miles to the west of Providence. His well-to-do parents lived in the parish of Portland where the lad was sent to a private religious high school.

That was where Puncus' troubles started. According to his parents, Puncus had fallen under the spell of a cult leader. He refused to have his hair cut and started smoking ganja. Reverend Watkins, the principal, quickly arranged a transfer for the lad to another school in Galina. There, Monsignor Ricardo Silva took charge of St. John's education, this time in a boarding high school.

St. John had not attended his new school for long when his troubles resurfaced. This time it was over his eating. The situation had gone on long enough for the Monsignor to ask the assistance of his friend, Reverend Watkins. The men met at the school in Galina and discussed the situation. After deciding on a strategy, they sent for Puncus.

The office where they met was far too big for the trio. The older men were already there at the long side of a large rectangular table. Puncus sat facing them. The windows were high up, and though light came in, it shone on the opposite walls and not directly on the table.

The silver-haired Monsignor nodded at Puncus and started. "Good morning, young man. I am sure you know Reverend Watkins."

"Good day, Reverend, and you too, Monsignor."

"How are you, young man?" the Reverend asked.

"I am happy to see you, Reverend."

"Your parents, good members of our church, asked me to intervene on your behalf, again," Reverend Watkins continued. "We understand that you refuse to follow a very simple rule of the Church. And you do know . . . I did tell you . . . that if you want to stay in the school you must follow the precepts of the church."

"Yes, Reverend, you did."

"So, I am here to see for myself just what the problem is and if I can help."

"Thank you for coming, Reverend."

"My wish is to help you. Do you understand, young man?"

"Yes, Reverend."

"Good. Now, before we start, let me ask, how are his grades, Monsignor?"

"Excellent, Reverend. St. John tops the senior class."

"Well, congratulations, young man. Your parents will be proud of you."

"Thank you, Reverend."

"So, let me ask, what exactly is the problem here?"

"Stated simply, Reverend, Puncus refuses the holy sacraments," replied the Monsignor.

"Is that so, young man?"

"Not really, Reverend."

"So, what really is the situation, St. John?"

"I refuse to be a cannibal, Reverend."

"What in heaven do you mean?" The Reverend asked.

"Just that, Reverend. I, Puncus St John, cannot be a cannibal."

"What do you mean? Will you become a cannibal if you partake in the sacraments?"

"Yes, Reverend. As long as I eat the flesh and drink the blood of a human."

"Ghastly!" remarked the Monsignor.

Silence followed.

"You partake to get forgiveness of your sins!" The Reverend finally said.

"I have no sin, Reverend," St. John said with a smile. "All I do is follow my heart."

The Monsignor looked at the Reverend and whispered to him. The Reverend nodded and whispered back, "I understand."

"Well, I must say. You are a very hardened, corrupt young man. We have others here, I mean good, obedient students from respectable homes, to protect from you," the Monsignor said.

"Have you been talking to that cult leader of yours again, young man?"

"Cult leader, Reverend? I talk to everyone. Why don't you ask me if I talk to the Doctor, too?"

"Do you mean Doctor Devinder Singh?"

"Yes, Reverend."

"What's he got to do with this?"

"Maybe more than you know."

"Don't be impertinent! And you'd better leave the doctor out of your confused mind."

"Well, if you say so, Reverend."

There was a pause while the men whispered to each other again.

"You do know, Puncus, why we transferred you to this school, don't you?"

"Yes, Reverend."

"So, then," Reverend Watkins continued, "If you associate with that cult . . . and I refuse to dignify their name here . . . you and your parents could be in trouble with the law. That is the very reason we moved you from Fellowship in Portland to this small town of Galina."

"And we will do everything in our power to assist in your education, Puncus," the Monsignor added.

"So, tell us. Is the cult here in Galina, too?" The Reverend Watkins asked.

Puncus did not reply.

"We are waiting on your response, young man," the Monsignor said.

Still St. John remained silent.

"Maybe we should turn this situation over to Detective Graham," the Monsignor added. "We cannot harbor wrongdoers here."

"Maybe we should. His silence seems to speak for his guilt."

"Well then," said the Monsignor. "Young man, if you will not cooperate with us, if you will not accept the precious sacraments and tell us whether or not you are in league with that cult, you leave us no choice but to notify Detective Graham."

Still Puncus did not respond.

"Most of all," said the Reverend. "I would hate to bring bad news back to your parents and the community of Fellowship. So much is expected of you, St. John!"

"Then I will leave," said St. John.

"Leave?" asked the Monsignor.

"Yes," replied St. John. "I will leave your school if you will return my tuition."

The men laughed, then whispered again.

"You don't have to leave, young man," said the Reverend.

"Does that mean I do not have to eat the sacraments?" St. John asked.

"No! Not at all. It means you can partake of the sacraments and stay!"

"Is that the only way, Reverend?"

"Yes, absolutely. That is the only way!"

A pensive silence followed.

"Okay then," said St. John, breaking the silence, "you can return my tuition and I will leave."

This time the men did not laugh. They whispered to themselves again.

"All right, St. John. Meet us here at noon tomorrow, and we will have everything ready for you," said the Monsignor.

The Monsignor sounded honest and reasonable. Yet all that St. John heard was "Detective Graham." He knew of the Detective's thoroughness and the number of boys from the village that were locked up on his account. The only other thing Puncus heard was "escape."

"Okay, Monsignor," Puncus said, "tomorrow at noon."

With that, the meeting was adjourned. As Puncus reached the door, he turned and asked, "May I address the school tomorrow at lunchtime, Reverend?"

Again the men laughed. "Don't plan to," said the Monsignor.

"In that case, please give this message, just in case they ask for me."

"What message, young man?" the Monsignor asked.

"That I love them."

Again the men laughed, louder this time as Puncus closed the door behind him.

Soon after sunset that evening, Puncus, leaving all his possessions behind, left his dorm and started to run. His next stop was the remote village of Providence.

Not knowing what to do, and certainly no longer welcomed in his father's household for the disgrace that followed, Puncus settled into Providence and started the saloon.

Puncus had never before cooked or served food. Yet he thought he could operate a tavern. His strategy then was not to charge for the food or drink but only for the need to congregate, or the more tangible thing, the seats, which he knew were sturdy. Puncus had wagered on another of his beliefs: if one person stayed in any place long enough, another would come along. He was that first person, and his theory proved true when others joined him.

Quickly, Divine named his operation the *Sun Rise Tavern*. Shortly after he posted his first sign, a young lad scarcely older than Puncus sat smoking at the bar. He questioned St. John about how he derived the name for the tavern. Puncus told him how he was expelled from school for his thoughts and how he came to believe in nothing except that the sun always rises.

"And that's the only thing I believe in now," Puncus ended his explanation.

"What?" asked the customer, who may have had too much drink.

"Sunrise!" Puncus had reassured him.

"Yes, Puncus. But you can't have a sunrise without a sunset!"

"So what's the difference? I could call it the *Sun Set Tavern* as well."

"I suppose you could, Divine. But either way, your sign would still be half right or half wrong."

The next day Puncus hung a new sign that read:

The Sun Rise – Sun Set Tavern
(Any questions?)

The name *Any Questions* stuck, and folks gathered there, either to give or take questions or to snicker about anything that happened in Providence. Perhaps they even pondered why Byah became mute after that fateful conversation with Puncus St. John.

Aren and Vijay were no exceptions. Each evening they would first meet at the *Any Questions* and, as it grew dusk, walk down to Providence Pond to watch their property.

Nweka

To Bem Covey, the plan was simple and straightforward. He had it all worked out and had made up his mind, vowing never to change. Vijay Boydell, who had wronged him, had to be punished. As it stood, only Boydell's admission of guilt remained. Only this separated Boydell from his fate. Bem considered Aren to be reasonable. The proof of Vijay Boydell's wrongdoing grew within Afia. So in Bem's mind, it was all over. They would convene at Providence Pond, talk, have dinner, and settle the matter according to Bem's plan.

By mid-afternoon the guests started to arrive at the pond. Aren Tyler had brought his only child, Lev, with him. Lev, a lad of about seven years old, was epileptic, or so his family thought. Aren, either out of love or concern for his son's welfare, took Lev almost everywhere he went. Only rarely would he leave the lad at home with his caretaker.

The picnic was scheduled at Providence Pond where the lad's first seizure had paralyzed him almost to death and where his mother lost her life saving his. It was whispered that a great beast had reared from the deep, frightening Lev into his first convulsions. No one else had ever seen the monster, but fear of it had not diminished in Providence. From then, Lev was always forbidden from the pond, the thing he cherished most.

Esi, who had spent the night with the Coveys, went with Afia to assist Puncus in preparing for the party. While Puncus and Esi cooked, they talked and became more appreciative of each other. After assisting Puncus and

Esi, Afia returned home to be with her husband. The two couples would reunite later and walk from the *Any Questions* to Providence Pond.

With the preparations done, Puncus and Esi walked downhill toward Providence Pond. Afia and Bem, who had just joined them at the *Any Questions,* sauntered some distance behind.

"You know, Bem," Afia started, "I had the strangest dream last night."

"I had an unusual dream, too," replied Bem. "And I have been struggling all day to remember what I dreamt about." His reply was not friendly. It was measured, concealing his frustration with his poor memory and mounting anger toward Boydell. "What did you dream, Afia?" Bem asked.

"It was something about a bird. Let me see . . . a birdman. No, no! It was about this old man changing into a bird. I can't remember anything else. The only thing I do know for sure is that since I was a girl I have been having that very same dream."

"That's strange, Afia, you thinking of a birdman. I wonder what that means."

"I don't know, Bem, maybe . . ."

"Oh, I remember now!" Bem interrupted Afia. "Mine was about you, Afia. You were in this strange place. I do not know where it could be. But you were the head of a large family. The only problem is that some of your children were older than you!"

"That's strange, Bem. My own children? Older than me?"

"Yes, Afia, older."

"Maybe you were thinking about the baby and what will happen, Bem."

"You could be right, Afia. But I didn't think about the baby or our family until you mentioned it."

"But that might be on your mind. I wonder if that is why you seem so jittery, Bem?"

"I can't say. But you could be right. I hope you understand, Afia. This is very hard on me."

"I am sorry, Bem. It is hard on both of us. But it's all my fault."

"No, Afia. Vijay Boydell is at fault. But perhaps it's best to wait until we all meet before discussing it. What do you think?"

"Okay, Bem. We can wait."

The large pond glimmered beneath the evening sun. Colorful cranes paused as if in wonder while ducks floated effortlessly among the water lilies. Against the hill, vibrant silver-green bamboos shimmered against the lush red of the poinciana and yellow rose apples. Closer by, the sweeping arch of the fruited guango gave comforting shade to sleepy cattle. Only the calves still cavorted, as if fighting the fading rays of a plum-ripe sun. Under their mother's watchful though contented eye, all was well.

"Hello, Bem," called Aren Tyler, hastening to hug him. Tyler and Vijay Boydell were at the pond, awaiting Bem's arrival.

"Good to see you, too," said Boydell, also reaching out to shake Bem's hand.

"Yes, thank you," said Bem. "It is good to be back. And you all know Afia's friend, Esi?" he asked, presenting her with an unusually loud laugh, hoping to disguise his anxiety.

"Just don't stand over there by yourself, Byah, come on over and say hello to Bem," Afia said, trying to move the emotional spotlight from Bem.

Byah responded by spanking a few quick greeting notes on his drums as he approached the party.

With the casual salutations, including Lev Tyler's and St. John's, passed, Bem said, "Thank you for coming to the party. I am happy that Esi could be here, too."

"I knew you would like her to be here, too, Bem," Afia added, standing closer to her husband.

"Bem," Aren asked, "Aren't you going to tell us of your adventure?"

"I went to the seminary, Aren. You know that. But there is more serious business here," Bem said, patting Afia's stomach.

"Do you have serious business with Afia, Bem?" asked Vijay, a sudden choking feeling shutting off his voice.

"Yes, and we should get right down to it before going further."

"So let's hear it, Bem," Aren said.

"Afia is pregnant!" Bem replied.

During the deepening silence that followed, Bem looked accusingly at Vijay Boydell. In like manner, Boydell looked at Aren. Aren momentarily looked at Esi, but very quickly changed his glance back to Boydell. All eyes were focused on Vijay Boydell.

"So Bem!" said Puncus, "it seems that we are celebrating your return and a new arrival at the same time. That's wonderful! Let's burn some incense."

"Go smoke your herb by yourself, Puncus!" Bem replied.

"Why, Afia! You didn't tell me you were pregnant!" Esi said, hugging her friend. "I am so happy that you are."

"It's not that simple, Esi," Bem said, looking at Afia's tearful face.

"Vijay . . . Afia told me you had some business with her in my bed. Is that right?" Bem asked.

"So did Aren. Why accuse only me?" Vijay replied

"Vijay Boydell, you slept with Afia, and you know it. So leave Aren out of this!" Bem replied.

"What's this all about?" Puncus asked.

"A baby! Can't you tell?" Esi answered.

"Then we should be rejoicing. Why are we so angry?" Puncus said.

"It was not Aren who visited me," said Afia, staring at Vijay. "It was you, Vijay Boydell. It was you, and don't deny it!"

Aren said, "No! Good Lord, not me. I dissuaded Vijay from going to your house, Bem."

"I fully believe you, Aren," Bem said.

"So, what if I did go there?" asked Vijay.

"'What if you did'? That's how you put it? 'What if I did?'" imitated Bem.

"Yes, what if I did? What? Is Aren going to lock me in his Barton House jail? Or do you expect me to pay you so I can stay out of jail?" Vijay asked as he grinned.

"Just as I thought," said Bem. "You admit to your guilt!"

"Okay, Bem. I admit. So what?"

"I am going to punish you myself," Bem said, pulling out his concealed revolver. "It's finally my justice," he continued, pointing the revolver at Vijay Boydell and signaling him to move away from Aren.

In slow nervous steps, Vijay Boydell moved back. Stumbling, he fell. Suddenly, over the click of Bem's gun came the mighty word: "Mercy!"

Eyes turned, seeing a tall, angular man. His round, clean-shaven head glistening in the sunlight. Boldly, he approached the group.

"Mercy!" he repeated, his elegant, ancient, black frame getting closer.

He joined the assembly. He was a stranger. Only Afia and Puncus St. John seemed to have any knowledge of him.

"Good evening," greeted Puncus faintly. "How did you know I was . . ."

"Who are you, and what are you doing here?" Bem challenged.

"Maybe I should talk to him, since he is trespassing on my land," said Aren. "What is your business here, sir?" he asked.

The stranger didn't reply at first. He moved toward Boydell, offering his hand and helping him from the ground.

"This is a long story," replied the stranger. "My plan is to start a Family here."

"Start a Family?" Aren asked.

"Yes."

"Where is your wife?" asked Afia.

"And your children?" asked Esi.

"Let him talk. Let him talk," said Aren.

"You may put away the gun now, Bem."

"How did you know my name?" Bem asked.

"I know all of you," the stranger replied. "For now, please put away the gun."

"All right," Bem said, handing the gun to the stranger.

"Now," the stranger continued. "You asked me who I am and what I am doing here. That's fair. I suppose most of you have never seen me before, so let me tell you."

"Please do," said Aren.

"I am from the Bantu line out of Africa," the stranger continued. "In Portland, where I live, I serve as a King to my Family."

"A King for your Family?" Afia asked.

"Yes, Afia. A King for my Family."

"Is your Family a . . ."

"Please, Afia. Let him talk," Aren interrupted her.

"Thank you, Aren. So . . . let me ask. Has the news of Paul or George Gordon reached here yet?"

"Paul? Do you mean the Baptist deacon, Paul Bogle? And his pastor, George Gordon, as well?" Afia asked.

"The ones that started the rebellion . . . and the Governor had to hang?" Vijay asked.

"Yes, the very ones! They were good men, Vijay."

"They fought well in the rebellion at Morant Bay, as far as we could tell," Aren said.

"Yes, they did. And for good reasons, too, I can assure you. I can see you follow the news, Aren."

"I try to, sir. But," Aren continued, "as I recall, that was somewhere in the 1860s, right?

"Yes," the stranger responded.

"So, let me see," Aren said. "This is the summer of 1886, so that must have been about twenty-one years ago when they were hanged."

"Yes, in the year 1865 to be exact!"

"So, what's that got to do with us?" Bem asked.

"I am one of their original followers." The stranger continued. "I could have been hanged, too except that I belonged to a different Family, a secret sect. The Governor didn't know about my group at that time."

"So you escaped. We can see that!" Bem replied.

"Anyway," said the stranger, "the Governor later learned about us and started to persecute our Family."

"Did you say: a different Family?" Afia asked.

"Yes, I did."

"The Baptist Church is not a Family."

"Yes, yes. I understand. The Baptists build churches. We build Families."

"What do you mean?" Afia asked. "Do you build religious Families?"

"Yes, Afia. Ours is the Kumina Family. Have you heard about us?"

"No," replied Afia, looking at the others as they shook their heads in doubt.

"No wonder," the stranger replied. "I am the head of the survivors. We tried to save Paul Bogle and Gordon."

"So, what happened?" questioned Aren.

"Things were changing too fast, Aren. We just couldn't save their bodies, but their souls are with us," he said. "Their spirits will be with us forever!"

That last bit of information caused more confusion than enlightenment. The small gathering became silent.

"What did you say your name was?" Afia asked.

"Asa. My name is Asa, and I work as King for my Family."

"Asa?" she paused. "Asa! Are you the Bongo, the war-man, that same Asa?" Afia questioned.

"Why do you ask that, Afia?"

"My nana . . . my grandmother, explained that . . ."

"What did she explain, Afia?" Asa asked.

"That during slave rebellions, one Asa, an old African warrior-spirit, roamed the battle fields. He cared for the living but carried away the dead."

"What else did she say, Afia?"

"Nana told me that although Asa traveled by foot, he was so fast that no one, not even horsemen, could catch him."

"Yes, Afia. And the Morant Bay rebellion was one such battle."

"I follow you now," Afia said, nodding her head.

"That's good, Afia. You see, there was always talk of Asa from the Congo, and the battles on the plantations. What your nana told you was right."

"So you are that Asa!"

"Yes, Afia. I am Asa from the Bongo Nation out of Africa. And now there is this latest rebellion I mentioned."

"The rebellion in Morant Bay. Is that what you mean, Asa?" Afia asked.

"Yes, that war. I went there to get the bodies of Paul Bogle and George Gordon."

"Okay. I understand you better, now. You are really a warrior. You go to the battlefields to help the living or collect the dead."

"Yes, Afia."

"Why on earth! Why do you need dead bodies, Asa?" Aren asked, looking down at Lev.

"I save the dead ones. We need good bodies for living souls." Asa continued.

The silence that followed hung like a mysterious cloud. Asa understood. Maybe he should stop there or lead somewhere else.

"So did you come here to collect his body?" Bem asked, looking at Vijay.

"Not as yet," Asa responded.

Silence returned to the group. Aren pulled closer to Lev, wondering what must have been going through his son's mind. This was all so sudden and strange. It was one such monstrous event that sparked Lev's first bout of epilepsy at that very pond some years before. Aren remembered it as he nestled closer to Lev. The silence hung like a deepening mist.

"Asa King, then. Is that what we should call you?" Afia asked, reviving the conversation.

"My Families call me King. But, since you know of my duty, Asa should suffice."

"Okay, Asa King. That's a little clearer now," Afia replied.

"But, Asa, why Providence? And why us?" Afia asked.

"First, you sent for me," he said, looking steadfastly at Afia. "I was in

Galina, where I have another Family. Your call for help came to me there, Afia. So on my return to Portland, I stopped to help."

"Who sent for you?" Afia asked.

"You!" Asa said, focusing his gaze on Afia. Questioning eyes fell on her.

"Me? I am in enough trouble as it stands. Please leave me out of this!" Afia said. Suddenly, she remembered her dream and a look of cognizance brightened her face.

Asa laughed. "Do you remember dreaming of a birdman?" he asked Afia.

Bem, remembering Afia's dream, looked at her and then at Asa.

"Who are you?" asked Afia as a grimace creased her forehead.

"I am your guardian. You called for me last night. I am here to prevent your death."

"My death?" Afia questioned.

"Yes, all of you are as good as dead. That's how Bem planned it."

"What's that I heard, Bem?" Afia asked. "'You are all as good as dead?' What does that mean? Did you intend to kill me? And what about my baby and Esi? What did they ever do to you, Bem? And not to mention the time we've spent together since you are back. What were you thinking, Bem!"

Bem looked at the group, feeling shame and guilt. His visit to the Seminary, it was clear to him, had not changed him much. Bem did not know what to say; he stood grieving but unable to let go of his hurt. Afia, feeling the new life move, was more ready to forgive, though she still felt fear.

Following a long, brooding silence, Aren asked, "But that's all behind us now, Bem, isn't it?"

"Yes," he said, looking at Afia and seeing her lips quivered into a nervous smile as she held Esi's hand.

"I am sorry. I should have put what I learned at the Seminary to work," Bem added, looking at Vijay.

Puncus stepped forward and hugged Bem. "That is all behind us now," Puncus said, nodding at Afia.

Bem looked at Asa as he moved toward Afia, placing his arm around her waist and kissing her cheek. "I am sorry, Afia," he whispered.

Afia, smiling, looked at him but said nothing.

"And you, Vijay Boydell? What was your plan?" Asa asked. Bem and Aren looked at Vijay Boydell and then, in amazement, at each other.

Asa took Boydell's concealed revolver and threw it to the ground. He also, unknown to everyone, had come prepared for battle.

"It wouldn't have gone as you thought," Asa said, looking at Bem and Vijay. "You were all as good as dead," he repeated.

After a brief silence, Asa cleared his throat and continued, "Looking forwards, I am here to set up a Family; and you called me, Afia. You needed help."

"We thank you for coming here," said Aren.

"No, no! Thank you for being my stock." Asa said. "I will build my new Family from you."

"Stock? Friends, maybe." Vijay Boydell replied.

"Friends? You are my new Family stock. We are all together, now." Asa laughed. Everyone quieted.

"This might be a good time for our first Family meal," said Puncus, breaking the silence.

They ambled toward the table, and seated themselves. Afia, still fearful, made sure that Asa sat between her and Bem. Esi, on her other side, huddled close to her friend. They soon served each other and began eating.

"I will return when my children are old enough," Asa said.

"Where will you stay?" Bem asked.

"A home has been provided."

"A home has been provided?" questioned Aren, looking down at Lev and wondering how his son would adjust had they to share their luxurious Barton House with Asa and his family.

"You mean a home will be provided; isn't that what you really mean?" Afia asked.

"You may say that if you like. To me, it's all the same. But enough of that. Let's eat," said Asa. "We have work to do."

"What about the baby?" St. John asked.

"It's a girl," Asa said.

"A girl?" asked Afia. "I will have a girl!" she said, wiping her eyes.

"Yes, a baby girl, Afia," Asa reaffirmed.

"I will have a girl, a girl!" Afia said, caressing her stomach with both hands in delight.

"What about the baby?" Bem Covey asked, looking at Vijay Boydell. "The name and care of the baby. You are responsible, Vijay."

There was silence. Bem thought that Vijay should care for the child.

Boydell thought the girl should have his name, but that Bem should care for her. What should her name be? Afia knew the baby should stay with her, whatever else happened. She loved Bem, and he had vowed not to let anything split them apart. Such thoughts of ownership and rights deepened the pensive silence. Asa said he was there to create a Family. How perplexing! The situation called for wise judgment. Asa also knew that positions would soon be staked out and, once voiced, couldn't be easily reversed.

"The baby will take my name," Asa began, "and you, Boydell, will donate five acres for the girl's care. When she comes of age, Bem, the land becomes hers."

"Quite fair," said Puncus St. John.

"Bem," Asa continued, "the girl should live with you. And you, Afia, will care for her."

"That should make you happy, Afia," Esi said.

"You, Aren, will see that this agreement is kept."

"I would be delighted to, Asa."

"Good!" replied Asa, looking at Esi. "There is only one more thing."

"I wonder what that could be?" Afia asked.

Looking again at Esi, Asa said. "Your child, Esi, will carry Boydell's name. And this is the start of my Family," Asa ended with a broad smile.

The pronouncements seemed fair, with everyone in agreement. Asa looked around the table. Nodding heads gave the confirmation he expected. Silence, tinged with guilt, curiosity and relief, prevailed. Slowly an air of normalcy returned.

"I have no relationship with Vijay Boydell," Esi protested, hiding her true feelings for him.

"Yes, she hates me! How can her baby carry my name?" Vijay Boydell questioned.

"In time, it will be so," Asa said.

Asa looked on, reading the silence. He ate, gave thanks for the food, and was about to leave.

"Where are you going, now?" asked Aren.

"Back to Portland. You must remember. I have a Family there, too. I will get back here as soon as I can."

Asa stood before the group, rays of sunlight lighting his face. He appeared to be close to a hundred years old, so deeply furrowed his face was. His body, in contrast, was young and limber like that of a twenty-year-old. His certainty of gaze deflected any questions of age.

"Do you wish to spend the night with us?" Bem asked. "You could stay in Hell . . ."

Afia quickly interrupted, "The guest house, didn't you mean, Bem?"

"Yes, Asa, you could stay in our guest house."

"No, thanks, Bem. I must be back now. I have been called back."

"But the invitation stands, Asa. When you return, you can live with us, in the guest house," Bem said.

"Yes, we would be glad to have you, Asa," Afia added. "And your children could play with our daughter and Lev."

"Thank you both," Asa said. "All that has already been arranged. Moreover, we can talk about that when I return. He looked towards the darkening west and said, "They are calling for me. I must leave now."

"And do you expect to be in Portland tonight, traveling by foot?" Vijay asked, knowing that he himself couldn't cover that distance using his swiftest nag.

"Yes, Vijay. I will step it. I will be in Portland long before you get home," Asa said with a teasing smile.

"Can you prove any of that?" Afia asked.

Suddenly, the man standing before them seemed like a giant bird, and in a moment, he became a man again. He looked at them and smiled. Silence ruled.

"Let it thus remain," he said.

Aren placed an arm about Lev's shoulder, pulling his son to lean against him. He would have nothing panic his son to the point of an epileptic seizure.

"I will follow that man!" Puncus said, holding a satisfied smile.

"I must be Stepping off now," Asa said.

"Please stay a while longer with us," Puncus invited.

"Yes," Afia added, "unless your wife or your Family would mind it."

"My wife!" Asa leaned back and laughed. "I have a Family in need of a great Mother, Nweka, like you, Afia."

"Nweka? Me, me your Nweka, Asa?" she asked, with her palm over her heart.

"She has a family, here," Bem said, "and now, if you are right, a daughter to raise."

"This is true," Asa said.

"Then how can you speak of Afia as your Nweka?" Bem questioned.

"When her work here is done, Bem, and you are on the other side, she will be our great Mother Nweka, in Portland."

Puncus, laughing, said, "Hello, Mother Nweka."

The rest of the group looked at Afia, not knowing what to make of Asa's ominous pronouncement.

Afia cringed and, folding her arms, stepped back with a puzzled grimace as if examining her new role. Me, Mother Nweka? She asked herself. What qualifies me to be his Nweka? Why can't I stay here and be Afia with my family!

Bem, sensing Afia's uneasiness, moved closer to her. Putting his hand around her waist, he looked pointedly at Puncus and said, "Not so fast, St John!"

"Yes, not so fast," Asa repeated. "There is time ahead of us, and I must be leaving, now."

The group stood and bade Asa farewell, remaining for a while after his departure. In mild amazement they watched as he Stepped off.

More amazed than all was Lev. He was feeling as if still in an impenetrable nightmare, its pangs of anxiety – of fear and certain doom – hovering about him. He eyed the old cotton tree, high and silent on the far hillside, growing gloomy and more foreboding. He remembered it was rumored to be the haunt of frightful phantoms and beastly demons.

Yet, when Lev looked up again at his father, he saw a comforting, reassuring smile emanating from Aren's face. It told him all was well, despite the menacing cotton tree and the eerie Asa King.

Finally, the group returned to the food, and a slow, easy calm hovered. They had more questions than they had answers. Nevertheless, they ate in solitude, catching the last glimpse of Asa as he disappeared behind the far ridge of the distant hill.

Little did the party know that indeed a new Kumina Family had been born at Providence Pond that day.

Master M. Congo King

In the remaining light the party ate but was still unsatisfied. They felt that their lives were in the midst of deep transformations. With apprehension they lingered, looking at Puncus St. John.

"You should have told us, Puncus!"

"Told you about what, Afia?" he asked smiling.

"About your Kumina Family and Asa."

"I have been telling you all this time . . . by the way I live."

"Well, that's not enough!"

"Yes, and what about this new name, Afia, she is supposed to have?" Bem asked.

"And Asa?" Lev asked. "He seems like a duppyman, I mean a ghost, when he is walking!"

"Okay, Lev," Puncus said, smiling reassuringly at the lad, "Let me start with you. Asa is my leader, almost like Reverend Watkins is here in Providence. But, Lev, Asa is a different kind of leader. I met him in Fellowship, a little village just like ours in Portland."

"He is not like Reverend Watkins," Lev said. "Asa walks funny!"

"One day, Lev, we will Step like him," Puncus said, starting the laughter.

"Tell us about his wife!" Afia said.

"And where is his church?" Esi asked.

"Asa has neither wife nor church, if you mean a church like the Anglican one here. It is different with us. In the Kumina Family, we are the church!" St. John said, opening his arms to the table.

"So . . . where do you worship?" Vijay asked.

"Anywhere and all the time. What we do is give praise for life . . . and our part in it. That's how we worship."

"And what about heaven?" Aren asked.

"Yes and hell, too . . . what about that?" Vijay asked.

"Yes. And sin, and salvation: what about those?" Bem asked.

"So many questions. Where do you think you are, the *Any Questions*? Kumina belief is that heaven and hell are right here," Puncus said pointing at his heart. "It's all here on earth, inside us, you and me. But, it's our choice which one we live in, at any time."

"Is that all there is to it, Puncus?" Esi asked.

"That's one big slab of it, Esi."

"We could tell that you are associated with something special, Puncus. You live different from us. We go to church. We observe Christmas and Easter, and participate in the sacraments. We do not see you do anything like that!" Afia said.

"I have only one thing to say about that, Afia."

"What is it, Puncus?" Esi asked.

"When your life is your ritual, when you are guided by Love, there is nothing distinctive about how you live. Every minute, every day, you know that you are the church, the religion, and what you do defines you. All Kumina does is help us become who we really are. That alone is enough for a lifetime! I don't really want to do anything else."

"It seems to me," Aren said, "that your religion is made up as you go. There is no true center, no real message in it."

"Yes, Aren. A part of that is true. We are not bounded by doctrine or custom, only by Love, and what we are trying to become," Puncus said. "We live by Love as it guides us."

"That makes you sound like you are better than the rest of us, Puncus," Bem said.

"And everyone to his own way? That's confusion!" Vijay added. "Utter madness!"

"Or her own way, Vijay . . . as guided by Love," Puncus said smiling. "That's an important part of it. And, moreover, we are responsible to ourselves for how we live."

"You make it sound very straightforward, Puncus: simple and straightforward."

"Yes, but it is not as simple as it appears, Afia. We sometimes interfere with the process, with what love is trying to do through us. So our lives often get out of kilter," Puncus said. "We just need to let love have its way, that's all."

"Then, if it's that simple, Puncus, why is Kumina illegal? Why did you run away from Galina? Don't you know Reverend Watkins and the Monsignor told us about your little secret?" Vijay asked.

"So, they told you, ah?"

"Yes! And that's not all, Puncus. Why did Detective Graham ask so many questions about you when you first came to Providence? Why? Why is all this happening if Kumina is as pure as you make it out to be? Why, Puncus? Why did you run?" Vijay questioned.

"To be direct, Vijay, I ran so as not to compromise my beliefs. That's the first thing. And I hope that the Reverends told you about that, too. I ran so as not to betray the Family in Galina. That's the second reason. And you say *ran*? Really, I was led here so that there could be more Kumina Families when, if I had stayed in Galina, there would have been none. But I challenge you, Vijay. What crime did they accuse me of?"

"None, Puncus. No crime at all. But," Vijay continued, "there must be something deeper, Puncus. Kumina is always in the dark, always on the run. Why?"

"That's because the authorities do not really understand us. They think we are demonic," Puncus replied.

"Well, anyone who cares for dead bodies as if they were alive must be demonic!" Bem said.

"Only if you believe in devils, Bem. We don't!"

"So what do you believe?" Esi asked.

"I have been telling you. We believe in Love, in life, in the Family: in you and me, in now!"

"Then, what's with the dead bodies?" Bem asked.

"We honor them as we honor life. They are garments for the spirits that visit us."

"Hold it right there, Puncus. Hold it right there. That's demonic!" Vijay protested.

"All I am saying is that when the spirits of our ancestors come back to visit us, we provide bodies for them. That's what a Mother, a Nweka, will do. She cares for the bodies of our beloved."

"What? Asa collects dead bodies and the Nweka cares for them? Is that what he wants Afia to do?" Esi asked.

"Yes, Esi. Afia will hold the Family together. Without a Mother there can be no Family," Puncus replied.

A deathly silence hovered over the table. For a moment it seemed to Afia that the dead bodies formed the connection between this life and the hereafter and she would be working at that junction. The thought intrigued her. "And his children, his children!" Afia wondered.

"There are only two of them. I met them in Galina, and Fellowship."

"Do you go to Galina, Puncus?"

"Yes, Esi. I told you I am a Kumina member. I attend the Dances there, and in Portland, too."

"No wonder you Dance so well," Afia said.

"Thank you, Afia. There is nothing like a good Kumina Dance, you know."

"But it's your cooking that bothers us, Puncus," Esi said, bringing laughter to the table.

"So . . . who are Asa's children?" Esi asked, ending the merriment.

"Oh! There is Master Congo. Master M. Congo King, I should have said. And his older sister by a few years, Miss Hene. Master Congo is scarcely older than Lev, here," Puncus said, pointing at the youngster. "But already he is in training to lead our Kumina Family in Providence."

"And Miss Hene . . . did I get her name right?"

"Yes, Esi. You did. Miss Hene is going to be the Mother, here. She also will train Afia in our Kumina ways."

"What will Asa do after he brings Congo and Miss Hene here?" Esi asked.

"Oh, nothing! But that's where their lives really begin. Congo and Miss Hene will be all on their own, and the fate of this Family depends fully on them."

"And won't Asa come back to help if things go wrong?"

"He rarely ventures back in, Esi. Once he starts a new Family, it is on its own. But this I will tell you. Congo and Miss Hene will have been well trained before coming here. Asa will see to that!"

"Why is that so, Puncus, that Asa will not come back to visit?"

"First of all, Esi, each Family is its own center. And all the Families are loosely connected. Asa will not be responsible for this Family once Master Congo and Miss Hene are here."

"But why is that, Puncus?" Esi asked.

"It's a matter of responsibility, Esi. First, we must learn to take care of ourselves. There is also the practical side . . . a matter of survival. Look, Esi, the authorities may kill Asa like they did Paul Bogle, but they will not kill Kumina."

"That's very reassuring!" Vijay said.

"So . . . if you have no church, where will Master Congo preach? What will he do?" Aren asked.

"He will make converts by showing us how to live. The role as the leader is to expand the kingdom of Love by the example of his life. We do not preach and give sermons. We just live! Me? I dance at the *Any Questions*. Our way is so simple; no wonder most people don't understand it."

"You mean 'no wonder people fear it,' don't you, Puncus?"

"Okay, Afia," Puncus said, joining the laughter.

"So, what about you, Puncus? Why don't you show us how to live?" Esi asked.

"Ah. I have been! I answer every question put to me, and I Dance. I am sorry if it does not seem like leadership to you. But Master Congo, as young as he is right now, I can see a true leader in him. There, I tell you, is a leader. He will show you!"

"This is all so new to us," Afia said.

"Yes, I understand," Puncus, replied. "You see; we all have a different way of leading: each from his own center, independent: as guided by love. We report to no one. But if we need help, we find it in each other, from the Family."

"Quite interesting!" Afia said.

"Congo's long training with Asa," Puncus said, "will make his leadership better, much better than mine. My only hope is that he lives as he has been shown."

"This Kumina thing does not sound so bad now that you explain it, Puncus," Bem said, breaking the silence.

"Not 'thing,' Bem, Kumina Family!"

"Okay, Puncus. Thank you," Bem smiled as he cleared his throat, bowing his head.

"Nweka seems like somebody I could be! Afia remarked, and then continued, "When is Asa returning?"

"I am not sure. But, you know, there is talk of a smallpox outbreak in Portland," Puncus replied. "That's why Asa is hurrying there tonight."

"Yes," Vijay said. "The infection started in Kingston and is slowly moving this way through Portland."

"We have all heard about it. That may keep Asa busy. After things settle, I am sure Asa will be here with Master Congo and Miss Hene."

"Can you be more specific about the date, Puncus?" Esi asked.

"I can't be exact. But the new century is only fourteen years away. By that time Master Congo will be in his mid to late twenties. That's about the age Asa likes to start a new leader."

"You say only fourteen years?" Esi asked. "That seems like a lifetime to me! By then we may all be dead and gone. Why should we even be concerned about this?" Esi said, poking fun at the whole affair.

"Yes, dead but not gone." Puncus replied, joining the laughter.

"But that should be eventful!" Afia said, "having our own Kumina Family here."

"I assure you, Master Congo is a wonderful young man. He will bring the world to Providence Pond!" Puncus said.

"That would be some feat!" Afia said in fit of laughter.

"But well worth it," Aren responded.

"If it can be done, Master Congo will do it!" Puncus said, joining the laughter.

"You seem to have a lot of faith in Master Congo, Puncus."

"Yes, Aren. Faith in him, Asa, and the process."

To break the long pause that followed, Puncus pointed to Byah, who started drumming a short piece as Puncus danced unconcerned.

"All very strange! Strange but delightful," Vijay said, shaking his head.

"But I am feeling much better, now," Bem added.

Lev rested his head against Aren's shoulder. His father nestled closer to him as Afia smiled at the lad.

"Are you feeling all right, Lev?" Esi asked.

Lev did not reply. He simply smiled and looked up at his father with his arms still crossed in front of him.

"If you permit me," Aren said, "I would like to go back to something Asa mentioned."

"What is that, Aren?" Esi asked.

"It must be about my baby's land," Afia said.

"Yes," Aren agreed. "Do you know which parcel you will give to Afia's daughter, Vijay?"

"You mean my daughter. Right, Aren?" Bem said, laughing as he looked at Vijay. A spirit of cordiality was slowly coming to the table.

"What are you going to call her, Afia?" Esi asked.

"Ama! I don't care which day of the week she will be born on," Afia said laughing.

"I like that name, Afia!" Bem said. "And what will you call your child, Esi?"

"She will be a girl like Ama and they can play together."

"That's sweet of you to say, Esi. We will be just one big family here in Providence."

"Yes. But we'll have to get married first, Esi," Vijay said.

"Well, if Asa said we are going to get married, we are going to!"

"So does that mean you will marry me, Esi?"

"Yes! Of course, Vijay! And we will call our daughter Charm. Do you agree?"

"Yes, of course, Esi. That's a nice name!"

"Ama and Charm. How lovely!" Afia laughed. "Sisters of best friends, always together!" Afia said, hugging Esi.

"Which parcel?" Aren repeated, interrupting the laughter and bringing back a sense of reality to the table.

As Aren spoke, he glanced at the full face of the rising moon. The radiant disk had just climbed the crest to the distant hills, sending golden ripples across the hushed, mysterious pond. Following Aren, the friends looked from the innocent moon down to the water, wondering why they had never seen the pond like that before. It appeared alive, yet silent and powerful, with a haunting presence. Lev nestled closer to his father, pondering anxiously where beneath the gentle waves his mother might still lie.

"The one next to Hell . . ."

"Don't bring that up now, Vijay," Bem interrupted. "Just let's say 'the guest house.'"

"Okay, Bem. Your Ama will get the parcel next to your guest house," Vijay said.

"Good! Now we are one big Family," Aren said, lifting Lev onto his lap and looking at Bem and Vijay.

"It's a deal!" Bem said, reaching to shake Vijay's hand.

"Let's all hold hands," Puncus invited, laying his slender hands first out on the table. Esi took one of his and Afia held his other hand. Vijay and Bem did likewise, until all the hands were joined.

"Whose hand should I hold?" Lev asked, looking up at Puncus.

"First you have to lay your hands on the table," Puncus said, smiling at Lev.

Lev unfolded his arms and laid his open palms on the table.

They all held Lev's hands. They held hands, pondering the events of the evening, until Puncus said, "Thank you for joining the Kumina Family. So in life and in death we will remain."

It was then that Puncus St. John got yet another call: it was time for him to Dance at the *Any Questions* and Byah would not let him forget. With the golden light shimmering across the pond in yet another Dance, Byah started drumming. As if called to duty, Puncus arose and Danced a strange jig not before seen in Providence. He Danced and Byah drummed. The new converts watched in awe . . . wondering if some day they would awake from their sweet trance. But it did not matter. For now, they were satisfied that Puncus St. John was their Dancer!

Under the open light of the heavens, and feeling united, the small group walked up from Providence Pond, hoping that the time would go quickly until Master M. Congo King would be with them.

Part 2: The Family
(1900 to 1910)

Reconnections

Within a few years of Asa's appearance at Providence Pond, a potent smallpox epidemic swept across Jamaica. The disease started slowly, then reached its destructive zenith toward the end of 1890. It finally waned with the approach of the new century. Since the rural populace had neither medication nor magical antidotes, the disease expired more slowly there, leaving fatal strikes in its dying wake.

With the contagion finally over, Providence anguished more from the fear of its return than from the perished souls. Still, there remained sorrow and great hardship. New hopes were rekindled from the fragments of dreams that persisted. Trying times indeed! But neither would the sun nor the rain neglect Providence forever.

Soon after Asa's visit and prediction, Vijay and Esi had married. The new couple lived in Providence. Not long following, Vijay's parents died. With Esi pregnant, the family returned to his parents' home in Free Hill where Vijay's sister lived.

Just before the close of the old century, both Vijay and Esi succumbed to the disease, leaving Charm, their newborn daughter, in the care of her aunt.

Following Vijay's death, Bem Covey leased the Boydell property in Providence. With Bem's death occurring not long after, the Boydells quickly transferred the management of their farm to Aren Tyler. Aren's tenure didn't last long either. He also fell to the disease. In only two decades, Providence had been resized like a juiced fruit.

Like clear blue sky, Afia and her family persisted; more than that, they increased. Ama King, by then a beautiful maiden in her early twenties, was Afia's firstborn. She was Saturday's child, so named by Afia following Akan tradition. In the ensuing year came Ulu Covey, Ama's sister. While Mr. Covey was alive and capable, three others were born: a boy, Rex Covey, and two girls, Kisi Stevens and Celestina White. Neither time nor marriage, it seemed, had diminished Afia's desirability or her sense of independence. Nothing killed her power of choice! The last girl, like Bem, however, soon died from the same infection.

Unruly Rex Covey had, from the early age of thirteen, been dispatched to New York, where he attended high school and, subsequently, college. He seemed stuck there forever. Afia's third baby, Kisi Stevens, born on a bright Sunday morning and whose father was British, kept the home with Afia. That was what Bem's remaining household looked like when Asa King returned to Providence.

Ulu, queen of the Covey household, to her father's eyes at least, had escaped the pangs of the pestilence. When she was not sequestered in her exclusive St. Hilda's all-women boarding school, Ulu vacationed in New York, where she stayed with Bem's elder brother. There, she subsequently finished a secretarial and business-school curriculum. Upon her return to Providence, Ulu managed the family's estate with Ama's assistance.

It was Ama who met Ulu at the bus stop in Jacks River to escort her home on her return from New York. That was a sunny day. As Bem would have expected her to do, Ama took Ulu's horse to retrieve her sister. Ama had fed and watered, then brushed the nag to a sleek auburn glow, saddled and led it along the three-mile journey to meet Ulu.

When at last the late bus screeched to its stop, Ulu descended to the platform with royal poise. After ceremoniously kissing Ama, she lovingly kissed, cuddled, and whispered to Rock, her ride, before mounting him. They headed home with Ulu in front. Ama struggled and toiled behind with Ulu's oversized luggage, wondering why she had been left alone with it. Ama also pondered why she, the eldest daughter, had not been sent to school. Would that have been her fate had her father headed the household? So she trudged along behind her revered sister until they reached home where she would care for both Ulu and Rock!

Even though Afia had borne their first child, Vijay's death didn't bother her. Afia had never loved him and had long considered Asa King the spiritual father of her firstborn. That was made easier for her because

Bem would rather not think of Vijay nor have his name mentioned, at least not in their home.

It was the knowledge of Esi's death, though, that unnerved her. Afia loved Charm and longed for her custody. In fact, Afia had approached the Boydell family requesting Charm. Her argument was that the sisters, Ama and Charm, should live together, and that she, knowing Esi better than anyone else, would be best suited to mother the girls. That was not to be. After much deliberation, the Boydell thought it best to raise Charm in Free Hill.

This shunted any opportunity Afia had to keep Charm and Ama in easy contact. As time passed, all of Esi that remained with Afia were memories and ardent hopes that the sisters would someday be reconnected. This, however, was never to be. Life for its own reasons forged seemingly distant, parallel paths for the siblings.

Despite all, life's urge to persist, its unrelenting yet directionless push, conveyed hope and renewed vigor to the nascent century. It was that stirring which brought the almost dead elementary school of Providence back to life. It had been closed during the epidemic, but now the teachers had been recalled. New minds of Providence clamored for the reopening of their school and were rewarded with that and a new principal, Headmaster Henry Isaac Love. He was young and dashing. Only recently graduated from Teacher's college, he had taken on his first appointment with bold, brilliant dreams. His charm and wit made him an instant celebrity, and he intended to take full advantage of it with the approaching school year just a few days away.

For his September reopening ceremony, the Headmaster invited Monsignor Ricardo Silva, Anglican Reverend Bernard Watkins, and the eminent Doctor Devinder Singh to offer their blessings and reassure the public that the evil epidemic had passed. Coupled with the physician's dedicated work and new medicines, Providence's health had returned and, with it, the rigor and excitement of the ensuing year. The entire village of Providence attended the function with eager support for the reopening efforts.

This could not be otherwise. Children, fearing the disease, had refused schooling; and parents, preferring living children to dead classrooms, encouraged the refusal. Parents, however, knew the promise of education and overwhelmingly supported the reopening ceremony. They dragged their youngsters along with them to be assured, as they were, that the ter-rifying monster had really departed Providence, and whatever remained of it would finally be expunged by the holy men.

At that very function, Headmaster Henry Love, whose curious sur-name had been sometimes snickered at and smeared in prosaic, sexual terms on the farms, attempted a clarification. Love made his explanation from the lectern in a boastful yet light-hearted manner. This he did without malice or mention of the community's ridicule of his name.

Jokingly, he pointed out that, although his grandfather had emigrated from Scotland, his name was originally Germanic, where the "v" was ini-tially a "w". In the German, he explained, his name meant lion and, as a nature-symbol, was the marbled head of the beast standing guard outside houses and official buildings. With a tinge of seriousness, Henry Isaac Love explained that his name, lion, had mythological associations with the Roman and Greek sun gods.

Following the Headmaster at the podium, Monsignor Ricardo Silva complemented Love on his scholarship, adding that the religious lion pre-dated the Greek epoch and pointed rather to the Egyptian goddess from whom the Jews copied, whence the godly symbol entered Christianity and assumed its current hackneyed usage.

"My mission here," Reverend Bernard Watkins started, "is to offer support and guidance: to enforce spiritual control on this community. Why you may ask? As my Bible says," he said, shaking the Good Book at the audience, 'the wages of sin is death.' That, we have just witnessed. No doubt it was our sin and waywardness that brought this evil epidemic upon us. It was the cleansing grace of our Lord. It was a warning that we men of cloth did not force a strong spiritual discipline on our flock. If we once failed, we will not anymore. From henceforth, we will walk the 'straight and narrow' and keep all evil from this very house."

He held his Bible close to his heart and said, "Let us pray." Their recitation of the Lord's Prayer closed the meeting.

After the ceremony, the Headmaster, seen with increased association to the deity, became a more potent magnet, pulling the entire community to himself and the school. Young women wouldn't be slow, either, in offering themselves as willing sacrifices to that god. Among the elite of Providence, Love's full luster was heightened.

The snickering and derision at the *Any Questions* or elsewhere among the lower echelon increased. At the tavern, St. John remained quiet, hoping that his caution would not further fan the flames of ridicule. His silence, treated as consent or encouragement, did not help either, and soon Headmaster Love became most talked about in Providence.

Lev Tyler

Yet Headmaster Henry Isaac Love wouldn't be the only new center in Providence. That spark of change also brought Asa's return. He didn't come alone this time. The Family he promised accompanied him. It consisted of his two offspring, Master Congo and Miss Hene King, both in their early twenties.

Asa arrived with a wizened, emaciated body, signaling the call of death; even though, as before, his behavior and general rapport denied it. In marked contrast, his progeny sparkled with health and enthusiasm. They were penniless, though. That was advertised by their meager, worn-out clothing and hunger that begged in silence, not shame. But regardless of their appearance and lack of material worth, Asa's Family did announce, by the glow of their countenances, that they were, indeed, spiritually rich!

In sharp contrast, Lev Tyler had grown into a tall, fine-looking, young man. He wore his hair low and shaved a delicate pattern from his facial hair. It made him look rather distinctive but without an air of arrogance. In manner, he was soft spoken and given more to asking questions than to quick judgment.

In his early twenties, Lev had the responsibility of administering his father's property together with the Boydell's. Barton House jail was also his responsibility. With the paltry help he mustered from the surrounding villages, it was hard.

Nevertheless, there wasn't much choice for the young man. Lev could run, or accept the challenge. He did the latter, and his new position brought wealth and respect. Not that Lev needed or yearned for either. What he liked was the work, the open sunshine and the close, unhindered association with the villagers. Lev was kind and thoughtful to his workers, and they in turn cared for him so that he did not miss the love of his parents.

He had never taken a wife and, except for servants, young Lev lived alone in the palatial Barton House. He longed for a consort, and for friends. Even though he had scant memories of his mother, his father's demise had weakened him. Lev had never quite recovered from it. He didn't need more servants, for they had to be managed. What he needed was a father, a friend, and a partner. Lev Tyler needed a family. Could it be that Providence in one stroke would link and forever combine these very dissimilar yet needy families?

Asa, on his return to Providence, would first visit the Coveys. That was where he had grafted himself into Providence. That was where the first stock of his Family lay dormant; and he had to make the reconnection, linking Ama King and his arriving progeny into one Family.

Family Principles

For Asa, knocking on the Covey's door that Friday was a simple matter of completing the contract that was started at Providence Pond about twenty years previously.

"Come in!" shouted Kisi, Afia's youngest daughter, from her comfortable seat at the kitchen table.

It was early morning and Ama was preparing the family's breakfast. It was simple enough, cut fruit and hot cereal. Yet, it had to be done. Lev and Puncus, at Ulu's invitation, had already been seated along with Afia and Kisi. They were gathered, as Lev had requested, to plan the summer's festivities at Providence Pond.

When the knocking repeated, Ama, who had just brought food to the table, yelled, "The door is open. Come in!" With this, she walked to the front door, wiping her hands on the long, fruit-stained apron hanging from her dainty waist.

"Yes?" she asked, staring at the strangers.

"Yes!" replied Asa, nodding as he smiled, "I was expecting Nweka, our Mother."

"Who? Who did you say? " Ama started to ask, when Afia shouted from behind Ama as she approached the door.

"Good morning! Is there something I can do for you?"

"Good Morning, Nweka," the stranger replied.

"And who are you?" Afia asked, somewhat hesitantly, stepping back from the sight of his gaunt face.

As Afia spoke, the stranger's face, his entire body, seemed to change before her, momentarily taking on the form of a giant bird, and then appearing human again. Ama must not have seen it, for she simply stood there, wiping the sweat from her forehead.

Momentarily weakened by fright and disbelief, Afia clutched the door for support. Ama, noticing Afia's apparent giddiness, moved to assist her mother.

"It's all right, Ama," Afia said. "I'll be okay."

Afia looked up to the stranger, this time with a smile of awareness and slight embarrassment, and asked, "Won't you please come in?"

"Yes," replied the stranger, hesitantly.

"Well, Asa, come in!" Afia repeated with more assertiveness.

"Thank you," Asa said as he turned around and ushered a younger man and woman through the door ahead of him.

"Goodness!" said Afia, seating them at the breakfast table. "And who are these wonderful young folk?"

"Gracious!" shouted Puncus St. John, as he leaped to his feet and rushed to hug the three strangers. "How are you, how are you?" he asked as he kissed the stranger's face.

"Excellent, Puncus! All is good," said the stranger who, turning to Afia, said, "Please excuse the interruption."

As he spoke, Puncus Danced as if oblivious to his surroundings, so delighted he was. As soon as he seated himself again, the stranger patted the shoulder of the young man seated to his right. "This is Master Congo, my second. He is like the great river," Asa said with a whimsical smile. "And the young woman, his older sister, her name is Miss Hene."

"Miss Hene, did you say, Asa? What a lovely, unusual name!" Afia remarked.

"Yes, Afia. I thought . . . I would get a boy as the first child. So I chose the name Hene before the birth. Miss Hene is a few years older than Congo. Hene is actually the Twi word for king or chief. My first-born I wanted to lead the new Family. But as you see, providence brought us a girl. So to cover my mistake, or maybe my pride," Asa said with a grin, "I named her Miss Hene."

Afia, looking at the young woman, placed her hand over her mouth and started to laugh. "So, Miss Hene, you are really Miss King King?"

"Yes, Afia. Or Miss Chief, if you prefer," Miss Hene said, joining in the laughter.

"And who, may I ask, is the gentleman seated before me?" Miss Hene asked, looking into the gentle, captivating eyes studying her face.

"Oh, this is Lev. Lev Tyler. Do you remember him?" Afia said, directing her question to Asa.

"Yes, of course, he was the lad at the pond. What a gentleman he has grown into!"

"Indeed, indeed. He is a good man for Providence."

"I see, I see," Asa remarked, eager to learn more of Lev.

"And here are my daughters. This is Ama; she met you at the door," Afia said, pointing at her daughter. "And," she continued, "standing there beside Ama is Ulu, and the other seated beside Miss Hene is Kisi. She is the youngest, and she is just like me when I was young, they say." Afia ended in playful laughter.

"Quite a lovely family here!" Asa remarked.

"Thank you, Asa," Afia said.

"Yes," replied Asa. "And Puncus met Master Congo and Miss Hene in Portland."

"Hello, Puncus," Miss Hene and Congo said in unison. Puncus nodded and returned their greeting with a broad smile.

"Now we are together again," said Asa.

"Together again?" asked Ama, looking at her mother.

"Oh, yes, Ama."

Ama, like the other young folk, was thrown into confusion. Afia tried to explain. "This is Asa, Asa King of the Bongo Nation. You remember the family stories about him, don't you?"

"Oh! Asa King the Bongo-man? My father who is not my father?" Ama asked.

"Yes, that man. And if I have it right, this is the rest of your kin, your brother and sister, Master Congo and Miss Hene," Afia answered.

"Yes, yes, Ama. Very much so," confirmed Asa.

In silence the strangers eyed each other closely. New bonds formed. Yet there was a curiosity deep and questioning, looking for acceptance.

For Lev, the silence was not as awkward as it could have been. He scrolled back in time, capturing the eerie moment at the pond when the stranger, Asa, seemed to have fallen out of nowhere to settle a most dreaded paternal problem. He hadn't forgotten it, but remembered a different face and body with the same voice, manner, and authority.

Lev carefully eyed the visitors sitting before him. Congo, not much younger than he, seemingly absorbed with Ulu, abounded with energy and delight.

Yet, it was Miss Hene's countenance that captivated Lev, making him feel guilty at staring so squarely at her face. He felt intimidated. Lev thought she had an air of magic or mystery about her. Miss Hene appeared aloof and childish at once, smiling easily. She remained deep, unfathomable.

Miss Hene noticed Lev's uneasiness when her eyes on occasion met his. His eyes spoke of pain, a man of abundance, yet loneliness. She didn't know how to respond to him. When she blushed, she forced her face upwards, prolonging her smile. Lev's head unconsciously followed hers, seeking contact with her caring, loving eyes.

The agreement to which Vijay Boydell had entered at the pond held. Ama had been provided for. She knew of the agreement, and that Asa King, the man whose name she bore, meant her well even before her birth.

Ama's eyes meet Asa's across the table. Theirs was a comfortable gaze. Her eyes swallowed his, as if she were thirsty for them. She wanted to thank him, to reach out and touch him. She looked at Master Congo and Miss Hene and wondered what they were like. She had another Family, of which she had only heard. Now it was before her.

Ulu's steadfast look, sometimes at him and at other times seemingly through him, had awakened Congo's enthusiasm. She knew he was from the Bongo Nation, the plantation workers who were snubbed during slavery because of their loud, drumming music. That same Bongo group, Ulu knew, was also derided as country because it was made to live in the backlands, far from British civility. Ulu thought of the Bongo as more given to artistic pursuit and music than to warfare and business and leadership, as the Ashanti from whom she was descended. Ulu looked at Congo with scorn. Without knowing it, however, Ulu had made herself his prey, and he an unwitting hunter.

Congo's prolonged training and close connection with the highly disciplined Asa had prevented him from accepting or adequately attending to his manhood. What Congo, in his late twenties, had long deferred now crept from beneath with monstrous force and agility to haunt and shape his life.

Afia noticed the look, and her eyes focused on Ama as she asked, "Should we eat?"

"Yes, of course," replied Ama. With that, Ama scurried nervously into the kitchen and started serving.

"This must be the Family you spoke about, Asa," Afia said.

"Yes, a part of it. I have other Families in Portland and St. Thomas."

"We could think of it this way," Miss Hene said. "Asa has settlements in those parishes and we are here to start another settlement in Providence."

"That still does not answer anything about his wife," Afia said.

"I do not have a wife. I am in need of a Mother," Asa said.

"A Mother!" Afia questioned. "You already have grown children."

"My Family in Portland needs a Nweka."

Afia's mind flashed back to the evening years ago at Providence Pond. Asa had not only saved her life then, he had given her a new name, Nweka. After much musing with the party about her new name, Afia finally submitted to the then-novel role of Mother. But much time had since passed.

Afia's thoughtfulness filled the room with silence. She mused: Nweka, not Afia. Nweka? Nweka! I like it. And Portland, why not here? But, my life here is over. I have always known that! So am I to leave my home, my friends? Oh, what friends? And no husband! Esi is dead and so is Bem. But Mother? Nweka? Is that what I asked for? How did this all happen? But . . . maybe that does not matter. After all . . . after all my wild years, maybe it's time I finally settle down . . . give up being me, Afia, and be obedient. Maybe its time I become his Nweka, as I wanted to when he first visited us at the pond. Nweka! It does not sound so bad after all!

"Asa! I will be your Nweka," she finally said, as if seeking confirmation that she had made the right decision.

"Congratulations, Nweka!" Puncus said, springing from his chair and taking Miss Hene with him into an impromptu dance. "No more Afia, no more Afia. We have a Nweka!"

"Yes," said Kisi. "But I want to be with my mother, with Nweka."

"Nweka is still your mother, but now she will be Mother to a much greater Family," Asa said.

"You are our daughter, Kisi," Nweka added, "and you are invited to join us, too, in Portland."

"And leave everything here, behind?"

"Yes, Kisi, that's how we Step," Asa said.

"You mean travel, don't you?"

"If you say so, Kisi," Asa said smiling. "I see there is much explanation to do here."

"There surely is," Lev replied. "For example, you haven't explained where you will live, Asa!" Lev said.

"Nweka and you, Kisi, let's talk about Stepping later. It seems that in Lev's eyes, settling our living arrangements is what we should do now."

"Well, it would certainly be nice," Lev said.

"You would not remember this, Lev, but at the pond Bem and I invited Asa to live in our guest house," Nweka said.

"But," Lev asked, "isn't there someone in the guest house already?"

"Ah!" remarked Nweka, with a sudden lift of her hand, "I simply forgot! It's better to leave that alone for now."

"And, moreover, Barton House really needs new management. I am tired, really very tired of it," Lev continued, "so Congo and Miss Hene would be of great help."

Nweka looked at Lev. He seemed to be out of place offering what might not be needed, and in such a presumptuous manner. She did notice that the Kings had come to the door with nothing except the clothes they wore. Had Lev noticed that too? Well, if he had, how pompous he had been in his offer. On the other hand, if Lev hadn't noticed their seeming neediness, then how selfish could he be? Maybe Nweka felt a touch of jealousy at Lev's offer. Maybe she wanted the Kings to stay with her. Whatever the reason, Lev's abruptness or seeming poor manners needed some cushioning, she thought. Nweka, however, didn't dare offer it. She looked questioningly at Lev. She saw his eyes working Miss Hene's face as though he had yet another reason for his offer. Nweka's thoughts and observations forced her into silence.

"Yes," said Asa, "Aren did offer, and we would be glad to accept your hospitality, Lev."

"Then thank you," said Lev with great relief and enthusiasm. "I would be glad to have you!"

With the question answered, Congo again studied Ulu's face. She seemed to want to get away from his stare. She looked down at the table. Congo watched.

Lev looked at Ulu, who had been like a sister to him. She often assisted him while he entertained at Barton House. He wanted some kind of approval from her. Ulu remained detached, silent.

"You are so quiet, Ulu!" Lev said.

"Well, it's not unlike her," said Nweka; "she is always thinking, planning, you know."

Congo continued examining Ulu's face.

"She is the bright one," Nweka said, breaking the tension.

"Thank you, Nweka; I mean *Mother*," Ulu responded, blushing.

"If I may say something," Congo said, "all she is missing is a man . . . a husband, I mean." With his innermost thought aired, Congo twitched in embarrassment. He looked around the table, noticing that everyone else shared his astonishment. He wanted to hide.

"What *you* are missing, *Bongo*, is your manhood! And maybe a woman to train you, properly," Ulu snapped. "And you might as well drop your country life right here!"

Congo's athletic frame rebounded in the chair as if it had been stung. His predatory senses awoke, but his head prevailed. He had mistakenly awakened his quarry, the woman his eyes stalked, and its shocking response was rebuttal, not flight. Congo would require a new strategy. It wouldn't be long in coming, he thought. For now, he remained silent.

Congo had lived too long under the tutelage of the powerful Asa King, Puncus thought. Congo, it appeared to him, needed time to find his true voice.

"He has been trained for his life's work," Asa said.

"Some training! What he must know is that Providence is mainly Akan. We are Ghanaian, Ashanti, Twi, Fante; and I have not said Bongo yet." Ulu said.

"Congo will fall in line, Ulu. That I assure you, "Asa said. "He will fall in line and get his work done."

"And what, may I ask, is that?" questioned Lev.

"To be a missionary. To grow this Family."

"What did you bring with you? To grow a Family?" Ulu echoed. What do you have, I mean, to . . ."

"Ulu! That's enough," Nweka interrupted.

"Please, let her," Asa replied.

"So, answer!"

"Faith, Ulu! Faith and a vision are what we bring," Asa said.

"Well, at least you can all work on Lev's farm. He seems willing to have you."

To end the discomforting silence and get back to Lev's question, Miss Hene said, "He needs to grow a Family here."

"Yes, to grow it. He has been trained," reaffirmed Asa.

"A missionary? Did I get that right?" Kisi asked.

"Yes!"

"Are you going to build a church, here?" Kisi asked.

"The foundations have been built already," Asa responded.

"What is the name of your church?" Kisi asked

"It is not really a church. Our Family has a simple principle, something to bind us together," Asa replied.

"What's your Family principle?" Ulu asked.

"Love, Ulu," Puncus replied.

"And what name do you call your church, or Family, or your whatever . . . ?" asked Lev.

"Kumina! That's the name of our Family, and we communicate through love," Asa replied.

"Communication is important," Ama remarked.

"Yes, it is. So we teach the Family to commune and show love between the living and the dead."

"The dead?" Kisi asked.

"Yes, especially with the dead. You see, Kisi, love persists. Bodies die, but love continues," Puncus answered.

"So?" asked Nweka.

"Well, to take it further, I must add that this world and the next need each other. They support each other."

"And how is that?" Kisi questioned.

"This is very complicated, Kisi, but let me try and answer you," Asa said.

"Please do."

"You see, Kisi, we have bodies which the Family cares for. These are bodies of our dearly beloved."

"You take care of dead bodies, Asa?"

"Not really dead bodies, Kisi. But bodies of our dearly beloved, whose spirits have joined the Light. We care for the bodies so that the spirits of those who have crossed over – those who care for us enough to revisit us – can use those bodies on their return. The spirits of our dearly beloved may have gone on, but not forever."

"Are you sure of this?"

"Yes, Kisi, as sure as can be! We commune with them and they prophesy for us."

Silence fell over the table. Eyes were focused on Asa. "For those who saw me before, you will see that I have a different body than when I came first," he said, pointing at himself. "When this body fails – gets sick, injured or is about to die of old age – I need to take on another. But my case is unusual. I should have crossed over long ago. But I was selected to build families and spread this word of love." Asa paused for a while, giving his audience time to digest his words. "So you see, Ulu, I have trained Master Congo here to lead this Family. I am a King in the movement, the only King, and Congo is now a Master. We have Families in Portland and St. Thomas, and I am building in this direction, in St. Mary. Next we will go to St. Ann."

"What did you call him? Master Congo? You refer to him as Master when he has nothing! Why do you call a penniless person Master?" Ulu asked.

"Congo is a Master in the Family, Ulu. I am King. That means that Congo can officiate in my place."

"What's that exactly? What will Congo do?" asked Ulu.

"He will make converts, one at a time. You see, our lifestyle is different, and when we are asked to explain it, we do so by showing love: here above and there below," he said, looking at the floor as if it were the ground. "All of our life is between here and there. Congo has been trained to collect bodies, care for them, and walk the dead, so they can prophesy for us, so that we can know how things happen: the past and the future, everything."

In the eerie, foreboding silence, Asa gathered his thoughts. "And Miss Hene. She has been trained, too. She is the Mother of the Family. They, working like Mother and Father of the Family, will help each other. Congo gathers and prepares. Miss Hene attends. And I will be here for the first Walk. But from here on, it's all up to them."

Ulu searched her mind. She had heard and read of the new movement. The government was against it, describing it as a cult, and had placed it high on the list of similar movements to be attacked and destroyed. To her, the Kumina Family was clearly illegal. Ulu was a staunch Anglican. In fact, the Reverend Watkins was a family friend.

Ulu quickly dismissed the thought of having a Kumina settlement in Providence. She had no liking for it and knew it couldn't co-exist in Providence, not if she was living there. For her, it was as good as dead. Yet she said nothing. At that time, there wasn't anything to say or do. There was nothing to fight, save a novel, perhaps crazed idea and a few empty words. If, however, a seed sprouted, then, as Ulu thought, her job would be its immediate destruction.

If, on the other hand, Ulu could pollute the soil or destroy the seed, how much the better! If Congo were the leader – the conveyor of that seed – then she would certainly see to his demise, stooping even to the use of deceptive, rogue love. She would so entrap him to save her beloved Providence. For now, Ulu saw only a waiting game. The immediate question occupying her mind pertained to Master Congo's constant ogle, his intense studying of her face. Did he wish to make a convert out of her?

"Asa," Ulu started, after her moment of reflection, "I know you saved my mother's life. In a way, that makes this family owing to you. But we do not want any trouble in our little village."

"Quite so, Ulu."

"But your Kumina movement is illegal!"

"Yes, the law makes it so. And another law could undo that just as easily. We offer love, not death, Ulu."

"What is your code, Asa? You may say whatever you want about the law, but where is your doctrine written? You do not even have a church. How do you live, and what can we expect from you?"

"Our Families live as Love directs, Ulu. You are right. We do not have a church. We do not have a written code."

"We would be restricted by a written code, Ulu. With such a code we would be stuck in time," Miss Hene added.

"What you would have with a written code is the certainty of what you believe – something to pass down from one generation to the next. And moreover, Miss Hene, some things do not change."

"We do agree on that, Ulu. Love as a principle, for example, does not change. And we do have that. As we live out our lives, we demonstrate what we believe and that says who we are!"

"If you must think of a church, Ulu," Congo added, "each Kumina member is the church, and each life a gospel!"

"Master Congo is right. He is right because we are connected, because we live from within. Does that make it clearer to you now, Ulu?" Asa asked.

"I suppose so," Ulu responded. She glanced at Kisi and then at her mother. Why were they so complacent? she asked herself. "But I tell you, no family of mine, and certainly no husband of mine, will ever be a Kumina member. If anything, he will join my church and follow my creed."

"If I may add this . . . we go to all churches, Ulu," Congo said.

"I didn't mean *you*, Congo. It seems you would do anything to get your way!"

The conversation came to another pause. Lev couldn't think. His mind was absorbed with Miss Hene. From her carriage and her words, he knew she was a person of distinction. But what was this Kumina Family, and she, its Mother? Would she have time to attend to the things he had in mind for her, the employment he promised? Or, that aside, would she have time with him alone, perhaps sipping tea? Everything seemed immediately confused. Was there a way out? He looked at Asa, who gestured as if he wanted to leave.

"So, Master Congo," said Asa, "attend to the duties Lev puts to you. But remember who you are, and what you were made for. You are a Kumina Master, and to help wherever you can is good. So work with Lev, but return to your center. That you do without delay. Be constant in your purpose, honest and patient. Miss Hene, Mother and Chief, please work with Congo. And be not boastful, cunning or vain. In all things, judge with love, tasting the judgment as if it were your own before issuing it."

"You speak as if you are leaving us again, Asa," Puncus said.

"Not before I know Lev is comfortable with Master Congo and Miss Hene." And returning to his children, Asa continued, "You must serve to know humility, so it is okay to help Lev with whatever he asks of you. But you must never forget your purpose. Let whatever you do enhance and not detract from that purpose." Asa looked first to Master Congo and then to Miss Hene.

Lev's eyes roamed the valleys. There was so much to do, too much for him. He needed help. Miss Hene's comforting eyes assuaged his fears. He was still listening to Asa but he saw her. Without excusing himself, Lev stood up and walked into the kitchen. Miss Hene's eyes followed him. She hadn't noticed he was so huge, a towering six-foot frame, and matching square, wide shoulders. Nor would Miss Hene have wagered Lev could move with such ease and elegance.

"Water, anyone?" Lev asked, and returned to the table to serve upheld glasses. "And if I am not pushing things: maybe, Master Congo, and Miss Hene, you can both come to Barton House with me, spend the night, and in the morning, we can discuss your duties."

"Excellent!" said Ulu, feeling strangled by Congo's stare.

"Yes, thanks," said Congo, looking at Miss Hene nodding her approval, "we would love to go with you."

"I will go with you, too," said Ama. "Lord, how do these things happen?" she asked rather vacantly.

"Why, Ama. I simply asked for help and someone answered," said Lev. "That's how it happened."

"It must be more than that," Ama laughed, with Asa eyeing her intensely.

"Will you please join us, Ulu?" Lev asked. Ulu hesitated, not wanting to give Congo the upper hand, not wanting him to think he had subdued her by his staring eyes. Ulu accepted, leaving Kisi, Asa, Puncus and Nweka behind.

"It's nice to meet you again, Congo, and especially you, Miss Hene," Puncus called. "And after you are settled, come over to the *Any Questions*. Lev will tell you where it is. Come over. You'll meet the town's folk there!"

"Okay, we will," said Congo waving good-bye and hurrying to catch up with Lev and the others.

He did not join them right away for fear of interrupting Ulu.

As they walked, Miss Hene asked Lev about the old house not too far from the Coveys. It was on their property and was almost overgrown by trees. It had an interesting façade and seemed as if it could be a cozy residence. Lev explained that it was the house the Coveys intended for Asa on his return to Providence.

Ulu picked up from there, explaining that her family had not tended the house for years because of its use by a sisal-head white girl whom no one in the village knew. She suddenly appeared and, to the apprehension of the family, never left.

Before Asa's return, Reverend Watkins attempted the girl's removal. On the appointed day, the Reverend walked through the already opened front door of the cottage and entered what he considered to be a living room. The girl quietly slipped from a bedroom to join him. She looked quite normal with long, white hair spreading across her shoulders then cascading to her waist. Her face was simple, matching her faded red dress with missing buttons and her unkept nails. They looked at each other and, as she smiled at the Reverend, he beckoned as if inviting her to join him in prayer. She accepted his gesture, not knowing that he intended to expel her from the house, if not from Providence.

But when Reverend Watkins completed his plea and opened his eyes, he saw the girl kneeling with her back toward him still fervent in her prayer. Distraught but not discouraged, Reverend Watkins, with both hands, held out the holy Bible toward the girl, hollering for her banishment or her damnation. Just then, the girl stood up, dropping her dress to the floor, and faced him, holding a large, black, wooden crucifix in her hands. Alarmed, the Reverend jumped back. She advanced and he scrambled to the door, slamming it shut behind him and scurrying out of Providence. Reverend Watkins never returned to the house but condemned it as Hell House and recommended that it be burnt. Afia saw no reason for that. The family, however, ceased caring for it and the house lay alone, seemingly abandoned.

Ulu assured Miss Hene that she would not live there.

Choosing Congo

The remainder of that Friday and the ensuing night at Barton House, if not as revealing, were more eventful than the preceding morning. The women visiting Barton House gossiped and grew in deeper understanding.

Master Congo was shown his domicile, the headman's cottage at the far side of the great house. It stood in close proximity to a massive apple tree. An old graffiti-carved wooden table and a few long, weather-beaten benches sat beneath the ancient fruit tree that constantly beckoned the weary to its sweet sustenance and comforting shade.

Lev spent most of the evening there with Congo, sketching out the rudiments of his new responsibilities. When Lev found he was repeating himself, he looked at Congo and said, "You know, Congo, I believe we can make this work. What do you say?"

"This is not what I have been trained to do, Lev. But I should be able to do it, with a little coaching from you."

"That you will have, Congo. And you will find the men very helpful," Lev said, patting Congo's shoulder.

"That's good."

"I know you will succeed, Congo. In fact, let me make a proposal to you."

"You had better wait for a few weeks and see how I do, Lev."

"Not at all. I am confident you can do this job, Congo. So, here is my offer."

"Okay. What is it?"

"I offer you a quarter of whatever increase the property makes from this day."

"Oh, my goodness! That is quite generous of you, Lev. But a full quarter?"

"Yes, Congo."

"Why do you want to give that much, Lev?"

"Don't be so eager to judge, Congo. The rest of the offer is that you get nothing save your board and food if the yields do not increase."

"Oh!"

"So think about it, Congo, and let me know in a few days."

"If it's okay with you, Lev, I will accept your offer now," Congo said, reaching out for a handshake.

Lev was happy Congo accepted his offer. For the first time in his life, a burden had been lifted from him. He would just as easily have offered Congo a half of the increase had Congo asked. Overjoyed, Lev embraced Congo and walked out of the cottage.

Soon after Lev's departure, Congo turned his attention to his new residence. He had never lived in any place quite as large or as comfortable. In the commune at Portland, Congo had shared a bedroom with three other men. Now he had his own bedroom: his own bedroom with a mirror and an extra room to spare! He hadn't been able to help noticing the mirror as Lev showed him around the house. It seemed handmade. Congo, with a natural ability and pressing desire to paint, could hardly keep from noticing its oval form and the highly polished mahogany that framed the beveled edges.

In the kitchen Congo saw a wood stove. He knew how to cook, even delighted in doing so. But Congo's repasts would be brought from the great house, diminishing his need to fend for himself. Ama, if not Miss Hene, would see to that. He had his own horse and men to manage. Congo, who just moments ago had nothing, not even a change of attire, now had clothing from Lev, his own ride, and an increasing sense of material worth!

Congo walked back into the bedroom and sat in the old wooden rocking chair by the window. He wanted perspective. He thought about Lev and Asa. He wanted to work for Lev without being disobedient to Asa.

Congo had been trained for leadership and was eager to show what he could do. He had not been so tested before. Moreover, Congo had a personal stake in the increase of Lev's estate. He was beginning to see where that would lead: to his own land and a house on it.

It was now incumbent on Congo to guarantee not only a smooth relationship between himself and his new boss but increased productivity from Lev's estate. Congo stood up and looked out at the vast holdings. It occurred to him that the labor to increase its bounty would devour all his energy, but it didn't seem to matter. Congo saw a way of getting what he wanted.

Stepping

Miss Hene couldn't sleep. Meeting Ama, her younger sister, greatly excited her. She adored Ama, immediately falling in love with her. Ama she imagined to be gracious, earthy and kind. Ama fixed her hair by parting it in the middle from her forehead to the back, making a large braid by either ear. When Miss Hene touched Ama's hair, she was amazed by its soft silkiness, much more delicate and pliable than her own rough and matted African braids.

The unusual and unsolicited petting of her hair didn't bother Ama. Her light, Indian complexion, soft, straight, and shiny black hair had long ceased to be a concern for Ama. Her playmates at elementary school had constantly marveled at her looks compared to her mother's strong, dissimilar African appearance. Her King surname didn't help Ama's classmates either, since other Kings were unknown to Providence. Ama loved herself down to the smallest iota of uniqueness her mixed heritage brought her.

Since she was ignorant of her true biological paternity, Ama had imagined Asa to be of European and Indian ancestry. Now that Asa had finally appeared and exhibited such a striking African form, Ama started to question her heritage again. Nweka and Asa, however, did speak of the different body Asa presented on this last trip. From that conversation, Ama gathered that the mysterious Asa might have changed bodies more often than Ulu changed clothes, and that, perhaps, a discussion of bodies with him would be fruitless. As before, Ama decided to leave the matter alone and simply live.

Ama liked Miss Hene, even though she had touched her hair with childish curiosity, reawakening youthful memories. She liked her quiet, deep, loving eyes. It was Master Congo, though, who now concerned her. Like Miss Hene and Ulu, he was her sibling. Why was he sleeping alone and in the servant's lodging? Congo seemed so full of life and certain of himself; Ama wanted the best for him. Moreover, since Asa had given her his name and had seen to her care, why shouldn't another of his children share the same accommodations afforded her or Miss Hene? Ama wanted togetherness, not a rift in her family.

As the women talked, Ama's mind sought ways of bringing Congo into the fold. She liked Miss Hene and Congo, both of whom she immediately took as blood siblings. Of course, Ulu, as sophisticated an air as she breathed, and with the tensions from their first meeting, would certainly not have Congo in the house. On second thought, Ama realized that Ulu and Congo were not related, not in the least. It occurred to her then that, if Congo were to be brought in, so to speak, and be made a part of her family, it would all be up to her. That event would happen of its own accord.

Miss Hene, remembering the conversation in Afia's house, alternated her attention between Ulu and Ama, noting marked personalities in the two sisters. They were both beautiful, but differed in their very foundations, with Ulu being broad and stocky and Ama slim and delicate. What Miss Hene saw was that Ulu's ambition couldn't be hidden. Ulu was soft-spoken, very honest, and equally blunt. She liked knowing where she stood, and Ulu, with her fixed positions on every matter, made things easy for Miss Hene.

It was Ama's indecisiveness in that very first meeting that challenged Miss Hene. To her, Ama spoke as though nothing really mattered, as if every action were the right one, making the world perfect. This caused Miss Hene to wonder how many perfect worlds existed at once in Ama's universe.

The women talked through the night. As the first hint of gold crested the distant hilltops declaring another dawn, they succumbed to their weariness and sank into deep, restoring sleep.

Lev's contemplation lasted well into the night. What or whom had he taken into his dwelling and unwittingly made a part of his household? Who was this Master Congo, the man now supervising his farm and to whom he would disclose details of his life and business he had only shared with his father?

The mystical air Asa exuded was not any more comforting, either. In fact, the longer Lev dwelt on it, the more it unnerved him: Walking the dead? Walking the dead! Why not walk the living? Oh, they can walk themselves! Was that a religion? No, Ulu said it was a cult, a cult persecuted by my government. Ah! Was Asa in hiding? Yes, that was mentioned. And now, in hiring Master Congo, am I inadvertently aiding criminals? Criminals! What? Criminals in my own house? Are they criminals for walking the dead? No, but they surely are lunatics for trying. That's a crazy cult, but not criminal. Can that be done, though? Can the dead walk? And who is this Miss Hene? Why couldn't I stop looking at her? She must be pretty. No, beautiful! She has such an amiable face. Is she in the cult, too? Well, yes! She is the Mother of it, that Kumina madness, whatever it is. I must talk to Ulu . . .

And so, his thoughts ran and ran. When none of his questions found favorable answers, he plunged deeper and more hopelessly into his soul, questioning still, until his mind, exhausted of energy, forced his body into twisted, tormented sleep.

While sleep hovered over Lev's household, Asa Stepped. He Stepped, but not alone. Nweka and, to no lesser extent, Kisi, had grown highly interested and animated by Asa's phrase, 'walking the dead.' What exactly was that? And where were those mysterious places in Portland and St. Thomas where such hitherto unknown events existed? Curiosity kept Kisi from dropping the subject, even when Asa had first bade them farewell and prepared to depart.

"So," asked Kisi, "are you really leaving this late?"

"Yes. It's not really late. And in any event, there are things I must do at home before sunrise."

"And how do you intend to get to Portland or St. Thomas before sunrise?"

"Stepping, of course. By Stepping. I can Step there before dawn."

"Stepping? Is that like walking?"

"No, Walking is for the dead. I said 'Stepping'. That is for the living. I will Step it."

"And what is this Stepping that we living cannot do?" asked Nweka.

"I didn't say you can't Step."

"But we couldn't get to Portland before three days by walking."

"I said Step. Stepping."

"Is that something you can show us, Asa, that Stepping?" Nweka asked.

"Yes."

"And you said you don't have a wife?"

"A wife? Why, Nweka? No! But, we are in need of a Mother."

"So, Asa, if you are not married, who do you love, the Mother?" Nweka asked.

"I love . . ."

"Can we start Stepping now?" Kisi interrupted.

"Yes, Kisi. Let me show you." With that Asa walked with Nweka to the front porch.

"Wait for me," shouted Kisi, hobbling from behind.

"You, too, Kisi?"

"Yes, Asa."

"Well then. Let me stay in the middle, and each of you hold one hand."

"Like so?"

"Yes, like so," he responded, holding each to one side.

"Now, open your eyes."

"That's easy!"

"I mean your inner eyes."

"Oh!"

"Good."

"What next?"

"With open eyes you follow the rhythm."

"The rhythm?"

"Yes."

> *Stepping, Stepping.*
> *Keep on Stepping.*
> *Stepping, Stepping,*
> *Always looking.*
> *Stepping, Stepping*
> *Looking, Stepping.*
> *Stepping, Stepping,*
> *Keep on Stepping,*
> *Stepping, Stepping,*
> *Stepping ahead.*

He chanted and Stepped. With each downbeat of his rhythmic voice, his feet, his alone at first, bounced from the ground while he held the women close in his arms. With each stride, each Step, the road rushed increasingly faster toward them. He paced, Stepped, kept on Stepping as Nweka apprehensively watched his face.

When Kisi finally got the courage to open her eyes, she saw in the placid, silvery moonlight, trees, animals, hills and rivers, everything rushing to her but ever faster than when she ran. Faster, faster than her mounted nag. She liked feeling air-bound, flying, sailing, striding, bouncing. No! Simply Stepping. Stepping home.

Strange Flight

While Asa Stepped Nweka and Kisi into their new lives, far, far away from Providence, Lev lay unnecessarily perplexed by a fate much larger than he could ever have imagined. His unsolicited preoccupation with Miss Hene, his new role of hosting a Kumina Family, the sudden shattering of his old, comfortable world, and the sprawling dawn he had now awakened to, far overshadowed the despondency and weariness that of late had plagued him. While the rest of Lev's household gossiped or, unaware of his turmoil, slept in childlike slumber, Lev yearned to get to the end of his daunting enigma.

This was not the case with Congo. Where Lev saw anxiety and fear, Congo saw opportunity and the chance of a new life. He quietly put Asa aside and plotted a different path for himself.

Asa's training left Congo strong and fearless. He was young and ready for the world, but on his terms. It was simple what Asa wanted him to do. In fact, so simple and one-dimensional, he got bored just thinking about it. Of course he loved Asa and respected the principles Asa represented. But a simple spiritual life seemed trite and uneventful to Congo.

In Portland or even in the Families in St. Thomas where Congo visited with Asa, he saw poverty. He had often wondered what could be done to relieve that plight. He loved the gentleness of the people, their fondness for simple stories and ready hospitality. Congo liked that there were no jails, no fights over property, and that whatever family squabbles existed, Asa would easily quell.

Still, Congo did not understand why Asa was so unlike Lev, lacking in property and earthly prestige when he understood so much. Why hadn't Asa a wife when he had performed so many marriages and assisted so many families? Why, why, Congo asked, wasn't Asa like the affluent families of Providence or Fellowship?

It wasn't long after Lev left his room that Congo began visualizing an alternate way for himself. He would please Asa. But Congo would also please himself. After trying on the clothes Lev had brought him, and the space, his house, Lev had allowed him to occupy, Congo felt the taste of ownership. He suddenly knew exactly what would fill the missing corner of his soul – a corner, it seemed to Congo, that only worldly things could fill.

Asa had always thought that with spiritual enlightenment came whatever else the soul desired. Congo listened again to that piece of Asa's teaching and vowed then to use his spiritual gifts to add to his material side. Thus, he would be complete, needing nothing!

Congo walked from the window and looked at himself in the beveled glass mirror. A puzzled, confused face greeted him. At this he grunted and, closing his eyes, walked back to the window and stared at the darkness. Thoughts of money and Ulu again flooded his mind, bringing some modicum of relief.

Money and property were not primarily what he had in mind, though he wanted those. His first taste of ownership would be Ulu. That he decided. He would get her, claim her first. Then he would set about creating wealth and building the Family Asa desired. With that understanding and the flames of his heart quelled, Congo lay on his bed and slowly drifted to sleep.

There, another world rose up before him. Congo soon found himself confronting someone who looked like a wizard. The meeting took place at the foot of a hill owned by the wizard. Congo's task was simple but crazed.

He was to climb the hill, only to ask permission from the wizard for the climb. The wizard stood beside Congo at the base of the hill, so why should Congo climb?

"If I may, old man," Congo started, "I need to ask your permission to climb your hill."

"No need to tell me that, young man. Everyone needs my permission. It's my hill you see," said the old man, waving out the panoramic form of the hill with his walking stick.

"So, will you please give me your permission for the climb?"

"Permission is given only at the top of the hill, young man."

"But we are here, and I am asking!"

"Yes! And why tell me what I already know?"

"If I get your permission here, I do not have to make the climb."

"I know. I know!" repeated the wizard. "You exhaust me with your knowledge."

"Please," said Congo. "Save me the trip. Give me your permission."

The old man reared back in laughter. "Do you really need my permission, young man?"

"If I didn't, sir, I would not ask you."

"Then, young man, meet me at the top of my hill!"

Congo closed his eyes and shook his head to dispel his frustration. When he opened his eyes the wizard was gone, but standing before him were two great birds. They were fiery red and stood taller than he. Congo was at first alarmed but, accustomed to Asa's various forms, thought it was his father.

"Why are you so distraught, young man?" the birds asked in unison.

"My name is Congo. My task is to get to the top of the hill and ask permission to walk up the hill."

The birds laughed. "That's why we grew our wings. We just fly up or over without caring about the magician."

"Oh! Then could I fly with you?" Congo asked.

"Sure, Congo. All you have to do is hang on to our feet. We will fly you up there!"

"Thank you!"

Almost immediately the birds hovered overhead, and Congo with each hand held on to one foot of each bird. Without knowing it, Congo was air-borne and looking down on the vast estates below him. The mother birds flew and Congo surveyed. He was happy.

After flying for some time, the birds said in unison, "Over there, Congo, in the thicket of the bamboo is our nest. There we feed our young. You can still hang on if you want, but you will be their next meal."

"You said you would take me to the top of the hill!"

"We passed it long ago, Congo."

"Why didn't you tell me?"

"Don't you know where you are going?"

"Yes!"

"Well?"

"If you would only take me back!"

"We have no time for that. We must feed our young!"

"Then put me down!"

"We can't! But you can let go, anytime."

"I would fall and die if I let go!"

"So?"

"I do not have wings!"

"Get some."

Congo looked ahead. He could see the young birds in the nest jostling and screaming for food. Beneath him lay a large, rugged, unforgiving ravine. The "So" of the birds rang clearly in his mind.

Yet, without delay, Congo let go. In free fall he felt the wind rushing, whistling against his face. Down he fell, tumbling, whirling, spinning, and falling until helplessly close to earth, he found that his once folded arms were wings. He stretched them out, soaring, but not in time to prevent a very hard landing. Congo fell right back where he'd started. He looked up to see the old wizard laughing at him. Amazed, Congo watched the wizard as he slowly changed into Congo's image, taking on first his face and body, then dressing even in the clothes Lev had recently given him, finally becoming Congo. Immediately, the hill vanished. Congo was numb!

Sweating and with a loud scream, Congo awoke in the strange, dark room asking, "Where am I?"

Seconds passed as he sat shaking the sleep from his head, trying to remember his recent experience. He could not. Soon, however, he realized he had fallen out of bed and onto the cold floor.

The slow moments passed and gradually Congo remembered where he really was, in his new home. Letting go of his dream, he crawled back on the bed and fell into gentle, forgetful sleep.

Ama King

Ama's youthful sparkle was particular. It was true and resonated from a single center deep within her inner core. Ama King enjoyed the attraction it brought. It elevated her self-esteem. The threat to her inner worth came not from sibling rivalry but from Bem's promotion of the younger Ulu above her. Ama was as intelligent as Ulu, and at least as deserving of a high school education. Bem denied her that and the other benefits given to his true progeny.

Whenever Nweka had sought Ama's education, Bem distracted her by proposing to sell Ama's land to defray the cost. Nweka interpreted the land to be more than mere birthright or security, but rather, a bond. Her determination that the land remain with Ama until her mother's death or beyond gave Bem his victory while denying Ama her education. Unlike her mother, Ama bloomed late, but it was in time for Henry Isaac Love and Farmer Leroy Kendal. Ama imagined herself a planet around which these two suns of Providence would eternally revolve.

Ama's love for learning didn't die easily. When news of the reopening of the school broke, Ama wondered what prospects it would carry for her. She thought of continuing her education, knowing quite well she would bear its full cost since she had already graduated from elementary school. Ama's solution was to barter her custodial service at the school for the Headmaster's assistance as she studied independently. Her plan worked. Headmaster Henry Isaac Love, enthused by the idea, invited Ama to use the library during the summer while there was not much work. Ama was ecstatic!

For her delight, Ama not only read but took the time to start a diary. She did more than sweeping or cleaning, delighting Headmaster Love. She had a soul, he thought. That and her adorably good looks bonded her to him long before she noticed or cared.

At first their only exchanges were polite hellos and good-byes with the Headmaster inquiring about her reading and often suggesting complementary material. As the summer aged and their acquaintance grew, the Headmaster exposed tidbits of his past and offers of further help, even after school started. Still, Ama remained unaffected by his charm.

Her superficial barriers soon crumbled, and her head was thrown into a spin when he first held her hand. It did not stop there. The Headmaster took her other hand, cupping both into his, without any hint of letting go. At last, Ama felt his warmth.

That, their first interlude, might soon have been forgotten if, on the following Friday, Henry had not quietly approached Ama from behind and soothingly massaged her shoulders as she read. Ama wilted under his touch. Delicately arching her shoulders, she slid her fingers over his hands. Henry bent slowly, dabbing his face in her hair and at the side of her neck. With gentle ease, he started kissing her.

She accepted him and at once made love to him on the library floor. At twenty years of age, this had been her first kiss. She later refused his sexual advances, though, preferring to have him read poetry to her or tell her of his family and his aspirations. He always painted her centrally in this, in the coziest of settings. Maybe he shouldn't have bared what Ama conceived as his soul to her. From then on Ama craved only him, his poetry and the ring he promised her. This she contemplated as he soothed her with tender ramblings of love. Her fingers pined for that unyielding ring. Henry encouraged this in silent, private moments, affirming, Ama surmised, the strength of their bond and mutual understanding.

But Headmaster Love was not without rival. Farmer Leroy Kendal was also attracted to Ama, although his eyes saw a mother and the tender, delicate touch of a lover, a wife, and friend.

In the market place where their eyes first met, Leroy Kendal's new puppy, his bundle of life, slowly slipped from his hands as he stood staring at Ama. She walked by him, nodding hello. He reached for her hand, saying, "You are my wife, you know."

His attempted, amazed smile was stiff and awkward, looking almost like a frown. The scant scent of tenderness and love about Leroy he derived from a small Shepherd he had just found. Leroy carried the lonely, whimpering pup in his arm. It looked up timidly at him as if to its terrifying canine father. That image of father and son burned fearfully in Ama's mind.

Ama didn't know what to make of it. She liked poetry, but she had spent many days toiling with Bem on the farm. She knew, understood, and respected that trade and what it made of men. Yet, his direct stare, his speaking of the future with boldness and clarity, and his unilateral claim of her were unnatural, maybe even uncivilized. When she refused his arm and walked away, Ama could hear him turning and sensed that his eyes, but not his touch, still followed her.

Ama, however, couldn't wait for the following week's market. Her enquiries gave his name and told her he was the new tenant of the Boydell property. He was unmarried and had recently come to Providence seeking his fortune. In the market, Ama allowed him to approach her, requiring by her manner a gentleman's advance. He quickly apologized for his earlier crude, abrasive remark, explaining that he was so engaged by her he didn't know what it was he thought until he had voiced it. Ama, sensing his honesty, quickly forgave, lulling him into courtship. He accepted, and she liked it. Beneath his rough exterior, she imagined him a gentleman farmer, a unique, perhaps bizarre, yet natural creation.

The paradox of two giant suns circling such a miniscule planet was the problem Ama brought to Lev. He listened and tried at first to joke it away; but with Ama's insistence, he researched it. On his conviction of its truth, he settled on finding a resolution. That was the second reason for the party he was planning. Lev wanted to observe the two men, their interaction and behavior with Ama, before advising her. She couldn't wait.

Delayed Invitations

The amiable, even-handed Lev Tyler hadn't neared broaching the reason he visited the Coveys when Asa arrived. Lev didn't need an invitation to visit the Coveys, nor they one for visiting him. The friendship that existed between their families long before King's first arrival had only been strengthened by the malady that destroyed so many other families and finally drove the Boydells from Providence.

There was more, though. Ama and Lev had become close friends. Lev's father, Aren, had always treated Nweka as a sister and Ama as his daughter. Lev, even though a dozen years older than Ama, had taken her as his sister. Ama, adoring the protective attention of the affluent male, easily adopted Lev as her brother.

With Ulu's return from New York two weeks before, Lev thought that his hosting a buffet at Providence Pond would be not only appropriate, but also necessary. It had been a long time since the families were together. Moreover, for the newer members of Providence, there existed an even greater need to build or extend new relationships. For Headmaster Henry Isaac Love, that task was almost done. He had been there for three months and, because of his friendly, dashing personality, had been known to most. This, however, was not true for every newcomer to Providence, especially if by occupation they were removed from the public eye.

Getting well known was not so easy for Leroy Kendal, the farmer who recently had leased the Boydell estate. Leroy was a short, shy man, with a brutish stare peeping from small, deeply set eyes. His craggy, yellow face rarely smiled; but when it did, it brought unexpected though delightful reassurances of congeniality and charm. Little could mere acquaintance suspect otherwise. His unusually small stature, diminutive especially for a farmer, disguised the heavy musculature which moved him briskly under his oversized clothes. He was taken seriously at first glance, and that gave him the sense of importance he sought, since, perhaps, it compensated for the social grace he lacked.

Before arriving at the Covey's residence that Friday morning, Lev stopped to invite Headmaster Henry Love and Leroy Kendal to the buffet. Lev had also asked Puncus St. John to have breakfast at the Coveys with him where they would plan the fare and entertainment that Puncus Divine would provide. The fete was expected to be a small, rather intimate gathering of less than a dozen people if everyone showed up.

Ama, at Ulu's request, had already invited the beautiful longhaired Laura Wong. Laura was Ulu's best and only real friend. She owned a store in Oracabessa, a seaport town some ten miles away and lived in the inland farming village of Free Hill, within an hour's ride to Jacks River. Ulu and Laura had never met, however, until they were roommates at the same boarding school where their friendship blossomed.

Laura's father, originally from Hong Kong, was a pimento trader and jeweler. Laura was his only kin. He had tried coaxing her many times to marry his protégé, Ho Chan. Laura rejected her father's wishes and, when his requests became commands, Laura openly rebelled, ceasing dialogue with her father in spite of his love for her. He soon relented and stopped trying to force the marriage. Laura, however, continued living in protest, for she had tasted the life of a rebel and liked it! Moreover, it served as a clear, potent signal to her father never to force his will again over hers.

With the restful Saturday morning behind him, Lev returned to invite Nweka and Kisi to the buffet. This was the reason he had visited the Coveys when Asa arrived. Asa's arrival and the absorbing intrigue that followed had prevented Lev from mentioning the subject of his visit.

As usual, Lev let himself in, shouting, "Anyone home? Anyone here?" He soon reached the kitchen and read the note Kisi had left behind:

Gone Stepping.

Lev didn't know what to make of it, so at the end of Kisi's note he wrote:

Buffet on Sunday.
Please walk.

Then, on remembering King's statements, Lev grew cautious and drew an "X" through his words, then wrote instead:

You are hereby cordially invited to a buffet party by the pond
given in honor of our highly esteemed Miss Ulu Covey and
other notable new arrivals in Providence.
Transportation will be provided.

Upon completing the note, Lev dropped the pen and scurried out of the house toward Providence Pond.

Easy Choices

Three simple springs bubbled from the southern slopes of the hills, then, uniting, flowed swiftly as one along a pebbled path before gently spreading out into the shimmering silver-blue pond. From the polished gravels and fine white sand on the western edge of the pond, thick blue-green grass opened into a cushion of silk that ran up the slopes, wrapping the roots of towering plums trees that sheltered the ridge from the fierce, celestial fire. Lev and his party sought comfort beneath the trees, bringing the sun, water, and shade to their gathering. On the far bank of Providence Pond, where the grass was high, green and tidy, as if manicured, it matted out towards a delicate bamboo grove. Beneath its bowers, the foliage spread into a delicate blanket of brown and yellow, as if laid for lovers.

Ama had already told her sisters, Miss Hene and Ulu, of her lovely, yet peculiar tangle involving Henry Love and Leroy Kendal. Laura Wong had not yet learned of it. After the main meal was over, Ama pulled Laura into the grove along the pond, where she intimated her burning ordeal.

Congo watched the women as they sauntered from the table toward a ridge rimming the pond. Capriciously, their brightly colored all-in-one dresses flirted with the gusty breeze and then restrained themselves, returning above their knees in wait of the next puff of wind. Together they looked like twins, Laura and Ama, in their snug-fitting, sleeveless floral chemises with deep cuts front and back, beckoning adventure. When Lev cleared his throat for attention, Congo's gaze returned to the table. There he noted that, like Lev, he and the other men wore white, chain-stitched, cotton marinas and short khaki pants, showing Leroy as the most muscular and well formed of the men, despite his small stature.

Lev then turned to Congo, as if to talk. Congo sat across the table from Ulu. He and Lev faced the pond. Ulu's wide-rimmed straw hat offered protection she didn't need. She also didn't need the air she got from periodically fanning herself with it. She, however, couldn't do without the attention it drew. Congo gaped at her.

Her face was oval and smooth, delicately powdered but with a dull shine. Large brown eyes observed from beneath wide arching brows, reflecting integrity and passion, though not tenderness or love. Ulu was kind. Her passion was born of business— a quid pro quo kindness. She would be an excellent professional partner, Congo surmised. Her high cheekbones and pleasant, polite speech added the currency that would make her excel in commerce, for it disguised her general's resolve to win while adding to her feminine mystique.

This time, Congo noticed only her desirability. He craved her attention as much as Asa wanted a Family. He looked at her and tried to smile when she did, hoping to share something. He knew not quite what. Ulu, however, guessed. Not wanting to give anything away, she avoided his invitations.

When he allowed himself to think and not salivate about her, Congo could feel his hands gliding over paper, sketching her face, the slight bulge of her forehead. He could see her, his creation, come alive on paper. Congo, enamored by her, easily envisioned Ulu's long, slender fingers reaching for her earrings or polishing her well-kept nails. He was lost in his fancy. She filled his imagination like a powerful question seeking an immediate response. Congo loved his indulgence.

Miss Hene must have noticed her brother's preoccupation, for she elbowed Ulu, as if asking her to stop it. "What is it, Miss Hene?" Ulu asked quietly, turning to look at her.

Congo interrupted, still not fully awakened from his artistic flirtations. "You are wonderfully attractive, and well worth my pursuit."

"Worth your pursuit! And what about you is of any worth? What audacity!"

"Ulu!" exclaimed Lev.

Congo awoke! He wanted to hide. Only the pond, the deep cool water could separate him from her spider's venom. With that, he broke company and dashed down to the shore. Laura, thinking that a race had started, turned from Ama and, running after Congo, yelled, "Come on, let's go!"

She dashed beneath the cooling water, chasing Congo. At first he didn't know who had accompanied him. On seeing her elegantly sculptured face and her captivating smile, he swam toward her, beckoning Laura into a race to the far side of the pond. She accepted.

"You are crazy!" he said, smiling insanely at her as soon as they lay with their backs to the sky lost in spontaneous attraction and puffing like tired trains.

"Not crazy! I am not crazy. You are stupid," she smiled playfully at him.

Reading her flirtatious giggles, Congo moved so that his body rested against hers. He held her hand which she let him examine gently, engrossed, yet delicately excited by the sudden sense of calm overshadowing them.

"I simply know what I want," she said.

He leaned and kissed her face. Surprisingly, she returned his kiss and he placed his arm around her back, his memory of Ulu having faded.

"Remove your arm!" she said, smiling at him, then kissed his face again. "I do not want Ulu to see that."

The couple followed the grass to the bedding beneath the bamboo grove.

"There is nothing between us, Ulu and me, you know."

"You are so silly!" she said, laughing at him. "Nothing between you? Then why is she so angry with you?" Laura asked, laughing at him. "You come and lie with me. I will explain it to you."

"At your home?"

"No, silly! Here."

Congo laughed. "Oh, then, and what about your husband?"

"Do you see him here?"

"No! But that does not mean . . ."

"Do you think I would be here without my husband if I were married?"

"So, what happened to him?"

"I am not married, silly; and why all the questions?"

"So, you have never been married? I do not believe that, Laura."

"Okay, I am a liar and you are stupid!"

"Oh!"

"But you don't get any ideas, just because I am here with you."

"I have no ideas. None at all," Congo said and kissed her lips as she turned invitingly to him.

"You are so simple," she said, smiling at him.

Again they kissed. Noticing the comfort and seclusion of the grove, Congo nestled closer to Laura, her moist, bright skin and dainty pink lips meeting his tensed, shivering body. They didn't know why, what they felt or what would result, but without words, without fear or reservation, they connected in a hot, fleshy embrace and, following raw instincts, plunged into lovemaking. At first it was quick: sharp, inexplicably intense, with Laura pulling handfuls of grass suppressing her joy. But it was not over.

Laura raised her head, looked at Congo, and then glanced across the pond. On seeing Ulu, pensive but preoccupied, Laura returned to Congo. She pulled him onto her, surrendering to the savagery of her daydreams. At first he kissed; he kissed and caressed before gently, and in blissful cadence, he embraced and re-entered her. But this time, and to a slower tempo, Congo tenderly delighted Laura to another crescendo. Falling, but still clutching, they drifted into a short, restoring nap on the brown and yellow grass beneath the grove. Such was their first meeting.

Maybe it was because Laura was one of the few people Ulu admired, whose opinion really meant something to her; maybe it was because she thought Laura more attractive than she, more elegant and better poised; maybe it was because she liked admiration and attention but couldn't accept it from Congo; maybe it was his seemingly low estate; maybe, maybe she thought . . . but what on earth could Laura see in him anyway? This was the question which still rang bell-clear in Ulu's head as Laura and Congo lay bedded beneath the grove. What on earth could she see in him anyway!

Whatever it was, Lev, peaceful Lev, was happy the tension was gone. His thoughts were with Miss Hene.

The newness of the place, the chill of the sparkling clear water about her feet and the warm, invigorating summer breeze soon brought Miss Hene to a standstill. Something called her. She leaned against a large boulder in the stream looking first at the pond and then down to its very northern extremities. There her eyes followed the folds of land up to the crest of the hill, as the terrain leveled into verdant meadows. High on the distant ridge stood a singular cotton tree in resplendent luxury. To the right of the tree was the scant roofline of the Coveys' house. The smaller Hell House stood beside it. Offering perspective, the house appeared distant and tiny. The primeval cotton tree seemed almost to touch the sky, so robust was its bounty. Miss Hene watched that luxuriant tree: strong and firm in the wind, shimmering but not swaying, holding firm. She wondered just what ancient soul might have nested beneath its massive boughs, finding comfort there. She did not know. Yet, it pleased her so. Miss Hene fell in love with it, claiming the tree as though it were of her own making, her very child!

Ulu, with increasing fondness for Miss Hene, joined her and Ama as they played in the clear, shallow water flowing to the pond. That was Ulu's favorite spot. The sand-washed stones were white and smooth, making them easy to walk on. Small mullets darted, exposing their silvery undersides. The winds sprang up, bathing their faces with warm humid air as the three women sat in the shallows, lacing the cold water about their bodies.

"Why does Lev think I can run his household?" Miss Hene asked.

"For starters, you made a perfect Saturday dinner," Ama replied. "Moreover, Ulu told him so."

"You know, you are more than just a housekeeper," Ulu added.

"Then why does he keep looking at me like that?" Miss Hene asked. "Am I doing something wrong?"

"If I know Lev," Ama said, "my poor brother has found himself a wife and does not know what to do about it."

"A wife?"

"Yes, Miss Hene. A wife, if you will take him for a husband."

"It's my brother Congo and you, Ulu, I am concerned about," Miss Hene said.

"He has not found a wife here!" Ulu said with a smile.

"No. But something to take him from his charge."

"Ah!" responded Ulu.

"From what Asa intended," Miss Hene said. "He should be building a spiritual Family here, not taking responsibility of an estate and a jail."

Ulu showed some disappointment. She had guessed incorrectly that Miss Hene was referring to Congo's futile attention towards her. She walked further upstream, leaving Miss Hene and Ama together, but remaining close enough to overhear or rejoin the conversation at will.

On their first night at the Tyler's, Ama had disclosed to Miss Hene and Ulu the two marriage proposals she had received, one from Henry Love and another from Leroy Kendal. Ama didn't tell them how she would decide but promised they would be the first to know.

"So who will it be?" Miss Hene asked her.

"I do not know. Lev will tell me, won't he?"

"Your heart should."

"My mind tells me both, but I think it will be . . . well, I do not know," she said sighing.

"Come on, Ama. If you can't tell me, then tell Ulu," Miss Hene pried.

"What should she tell Ulu?" Ulu called.

"All that her mind is about," Miss Hene said, looking at Ama.

"Lev should tell me."

"What should Lev tell you, Ama?" Ulu asked.

"Who will make the better husband!"

"The Headmaster, naturally," Ulu said. "That's whom you should marry."

"Sorry, Ama. I know neither of them," Miss Hene said. "I can't advise you there."

"That shouldn't matter; it's just a husband," Ulu said.

"He could be wrong for you," Miss Hene advised.

"Oh! But he could be right, too," Ama replied.

"Yes, but don't you want to be sure?" Miss Hene asked.

"Yes, but whoever it is, maybe things will just work out, after I am married," Ama said.

Silence fell on the conversation. How do things really happen? Ama could remember Nweka's voice repeating in her head. She didn't know. She loved and admired both men. If they were simply going to be lovers, either one or both would be wonderful, she surmised. Of course, she had been to bed – or to the floor in this case – only once with Henry and never with Leroy.

The idea of multiple lovers, or simply of a lover with no further commitment or certainty, love for its sake only, pained her. Ama's heart, unlike Nweka's, wouldn't allow it. She had long left it up to Lev to decide between Henry and Leroy who would be the better husband for her. Ama never trusted her deductive abilities; neither had she harbored any right to self-determination. Life had provided so far, and providence had limitless abundance. So why the bother, as long as one lived with love? With two offers of marriage jostling in her mind and the thoughtful luxury of Lev and her sisters' wisdom to guide, how could she go wrong? She had already decided to make the question of her choice an open issue, and make it final depending on which advice suited her feelings. In effect, her game was to decipher which of her friends truly understood her by choosing her mate, thereby demonstrating that they could sincerely read her soul.

Like an eagle standing watch over its domain, Lev warmed his seat on the hill from which he oversaw the day's affairs. There were other unsettled issues calling for his attention. He was glad that Ama's suitors, like sentries, still sat there with him. He had served the men what they requested, brandy on the rocks, and for himself his own favorite, gin. He liked its pure, smooth swallow. Not that he needed the drink for his next task, but to help him savor the bouquet of delight he reaped from thinking of Miss Hene.

"Gentlemen," Lev said. "I have never been married, yet Ama, my dear sister, has asked me to do her a favor of greatest importance. I have committed to satisfying her and will now ask you to assist me."

"Will we have to drain the pond today?" asked Henry.

"No!" responded Lev with less certainty in his voice.

"Anything else here should be easy then," Henry responded.

"What is the task?" asked Leroy.

"You each have told me, and she concurs, that you both have asked for her hand in marriage."

The men nodded in the affirmative.

"I should ask you just what the task is," said Leroy in a more relaxed tone.

"To decide for her which of you would make a better husband, and I need your help."

"Let's go and drain the pond," said Henry, bringing laughter. Leroy looked on stolidly. He eyed Henry with some nervousness. He was not a man of words, but rather more practical, given to action.

"I would suggest something else I heard of," Leroy said, "if I knew you were serious."

"And what is that?" Henry asked.

"Let a wrestling match decide."

"Rather barbaric," Henry said. "Why not just toss a coin?"

"I do not have one," Leroy said, looking rather humbly at him.

In a merrier tone, Henry added, "And I am a professional wrestler; that may not be to your advantage."

"Your honesty is admirable," said Lev.

"What? Are you saying I cannot wrestle?" Leroy asked.

"Farmers do not wrestle, they farm. Professional wrestling is somewhat scientific, and there are rules."

"Well, then," said Lev, "maybe you can each say something about yourself, something I can discuss with Ama."

"Oratory!" remarked the Headmaster. "You, Leroy. You go first."

"Why not you?"

"Okay, I will."

"That is not a reason, Headmaster," Leroy rebutted.

"But you can't have it both ways!" Henry Love replied.

"Should I flip a coin then?" asked Lev.

It was decided that Leroy should begin. "The land I work on here is leased. Before this, I had nothing but desire to better myself and escape from Galina. I am a simple farmer, lacking in words, but strong. I have no children, no siblings, and my parents are dead. I have one more thing, love. That, I bet on Ama. Take or leave me, it stays with her till death." He paused nervously, as if searching for his drink, and then added, "When you bet all you have, it better win!" Leroy looked up to find the other men grinning. He joined in, then let the brandy find his lips.

"That will be long remembered," said Lev. "And you, Headmaster? What do you say?"

Henry sipped his drink, and wondered if he should recite one of the poems he had given to Ama. No, those were too personal. What about a love poem: Byron, Keats, or Wordsworth? He knew so many, such tender beautiful parcels of thought and feelings, uniquely framed with power and beauty. Why not just let a few words fly! Then he pondered why he should express his feelings in such a schoolboy manner. Why was he beginning to feel uncomfortable? Was there not something rather artificial about this whole affair? And shouldn't Ama be deciding in the privacy of her heart? He couldn't, however, simply fail by nonperformance. No champion of love should be so defamed. He sipped his brandy and started.

"Though I have loved, I have often questioned what love is. I find it, therefore, insincere when one claims to love totally, or to wager all on love. Poetry I know and that I share; give, give abundantly! I want a family, a wife, and children. That now I need for completion and wholeness. For a family, I have the means to provide in every way. That should make me a good husband, father, and man of high standing in society. With one additional quality: that I promise to stay beside my wife and children, born or unborn, and, like an army protecting the motherland, stand to protect, fight, and die for the territory! That, gentlemen, is why I deserve to have and own Ama."

Farmer Leroy Kendal looked first at Headmaster Henry Isaac Love then at Lev for compassion. He knew he had lost the oratory contest. His couldn't match the finery of the teacher's words. He wanted to bow out. Or, on second thought, ask for a wrestling match, something he could be proud of losing. What was this oratory into which Henry had tempted him? He had nothing more to say, except, "Care to swim?"

When it seemed that Leroy's invitation had gone unrequited, Lev said, "Well . . . thank you, gentlemen."

"I will take you on across the pond," Leroy challenged.

"You may not, Leroy. I do a mean breaststroke, you know," replied Henry.

"Let's go!" shouted Leroy, getting a head start on Henry.

Henry made a long shallow dive, emerging ahead of Leroy. He swam quickly and joined Congo and Laura who, by then, sat facing the sun, dangling their feet in the cool water. Leroy still struggled in the shallows.

On seeing the activities, Ama started towards the growing group consisting of Congo, Laura, and more recently, the two swimmers. Miss Hene started off toward the table – to the territory Lev still held – and began her clean-up, readying for the return trip home. Ulu stayed on the rock in the crystal clear water by herself, wondering why the party had moved around Laura, though she couldn't avoid thinking it was really Laura and Congo together that had drawn the attention. Not to be outdone, Ulu walked farther upstream, then turned slowly through the woods and walked towards Miss Hene and Lev.

"Well, Miss Hene, thanks for preparing this lovely party," Lev said.

"You are welcome, Lev."

"Here," he said, patting the seat beside him. "Please come and sit here."

Miss Hene accepted and, as she sat, Lev moved closer to her, touching her.

"Tell me, Miss Hene. What is Stepping?"

"Why, Lev. Where did you get that?"

"At Nweka's house. It was a note I read on the table."

"What note?"

"Just a note, in Kisi's handwriting. It said 'Gone Stepping.'"

"Gone Stepping?"

"Yes."

"Then they are all gone."

"Yes. That's what the note said."

"They are long since in Fellowship!"

"Fellowship in Portland?"

"Yes, That's what it means. They Stepped to Portland."

"Stepped to Portland," Lev repeated.

"Yes. It means they moved faster than a running horse. Stepping, Stepping."

"Ah! Can you Step too, Miss Hene?"

"No, Lev. Only Asa can Step. But if you are with him, he will let you Step with him."

"And you have?"

"Yes. Stepping, Stepping. What a thrill!"

"What a Family!"

"Yes, that is what Congo is to grow here, a new Kumina Family. I hope he starts soon."

"You speak as if you do not approve of what he is doing for me."

"That's his decision, Lev. And I do not want to judge or offer advice not asked for. Whatever Congo does, I'll still love and follow him. He has to lead as he sees fit."

"I understand, Miss Hene, but you take things so seriously!"

"We must," she responded, looking down. The moment grew solemn. "You know, Lev," Miss Hene continued pensively, "we are a small group. But I believe we have a message, nothing new, just a message of love, in our Kumina fashion. I will tell you this, Lev: Congo and my survival depends on the success of the Family Congo is to start here. To you, that might seem trivial, but for us, the Family to be built in Providence is all there is."

"Oh, I see. This is more serious to both of you than I first thought."

"So it seems."

"Then, you really do disapprove of the work Congo is doing for me. To you, it can only be a diversion."

"I am sorry, Lev. I only wanted you to know where I stand."

Lev looked at her, not knowing what to say. In the silence that followed, he searched for her hand. She looked at him, smiling.

"You are a wonderful woman, Miss Hene."

"Thank you, Lev," she said, kissing his cheek and immediately moving away to clear the table.

"I could send a servant to do that, Miss Hene."

"And what then would my employment be?"

"You could supervise the servants in the house, and be my guest."

"That's a rather awkward position for a guest. Don't you think so, Lev?"

"Yes. But I could let them know that is your position."

"And your position, Lev?"

"I wanted to ask you, Miss Hene, if you have any interest in marriage."

"Yes, I like marriages. Asa allows me to perform them."

"I meant . . . I meant . . ."

"What, Lev?"

"If you would marry me?"

"Yes. To whom?"

"Ok, if you would so have it . . . to you, Miss Hene."

"Yes, Lev, but not at this moment."

"When then, Miss Hene?"

"A fortnight from today, in the full moonlight, by ourselves. We will come here one night, walk as far out as we can into the pond, say our vows, dip under the water and arise, married, according to our Kumina tradition."

"What a Family!"

"So you agree?"

"Yes?"

"Yes!"

"Then it is so agreed, Miss Hene."

"Yes, Lev. Providing one thing."

"What?"

"That no one except us knows about it until after it's done."

"Is that a Family rule, too?"

"No, Lev, No! It is my wish. And do you have a wish, Lev?"

"Yes. That you kiss me, now."

"That would be telling,"

"Telling?"

"Yes, Lev. This is public."

"My property."

"Yes. Your friends and family are here, too."

At that moment, Ulu, whose action Miss Hene had been observing, walked to the table. Puncus St. John followed not far behind. He had helped Miss Hene at Barton House in preparing for the party at Lev's request. He came to assist in cleaning-up and taking his utensils back to the *Any Questions*. Puncus rejoined the group without much notice or need for salutations. Puncus hadn't planned, neither was Miss Hene expecting it, yet he kissed her cheek and, with his arm around her waist, announced, "One day, Miss Hene, one fine day, when our love is ripe, we are going to be married! Did you know that?" He smiled in gleeful self-admiration as he slipped into his accustomed solo dance.

"Behave yourself, Puncus St. John!" Ulu reprimanded. "You of all people, you should set an example!"

"Behave?" he replied with an astonishment that matched Lev's. Lev had not known of any amorous relationship between Puncus and Miss Hene, who had just agreed to marry him. Or, Lev questioned, was Divine simply testing his hand at blissful prophecy?

"Puncus St. John," Miss Hene said, "it was fun cooking with you, but don't you think I would know if I am going to marry you?"

"Yes, Miss Hene. I just told you!"

"Don't you think I would know, Puncus?"

He understood her and with a little, sad smile said, "Then, perhaps, you just don't know yet!"

Lev, feeling relieved, walked up to his friend, hugged him, and said, "Neither do I, Puncus St. John. Neither do I. But still, consider yourself lucky. Some of us do understand a little about you: and, maybe, that's enough."

"You are easy, Lev, easy!" Puncus laughed.

A moment of quiet returned and St. John dashed to his chore. Lev looked at Miss Hene with the impulse to shout: You are my wife, my wife! But observing Miss Hene's watchful stare, he refrained, saying instead, "They are gone, Ulu!"

"Who is gone? Nweka?"

"Yes."

"Nothing surprising there. She has always said she would leave with Asa if he returned."

"But she took Kisi with her."

"Just as well. They are so alike!"

"Is something bothering you, Ulu?" asked Miss Hene. Ulu looked down at the pond, not across it, wondering: What does she see in him anyway! What does Laura see in Congo that I don't?

"Just a headache," she responded.

"It's nothing the water can't cure." And with that, Miss Hene grabbed her hand, pulling Ulu down the incline and into the pond, their clothes floating like patches of lazy clouds against a casual sky. They swam back and forth, out into the deep and under, deep under the clear cold water, feeling only joy and exuberance, momentarily forgetting all.

Rituals

Whereas Ulu knew the land and its people, Congo started anew when he assumed the position Lev offered him. All his previous training and experience prepared him to lead a spiritual Family. He wanted to be true to Asa King, his father. He also wanted to demonstrate his competence in secular affairs to himself and to Lev, but perhaps more importantly, to Ulu.

Congo didn't know what to make of the affair between himself and Laura. Neither did he know what Laura thought of it. It happened with tremendous magic, suddenness, and pleasure. But would it continue? Even though Laura was completely satisfying to him, it was Ulu that tugged at another part of his heart. Was it because Ulu had set herself so highly, defining herself as an unattainable prize? Or was she the ultimate seductress, wanting yet rebuffing him, stating her available though unattainable shimmer? Congo didn't know, yet his heart ached for her.

With love pulling Lev's eyes toward Miss Hene and her alone, Congo was left to decipher a winning plan for the Barton estate. The task was daunting, but Congo had time and resources. He immediately befriended the men who worked the plantations and the dairy, learning as much as he could from them. With a mixture of strict discipline and friendliness, he gained their trust, and they his leadership.

That didn't come easily at first. Though friendly, Congo was characteristically proud, one may say vain, and at times given to boasting or self-promotion. The men saw it, and it confused their liking for him. What assisted in binding Congo to the men, and they to him, was his frequenting the *Any Questions* tavern at the end of the workday. He liked to mingle with the men, not only the ones who worked for him but other regulars, listening quietly to their shattered lives, their boasts and dreams. Those very talks and habits, Congo noted, kept them poor and dependent but strengthened the ties binding them. He considered this the sacrifice of their lives. It was the intrigue of this sacrifice that drew Congo to the *Any Questions.*

It was not only the rustic pull of *Any Questions* that drew Congo. He was familiar with Mento music and still liked it, as not dissimilar to his native Kumina rhythms. Congo, however, was especially drawn to the newer sounds of Rumba and Calypso, sounds that were foreign to his commune in Fellowship. Most of all, he was also fond of Puncus St. John, who brought the new provocative sounds to Providence.

Puncus carried an unusual, solitary air, making him seem saintly. Yet he approached life with a logic that was neither sweet nor easily discardable. His warmth, his kind and genuine good nature, were never disputed.

Men, and to a lesser extent, women, flocked *Any Questions.* To find out why, Congo once asked:"Say, Puncus, what brings your customers here, when they certainly don't agree with anything you say?"

"That's part of the reason, Congo. They come to ask questions, argue, and disagree with what I say. But the one thing they are sure of is that I do what I say."

Congo laughed.

"And I thought it was because you were a good salesman," Congo teased.

"I have nothing to sell, Congo. You know that."

"It's nice to know you do not try to sell your cooking, Puncus, but you certainly could sell this music. Tell me, who is your drummer?"

"Oh, that's Byah, Congo."

"He is good! Gracious . . . can he play a bailo rhythm! I would love to have a chat with him, Puncus."

"That would not help, Congo. Byah is mute."

"At least he would know I appreciate the sounds he makes with his music box and those bongos of his."

"You would, Congo, but Byah would not reply. He would only look at you and wonder why you disturb him. Then he would get right back to his conversations."

"With the drums?"

"With his drums or his Spirit. Either way, Congo, Byah does not talk to mortals," Puncus laughed.

"Strange fellow!"

"You might say that, Congo, but Byah has been with the *Any Questions* ever since it opened and he has never missed a day."

"What sincerity!"

"Some of us are like that, Congo."

"Yes, Puncus, if you say so. But tell me, St. John, what do you know about Ulu?"

"Oh, so she has caught your eye too, ah?"

"Yes, you could say that."

"She is a haughty one, Congo. She dumped most of us men. Me too. You have to be uppity to get her gaze."

"Is that so? Then tell me, Puncus, what does she like?"

"For one thing, not the *Any Questions*. Ulu would never come here," laughed Puncus. "But art. She likes art and music, neither of which you have . . . and she likes business, or maybe I should say money."

"Money, ah. That's out of my reach."

"Try talking with her sister, Ama. Now, that is a real person, just a bit indecisive, but genuine all the way."

"Yes, she seems so. And what a beauty!"

"Yes, just like her mother. It's a lucky man who gets her!"

"Right you are, Puncus."

"But you are in good hands, Congo. Lev is a stout fellow. Now, he is the type for Ulu. But I suppose Ulu has bigger plans. Talk with Lev, Congo, him and Ama. But whatever you do, take it easy with Ulu."

"Why do you say that, Puncus?"

"She is a temptress, Congo. She is an enticer and a heartbreaker, just like a spider. You had better remember that, Congo."

"If I can say this, Puncus, Ulu's got a strangle hold on me. But I love Laura."

Puncus reared back in laughter. "Two women and a Family! That's only a part of what Asa brought you here for, Congo."

"I know, Puncus, I know. But between you and me, Puncus," Congo leaned forward to whisper, "I want both: the women and the Family."

"That's not how Asa does it, Congo. He is devoted to the Family. You know that."

"Yes, Puncus. That is his way. I am the leader here and I will do things my way."

"But two women, Congo? You are way over your head there!"

"If I can handle it, Puncus, it's all okay."

"So a taste of the flesh and the taste of Spirit at once. Ah, Congo. You better watch out! That could spell trouble."

"If there is trouble, Puncus, I will fix it. But I must have both."

"When you are in trouble, Congo, it is you who must fix your situation. What will happen to the Family then?"

"Don't be so concerned, Puncus. I will find a way, no matter what happens. And moreover, I really want a taste of this world. Not only that, I want to run a different kind of Family here. You will see."

"You seem to have your mind made up, Congo. No need trying to convince you otherwise. But just to let you know. Me and the *Any Questions* are here too if you need us, anytime."

"Yes, thanks, Puncus."

"And one more thing, Congo. I believe in you. I know you are Kumina way down deep. So if trouble comes, that's what you will find and it will lead you."

"Well, thank you, Puncus!"

"Maybe that's what your really need," Puncus grinned, "a good dose of trouble."

"Don't go willing that on me now, Puncus," Congo said, sharing the humor.

The men talked more: Puncus, by slow degree, telling Congo about Lev and the history of Providence.

Puncus was intent. He sat, carefully observing Congo, the youngster who, not too long ago, was considered an annoying pubescent. He had now developed into a reticent adult commanding his elder's full attention. Congo, knowing Puncus' early struggles, first in Galina and then in Providence, wondered what his own personal path might be.

"So, what about your sister, Congo?"

"What about her?"

"Has she been spoken for?"

"Not really, Puncus, as far as I know. But Lev has an eye on her."

"Oh! She caught mine, too! How much she has changed from a tot in Fellowship!"

"Lev may have first place there, Puncus."

"Yes, Congo. He deserves her. But we are back together like before, the three of us!"

"That's Divine."

"This is the start of your Family!"

When Congo did not respond, Puncus said, "You know, Congo, I take Lev his wine. I provide a service to Barton House . . . so we talk there. Lovely lady she has turned into, Miss Hene."

"Thank you, I will let her know you say that."

"Let's see how things go between her and Lev, and whatever happens will be all right with me."

"If you say so, Puncus."

So, day by day, Congo plunged further into the affairs of Providence. He quickly learned the borders of the properties, soon learned what was incorrect, what needed fixing, and rapidly attended to them. The farm was improving. With Congo's assistance, Lev also gained the respite he sought.

In rapid succession, many of Lev's concerns – his lack of companionship, his heavy workload, his facing an empty future – ended, and Lev felt happy in pursuing his new dream of courting the elegant Miss Hene. Only about the larger projects requiring huge expenditures did Lev ever meet with Congo. Lev had worked his way out of the day-to-day operation of the farm.

The independence and trust Congo earned allowed him to pursue his other personal dream of drawing. On horseback or on hilltops, he searched for subjects, sketching them by day and filling in the details at night. He had the time, but he disliked his subjects. It pained him that in all the world of Providence, nothing, not even the pond, moved him sufficiently to bring any composition to completion.

His habit of strolling his beat on horseback at dawn soon brought him a fitting diversion. One morning as he returned, he noticed a dazzling form in the pond. He dismounted, hitched the horse, and moved closer, closer still. It was Ulu! She, too, was an early riser. She delighted in the warm pond water. Ulu would bathe, then commence her homeward climb in the chilly morning air. She noticed the billows of gray night-clouds transforming to gold and crimson, but never caught a glimpse of her admirer.

Morning after glorious morning, Congo returned to Providence Pond where he watched and delighted himself with Ulu's ritual.

A Scale of Size

Despite his proclivity for earnest work and unflagging devotion to his art, Congo found time for the politics of Providence. Especially, he found time for Ama, drawing on her warmth and knowledge of the farm and villagers. Ama was open and, not having placed value on her information, gave liberally. Congo gulped in every word with delight.

From her, he learned about Lev. Congo gleaned a range of guarded feelings and concerns Lev couldn't disclose to him – not because he didn't want to – but because Congo was a subordinate. Because they were men! In that regard, Ama was Lev's reluctant, though benevolent, courier.

Congo also spoke with great transparency concerning fears about his new tasks, potential repercussions for his disobedience to Asa, and his aspirations to ownership and power. Why? To him, Lev seemed admirable! Congo was less daring, though, with his feelings toward Ulu. Ama noticed them and cajoled, yet Congo remained clammed. Ama soon relented, not letting his privacy interfere with their growing camaraderie.

Even though a sibling relationship had been forced on them, they nevertheless found a core of understanding, mutual love, and respect that formed the basis of their relationship. Congo and Ama were sure to maintain the code they had magically found. The strong friendship forged years earlier between Lev and Ama laid the groundwork for a confident, fast-building friendship between the siblings.

Her complete trust in Congo made Ama easily disclose the full extent of the emotional relationship she had forged with Henry Isaac Love, much sooner and in more detail than Ama had divulged it to her sisters. With regard to the middle-aged farmer, Leroy Kendal, Ama told Congo the manner of their meeting in the market place and that she had grown to like him, despite his stern, insensitive look. Not that he gave her reason for deep concern, but his seemingly tense manner, his drive and decisive mean gawk sometimes frightened her. These made her wonder if he could ever be tender or gentle enough, not for her sake alone but for that of her babies. For, as Ama disclosed to Congo, she intended to have many, and even more grandchildren, willingly sacrificing the rest of her life for them.

The often and easy outpouring of her soul to Congo at breakfast or dinner, which Ama prepared at his cottage or carried from the great house, increasingly drew them closer. It made Congo vow inwardly, then openly to her when it became a solemn promise, to assist her, were the need ever to arise. Congo made Ama feel safe.

This trust also made Ama rather forthcoming with her sister's secrets. He learned that Ulu had been born to privilege, since Bem had willed his entire property to her at her birth. And since Kisi had been fathered by an English port master, Bem hadn't reason to rewrite his will on her arrival. Rex inherited money from Bem, but it was left under Ulu's management although she never gave Rex a full accounting of his worth.

From Ama's further disclosures, Congo surmised that Nweka's hope of a fulfilling life might lie outside Providence; and that when she had Stepped with Asa, Nweka might have inadvertently done what was best for all.

Learning more about Ulu, both from his observations and Ama's anecdotes, gave Congo a more complete view of the woman who, it seemed, lived to insult and deride him. She had been accustomed to the best, just the opposite of Congo. To him, she was a mystery, then an icon: his measure of beauty and distinction. She was unapproachable, yet his desire was relentless.

Ulu had been resolute, unaffected by his posture. Then suddenly Congo learned from Ama what he would turn into his game. He learned of her love of praise and admiration. Not that she was bound by nature or habit to accept them, but the very offering elevated her. It added gold to her emotional account. Ulu also gained the option to accept or reject, and so elevate or denigrate the inner estate of the giver. Ulu loved that power. She adored offerings of praise and admiration! In fact, Ulu lived expecting them; and her toil and perseverance ensured they would follow her like her shadow. Poor Congo. The hunter without a prey: the admirer without a reciprocator. Lover without a love! But, perhaps the situation was not all without hope.

As desperate as Congo was or as seemingly unattainable as his task appeared, Congo was not given to self-pity or driven to climbing imagined mountains. He set out to be the brother and friend Ama deserved. He endeavored to tie himself to Love and Kendal, becoming brothers to each of them. Indeed, Ama's decision to marry could so make him a brother to either.

With Kendal the task was easy. Congo managed the property Kendal rented. That gave Congo an advantage, for he knew the full extent of Farmer Leroy Kendal's estate. Moreover, being plain in thought, intention, and speech made it easy for the relationship between farmer Kendal and Congo to move to an open and personal level with speed and comfort.

Henry Love's fast, slippery mind was more than a challenge to Congo. Unable to reach any reasonable depth of his soul through casual conversation, Congo decided on a more direct approach.

Surprisingly, Congo didn't have to poke far to penetrate the slick outer covering beneath which Henry Love had protected himself. Fear: fear of losing his game and not winning Ama, fear of having the plain farmer claim his prize. Because Love felt he had already placed his sure mark of ownership, he accommodated Congo's open interrogation with ease and reassuring good grace.

Congo simply wanted to understand him. So one Monday after school, Congo approached Henry Love's cottage. The Headmaster warmly welcomed him, setting out his best brandy. Love started: "Congo, you more than anyone else have asked me about my background, which I failed to explain adequately. But now that I know your intentions are sincere, that I know you are Ama's brother, that you have a position of responsibility with the Tylers and in this community, I must admit, my spirit has changed much toward you."

"Well, thank you, Henry."

"You are welcome."

"If I may say this, Henry, after Ulu's insult at the picnic, this surely comes as a pleasing surprise. So, I see now, Ulu doesn't speak for everyone in Providence."

"Oh, Ulu, she has her way. But, I assure you, Congo, I do admire her honesty. To put some old questions of yours to rest, I should tell you I can support your sister and whatever children we may have. I say that because every man is first concerned with whether his sister will or can be taken care of in marriage. In that, you are right. You see, Congo, I am not from here, but rather from Adelphi in St. James. You may not know it, but my family is well off. I do not have to work. I work because it is expected of every Love to be self-supporting. And, of course, that is a respectable way of life. My oldest brother has an ambition for politics, a position he is sure to attain. The sister I follow is a practicing physician, and my younger brother an apothecary, a short stopover before pursuing his medical training at Oxford, where I shall join him to study philosophy. I didn't disclose much of my affairs before, so as not to give the impression of boasting. Your sister is wonderful, and my father would be proud of my bringing a woman such as Ama into our family."

"Ah! I see."

"And I do hope, too, that you see the wisdom in my decision of not disclosing my family's worth. But I would be greatly obliged if you might be the one to tell her of my worth, my value to her."

"Yes, I see."

"Thank you, Congo. What you manage here could fit into my father's estate many times over with space to spare. And, of course, we wouldn't mind having a talent such as yours managing our estate either. To the contrary, my father would be delighted."

"That's quite understandable."

"In fact, I have been thinking of arranging a trip home with you, Ulu, and Ama."

"Please, not now, Henry."

"As you wish, Congo. The invitation remains open, though."

"Thank you, Henry."

With this discussion, Congo was thrown into a new light regarding the Love family. Clearly, the Headmaster was from a family of unusual means. Congo ended the discussion in a state of internal discord. He didn't know what it was that heightened his fear. Was it his distrust of Henry? He couldn't put his finger on it. The one thing of which Congo was un-questionably sure was the vicious riptide, the dark down-drag in his spirit that wouldn't let him go. He felt toyed with, measured, discardable, like fruit peel. This moved the uneasiness he had previously felt about Henry to a different footing. It became something from which he had to gain understanding and appeasement. He feared for his sister.

In his state of doubt and confusion, Congo couldn't disclose to Ama the new information gleaned from Henry. So he decided to play a neutral hand until he deciphered the buried messages, perhaps even poison, which Henry Love had planted for him.

To not unnecessarily burden himself, Congo returned to the cottage he now called home, working and reworking his sketches, making use of the fading western ember.

Perfect Secrets

Perhaps it was what Ama lacked most in her life that drove her to the keenest friendship with Congo. Maybe it was her lack of a father: a robust, male psyche on which she could exclusively depend. Maybe it was his seemingly easy-going ways disguising his rugged strength and determination that engrossed her. Whatever it was, Ama found Congo irresistibly attractive, and she fell easily into his charm. Yet their relationship never moved away from their sibling underpinnings.

Before Congo, Lev had been Ama's confidant. He had been the accepted brother to Nweka's household since Rex's departure to New York. Ulu, however, inveigled her way closest to him, stunting Ama's relationship with Lev. Congo's unassuming friendliness easily filled the void Ama had long hoped Lev would.

One evening, only a few weeks after the fete, as Congo engrossed himself with the sunset, Ama called on him.

"Please, come on in, Ama," he said to her as she walked into the cottage.

"You have so many facets to you, Congo. Just fancy you here all by yourself gawking at nothing. It seems so unlike you."

"Yes, Ama," he laughed. "I have a few things to sort out."

"So. You, too, ah?"

"Yes. I visited Laura, you know . . ."

"Oh! You have grown fond of her!"

"Yes, I like her; she is indeed interesting. But it's Ulu that I want."

"You do? You know, Congo, Ulu is very choosy. I should say spoiled. She has had everything she wanted. Now, she has returned from New York, behaving as if she is better than everyone here. She talks constantly of our brother, Rex, in New York. She really adores him. But I can let you into a little family secret: well . . . you are like family already," she laughed.

"What is it, Ama?"

"You know, our family is not all it's made out to be. You see, Congo, Rex is not in New York of his own choosing. When he was younger, he was very dishonest."

"Ah! What did he do, Ama?" Congo asked.

"For one, Congo, he was a thief."

"So what did he steal?"

"Money, Congo. He was always stealing money. So Bem had to send him away so he wouldn't get locked up for good at the Barton House jail."

"Ah. I understand better now."

"Yes. For his own good, I hope he stays in New York and does not return here to get into trouble again. Anyway, as I was saying, Congo, Ulu does not have to be such a show-off. Know what I mean?"

"That may be so, but there is a trap for every bird, you know."

"Yes. But if you like Laura and she likes you, why go out of your way for Ulu?"

"You are right. With her, it's like rowing upstream."

"And it really should be downstream, you know," Ama laughed.

"That's how it is with Laura. But I fear that."

"Why on earth, Congo?"

"It's just too simple."

"So, have Ulu and Laura both, and make your life hell!" she said, as she moved to kiss his cheek. They laughed, then went silent.

"You know, Ama," Congo said after the brief silence, "Miss Hene and Lev are to be married."

"Yes, I know. But how on earth did you know?"

"Of course, Laura told me."

"Laura, she must have gotten it from Ulu."

"Yes."

"Yes, Miss Hene told us. But it was to be a secret."

When Lev had promised to keep their betrothal a secret, he surmised that Miss Hene wanted his silence so she could spread the excitement herself. He wouldn't have disappointed her. Nor would he whisper a word of it. He, however, would have been disappointed if the word didn't get around. He also guessed that the time and place of their marriage, that much, would remain a secret. It had.

"A perfect secret, then," Congo said. "But tell me, when will it be?"

"Miss Hene didn't tell us; she just said it's soon."

"Well, since you have been forthright with me, Ama, I will tell you. It was last night, at the pond. But they will have a fete for it, next week."

"And how did you know, Congo?"

"There were these signposts all over Miss Hene and Lev's faces every time they were together. So, I put the clues together and, knowing Miss Hene, I made a guess. It happened in the pond. You should have seen it, Ama. It was so simple. They walked out into the pond, undressed, held hands and dipped under the water. When they emerged they held hands and walked naked back out, leaving the old clothes under the water and put on new, dry clothes, each dressing the other before returning to Barton."

"Whew! And nothing said!"

"Nothing said."

"And now, Ama. It's your turn."

"How did you know?"

"Know what? I meant it was your turn to decide who it will be and get married."

"Well, it's my turn, all right," she said, taking a small box out of her pocket and placing it in his hand. "Open it, Congo!"

"Ah! It's beautiful," he remarked, holding it to the light.

"Thank you," she said and moved to hug him. "He brought it over just this moment."

"Congratulations, Ama. Was it from Henry?"

"Yes."

"So, I suppose, he is the one then, ah?"

"Yes, of course. We have only to set the date." And without saying more, she rushed out towards the great house.

"It's our perfect secret," Congo called after her.

"Not for long!" And she ran into Barton House to share the news with Miss Hene.

Congo ate and went back to studying the evening light, the shades and reflections growing among the greenery. Congo's thoughts deepened as he wondered what fate would attend his amorous fantasies.

Rejection

Knowing that Ulu was alone, Congo went to see her. He knocked on the door and waited. Ulu, deeply engaged with her books and not expecting visitors, paid little attention to the low, cautious knock. Congo waited and knocked again with more boldness. That time, Ulu answered.

Congo stood before Ulu, handing her something, without speaking. Ulu looked at him. Well dressed, she thought, in Lev's oversized hand-me-down Sunday suit, but dressed nonetheless. He was dressed with top hat, a brazen red handkerchief in the pocket of his blue tweed coat and a yellow rose on his lapel. Congo would not have forgotten his wooden, hand-carved walking stick, nor his wide, open smile.

Cautiously, Ulu took the decoratively wrapped package, making sure not to touch his fingers. Suspiciously, she eyed his wide, childlike smile, then opened the package, still eyeing him. When the unwrapping was over, Ulu found herself looking on the back of what she surmised was the oval mirror from his cottage.

It was the work Congo had done of her. He had honed his native talent of painting for as long as he could remember. Yet he had never gained critical review of his work. He, despite the approval and encouragement Miss Hene and Asa gave, had always judged it poorly. Congo didn't have their support with this new endeavor. He, however, solicited first Ama's review, then that of Headmaster Henry Love. Ama loved it and thought it a fitting gift for her sister, since it had the appearance of prints and drawings Ulu had brought back from New York. That was his first test.

Congo trusted Ama's naiveté. Ulu, he knew, had a more sophisticated taste. Congo deferred to the scholarly Love, the test of urbane acceptability. Henry loved it and immediately offered to buy it, stating that it at once reminded him of the upcoming Picasso and the established Monet. The untrained Congo didn't know with whom he had been compared, but gestured as if he did. The Headmaster's approval, bringing with it a ready offer of money, was sufficient. Congo had watched him intently as Henry, gesturing and talking to himself, described the work. It showed Ulu frontally nude with her back toward the rising sun, as she stood in the pond with its silver-blue ripples undulating about her knees. The maiden's seeming self-enchantment within the halo of light and water drops from her head – seeming to halt time – did not go unnoticed either. Love admired the depiction, Ulu, the nymph, appearing hesitant to dry herself and leave the pond. She must, however, to avoid exposing her sensuous frame to the radiance of the approaching morning. Love spoke of it as a study of light, and then contradicted himself, arguing it was one of color, or timing, and then grudgingly concluded it was really about love. Congo had watched the Headmaster, knowing it would be his last trap for the highhanded Ulu Covey, the girl whose heart he had pledged to win. The painting was his praise offering to her. Congo handed her the gift with the artwork facing down.

Ulu turned the image to face her. After she'd studied it for a long meditative moment, Ulu screamed and threw the painted glass frightfully to the floor. The old wooden frame still held things together. Yet, the mirrored painting shattered with one part showing Ulu's face smiling anxiously in the fleeing dawn. Congo's study of her most private activity at the pond at once horrified, pleased and humiliated Ulu. Seething in contempt and confusion, she looked at him. Then, with an aloof, grudgingly forgiving grin, she slammed the door and ran to her bedroom.

Confused, though undaunted by her rejection, Congo remained looking at the door. Expecting that by some miracle it would still open itself to him, Congo waited in vain. Finally, in humiliation, he ground his teeth before retreating in silence.

On arriving home, Congo's solitude, his need to recover, was interrupted when he found Ama waiting for him.

"I am sorry," she said. "There was one thing I didn't tell you, or him."

"If only I knew which him, Ama?"

"Don't be cross with me, Congo. I didn't do anything wrong."

"What is it, Ama?" Congo asked, focusing intently on her.

"Oh! I am pregnant, Congo!"

"Goodness! We'd better sit, Ama." As soon as they were seated, Congo asked, hoping he had heard incorrectly, "Are you sure?"

"Yes."

"How can you be sure?"

"I asked Miss Hene, and she told me the signs."

"Did you tell her it was about you?"

"No!"

"She told me many stories of how pregnant women behave. Then I knew I was."

"And who is the father?"

"Henry! Why did you have to ask?"

"Because there is Leroy."

"Leroy? He is too much of a gentleman. And, moreover, Henry is the only man I know."

"You mean . . . been to bed with?"

"Oh! Only if you want to call it that. It was in the library, and only one time."

"Once?"

"Yes, Congo, once! I still do not know why I did it. But it was only once. And he has asked me many times since. And I have felt a need for him, too. But I wouldn't, not until after I was certain we were to be married."

Silence filled the room. Congo saw the mosaic clearer. Miss Hene was married. Ama was engaged and pregnant. Ama was sure Henry would marry her. Ulu was unmarried and not pregnant. She had just rejected him. Or was she simply stating that his offer, her price, was not well placed?

"If I may ask, what will you do now, Ama?"

"The only thing to do, Congo. Tell Henry."

"Yes, indeed. And set an early date for the marriage."

"Yes, maybe next month. It will be Christmas vacation then. He should have lots of time."

"He seems to be from quite a respectable family, Ama. He will need to send out invitations." Congo wanted to add 'and get permission from his parents,' but he restrained himself, not wanting to dampen her jubilation.

"Yes, all the better to tell him soon," Ama said. "I will go to the teacher's cottage on Saturday morning and let him know we better set a date soon.

And let him know he will soon be a father."

"That should be good."

"Yes. The news will make him so happy. I am so sure it will."

"It ought to, Ama. And I am happy for you, too."

"Thank you, Congo. You make me feel so safe and happy," Ama said, hugging him and kissing his cheek.

"Would you like me to go with you?" whispered Congo.

"Shouldn't I do that by myself?"

"You may, but this is a Family matter now, Ama. And your Brother can go with you."

"Yes, of course. He will be your Brother, too! And with Miss Hene and Lev getting married, we will be a big happy Family."

"It does appear so," said Congo, with a glimpse of Ulu flashing across his mind. "I will bring the buggy over and get you on Saturday morning."

"Wonderful! Again, I thank you, Congo," and she kissed him again. This time he held her especially close to him, and kissed her face over and over again. Ama felt closer than ever to him.

"I will be going home now," Ama said.

"May I walk you home, Ama?"

"No, thank you, Congo. I just want to be by myself." And with that she sauntered home singing as she contemplated names for her baby.

Indifferent Tigers

Headmaster Henry Love considered his meeting with Ulu as his real entrance into Bem's household. Ama, and to a lesser extent, Congo, he viewed increasingly as mere stairways. His first substantive look at Ulu was during the party at the pond. He admired her composure and elegance. Like a polished gem in a quarry of raw stones, she stood out, beckoning his attention. He would be less than perfect not to reach out and give it. Why previously he had not noticed it eluded him. That, however, served only to further motivate Headmaster Love in covertly mining his new find. So, at his ardent suggestion and to her delight, he started calling on Ulu. Of course, that was philanthropic and inevitable, Ulu being a future sister-in-law and his intellectual counterpart.

Ama didn't know of the visits. Her job as custodian and her protracted reading hours kept Ama at the school long after its closure. Moreover, the meetings between Ulu and Henry occurred at Barton House, as Lev and Miss Hene entertained themselves at the pond or riding until dark. Ama, however, was sufficiently comfortable and secure with Henry so that his visiting Ulu, had she known, would simply have been considered purely social and innocent.

Upon reaching the Barton House, Henry Love handed his horse to a servant and walked along the graveled path to the mansion that held the woman who, above all else, he adored. The flight of birds above the house caused Henry to look up, seeing for the first time the immensity of the structure standing ahead of him. He wondered what had caused the original owners to construct an edifice of such grandeur. The house was made of gray cut stones with doors and windows framed in elegantly trimmed oak. Even the attic above the second floor seemed to have been constructed with some future use in mind. The wide green lawn was neatly trimmed, as were the fruit trees whose blossoms brought bouquets of honey and pollen to the warm evening air.

"Have you had supper, Henry?" Ulu asked as she greeted him.

The close, enduring friendship between the Tylers and Coveys made Barton House a second home for Ulu. Until recently, there was the absence of a woman in Barton House. That vacancy Ulu's personality filled like perfume in a room. Neither Miss Hene's humility, her new, bucolic style, nor Ama's occasional visits impeded Ulu's flamboyance. Moreover, Lev liked it, her hosting his parties, discussing the needs of the house with the maids, or seeing that Puncus brought the right wines to the cellar. Ulu had talent and time and a willing brother on whom to hone her housemaking skills.

"Yes, thank you, Ulu. But a drink would be rather refreshing."

"At your service, sir," she said and sauntered into the kitchen to prepare a drink for both of them. He followed her, observing her nimbleness, the movements of her body and hair. Her beauty amazed him.

"Here," she turned, handing him a beverage made of tamarind and ginger.

"I do thank you, Ulu," he said, as he sipped it and followed her to the rear windows which framed the expansive farms below. "I like Providence," he said, more so in admiration of her.

"Yes, it is a wonderful place."

Ulu's face was almost pressed against the window. Henry set his drink on the table and, approaching her from behind, placed his arm about her. She turned to smile at him, and he attempted to kiss her. She smoothly turned her face from him and gently removed his arm from her shoulder. She held his hand.

"This reminds me of home," Henry said, turning to look at the high ceilings and mahogany-paneled walls. From the living room he glanced up at the polished cedar stairs and casement, even at the study that held books from the original owners. It was splendid, a gem of design and workmanship. Henry Love thought no less of Ulu as he savored the feel of her hand on his.

"What a lovely gentleman you are, Henry!"

"Thank you, Ulu." And he leaned forward, attempting to kiss her again. Again, she turned from him.

"Ama has your ring," she reminded him with a giggle.

"Yes, of course she has! I needed a friend, and Ama can be entertaining, you know."

"Oh?"

"I became attached to her as we read poetry."

"What are you telling me? Is that what your ring is all about?"

"No. A man in my position has much to protect. And for Ama, it says she is spoken for."

"So do you intend to marry her?"

"You are quite abrupt, aren't you, Ulu?"

"What are you saying, Henry! There are other interests at stake, here, you know."

"Well, let's say we are in a pre-engagement stage of things."

"And does Ama understand that?"

"For her sake, I hope so."

"It might be necessary for you to clarify your position to her."

"I may have to. But our readings of love sonnets go deep. Ama has a good mind. And I like her. So I gave her a ring, and we talk of marriage. We talk of marriage," he repeated.

"I see. A man in your position still needs the companionship of a woman. And you see the need to make your position safe."

"More or less."

"You, Henry, understand that. I may understand that. But does Ama know what you are thinking?"

"She is a wonderful companion, and I would hate to shatter her faith by abruptly or unnecessarily discussing what should be an almost traditional understanding."

"Henry, I accept your position. It is decent and honorable. But you must understand, Ama may think otherwise. She may be expecting marriage. I do not blame you. Of course, you have much at stake, but you are a man. On the other hand, how can Ama expect marriage from you? She has little or no schooling and she is not even a Covey. She has so little going for her, how can she expect you to marry her?"

Henry was struck by her analysis. He also felt relieved that he didn't have to disclose more of himself and his ties with Ama or his sudden and heightened interest in Ulu. His offering Ama a ring denied her any opportunity to unnecessarily complicate their relationship by further indulging Leroy. By so doing, Henry made Ama's relationship with him exclusive. That was now clear to Ulu. She didn't rebuke Henry, even though she considered his behavior opportunistic. She rather liked his advance and sought to encourage it.

"Would you like to sit, Henry?" Without getting a reply, she held his hand and walked toward the sofa. "It's not clear what your intentions are toward me, Henry," she said as they were comfortably seated.

"Oh, I could assure you, Ulu. Ours would be on a more genuine footing, based on your family background, your education, and experience. And you must know, I do admire your beauty and elegance."

"You are just saying that."

"No, indeed. You do see how well we get along. I am amazed at how properly suited you are for me."

"Well, thank you, Henry. But there is something you may still have to settle."

"Do you mean my connection with Ama?"

"Yes, of course. That and any other."

"Well, since you insist," he chuckled, "I will clarify things with Ama."

"Yes, and when that is passé, you may . . ."

"Is that a painting?" he interrupted. As she spoke, his gaze focused on an oval form leaning against the far corner of the room.

"Oh, that!" she remarked and moved toward it. Henry followed.

"It's you, Ulu," he said, his eyes still fixed upon it. Did you commission this in New York?" he asked, not wanting her to grasp his knowledge of its origin.

"No. Indeed not. Congo gave it to me."

"Who? How would he ever come by this?"

"He painted it."

"No! He does not have this kind of talent."

"What do you mean?"

"It's exceptionally well done. Moreover, there is a semblance of Pablo Picasso here. If Congo did it, I can tell you Congo is a master of hue, balance, and light. Just look at the water drops coming from your hair, and how he brings the sunlight into your face. There is a talent here, Ulu."

"Well, thank you, Henry. I must treasure it!"

"Yes, I would, and get the painting repaired. That may bring it together."

"Can you believe I accidentally shattered it?"

"You did?"

"Yes, in a state of madness, I suppose," Ulu said.

"Tsk, tsk, tsk" Henry remarked, kissing his teeth. ". . . you make me wonder how these things do happen!" Henry said as he shook his head sideways.

"Now you are sounding just like Ama! She must have gotten it from our mother. I suppose Esi, her best friend, brought that question with her to Providence. And ever since Esi's death, that question has been Nweka's and now Ama's response to every mysterious event. Haven't you noticed that, Henry? You must be spending too much time together," Ulu said, laughing.

"I meant it in a frivolous sense."

"I know. But there must be an academic side to it. Don't you think, Henry?"

"Yes, there may be. One view is that it takes three things coming to a point at once."

"What on earth do you mean? You'll have to enlighten me on that," Ulu said with bewilderment.

"Three things coming to a point," he repeated. "Two objects and an impulse."

"An impulse . . . ?"

"Such as a desire or wish."

"Or love?"

"Quite so."

"What? Did you mean – me – " Ulu asked, pressing her open palms on her chest. "An impulse, and you: two objects and an impulse?"

"Or rather, Ulu, you and me brought together by an impulse." His flirting smile grew into laughter that she shared. "That's how things happen," he finished.

"Are you saying, then, that Congo also has a love impulse for me, Henry?"

"A drawing impulse, I would rather say." They laughed again, Henry dismissing Congo as a credible and eminent suitor. That seed – Congo as her potential suitor and Henry's rival – was exactly what Ulu intended to plant, thereby bringing out Henry's desire for her. Henry nestled closer to her, touching her cheek and then pointing at the picture. "Look, it says 'Ulu' here, as though it were a self portrait."

"No. I certainly didn't paint it. Congo created it, Henry. I suppose he does not even know his name belongs there."

Henry laughed, and Ulu soon joined him.

"Silly man. He is really a very silly person," Ulu concluded, making it clear to Henry that he could be her only suitor of significance.

A Simple Elevation

Later that day, Lev sent a servant inviting Congo to Barton House on the approaching Friday. At first Congo was startled, since he had always declined Lev's invitation to the house. He spent all night thinking of the summons and what it might hold for him. He hadn't been given any signs of Lev's displeasure with his work. So why was there another invitation?

It didn't take Congo long to determine what was taking place. By the time he arrived, Lev's entire family and guests were there. Lev met Congo at the door and invited him into the parlor, which sparkled with light and delightful good humor. It was then that Congo realized the size and import of the gathering. All the teachers, clergy, the doctor and his wife, much of their staff, Detective Charles Graham, and many others were present, making it a substantial gathering.

On the invitation sent at Lev's request, Ulu had stated:

> *Your pleasure at Barton House*
> *next Friday evening*
> *would be greatly appreciated.*

Such an informal notice was sufficient. So, too, were the thirty invitations Ulu sent. Ulu purposefully excluded Congo, letting him know that perchance he attended, it was not on her account. Privately, however,

Ulu wanted Congo there, if for nothing else than to publicly demean or insult him.

She intended the party to be a simple, unceremonious gathering of friends. That was what Ulu negotiated finally with Miss Hene, who still hadn't learned all of Lev's friends or been inclined toward celebrating.

Yet Farmer Leroy Kendal got it wrong. He was never keen on going to church and, having no children, hadn't interacted much with the school. Except for his closeness to Congo or his trading in the market, Leroy Kendal rarely appeared in public. He was by nature reclusive, preferring to invest his extra hours on his farm. For this social event, his first since the picnic, he got it wrong. He came to the party dressed in the most luxurious English tweed with matching accessories. Still awaiting Ama's response to his proposal, and seeing this as another chance to silently persuade her, Leroy Kendal spared no cost in attending to his attire or appearance. His well-groomed statement was intended for Ama. Whereas Ama had always seen the Headmaster formally attired, she had never seen the farmer except in work-clothes. Moreover, Leroy wanted to make sure he measured up to everything for which he surmised Barton House stood. He did not know it also stood for humor – loud boisterous humor – the kind his very inappropriate image would provoke.

The Headmaster started with a snicker, but Ulu's grace spared Leroy. On noticing Leroy's unfortunate attire, Ulu discreetly removed the farmer to Lev's bedroom, apologized profusely for her mistake in not spelling out a dress code, and found casual clothing for Leroy. He sipped the wine Ulu brought while she mothered him, hastily making his attire fit the party.

Leroy was still unaware of the progress Henry had made with Ama. Ulu, however, sensing the farmer's distress, considered it best for Ama to inform Leroy herself and to do so at a more appropriate time and setting. So on the subject of Ama's engagement or, as Ulu understood it, Ama's arrangement with Headmaster Love, Ulu remained silent and Leroy, ignorant.

Miss Hene was radiant with smiles. Congo had never seen her like that before, and Ulu, as soon as she returned to the room, glided back and forth attending to the desires of her guests. The idea for the party was Lev's, but the planning, Ulu's. She had hired the finest cooks and musicians, and it showed. She moved seamlessly between the servants and guests, ensuring everyone's happiness.

With champagne and wine flowing easily and the musicians playing waltzes, it was effortless for Lev to lead the dance floor with Miss Hene. As they danced, Ama and Miss Hene, with their partners, met in the middle of the floor. Leroy found many easy dances, and Laura avoided Congo as she had promised Ulu. With Ulu making herself busy, Congo found companionship among the teachers. Ulu watched with whom Congo danced repeatedly, interrupting any of his conversations she considered unduly long. Congo didn't notice. He sipped wine and paid attention to the mental image he carried of Ulu, not daring to provoke another of her outbursts.

When it was time for dinner, Ulu made sure to place Henry and Ama side by side, with Congo sitting between Ama and Leroy. She trusted Congo to hold that configuration, if not for her, then certainly for Ama's sake. Laura sat facing Lev and Miss Hene at the head of the table, while Ulu seated herself by Laura, outside of Congo's stare. Ulu didn't care who occupied the other seats.

"This is a happy moment for us," Lev started, as he stood beside Miss Hene. Ulu signaled to the bandleader to lower the music. "This is indeed a happy time for us," Lev repeated, as he bent and kissed Miss Hene. "She, you see, has brought much happiness to me. And I must say thank you, Miss Hene for marrying me."

Miss Hene bowed her head with a smile, saying in a whisper, "You are welcome."

"And, before I go further, let me thank Ulu," he said, pointing at her, "for preparing this wonderful party. Ulu volunteered from the start and she did all the work, all the cooking, by herself. Isn't that right, Puncus?" Lev joined his guests in the laughter that followed.

"Now," said Lev, "I must also thank all my guests for responding to our impromptu invitation and giving us their time here."

Lev paused as he spoke and, looking around the table, acknowledged his guests with pleasant bows.

"Thank you all for coming here to celebrate with us, and for sharing our perfect secret. We are married," he said gleefully. "Yes, Miss Hene and I got married two weeks ago and have decided to make it public only now, with this little get-together. So, thank you again for coming. I do not want to take much of your time; and, moreover, we – Miss Hene and I – will be leaving this very evening on our honeymoon. In fact," he said, looking at his watch, "we will be leaving as soon as I am done talking here."

"Here, here!" said the Headmaster with his glass raised for a toast.

"For he is a jolly good fellow . . ." started Farmer Kendal, his craggy singing voice soon fading for lack of support.

"Thank you, thank you all very much," Lev said, nodding a pleasant smile as he looked steadily at Leroy. "All of my business affairs will be left to Congo. If anyone should have need of anything, please see him. He will have keys to Barton House. And – I hate to mention this now – he will be in full charge of the jail, too." Lev continued jovially. "Of course, none of you here should ever have need even to consider that. But I just want you to know he has full responsibility for everything. Our trip will last over three months. We will make an island tour, as Ulu has advised us to do. For me, a simple country bumpkin, this is good news. I have been locked on this property from birth, and this will be my first time traveling. Thanks, again, to Ulu for helping us plan the trip."

Lev paused, and the flash of a remembered anxiety that smeared his face soon gave way to a most pleasant smile. "I am getting more comfortable with this," he said. "But there is one I would personally like to thank for all of this, and that is Asa. Yes, Asa King. You may ask who Asa King is. I am sure Master Congo will be talking to you about him when he is ready. In the meantime, though, I have learned a lot from Miss Hene and still have more to learn from Asa, I am sure. He came here, bringing Miss Hene and Master Congo, without whom none of this would have happened. He is my mysterious father-in-law, and I would have liked him to be here."

As Lev spoke, the door to the parlor opened and Shep trotted in. Lev looked in surprise at the dog appearing without Leroy's leadership. There were always together. But Lev surmised Shep to be lonely and coming in search of Leroy, his master. The dog came to the table, and Lev patted his head while the canine licked Lev's and Miss Hene's hands. He then walked back out of the room, paying scant attention to Leroy.

"Perhaps, one day, Asa will come here for my sake. But enough of that," Lev said somewhat absent-mindedly. Soon his pace quickened and he seemed focused again.

"I want to thank him for planting his Family here and making life so wonderful for all of us. But enough of that, too, and everything else. Let me leave you now. But, maybe a toast before I leave is in order. Would you all, please? Let's drink to the long life and constant happiness of my gracious love and bride, Miss Hene."

After the toast Lev continued. "Now the music will play as long as

Ulu decides, and there is enough food here for all. So please, just have a ball, while we are on our way. Thanks again for being here and, until we return, good bye, all."

Lev, accompanied by Miss Hene, moved from seat to seat, embracing, kissing, and shaking hands with all the guests. Lastly, he got to Congo and Ulu. They placed their hands in Congo's and Ulu's and said, "We thank you so much. Everything is in your care. We love you." With a final kiss, Miss Hene bade them farewell.

The merriment had no reason to stop because of Tyler's absence. In fact, it got better. The preoccupation of not previously knowing the reason the party was given abated, and, with music, food, and drink in excess, the revelry continued until far into the night.

With Leroy excluded from dancing with Ama and Henry laying absolute claim on her, Leroy Kendal ate, drank, danced with many women, teachers and nurses alike. Having market to attend early the following morning, he bade untimely farewell and departed. Soon after Leroy left, Congo, seeing how happy Ama and Love were, whispered congratulations to them, then said goodbye.

Congo was content that he hadn't the courage to approach Ulu, even if the drinking and merriment had softened her to him. Laura, however, found Congo's unhappiness disconcerting but avoided the temptation to entertain him, busying herself, instead, with other friends.

Ulu felt triumphant about everything. Even Congo's unhappiness had worked well for her.

A Day's Fate

The servants had offered to take Ama and Henry to their separate homes in Lev's carriage. The Headmaster declined their offer and assured them he would safely walk Ama home. As for himself, he was fit enough to fend, not that there was any hint of evil in peaceful Providence.

Headmaster Henry Isaac Love's intentions were otherwise, however. With Ama's untested head full of the dulling red wine, with his ring on her finger, his baby in her body, and feeling safe and secure with him, she easily accepted the invitation to spend the rest of the night with Henry Love. She couldn't dispel his charm. Neither did she want to. To her the marriage was a thing of certainty. For Love, the ring was a mark of ownership, for he had found and paid her price.

The spirit of the party prevailed in Love's cottage until late Sunday afternoon. The next day's responsibility suddenly dawned on him as though he had gone to sleep in a cave but awakened in an open field under the stare of the midday sun. For Ama, unaccustomed to long, late revelry, she was slower in coming to life. She had scant recollection of the weekend. She remembered sipping wine and asking for the bedroom. She remembered little else.

As she recovered, Ama felt tired and bruised in mind and spirit. Love had made coffee and brought her some. He was on his second cup, rosy in his face and full of self-delight.

"Here you are, Ama. Have this."

"I can't take anything now," she said, wiping her face as she yawned.

"I understand. It has been a long night. And what a party!"

"You seem happy. Are you happy, Henry?"

"Yes, Ama. And you should be, too."

"Oh! Maybe I am, and just too tired or still too drunk to tell."

"Tired? You seem to have slept through it."

"Maybe, my love. It must have been the spirits. I am not accustomed to them."

"Yes, I noticed that. You kept passing out. But as soon as you did, you would come back around. And if I gave you more wine, you would drink and pass right out again. Oh, that was funny!"

"Oh! Is that what it was, Henry?"

"Yes. That, or something close to it," he said, smiling.

"I do not know why, but I feel sore, bruised, you know, like the first time we made love. Do you remember that, Henry?"

"Yes, of course! It was in the library. I watched you; read poetry to you; waited and waited for you. Then, and I still do not know why, on that rainy Friday evening, you relented."

"I loved you, Henry. And wanted to make sure you loved me. That's why I waited. All the poetry you read to me, all the nice things you said to me, about the sunset, my hair, my nose, how I walked, all those lovely things you told, finally moved me, Henry. So, when you touched me that evening, I simply melted. I couldn't resist you any longer. I had to have you. And I hope you liked it, too, Henry."

"Yes, and I have wanted you ever since, more and more. I didn't know why you held back from me so long. Why did you, Ama?"

"Oh, silly Henry, I have not been holding myself back. But I needed to know what your intentions were. You have never told me in your own words that you love me. You always said it in poetry, let someone else speak for you. But you do love me, Henry, don't you?"

"That was my way."

"Yes, now I understand. But that was not mine."

"So conventional!"

"I was seeking honesty."

"Honesty? Nothing is as pure, as honest, as poetry."

"Your words should be."

"My words?"

"Yes, your words, simple words from your heart, from your lips. Do you understand, Henry? So will you tell me again, please?"

"Tell you what, Ama?"

"That you love me, and me alone. In your words, Henry."

Headmaster Henry Isaac Love sipped his coffee.

"You ought to have your coffee, Ama."

"Yes, thanks, Henry," she said. "If you just tell me you love me."

"Ama. I do not have to claim to love you. You are mine now."

Ama looked puzzled. "What? You own me, Henry?"

"Yes, with the ring, and a promise of marriage, I do own you."

"We have a ring and a promise of marriage. That's what we have. Is that all we have, Henry?"

His intention, which progressively became clear to Ama, was to use the ring and a never-to-be-fulfilled promise of marriage as his passage to free and uninterruptible sex with her.

He paused in reflection. Henry Love had never seen a disagreeable facet in Ama previously. Was her association with Congo responsible?

"And I do not know why I feel so uncomfortable, Henry. Did we make love last night?"

The Headmaster laughed. "Wine and sex, that's all we had, Ama. How can you not know?"

"Sex?" she paused. Then started "How could you, Henry?"

"I thought you knew and liked it! Why did you come here in the first place?"

"Oh Henry! To be with you. I love you. We are to be married and I am carrying your child. I came here to tell . . ."

"My child?"

"Yes, Henry. I'm pregnant!" She paused, then added, "Congo knows. I told him all about us."

"You silly girl! You went ahead and got pregnant? And before coming to me, you tell others."

"Why, Henry? Why are you so angry?"

"Angry? You fill me with disgust! Do you know what this means? I will lose my Headmastership and prestige. Do you know how much work went into it?"

"Henry, we can get married anytime. We practically are already."

"Married! Me marry you? Oh no, Ama. You must have been mistaken! Who on earth would marry you?"

"You, Henry." Ama said between her sobs. "You gave me a ring and asked me to."

"I bought you with a ring, and asked you to bed. Do you always have to be so simple-minded, Ama?"

"Oh Henry! How can you be so cruel?" As she spoke, Ama fell to the floor in a formless mass, crying.

Henry bent over her and whispered, "It's best if you leave, Ama!"

When it appeared that all Ama had strength for was crying in her helplessness, Henry rose over her and said firmly, "Your tears can't buy me, Ama, so don't be foolish. Just get yourself together and go!"

Ama did not move. How could she? Her world had died. Henry helped her to her feet and led her outside, into the open sunlight. She was not even fully dressed, having on only a thin disheveled slip.

Henry could not care. He had his career and the school to protect. He had just gotten rid of his last hindrance. In his view, it was time for him to finish cleaning up the mess he had carelessly started and focus anew on the future.

Ama didn't know what she did next. Her last memory was of Shep licking her hands and face as she lay puddled on the ground in the broiling noon sun outside Henry's cottage.

When Ama awoke later that day, she found herself in Congo's cottage, prostrate on his bed, crying, crying.

Congo, however, was not there. Neither was Shep.

Celebration

My dear sister, Ulu:

I do not know what force governs Asa, but bless it, Ulu, for it has centered, strengthened, and given him a vision that has created and shaped my life. I owe him all that I am and will be, for he has taught it to me, and now I see how it binds Lev and me together, like one . . . one mind and body.

But, Ulu, I shouldn't start there. I must tell you thanks for your friendship since we, Congo and I, came to Providence. We came as strangers, and your family entertained us, treating us as brethren. Even though we . . . I should really say Asa . . . has done the same everywhere he goes. I have always been on the hosting side. Never before have I been away from my own home in Portland, looking for a new home in Providence; and here I have found not only kindness, understanding and open arms, but sisterhood and love.

This thing, this feeling between Lev and me, has developed so suddenly, we didn't have time to talk about it. I was not even sure I should marry him. Not that I didn't love him, of that I will be forever sure. What's surprising is that I didn't stop to think whether marrying him was wrong or right. I simply did it.

He is a wonderful man, Ulu. My feelings splice into his, and his into mine. It is so comfortable and reassuring. And when we make love, it is as though we are taken out of this world. Every time is an event unto itself. It is a wonderful transportation, to a place we know not. I will try and tell you, Ulu. We start *in simple ways, holding hands, talking, and sharing. It may be at tea or just lying on the floor. I do not know what sets it off . . . but there is a mood, like a cloud that comes over us. And we forget, yes, everything around us, and we live only for the moment. We become lost in a world of feelings and thought, and the more we feel, the more we move along this journey, until we become exhausted and fall in each others arms. I wonder, Ulu, is this the fall they talk about in your church? Is this a fall from passion or love? Or was the fall when we first saw each other and lost all our fear, and admitted our love? What a fall! It's a sweet place to be, Ulu, and I wish it for you, soon.*

I wonder. I wonder. What makes his touch so exciting? What brings such revelry to his song, his whisper, and his presence? And will it last? I wonder. I wonder. What brought us together, and what magnet holds us still like glue?

I cannot tell, Ulu. I only ask whoever so blessed us to cover everyone everywhere tonight with this love. I know it can stretch!

And what about you, Ulu? Will love bless you tonight? You will tell me, won't you, Ulu?

I hate to break this feeling. It gives me still so much pleasure to simply think of Lev. I must not leave him too long, or I may die. I mean, I fear losing the feelings I get from him. That would be a kind of death, and I should avoid it. I write to you this way because I want you to know we are truly happy. What would make two strangers find such deep peace and comfort in each other? When we are together, there is only silence save for his voice, I hear nothing else. It has become too easy for me to totally devote my being to him and be his willing slave. This matter of love is unfair. For without his asking, I want to serve him. I trust my feelings totally to him. And, although my love comes so late in his life and, he has known no other, as he so confided to me, I wish to devote all my time, my being to his pleasure, as much as he wishes. Oh Ulu! I love him, and I am happy to serve him as his wife, in complete surrender. And with all my heart, I wish to God you could find love tonight, Ulu, if only for the night.

But as cruel as it is, I must break from my selfish thoughts and ask what has happened to Barton. Of course, Lev should be asking. But he is tired, Ulu. He does not want to think of property any more. He is sick of it and has asked me to mention it to you. He refuses to write to Congo. And not out of bad manners. He simply is sick of it, and is so happy Congo is as capable as he is.

We go from store to store in Kingston, and he takes me to the best places. I have bought furniture for the entire house. I do not know why, for we already have the finest things I have ever seen. But he wants me to have a piano, a new wood stove, and all new drapes and curtains. Well, what should we do? I believe Lev is in love. He worships me more than I ever dreamed of. He is my man, mine: and he does not fully know. Should I tell him so?

Yet, Ulu, here is something you may do for us. Please store or give away the old furniture, every bit of it. We have new pieces for every room. I do not know why Lev spends so much time buying. He told me I am his first love. I disagreed with him, and told him I am his last. He is still grinning about that: kind of silly, ah? But back to the furniture, Ulu. The present furniture came from England, for the Bartons. It has been in the family for over one hundred years. And now that Lev has a family, he wants everything changed. I tell him it's because he is in love. He thinks otherwise . . . that he wants change. He has changed . . . but does not know just how much yet. He is asking more and more about Asa, and our Family. Bit by bit, I teach him, and he swallows it all up. Perhaps, some day, you will be so taught, Ulu. Bless you.

There is so much to tell you of our travels, Sister. We have many memories and moments to share with you.

How is it with Ama? Did she decide whom to marry? It seemed she wanted Kendal, but Love was ever before her. So much so, she mightn't choose rightly. This love can be a mist, a deep dark cloud sometimes. But Ama will sort it out, and her man will make himself clear.

Please give her and her beloved our best desires for them. We love you, and will be home soon.

Miss Hene

P.S.

Now that we can get the news, Lev reads the entire <u>Gleaner</u> to me on Sundays. It seems, Ulu, there will be a war between our country and Germany. I hate the idea of war and hope it will not affect our country or our little Family.

Lev sends his love for all of you.

Peace and love, my Sister,

MHT

A Flash of Fire

Congo listened to Ama's story time and time again. He watched her relationship grow from fascination to flirtation, then to denial, and finally a deep fall into love. Before he had come to Providence he would have seen, listened, but not understood the fire torching Ama's spirit.

He had never been flirtatious. In the Jamaican hillsides of Portland and St. Thomas where he spent his early life with Asa, he had seen the power of seduction. Congo, though often tempted, could never have yielded, for the ever-present Asa would never have allowed it.

He loved women because he thought he understood them. Actually, Miss Hene taught Congo all he knew about women, and he was never sure what he had learned and how to apply it. It was not until he was out of Asa's watch that he allowed the temptations of wealth and lust to enter his soul. Even then they did not reveal themselves as such to him. By admitting their disguises, Congo simply delighted in the pleasure they brought. The long, empty void in his soul was now being rightly filled. Now Congo understood Ama's plight!

Congo had already had his days and nights with Laura. He prided himself on his newly found prowess; he celebrated it. What needed testing was his novel code: in mutual understanding, to share love with respect and full responsibility. But wasn't that true of all men? Didn't all men honor that code? And, if not, what was their way with women? The neophyte still had to learn.

With Ama's sobs ringing in his ears and his code tugging at his heart, Congo reached the teacher's cottage. He knocked on the door. He was not there to judge but to understand and mend.

The teacher, vexed and confused, stood in the doorway and asked, "What do you want?"

"Just a few words with you, Headmaster, concerning my sister."

"Go away," Love replied, slamming the door.

Congo knocked on the door repeatedly. Never did the Headmaster respond. Congo, thinking more of Ama than either himself or Love, kicked the door in. "What did you do to my sister?" he demanded.

"Get out, Congo! Get out and don't behave as stupidly as Ama! You must know better, don't you?"

With that, Congo slammed him against the wall, pulled a string from his pocket and tied Love's hands behind him. With Love thrown on the floor, Congo tied his feet, with some distance between them. Not saying more, Congo pulled Love to his horse, strapped him on the saddle, and led the horse with the Headmaster on it through the town's square, then to Barton House jail. Such savagery!

Congo, unflinching, threw the frightened Love in, slammed the door, and said, "Let me know when you want to mend things."

"Congo, you can't leave me here."

"And why not, may I ask?"

"I am the Headmaster. I must be in school tomorrow."

"For getting my sister pregnant and not marrying her, you cannot be the Headmaster."

"I cannot marry her, Congo."

"Why not? She gave you her word!"

"My father has a bride for me already, an English lady. We are to be married in November."

"Outrageous! And what about Ama?"

"I will pay for her silence."

"Yes, how much?"

"Twenty, fifty pounds, you name it."

"And what would that make her?"

"Rich, Congo. Richer than she has ever been."

"Not quite so in my book, Love. And moreover, what would that make you?"

"Why, Congo? I would go free, and things would mend. Isn't that what you want?"

"So is that what your freedom is worth?"

His silence prevailed.

"And what about the child?" Congo asked.

"My father will care for it."

"And you, Henry?"

"I will be married."

"What convenience!"

"Grow up, Congo. That's the way of the world!"

"Not our world, Henry. Here, love and respect count for something."

"I need to get out, Congo."

"It is not Lev's intention to keep men here. I am to review cases and set a fine. That's the Tyler system."

"Good then. What is your fine, Congo?"

"One thousand pounds." Congo set the sum more than ten times what he thought it should really be. Of course he was angry.

"Give me writing paper," Henry said.

Love penned a telegram to his father and gave it to Congo.

"Here you are. Send this now, and you will get your money by nine o' clock in the morning."

"Do you have money to send your telegram?"

"Here." Love handed Congo thirty shillings. "Let me know if it costs more than that."

"This is more than enough."

Congo turned to go.

"Here, Congo." He scribbled on the remaining paper. "You will know what to do with this." Love gave him a note which read:

> To The School Board of Providence,
> I hereby offer my resignation.
>   Henry I. Love

Congo marveled at the small, illegible manner of Love's signature. He took the telegram and looked at the Headmaster. When their eyes met, Henry said, "I will leave for Panama, tomorrow."

"You need to tell that to Ama."

"No! You tell her."

Congo laughed, shook his head in disbelief and left.

Final Assignment

The tolling school bells hadn't finished ringing 9:00 AM on Monday in the fateful year of our Lord 1903 when Congo appeared at the jail. The money for which Henry Love asked had arrived. Congo took it to Barton jail. He had Ama accompany him. She waited while Congo went into the cellar to release Love. He said nothing, simply came up out of the jail to see Ama standing there.

Still Love didn't speak. Congo handed him the money.

"It's yours," Love said. "I am free now."

"Yes. But I have no use for it. I doubt Lev will take it, not for Ama's sake."

"Best give it to her then." Love said, looking askance at Ama.

Congo turned to hand the money to Ama.

"I would prefer to die hungry and homeless than to take it!" Ama said, spitting on the ground.

"Take it," Congo said to Love. "Take it; get out. And do not come back here."

Love took the money. With his face flushed with dishonor, he looked at Ama and walked away.

"Such a shame," Congo said mutedly. "Such a shame."

Ama watched him as, dejected and in disgrace, he left all he owned behind, walking alone out of sight: never, never again to be seen. Ama, not knowing what to feel, did not cry. She stood in silence and shock. It had all been so sudden.

The memory of the moment had so deeply burnt itself in Ama's mind that, in the future, it was all she could completely remember of the vaga-bond Headmaster, Henry Love. It was with tears, only long, sad tears of this memory, that she would tell her yet unborn child of his father when he paused from suckling and dared to inquire: "Mammy, who is my father? What did you say he was, again?"

Many, many years later, Ama had found and memorized *Outcast* by her favorite poet, Claude McKay. She and Henry had never read him together. Ama at times, though, recalled this very moment and wondered with a lonely, agonizing heart if the lines were written especially for her love, Henry Love:

> *Something in me is lost, forever lost,*
> *Some vital thine has gone out of my heart,*
> *And I must walk the way of life a ghost*
> *Among the sons of earth, a thing apart.*

Ama questioned if, in time, those words had perchance reached and pierced his still sick heart and whether or not their prophetic words had so destined and led his feet.

When quite often and in pain, Ama recited the lexis, she exchanged the word "ghost" for one of her own, "vagabond", hurting still more that with her liberty she had destroyed what she considered otherwise the poem's absolutely sweet and perfect scheme.

Of this . . . all of this, Ama wondered alone and in sorrow.

Furniture Arrangement

Lev Tyler's happiness with Miss Hene and hers with him didn't end at the party or on their honeymoon. They were madly in love, had repeated their vows each morning and night like a prayer. Neither did their sense of exploration fade. They spent time learning each other and mutually gave selfless affection. Lev took Miss Hene to all the capital cities, from Annotto Bay through Port Antonio, Kingston, Mandeville, and Negril. They planned and traveled the entire island.

As Ama grieved and her pregnancy grew, making her increasingly indisposed, Ulu turned to Congo for help instead of to the kind, easy-going Ama, who could never refuse.

Congo did what Ulu asked, not volunteering anything. Ulu arranged and rearranged the new furniture as if trying on hats, Congo thought. She arranged and disarranged and, at length, frustrated and fatigued, sat despondently on the most elegant sofa. Congo, with an eagle eye and a penchant for organization, had an image of how the furniture could be arranged.

Ulu's eyes were closed from weariness, oblivious to Congo's endeavors. Within a few minutes, he had everything placed with the taste of an artist. Congo said nothing, but sat admiring Ulu's form on the sofa. His quietness startled her. What was he up to? Slowly she opened her eyes and looked around. In disbelief, she again closed them. Then she said, "What a lovely fit, I must say."

"Yes, it is. They certainly have good taste!"

"I am sure it's Miss Hene."

"It could well be; she has a certain talent."

"Yes."

Congo said, "I must be going, Ulu."

"I thank you for your help, Congo."

"You are welcome, Ulu. I learned from you."

"What did you learn from me, Congo?"

"How to arrange the furniture, Ulu."

"Congo, I was saying thanks for what you did for Ama," Ulu said.

"Oh, I see. I love Ama. I will always stand by her."

"Yes, she told me you promised to adopt her baby and be its godfather."

"Yes, that I will do, Ulu. But not only that. I will build a house for her on the land Boydell gave to her. Lev told me about it. So she will have a house of her own, too."

"You know, Congo. I must tell you something about our family. Even though Ama was the first born, she is not a Covey. She is a King like you. I am sure you know that part of the family history. What you may not know is that she has not been treated like one of us, I mean like Rex Covey and me. Kisi and Ama are not Coveys. Ama has nothing to look forward to here. Bem left the property to Rex and me. Rex is in New York and everything is under my care."

"I know that, Ulu."

"What I really wanted to say is that the offer of marriage from Love was the first thing of importance anyone ever gave to Ama. And with that gone, no one has ever given her anything."

"I understand."

"But, that said, I must add that I do not blame Henry one bit."

"You may not have to blame him, just support Ama. This is very hard on her."

"What I have been explaining to you, Congo, is that Ama has nothing. Do you understand that? She works as a janitor at the school. She calls herself a custodian. The Headmaster was from an upper class family. Moreover, he is young, talented, handsome and well educated, if I must add that."

"So what are you saying, Ulu?"

"Simply, Congo, that there was never a match between Ama and

Henry. Do you see where I am taking this? She was more than silly to expect Henry to marry her. And whatever trap she set for him simply backfired on her. She initiated it. I can just imagine. And he, being a man, fell for her body. Now who is to blame? Ama, of course! And now she runs around crying for sympathy. I have none for her!"

"You seem to dislike her, Ulu. Or maybe you are jealous the teacher didn't choose you."

"Jealous! Not in the least. I am practical. I believe in cause and effect. Ama must be taught a lesson, a lesson in taking responsibility for her actions. She must learn. It is for that very reason I cannot take her into our business, even if I had the mind to."

"That would require a heart, Ulu."

There was a long pause. Congo saw deep into the personalities of the sisters. He was in love with Ulu. He felt brotherly toward Ama, and would do anything for her. He didn't think it his place, however, to get into a family discord, the roots of which he didn't fully comprehend. He sat pondering.

"You know what it really is, Congo?"

"No, Ulu, I do not."

"Ama has no common sense. She trusts in everything and everybody; and she believes life will somehow work out fine, somehow, no matter what she does. Have you ever heard of nonsense like that? Trust, trust, trust, with nothing to back it up? How idiotic!"

"It seems you are saying she has the mind of a baby."

"Yes. It is something like that. So, Congo," Ulu continued, "your love, your understanding, are the only things she has now. And you offering to care for her child must be wonderful to her, to her self-esteem."

"I am not quite sure what you are trying to say, Ulu."

"Please come and sit beside me, Congo."

Congo struggled for awhile. "What was that you said, Ulu?"

"Please, Congo, come and sit with me."

"Thank you, Ulu."

She laughed, as if pleased with herself. "I have great confidence in Lev," she said, touching Congo's hand.

He jerked, trying to calm himself. "Yes, he is kind and trusting."

"And I also see what you are doing for him and his property."

"Thank you, Ulu."

"What if we were married, Congo?"

"If we were married? Is that what you said?"

"Yes. I would expect you to do the same or better for me. Could you do that, Congo?"

"If we were married? We are not even . . . really . . . friendly, let alone courting. So how does marriage get into this?"

"What I am asking, Congo, is that you court me," Ulu said, locking her fingers into his.

Congo went silent. "You know, Ulu, Asa left me here with some instructions. He wants me to start a Family. That's what I should be doing. In fact," Congo continued, "I plan to discuss that with Lev and Miss Hene as soon as they get back!"

During the pause that followed, Congo reflected on his dream of wealth, power, and attachment. He also thought of Asa and his commitment to starting a Family in Providence. He wanted everything, and there was Ulu offering the key to power and prestige. Congo looked at her and smiled.

Ulu knew this was her chance to snare the energy of the only man in Providence who could make her truly wealthy.

"If we were married, Congo, we would be a family," Ulu finally said.

"Asa meant a Kumina Family, Ulu."

"What is that Kumina thing you keep talking about?"

"It's a Family based on our spiritual belief."

"What exactly is that belief, Congo?"

"Love, Ulu. But many will say it is based on possession."

"Possession of what?"

"Not of what, Ulu. By whom?"

"By whom then, Congo?"

"By our ancestors. The Beloved. We prepare bodies for them and they come back into those bodies and give us prophecies and wisdom."

"And do you believe that, Congo?"

"Yes, Ulu. It is the truth! And what do you believe, anyway?"

"What on earth are you asking, Congo? You know we are Anglicans."

"Yes, but what do you believe, Ulu?"

"Well, certainly not what you do. I believe in His Death and Resurrection."

"Yes, and I believe you talk about a Day of Pentecost in your church, Ulu?"

"Yes, of course, Congo."

"Well, our Visitations, which we call Walkings, are like that."

"What? Do you have your days of Pentecost any time?"

"If you like, you could say it like that."

"What are these bodies you prepare?"

"Bodies of our beloved. We prepare and keep them for the Walking."

"So, you walk the dead, Congo?"

"You could say it that way, Ulu. And yes, they do Walk!"

"Is that it? What you believe?"

"Yes. But we use the drums to invite the loved ones, and they come. They understand and come. They enter the dead and they Walk. And in the Walk, they give wisdom and guidance."

There was a long silence. Ulu thought of the Christian traditions: Lazarus, Pentecost, and Christ Jesus! She wondered: How do I take him to church with me? "This takes some rearrangement," Ulu said.

Congo didn't comment.

"Congo?"

"Yes, Ulu."

"What I must ask you bluntly is this: Are you open to other views of religion?"

"Sure! Yes, Ulu. Why did you ask?"

"What I have in mind, Congo, is that you accompany me to church on Sundays."

"I have been to church before, you know. Asa sometimes goes to church on Sundays and Saturdays. It's not a crime," he said smiling.

"Okay, then, it is not as bad as I thought."

"You know, Ulu, I decided to help Lev for awhile. Miss Hene will help me build the Family when she comes back. I believe Lev will help, too. I just have to start it. And once I start, Ulu, there is no looking back!"

"I quite understand your commitment. But you know, Congo, when we are married, you will be in charge of the Covey estate. That will be some undertaking. And I want to expand and do other things. I imagine you are man enough to handle it; otherwise, I wouldn't be talking to you."

Congo remained pensive, silent. The temptation was too great for him not to entertain it. He would soon hand back the reins of the Barton estate to Lev. After that, what would he have? He understood Ulu's offer. What he saw was the opportunity to run a smaller estate and start his Family. He might even get a few members from the Anglican Church. The temptation was clear. The rewards seemed even sweeter. Silence loomed as Congo sought to find a way to close the deal with Ulu and, at the same time, start his Family.

"Would you like some wine, Congo?"

"Yes, thank you, Ulu. How befitting!"

She brought him the wine and let him stand to get it. She walked across the room, smiling, accepting his roaming eyes. She was happy he was following her. She moved from window to window, facing him only when she wanted him to see her sparkle. She talked and laughed and finally led him down the passageway to a bedroom.

Without saying more, she lay on her back, kicked off her shoes, allowed her bosom to lie partially open before him. Not that Congo needed that much encouragement. He rested beside her, letting his arm fall across her stomach as it searched for her fingers. He kissed her cheek again and again and said, "Heavens! I love you, Ulu."

"You will be good for me, Congo."

She returned his kiss, their lips meeting as they dissolved into each other. They made love and fell asleep. When Congo later awoke, he found Ulu kissing him. She smiled, said nothing; and they made love again, then slept until morning.

Congo was long gone before Ulu awoke.

Ama's Home

Congo knew that Leroy Kendal was, like himself, an early riser. So to find him at home, Congo had to leave Ulu's comfort in search of him. There was much that Congo wanted from this trip. He didn't know where to start; and once started, he didn't know how he would end.

"Would you like coffee?" Leroy asked as Congo approached his porch.

"No thank you, Leroy. But I will help myself from your grapefruit tree."

"Please do."

"Thank you," Congo replied as he returned from the tree, removing the peel from the fruit.

"Nasty! Nasty. Isn't it, Congo?"

"Do you mean Love and Ama?"

"Yes."

"How did you know about it, Leroy?"

"From women at market."

"Poor Ama. And things could have gone better, just for a little honor, I suppose."

"I quite agree. And what do you suppose Henry will do now?"

"We certainly do not have to worry about him. He should be in Panama already."

"Yes, that's where everyone seems to be heading these days."

"The new land of opportunity, I understand."

"Yes, but that does not give a man the right to do wrong just because he can run."

"Well, you know, you do not even need a passport to get there. Just a simple ticket from a captain."

"Yes, but he didn't have to go that route, not with all the education he has."

"His education is nothing compared to what his father has. He told me, and I have every reason to believe, they are rich."

"Do you mean from the fine he paid?"

"Yes, who do you know that could arrange one thousand pounds overnight?"

"I know what you mean. That is quite a sum, and he was about to walk away from it? What, he didn't have to pay?"

"Not a penny. Ama gave it back to him."

"Why on earth?"

"Maybe she had a statement to make."

"The statement should be that he supports his child. That's the common-sense thing to do."

"Yes, to you. I suppose Ama saw things differently. And since she was the one wronged, I allowed her decision to stand."

"I see. But in that sense, you are scarcely better."

"Maybe, Leroy. Time will tell."

"So what will Ama do, Congo?"

"That's what I am here to find out."

"Ah!"

"I suppose you still have an offer of marriage out to her. She still has the right to accept, except there is the child."

"The child is one thing. But didn't she accept his offer?"

"It was not genuine, Leroy. And moreover, he is gone, with his ring and all."

"Well, I suppose if he is out of the picture. So if Ama accepts, I would have to marry her."

"Ama wouldn't accept that, your having to marry her."

"I didn't mean I am obliged to. I meant I would love to marry her!"

"Good, then."

"So I will talk with her and set a date. But tell me, Congo. Why didn't Ama come and talk to me instead of you?"

"There's more than one thing going on at once, Leroy. Ama is not in a mood to handle many complications now. Can you see that?"

"Yes. It must be hard on her. And in her place, I mightn't know how to handle it either. So maybe, Congo, you are right after all, being here."

"Good." Congo paused. He took the first taste of the grapefruit, which was surprisingly sweet.

"You know, Leroy," Congo continued, "The Boydell ranch must be sold."

"Damn! Now you tell me. What do you suppose I should do?"

"We can find a way."

"There is no way I can buy that farm. Moreover, this is the first time in my entire life that I will make a clear profit. You know that, Congo, and all my capital is spent."

"Yes, Leroy. I know your circumstances."

"So what do you suppose I do? Ama does not have an income, and she is bearing a child. Now I have to go to work, find a house, get married, and take care of a child I didn't plan for." Leroy was visibly shaken. He got up with hands in his pants pocket and paced the porch. Congo handed Leroy a piece of the fruit.

"I thank you, Congo," he said, and as soon as he bit it, spat ferociously. "Sour as hell!" he cried and spat again.

"Not so bad for this time of year," Congo said and ate another piece.

"Then you eat it," Leroy said, handing the grapefruit to Congo.

"Leroy, I have been thinking."

"It better be good, Congo."

"Boydell left a few acres in his will for Ama."

"Boydell? How does he come into this?"

"Be patient with me, Leroy. You see, Asa is not Ama's real father," Congo said, clarifying a secret that had been closely held in the family ever since Asa's first visit to Providence Pond.

"My God, a jacket! Is Ama a jacket? Did Nweka give Bem bun?"

"Not so fast, Leroy." And as Leroy listened with interest, Congo carefully recounted the incidents whereby Vijay Boydell fathered Ama while Afia had been married to Bem Covey, and how Asa subsequently became Ama's father.

"I got it! So she is a Boydell, ah?"

"Yes, Leroy. But that is between you and me. The Boydells have nothing to do with her now. But they gave the land as hush-hush."

"So she is a Boydell, living as a King in a Covey house?"

"You can say that. But back to the land, Leroy."

"What about it?"

"Ulu has a small piece adjoining. I will ask her to sell it to you. I will vouch for you. There is a good chance she will accept."

"You vouch for me to Ulu, who will not even give you the time of day at noon? I warn you, Congo, this had better be good!"

"You are right, Leroy, but things are changing."

"Well, that is your business."

"Yes, Leroy. I just have to get a small fire under control."

"You mean with Laura? It's a good thing she lives in Free Hills."

"Yes, I agree. That's more than ten miles. Right, Leroy? Yes. I just have to close my books on that, and get things right with Ulu."

"Did Ulu give you that ultimatum?"

"No, Leroy. I just challenged myself to do it."

"Well, you do that and get back to me about the land."

"Good. Good, Leroy. But let's suppose . . ."

"Suppose what, Congo?"

"Let's suppose Ulu goes along with it."

"That's what we want, right? Yes, that size land would give me enough to make a decent living."

"That's the point, exactly! I am glad you see it that way."

"But that leaves one matter unsettled, Congo."

"And what is that?"

"I need a place to live."

"Yes. Ama's home."

"If you call it that."

"Lev has finished lumber for sale. I will draw up a house plan; and if you agree, Leroy, you will have the lumber on credit, and I will find men to build the house for Ama."

"Wonderful! But you keep calling it Ama's house."

"It has to be that way, Leroy. The land is hers."

"I see what you mean. But I am paying for the lumber, and the adjoining land will be mine."

"Well, yours and Ama's. Everything will belong to both of you after the marriage. But are you making this into a business, Leroy?"

"Not at all, Congo. But one must protect his interest here. You know everything will be on credit in my name."

"Still you make this a business, Leroy."

"All I ask, Congo, is that you put me on title. In that way, Ama can't just tell me to leave so she has my house on her land."

"One title with Ama's land?"

"Yes."

"Well, if you insist. I will do it after the house is built."

"Agreed."

With that, the men shook hands. Congo bit into the fruit and again handed a piece to Leroy. Leroy bit into it, with the juice flowing down his chin. "Not bad after all," he said.

"No, not bad after all," Congo echoed and signaled his departure.

A New Account

Ulu was his easiest customer yet. It didn't take much from Congo to convince her to sell her small and separate parcel to farmer Leroy Kendal. In fact, Ulu sweetened the offer by lengthening the amortization period from the three years Congo had suggested to five. Ulu knew instantly she would make more money by so doing, even though it was not her primary goal. Neither was it that Ulu had Ama's welfare at heart. Ulu's goal, to the contrary, was to endear herself to Congo by handing him an easy victory. It was yet another sign that his success mattered to her. By so doing, Ulu signaled to Congo that they could work as a team, and, most of all, that he needn't look elsewhere for a partner. She and not Laura would own his skills. Yet Ulu wanted more than that. She yearned for the wonder of urban life.

The bright light and broad city streets of New York remained with her, reminding Ulu just how dark and dreary Providence could be. Ulu had no desire for city life, yet she yearned for the closeness of the metropolitan buzz. For Ulu, the provincial town of Jacks River, lying on the outskirts of Oracabessa and Port Maria, would be her oasis. The latter two were thriving coastal towns. Ulu was especially delighted in Jacks River. The town lay between Oracabessa and Free Hill. This would give Ulu easy access to both places and particularly to Laura, who lived in Free Hill but operated her store in Oracabessa. Ulu imagined having the life of a country esquire in Jacks River, with all the benefits of city life. For now, that would be her home. Ulu thought she would retire in the hills overlooking Kingston harbor later in life, but for now Jacks River was her choice. Congo would marry her, facilitate their move from Providence, and set about building the business she envisioned. That was her plan.

Ulu accepted Congo's offer for the sale of her land to Leroy on condition that he marry her before the Tylers' return.

"Let it be our surprise present for them," she stated, "in the same manner they surprised us."

Congo, having tasted her pleasure and knowing he would settle for no one else, quickly agreed. What Ulu hadn't disclosed and what Congo had been blind to, was her fear of his reengagement in Lev's service upon his return. In every respect, Ulu wanted Congo for her purposes and hers alone. This left Leroy and Ama hopeful but unwitting winners.

Leroy and Ama's plain two-bedroom house with its modest living-dining room combination and a front porch was built within a few months. Rich, red cedar floors contrasted with the deep black mahogany furniture inherited from Lev and tastefully arranged by Ama. Congo helped with its decorating and promised Ama that he would be both her child's godfather and, were Leroy to falter in any way, his father in substance.

Almost as an afterthought, Ama mentioned to Leroy that the house lacked a nursery. Leroy quickly obliged by adding a small room to the back of the living room. One, on entering the house, would walk into the living room and straight to the nursery, which was separated from it first by a drape and then by an unfinished door that hid the drab walls behind it.

The children, as they grew older, however, would reject the room, preferring the greenery outdoors and the tracks to Miss Hene's house and Providence Pond. Consequently, Ama's dream room was transformed into a utility area. As such, it was never painted, decorated, or even used. Ama favored the sunnier, brighter front porch for her work.

The simple room, which would have cost more for its removal than it had for its building, remained as though detached from the main body of the house, like a useless appendage, a dried stump on a tree. It simply stood there, distanced, looking away from the main building through a small window on its southern side. Soon the bland utility space became lonely, a small, dark cobwebbed place, without purpose or beauty. It, however, held a small cot in its far corner, signaling still potential usefulness. Yet it stood alone.

Despite that tiny, yet prominent disfigurement, the house exuded the pride Leroy felt in its completion. With its red corrugated zinc roof, its blue painted walls and gold trimmed windows and doors, the house – Ama's house – brought a cozy essence of welcome and love. The blossoming branches of coconut, mango, and citrus trees that lined its grassy path framed its narrow connection to the rest of Providence.

Disclosures

My dear sister, Miss Hene:

Thank you for your letter celebrating your love with my dearest friend, Lev. He has been, as you know, the caring brother I never had. After father's death, he became increasingly attached to our family. I do not know all that went on between Asa, Bem, and Aren, but whatever it was has welded us into a family, and I am in the deepest of gratitude for it. You have chosen for your partner the best man Providence has ever had to offer; and I share in your happiness now, Miss Hene.

Since you have gone, Congo has worked tirelessly on the farm and with other matters pertaining to our silly sister, Ama. I still do not understand her; how she plunges ahead without a plan. That is so unlike me or how I consider life ought to be.

And because of her deportment, I must now bother you with the most horrible and distressful news. Miss Hene, you must learn that the very respectable and – I must add – our most likable and honorable friend and Headmaster, Henry Love, is not with us any more. Ama's acceptance and later abuse of his playful proposal of marriage has regrettably led to his sad downfall.

Ama, floating in her dream world made even more chaotic by his unexpected and maybe undeserved offer, didn't understand how men in Henry's circle make their proposals and how women of her estate should accept them. Ama was fully in the dark about the true intent of the ring Henry gave her. She didn't understand that his ring was simply payment, a marker of respectability *for their liaison. Their "engagement" offered them both cover for their affair. If Ama had understood her hand, she could have played it for money, prestige, and a house. And if or when the affair failed to suit her purpose, Ama could have dropped Henry graciously. In this way our sister could retain her self-respect, and Henry, his social standing and the female companionship he is, by nature, bound to have. I should hasten to add, Miss Hene, that the Headmaster is from a wealthy, progressive family. He could have easily afforded Ama a life, though clandestinely, that is second to none. If only she had planned. If only she had taken a moment to plan, Miss Hene!*

She could have ended it with taste, which Henry, I am sure, would duly have accepted. And to complete the picture, the Headmaster would simply have published the pain of his loss and her nobility in rejecting him, thereby relieving them both of any social stigma. How easy and straightforward! This would also have spared our quiet Providence all the publicity and sorrow her inexperience in matters of love has brought upon us. I pity Ama, the pain and confusion her thoughtlessness has caused!

Ama has brought such shame and loss to our family, and me especially, Miss Hene. I am surely glad Afia, or if you prefer, Nweka, and the rest of our family were not here to face this disgrace. Headmaster Love, I discovered, had more than passing interest in Providence. It was my hope to find out what business ties and social acquaintances could have developed between his family and ours. If only he had looked on me as someone of a more appropriate footing for his lifelong companion. Backside! It is all gone now.

I was not in love with Henry, Miss Hene. I want to make that clear. But maybe that does not matter. It is the proper linking of our families, his and ours, for social and even commercial matters that would be of interest. And as you know, there are large holdings in St. Mary that I believe would be of value to any respectable family from St. James. But it is all gone. And I must say, a wonderfully lost opportunity, which must not go unpunished. Ama must come to her senses and take responsibility for her actions! After all, she will be a mother soon.

Do not misunderstand me, please. I do not mean to say that we should punish my ill-advised sister. Not at all, Miss Hene. What I want to say is that – and you have heard this before – you reap what you sow. That does not exclude the innocent or the fool, both of which may correctly describe my sister. This does not exclude her. So I say, woe betide Ama when this pain circles back to linger on her doorstep. Woes betide her, Miss Hene!

Yes, I should tell you, Miss Hene. Ama's carelessness led her into a pregnancy with the Headmaster. She is carrying his baby and will not give it up, despite the soundest of advice. How horrible! She, an unmarried woman, wants to carry a baby that was conceived out of less than a convenient, and a bitter, unlucky affair. She still does not understand how that stigma will hurt herself and the child. Just think of it, the young child will be going to the very school where his father was the Headmaster, and not even with his name. I so hate knowing our family is being dragged through this.

That, more than anything else, I believe, forced our dear Headmaster to promptly resign his post and flee like a fatherless child to Panama. I ask, who knows him there? How utterly disgraceful! So now we are without a Headmaster again, and I fear the school may not reopen after the Christmas holidays, assuming it lasts that long. It took us, especially Lev, so much effort and pain to get this school here. And now, because of one silly girl, we may be forced to lose everything. I pity her!

But your brother, Congo, has prevented the worst. I didn't agree with him in the beginning: how he mistreated the Headmaster, dragged him through the village in handcuffs and locked him up in Barton Jail. You see, Miss Hene, your wonderful name and position has been tarnished with this as well. It was not Congo's fault. He had to do something. After all, Ama went to him in tears, saying how Henry had wronged her. What sour misunderstanding! The gullibility of your brother easily allowed her tears to open his heart so all he could see was her false pride and pain, and not her stupidity. So there you have it. Congo jailed the Headmaster one day, only to release him on the next when his father – and we do not know how – sent the exorbitant charge Congo laid out for his release. And must I tell you? After all the trouble it must have been to get the release money here, Ama refused it! Can you understand? She has nothing but a baby coming into the world and refused the only money Congo skillfully gained for her. Now, whatever will become of Ama, and her son?

Luckily, Congo made a deal with Leroy to marry her on the condition that Congo get some property for him. Oh! I must tell you, the Boydell farm was sold, and Leroy has to leave it. So, fortunately for him, I will sell him one of my parcels, which is developed and producing. With the proceeds, I will move to Jacks River. That is a good move for me, as it will advance my business plans in ways I will explain when we meet again.

But, through all of this, Miss Hene, I have seen a spark in Congo. I didn't believe in the beginning he had any value. But I was misguided. He made the most extraordinary painting of me. I must admit it was the Headmaster who guided me to its value. He made me recall my many visits to museums here and abroad and the countless paintings I have seen from all over the world, even works from the orient. I must admit, Miss Hene, I have never before seen any painting with such intensity and delicate, good taste. It was uniquely good. It was a drawing of me, taking my morning bath. It showed me rising from Providence Pond, with morning just mounting the horizon, and droplets of water from my hair and face sparkling silvery in the morning light. And that towel I held across my back with upraised hands – how magnificently he showed it! Ah! Your brother has talent.

But, Miss Hene – and I still do not know why – I threw the painting that was done on Lev's beautiful hand-sculptured mirror to the ground. I bashed it right before Congo, cracking it. Luckily, the framing still held it together and so I still save and honor it. I shall never show that to anyone, ever! I hope he has forgiven me for my poor behavior, but he seemed so silly, handing it to me. Maybe there was something else between us about which I was so ashamed I couldn't admit it at that time. So maybe it was better that way. I will, though, have that memory of him and me and the painting which I will carry with me forever. I wonder if that is a blessing or a curse. For try as I might, Miss Hene, I cannot erase it from my mind. If anything, it just grows richer and brighter and binds us as one!

Congo has certainly matured and shown his worth. I have accepted his courtship. And I must admit, he is most kind, tender, and considerate. Only one fear I have of him: he may still be silly with his favors and kindness. And what is hard fought for must be held onto. For a long time, Miss Hene, I have been convinced of this: love is a kind of business, and business, I am now learning, is like war. And how can one keep giving and giving? If one did that in war, would one ever win? And what victory is there in losing? His main fault is that he gives too much and does not know how to take. He must be taught how to take. Is that so hard? But maybe he will learn yet – he must learn – to take and hold. After all, that's how wealth is created, isn't it?

I ask only one thing, Miss Hene. I do hope you keep this letter from other eyes – there is another concern. It is Congo's attachment to Laura. For his sake, and hers, I pray to God it is a thing of the past, and something quite inconsequential. I will not belabor it here, but Laura and Congo have both assured me it is only friendship which binds them together. I find that amusing, actually challenging. For, Miss Hene, I do not understand what friendship between a man and a woman is, if it is not love or passion or, rather, both repressed. Is there something else, Miss Hene, something casual, that can exist between a man and a woman? I trust Congo and Laura to show us by their lives just what they mean. For now, I live in the comfort and assurance of their words, trusting.

But back to my sister, she has set a date for her marriage. Even though you are still enjoying yours and will have a newly furnished house on your return, you should come back with your full love for Ama. You are her only real friend as far as women go. Really, you, Lev, and Congo King are her only true friends in this whole wide world, if one does not count the Divine Puncus St. John.

Congo has done everything to arrange your house to be the most tasteful you will ever find. I couldn't manage it without him. I am sure his efforts will rapidly advance my business plans. So soon, Miss Hene, I will be rich! You and your Family are a wonderful asset to Providence. I am so happy Asa brought you both here.

And now, Miss Hene, I must go. Enjoy your honeymoon, and let us hear from you soon, again.

With all my love and many tender thoughts from Providence,
Ulu

Prelude

The comfortable agreement Congo had worked out between Leroy and Ama came accompanied with its share of awkwardness. It was an uneasiness born from the wounds of failure. Henry's sudden and disquieting departure from Providence, his botched relationship with Ama, and his disappointment to the community not only shocked but cast a deeply felt coldness of distrust and shame. It was not easy for love to mend the torn fibers of the heart, returning warmth and life to Providence. Yet love with full faith would try.

It was with much encouragement and cajoling that Congo got Ama and Leroy talking again. Not that they didn't want to, or that they didn't still care for each other. Ama had invested so much more of her energy and time with Henry Love than she had with Leroy Kendal that most had guessed she would marry Henry. So, too had Leroy. It was only his faith, his deep love for Ama and the lack of a suitable alternative that kept him hoping. Now that Henry had self-destructed, Leroy was all that remained. But his pride prevented his claim to Ama. Despite all, Leroy wanted to know he was of intrinsic worth, that Ama saw value and purpose in him, that he had been her first choice, that she had been his alone all along.

Having given his word and his soul to Congo's proposal, Leroy sought to reopen the dialogue and discover Ama's true heart. Ama would marry only if there was love. Could there be love now, love for and from the man she had rejected? She had to know. It was Leroy's need for primal acceptance and the tug on her heart that made it possible for Congo to bring them back to the table of love . . . well, Lev's bench at the pond, anyway.

Ama had set out the picnic lunch. She brought ale for Leroy and herself too. With her memory of Henry's ill treatment revisiting her, Ama sat eying her glass, eventually setting it aside for water. Leroy sipped his and, across the table from Ama, looked pleadingly at hers. Ama gladly offered it and then watched him observe her having her sandwich. With her handkerchief she wiped the froth from his moustache and waited for him to talk. It was not out of politeness or fear or tact, but simple habit.

"I must tell you plainly, Ama. Congo is a real gentleman."

"Oh, yes, Leroy. He is a true brother to me. And I must tell you, he has decided to adopt the boy."

Leroy replied as if he didn't hear her. "It's strange what has gone on between us, Ama. I had almost given up hoping for you. Have you ever sincerely thought of me as a husband?"

Ama looked at him, studying his words. "What's the name of your puppy?" she asked, petting its head.

"Why? Shep. You have met him before."

"Yes, the first day I saw you in the market. He was so young then! Shep is why I thought of you again, Leroy. You seemed to care so much for him."

"I am training him to be a good watch-dog, Ama. So thank you."

Ama bent to pet his head. Shep rose alertly, growling, and bared his teeth.

"Sit! Quiet!" Leroy snarled at him, briskly yanking his chain as he did. Shep sat and became quiet.

"You may pet him now, Ama." She looked at Leroy and nervously touched the dog. He looked back at her, licked his lips, and laid his head on his master's feet.

Ama smiled at what had just happened and looked up to Leroy, her nervousness giving way to open laughter. She thought of his previous comment and, feeling more comfortable, started her reply. "Yes, I must be honest, Leroy," she said, studying his face. "I liked you, really. But Henry had a way of making me see things as he did."

"What do you mean by, 'liked you, really'?"

"It's not easy for me to explain, Leroy. But you have an unusual way about you that is very attractive."

"You really mean that, Ama?"

"Yes, a manliness, something unusual, secretive, and strong. That is smart, Leroy, but not charming."

"Is that so?"

"But after considering all you say and what you do – especially what you do and how you talk to me and treat me – I must admit, there is a kind of sincerity, a frankness, in you that is admirable."

"Yes, people always say that."

"And at first, in the market, you did scare me, Leroy," she said, patting his outstretched hand. "But after all, you are a decent fellow. I guess it takes a girl some time to get accustomed to you. But I must admit, you still do not make me laugh."

"To get accustomed, ah? So will you say you are accustomed to me now, then?"

"It's more than being simply accustomed to you, Leroy. It's even more than liking you." She wanted to say *love*, but felt somewhat anxious at the thought of the word. Perhaps it was simply too early in their discussion for such a word.

Leroy smiled, temporarily removing the native sternness from his face.

"I have not changed from loving you, Ama. And if I didn't love you, didn't know I wanted you for my wife and companion, I wouldn't have looked at you so in the market."

She smiled. "But you scared me then."

"I am sorry, Ama. I supposed I stare too much. And what's worse, I do not know when I am staring. But I do stare, for it makes me see so much. Do you understand, Ama?"

"Oh! I didn't know," she said with a smile. "I didn't know you stare in order to see clearly. But you seemed so friendless then."

"I was new to Providence, then, Ama. Except for Puncus, I had no friends."

"Where did you come from, anyway?"

"Galina Point. I must say: Asa had a Family there. I was a part of it. But after Asa moved to Portland and our leader died, I lost interest and came here."

"Ah! Do you know Asa?"

"Yes, Ama. The movement is catching on, but the government is against it. The authorities say it's necromancy; they call it a cult and really want to destroy it. That makes it harder."

With that, Ama's last bit of reservation died. She instantly felt closer to Leroy. He knows Asa. Does Congo know that? Why doesn't Congo know? How wonderful! How very wonderful! She mused and promised herself then to talk to Congo about it.

"Do you have family in Galina?" Ama asked.

"Not anymore."

"What happened to your family?"

"I am the only one who survived the smallpox."

She sighed. "It was hard here, too. So, Leroy. Are you all alone?"

"Yes, Ama. You could say that."

"And you have never been married?"

"No, Ama . . . Well . . . yes. I mean . . . not really."

"Yes? So where is your wife?"

"You mean Patsy Blue? She was not really a wife. She was a girl who ran out on me. We lived together for about three years and settled down quite well, not married, no children. I didn't want to marry her and told her so, but I asked her to live with me. Her family was strange. Anyway, Patsy understood me. Things were all right with us in the first year or so. Then she changed, after her twin sister . . . but, not really her sister . . . or her twin either . . . died."

"Some of what you say is very confusing, Leroy."

"I will tell you a little more, Ama. Maybe that will help."

"Okay, Leroy."

"Patsy," he continued, "wanted to live a carefree life and kept inviting Puncus and this Byah-man to the house, and they would not stop playing that loud country music. I mean loud . . ."

"Ah! Do you mean our Puncus, Leroy?" Ama interrupted him.

"Yes, Ama! Puncus and that natty-head, Byah. All they did was play that loud Bongo music like they are still in the bush, and Patsy wanted me to be friends with them. I told Patsy I was not interested in knowing them and that she should not invite them to my house. But Patsy was stubborn and disobedient. She wouldn't listen to me, Ama. I spanked her over it and she turned it into a fight. I won and she left me. I believe she was hurt, but I do not know for sure, and I didn't care. She was wrong and knew it! After she left, I joined the Kumina Family in Galina. That was the first reason I joined them. I thought it would give me more discipline. And it did. That's how I got to know Asa King."

"Oh! Go on, Leroy. This is interesting, really!"

"But now that you asked me about my family, Ama, there is something I must tell you, not so much about my family, but about Patsy Blue and her family. They were twins, but not really. I should say there were two of them, Patsy and Zadie Blue. Their father was a good man. But there was something about his wife, the mother of those girls, that no one quite understood. She always acted strange, even before Patsy was born."

"Why was that, Leroy? What was so strange about her?"

"I'll tell you, Ama. Even though it bothers me still, I will tell you. The mother gave birth to a beautiful baby girl, the image of her, then died right after."

"There is nothing strange about that, Leroy. Sad, really sad, but not strange."

"The mother died just after she named the baby Patsy. She named her baby, gave up the ghost and died. And got buried just like that," he said, dusting his hands.

"Still, I see nothing strange there, Leroy."

"Let me talk, let me talk. I am getting to it."

"All right, then."

"So as I was saying, the mother died, and when the family returned to the house from the funeral, there were two babies in the crib. Two babies! The burial was exactly three days after the death and right in the backyard. So the family left the baby sleeping while they buried the mother. It was so close, Ama. You could see right into the crib from the gravesite. No one would ever suspect anything."

"You are fibbing, Leroy!"

"I swear to you, Ama, it is the truth. At least it is the story Patsy told me. But that's not all."

"Then tell it!"

"Here is the strange part, Ama. Patsy was the image of her mother, tall, slim at birth and tar black."

"Now that was very strange, Leroy. Strange!" she laughed.

"Wait, wait! It is the second baby they named Zadie that caused the uproar. This Zadie was short, plump, and milk-white! Zadie was milk-white with snowy blond hair and the grayest gray eyes in the world! No one knew what to do about Zadie: not the family, not Monsignor Silva, not Reverend Watkins. Nobody! Some even said she was the devil's child. They wanted to kill Zadie: you know, just kill her at night so no one would know? Others say Zadie was the spirit of the mother, returned from hell to love and care for Patsy; and so, Zadie should not be killed. Anyway, everyone was scared of Zadie. Young Detective Charles Graham, who was seeking a promotion, said that it would be a crime to kill the child, but to leave her and she might go back, just like she came. Zadie was not even christened; the Catholics were afraid, too. Only Doctor Singh, who was a friend of Asa, spoke well of the child. Zadie never once got sick. Yet she could not go to church or school, for she had no last name. She was just there. And that's the second reason I joined the Kumina Family. When I remembered how they treated Zadie as one of their own."

"In what way, Leroy?"

"They just showed her love, Ama, all the way. And they helped her father school her."

"So, you joined the Kumina Family because they taught Zadie to read and write, Leroy?"

"No, Ama. That was not it."

"So, what then, Leroy?"

"Well, Ama, with the mother dead, everyone was afraid of having anything to do with milk-white Zadie Blue with her gray eyes, who just popped up from out of hell. She was sure to die. But Asa King intervened and found nursing mothers to care for the babies. Now, Ama, Zadie grew up to be the prettiest girl you ever saw. Zadie was a dainty little girl, except for one thing: she didn't know she was white. And even though her eyes were so large and gray, they had no pupils. None at all! Some say she was blind. But she wasn't!"

"Didn't you say one thing?" Ama asked, breaking the seriousness with laughter.

"Be that as it may. You see, Ama, as Zadie grew up, Detective Graham fell in love with her. That was the time I took an interest in Patsy, as well. So the four of us would go boating around Galina Point. It was fun. The water is rough there, but we liked it rough. It so happened, Ama, that Zadie got pregnant from Detective Graham. Graham told Zadie he would marry her, and they planned a wedding. But, soon after, Zadie disappeared from Galina."

"What happened to her, Leroy?"

"Everything!"

"Come on, Leroy. What do you mean? What happen to Zadie?"

"I'll tell you. Some said Graham killed her. Graham said she vanished while he sat facing her. He said they were talking about a name for their baby, and, just when he mentioned giving the baby her grandmother's name, Zadie just popped up and vanished. Patsy and I saw Zadie go into the house with Graham, but we never saw her come out! As soon as Zadie vanished, though, Charles Graham darted out of the house asking us if we had seen Zadie. But we had not. And when we searched the house, she was not inside either. There were no signs of foul play, no good-byes. Neither were there shouts of joy, nor death. Yet Zadie had vanished. Nobody knew what to say or do. So the rumor started that Zadie was never, never from this world and just went back, you know, just went away."

"Gone away, just like that?"

"Yes, Ama."

"Strange! That's strange, Leroy."

"Yes, Ama! Zadie just disappeared. Some say she went back to hell so as not to have another baby to love on this earth again. Gossip had it that Zadie, who was really the spirit of Patsy's mother, did what she came on earth to do. Her mission, they say, was to love and care for her daughter. With that done and Patsy grown, Zadie went back home. No one knows what happened, and no one wants to talk about it. So all of a sudden Patsy didn't have a sister anymore. I told that to you, Ama. But I do not want to talk about it anymore, either. Not that it is so sad, but bizarre!

"And I tell you something even more, Ama. Not even Detective Graham will talk to anyone about it. It's one of those things that's just left alone. The higher-ups hold it against his record. They say he will never get promoted until he finds Zadie. They do not have any charges against him personally. No! But they say he is responsible for finding Zadie, which it seems he can't. So this really bright man, the youngest to hold that post, now has a stunted career. He is stuck and cannot go up or down. The authorities are holding him there until he solves this case. And one more thing, Ama, Charles is trying everything he knows to break out of it. He is desperate and will do anything he can to find Zadie. For that reason, Ama, I stay far clear of Detective Graham."

"Oh! I am sorry to hear all of that, Leroy. You lost Patsy, and your friendship with the Detective. You do not even have Zadie as a sister-in-law."

"No, Ama. And after that, Graham and I didn't talk. Not that we hated each other, but there has been some suspicion or uneasiness between us: I am thinking he must have done it, and maybe he is thinking the same of me. But we have no real reason to blame each other."

"That's a sad story, Leroy."

"So you see now, Ama. To escape Graham, or to keep his eyes off me, I had to join the Kumina Family for my own protection as well."

"Now I see, Leroy. So is that what makes you so gloomy and thoughtful sometimes?"

"I suppose you could say that, Ama. I miss not having a family, someone to care for."

"So where is Patsy?"

"I told you that already. Patsy is gone, Ama. I have no wife, no children; no one except Shep here."

"That's sad, Leroy. Really sad for you and Patsy," Ama managed to echo, disguising her pleasure in fully satisfying herself that Leroy was really childless and unattached. But maybe that's how it was supposed to be anyway, Ama thought to herself.

A long silence followed. Awkwardly, Leroy looked at Ama as echoes of the conversation rippled through his mind. After all he had said, he wanted to put Ama at ease. He wanted to forget what he had just reported about Zadie Blue and continue the conversation with new emotions.

"Thinking of it, Ama, you must be right. I suppose it must be sad, too. It is right, but you can be sure of one thing. I will not have to beat you like a child or train you like I do Shep. You are from a good home, and you will be an obedient, faithful wife. I know I will not have to, I mean . . . if you go through with it and marry me," Leroy said with a loud, lonely laugh.

Ama looked at him and smiled. He must be joking about that. Who beats a child, even a dog? she asked herself, looking down at Shep.

"And so, from Galina you came here, Leroy?"

"I came right here, as Asa suggested."

"Oh!"

"I came here and leased the Boydell property. I am very glad I came to Providence. Things are starting to look up again. This is the first year the property will turn a profit, and I am responsible for that."

"Yes, it is sad you have to give it up."

"But that is all right now, Ama. Congo has a better proposal that I much prefer."

"Yes, it sounds good. And Congo will do whatever it takes to make it work."

"But for the child . . ."

"What about my son?" Ama asked sternly.

"Nothing's wrong with it, Ama. It's just that we haven't discussed it."

"Not *it*, Leroy! My son. He is my son."

Leroy looked up at her with some fright. She had been unusually strong and possessive. He didn't know what it meant. He sat back and looked in her eyes.

"I know it's your child, Ama."

"My son!"

"How do you know it is a boy?"

"Miss Hene said so!"

"All right."

The conversation quieted for a brooding moment. Leroy looked up at her. "But we still need to talk about him, Ama."

"Of course we do. How we will love him, take care of him, send him to school, and give him all the things to make him a man."

"Yes, that is where I will come in. A boy needs good training."

"You train a dog, Leroy," she said, looking at the young shepherd curled obediently at his feet.

"I know what I am talking about, Ama. So take it from me. A man knows. A boy needs discipline."

"He needs love, Leroy." She paused for a while, her eyes searching for his. "Do you love me, Leroy?"

"Yes, Ama, with all my heart, I will always love you. I knew we belonged to each other from the first day I saw you."

She smiled. "It feels good to be loved, Leroy. And when I feel good, I will make you very happy."

He moved to her side of the table, sitting close to her. She looked at him, and he kissed her cheek.

"There is another way to kiss a woman."

He leaned toward her and allowed her lips to find his. They kissed. But not long after their lips met, she broke the kiss and turned to sit astride the bench, facing him. Leroy did the same. She fell in his arms, weeping as they embraced.

It was some time before she released him. By then his shoulder was wet with her tears. She looked at his gaunt, puzzled face through the haziness of her teary eyes. He motioned to kiss her again. She moved toward him, and let her lips stay pressed against his until he moved for breath.

"I love you, Ama."

"And our son?"

"I love you, and him, too . . . wherever he is now."

Ama released him, looked at his face, and reburied her body in his open arms. They remained by the pond until they were led home late that night by a cold, metallic moon.

Shep followed spiritedly behind, his tender puppy senses deeply aware of their first touch with love.

The Twisted Wheel

With a small ceremony one Sunday afternoon in late March at the Anglican Church, it all was made official. Ama King and farmer Leroy Kendal were married. Their first child was expected within a few months.

The ceremony would remain in full memory for a long time due to the special efforts of Laura Wong. From her, Congo had learned about Ama's additional sister living in Free Hill, Laura's domicile.

Vijay Boydell had, about twenty years previously, finally married Esi, Nweka's childhood confidant. Esi and Vijay's marriage produced a girl, Charm Boydell. The news of a much younger sister and the loss of the Boydell name to Providence made Ama anxious to find her younger sibling. Through Ama's pleading and Laura's assistance, Congo located the lass, scarcely seven years old.

Ama made sure that Congo brought her sibling to the wedding. Little Charm, her sister, was quite unaware of the import of the occasion, even though one day she would be the center of a similar affair. Although Charm was clearly the cutest little girl alive that afternoon, she wondered what the whole thing was about.

The aloof, sophisticated Ulu, who had planned the wedding, spent most of her time with Laura, who would slip away occasionally, worrying with Ama's lavish attire. Congo was too busy attending the nervous farmer to notice much else. Luckily for all, the Anglican minister, the old Reverend

Bernard Watkins, was patient and wise enough to handle the inefficiencies with reassuring calmness, even in the face of unanticipated arrivals.

The Tylers had interrupted their honeymoon to attend the wedding. Ulu had planned the reception for the Kendals at Barton House. It was lavish, lacking nothing.

Congo, with Puncus' assistance, had arranged a Kumina welcome-Dance for the new couple in the courtyard of the Anglican Church. The drumming was to start just at the end of the wedding ceremony. Initially, Ulu found the idea of the Dance distasteful, but since the Reverend Watkins did not mind it, Ulu quickly quieted her objections, warning instead against excessive merriment.

Ulu's final plan called for the Kumina musicians and dancers to start the drumming, then lead the procession from the Anglican Church to Barton House for the marriage feast. Even Ulu's plans, however, were subject to the whims of Providence. Nweka's unexpected arrival would see to that.

Nweka and Kisi, by the dictates of Kumina custom, had traveled ahead of Asa from Portland to Galina to assist in the preparations for upcoming religious functions. There, the Portland delegation would participate in the annual Kumina Easter festivities. From the Galina Family, Nweka got late but sure news of Ama's marriage in Providence. Such news from any source would have propelled their Stepping to Providence for Ama's marriage. So, uninvited and unprepared, Nweka and Kisi arrived at Barton House from where they were redirected to the Anglican Church.

Nweka and Kisi reached the church with great excitement. No explanations were needed. The exhilaration of their arrival quelled all questions of their sudden reappearance in Providence.

Nweka's arrival followed the completion of the Christian ritual. The bride had already approached the altar with the organ music hushed to a dying hum. Rings . . . even kisses, had finally been exchanged. Congo had given what he had never owned and Leroy seemed thrilled with unexpected gain! Laura looked bemused. The Reverend was forever gracious.

Following the brief Anglican ceremony, the overjoyed couple, led by Ulu and Congo, strolled away from the presence of holiness and entered the front courtyard beneath the canopy of a bright blue radiance above. There Puncus, along with his Kumina musicians and dancers, waited to welcome the couple into yet another Family. Nweka and Kisi had long found and stood with Puncus' troop, anticipating the marriage procession.

"Ama, my daughter!" Nweka cried, running to embrace the married couple. "I had to come!"

"Thank you, Nweka. And you remember Leroy, don't you?" Ama asked, presenting her husband.

"Yes, of course! So nice to see you getting married," Nweka said. She hugged and chatted warmly with Ama, but spent undue time with Leroy, welcoming him to the Family as she studied him, noting his rather thin neck and rugged features.

Suddenly Nweka turned away from them and asked. "Miss Hene, why isn't the wedding down by the pond, following our Kumina way?"

"Ulu insisted on a Christian ceremony, Miss Nweka."

"That's no reason, and you know it. I want the best for my daughter, Miss Hene!"

"We all want the best for our Family," Miss Hene replied. "But sometimes we bend to bring in others."

"Oh!" Nweka responded and, after a brief thoughtful pause, looked at Congo and asked, "And Master Congo, aren't you going to Dance?"

"Goodness, Nweka! Not . . . not unless Ulu . . ." Congo stuttered.

"Then come, Puncus," Nweka called, reaching her hand out to her old friend, "come, let's Dance."

Puncus signaled to Byah, who started the bailo drumming. The musicians followed his lead, and soon Puncus and Nweka were Dancing under the full stare of the late afternoon sun. Miss Hene did not linger; she and Kisi were soon Dancing the Kumina Jump that was still new to Providence. Congo looked on, clapping his hands, cheering them on. Shouldn't this be Congo's dance? Nweka wondered. Nonetheless, the small group Danced with great vitality and joy.

Having finished her Dance for show as well as for her own pleasure, and knowing that Asa must be waiting in Galina, Nweka motioned to go. "I will be leaving now," she said.

"You must come back and see us soon," Leroy responded.

"Yes, I will. But, Leroy, you better take good care of Ama and my baby."

"We will make sure he does," Congo said.

"You better, Leroy, or else I'll be coming back for you and that baby-neck of yours!" Nweka said, laughing.

The group, joining in the laughter, embraced Nweka and Kisi farewell.

"And Nweka, no need to fear anything about Congo," Puncus said. "He seems to be a slow starter, much slower than I expected. But he is still young at this. He will be Dancing. I know he will be Dancing soon!"

"Yes, for his sake, I hope so," Nweka said.

"And give our love to the Family at Galina," Puncus added.

"We will," Kisi said. "You know, we are not perfect in Portland either. We spend too much time traveling between Families, and not much gets done."

"I understand, Kisi," Puncus said. "This is a long, long road, but everything we need is along the way as we travel." He moved toward her and embraced Kisi. "Just give it time," he added.

He released Kisi to see that her eyes were filled with tears.

"Here," said Miss Hene, "since you do not have time to eat with us. Here, take this with you, one of Puncus' black cakes. We made it together!"

"Has Puncus finally learned how to cook?" Nweka asked. When no one replied, reconfirming to Nweka that he had not, she continued, "So . . . why teach him to bake?"

There was more laughter until Lev said, "They bake well together, Nweka. Here, take a taste," he said, tipping a morsel of the black wedding cake into her mouth.

"It's good," Nweka said as she swallowed. "Puncus and Miss Hene, ah?"

Puncus looked at Miss Hene and shared a gracious smile with her.

"But shouldn't the bride and groom be eating the wedding cake?" Puncus asked.

"Yes," said Miss Hene, approaching Ama and Leroy. She gave each a fork as Laura and Ulu served them black cake and wine. Leroy fed Ama and she in turn served Leroy. Ulu poured wine and, alternately, Laura held it to their lips so they could drink.

"Now they are married!" Puncus finally said, breaking into his solo Dance. Miss Hene soon joined him and they Danced with Lev looking on, contemplating his own marriage into the Kumina Family away from the Christian fold.

Nweka broke from the center of the twisted wheel of onlookers that had surrounded Ama and Leroy. As she stepped clear, she saw the face of Esi.

"Charm!" Nweka called. "Is that you, Charm?" Nweka asked the lass who stood gazing up at her. Before the girl could respond, Nweka bent down and scooped her up to her bosom.

"You are so much like Esi, your mother! I am very glad to see you, Charm."

"Who are you?" the Charm asked.

"Nweka. I am your mother's best friend. And I will be yours, too. All along the way!"

"Do you know where my mommy is?"

"No, Charm, not now. But Ama . . . she is over there . . . you know her, don't you?"

"Yes, Nweka."

"Well, Ama should be like your mommy to you and take good care of you."

"Uncle Congo does that, Nweka. He brings candy for me at home in Free Hill."

"Ah! That's just as good. Congo will take good care of you and keep you in our Family."

"All right, Nweka."

"Good!" Nweka said, kissing Charm and putting her down.

Not long after, and with more hugs and crying, Nweka and Kisi departed.

Soon after Nweka and Kisi left, Puncus, Byah, and the other musicians encircled Ama and Leroy. Again they restarted the drumming. Congo and Miss Hene resumed Dancing as they led the celebration to Barton House. Ulu ambled slowly behind.

Later that night the Tylers, once again, left the Kendals to the splendor and service of their beloved Barton House while they continued their interrupted vacation.

It was on the first Friday of June of that same year – the third in the new century – when Ama, with Miss Hene's hand, delivered her first child. Following Akan custom, Ama naturally named him Yoofi. And so that the lad would not forget his father: Yoofi Isaac King.

The tranquility of his joyous birth belied the fury of the early August hurricane of that same year. It gave Ama cause to ponder. What lay ahead of Yoofi, just what dreams would his life unfold, his mother repeatedly asked herself. Dreading the vision she saw, the grave image of misery – the deprivation and lonely servitude of her own fatherless youth repeating in his life – Ama closed her eyes and cried herself to sleep . . . even to dream.

And in her dream Ama returned to her childhood bed where Afia served her banana porridge, hot, baked dumplings, with a heap of Bra-Anancy stories. Her laughter awakened her, only to find Leroy pulling their honeymoon covers over them, then cuddling her in his arms. With a long, peaceful sigh, Ama returned to sleep.

Toddling Lessons

It was in their seventh year of marriage when Lev was his most contented, and no less so was Miss Hene. Having lived without companionship for so long, he had grown accustomed to existing without it. Lev didn't understand, nor did he care to know, what had drawn Miss Hene, for so he still called her, into the close communion they shared. The couple began dressing alike, thinking and talking alike, and finished sentences for each other. Miss Hene, though she fully enjoyed it, still so young in the adventure, didn't understand the miracle of marriage, how it created one mind where before there were two. The spiritual bond they shared was not the only thing that joined them together; there was their son, Kwame, who was their constant adoration and joy.

In the meantime, Ama had blessed Leroy with two boys of his own. Dean was born one year ahead of Agu, completing the Kendal's household.

Saturday's child, Kwame, was seven months younger than Yoofi. The four boys, playing most often at the Tylers, developed a true friendship that deepened the already strong ties between both families. They lived and spoke of themselves as brothers. That special relationship brought the Kendals to dinner at the Tylers on Friday evenings. After dinner, the children remained with the Tylers for the rest of the weekend, when Yoofi sadly escorted his brothers back home. This, however, gave Ama and Leroy the weekends for themselves; and they spent it selfishly remembering each other.

It was Miss Hene's advice that the children pass the weekend with her, giving their parents their own separate time. The suggestion was offered to settle the first real dispute arising between the Kendals. Leroy had complained that he hadn't enough of Ama's time due to – and this is what he stated – "Ama's non-stop nursing of Yoofi and the boys." He didn't really know how to approach Ama for fear of appearing selfish or jealous of Yoofi. Leroy cautiously broached the matter to Miss Hene, who mentioned it while Ama complained to her of Leroy's workaholic and drinking habits.

"You know, Miss Hene, Leroy does not spend his time with me anymore."

"Is that so, Ama?"

"Yes, all he ever does is work and work, then drink at the *Any Questions*, as if he is afraid of coming home."

"I did not know that, Ama!"

"Oh! Is that so? And I do my very best to have everything ready for him. Usually I have the boys fed, bathed and dressed for bed, and his dinner ready."

"I know that, Ama."

"And he is out so late that, when he comes in, all he does is eat, bathe, and pass out on the floor. I have to wake him and take him to his bed at nights."

"And what do you do while he sleeps, Ama?"

"Nurse the children, of course! But Yoofi makes it hard on me."

"In what way, Ama?"

"He bites me sometimes. And if that is not bad enough, Agu, my youngest, now fights him to suckle."

"And what about Dean, the middle child?"

"He does not nurse sufficiently. He watches the two fight over my breasts."

"How strange!"

"What do you mean 'how strange,' Miss Hene?"

"Well, Ama. How old is Yoofi now?"

"He is turning seven. He should start elementary school in September."

"And he still nurses?"

"Yes, he eats, then nurses. And Agu wants to nurse as long as Yoofi does."

"I can't say I blame him, Ama. You know," Miss Hene paused, "maybe I should have told you this previously."

"What is it, Miss Hene?"

"Some time ago, Ama, " she continued, "when Kwame was about two and – let me see, Yoofi would have been about five then – Yoofi came to me so I could suckle him. At that time, Kwame had just been weaned. To Yoofi, it must have seemed normal, since in the past I had nursed them together. Yoofi saw me sitting and came running to me, I lifted him in my lap, kissed him, and he started to search for my breast. It took some struggle for Yoofi to understand I wouldn't nurse him any longer. And you know something more?"

"Ah! Why not just tell me?"

"Well, Kwame started to cry. He wanted to nurse, again. So, I had to go through weaning him once more. And make sure, he knew that his nursing was all over. Since that time, Ama, I haven't the least bit of botheration from either of them."

"That is good for you, Miss Hene, but it may not work for me," Ama said after some reflection.

"And why is that, Ama?"

"I believe Yoofi knows when it's his time to nurse and when not to. It's natural, Miss Hene. Yoofi should know when he doesn't need to nurse anymore."

"Maybe you are right, Ama. But that day, I had to decide for Yoofi and Kwame, both."

"Yes, Miss Hene. I see what you mean. But all the children are growing nicely," Ama added.

"Yes, they are. But there may be something else Leroy does not like."

"Oh! What could that be, Miss Hene?"

"Well, Ama, maybe Leroy does not want to look at you nursing the seven year old. And maybe he wants your time."

"How can I give him my time when he is sleeping?"

"Maybe, Ama, Leroy is asking how he can get any of your time while you continue nursing Yoofi."

"Ah! Are you suggesting something, Miss Hene?"

"I am just telling you what you said."

"Oh! I should do something else, then. Right, Miss Hene?"

"If you want to."

"Yes, I should do something else. But it is a little more than that," she began to explain.

It had been a lot more. Leroy had grown rather impatient with Ama's inability to take control of that situation. Not only had he longed for her time and devotion, he disliked and distrusted the relationship between Yoofi and Ama. He watched how the condition under her eyes deteriorated. Ama would recline in bed to let the boys fight and suckle. Yoofi had grown possessive of one breast. The youngest, Agu, was by then the largest and most aggressive. He was born a large baby, making an eleven-pound entrance. His size and rapid growth made him much more aggressive than his older brother, Dean. Being more docile and analytical, the middle child was unable to make lasting claim to a breast. He was often left out, not fed during the nursing periods.

One evening as Leroy busied himself with other things, he noticed the unabated behavior. Without further question or comment, Leroy angrily removed Yoofi from his mother's breast to the dinner table and provided food for him.

"Why did you do that?" Ama asked.

"Why, Ama? We have spoken about this time and again. You promised to have Yoofi sit at the table with me. And if you must still nurse, then let Dean nurse instead of Yoofi."

"Is it because Yoofi is not yours?"

"I didn't say that. No! Not in the least, Ama."

"Then leave him alone!"

"Dean needs you more, Ama. He is not growing, and he sits there, crying and sulking instead of nursing, when Yoofi could be eating with me."

Ama wouldn't reply. She would let Leroy have his way, but cried as she nursed the other children. As soon as one stopped, Ama removed Yoofi from the table to let him suckle. At times, Leroy would remark, "You need to respect me, Ama. I am trying to get some discipline in the boy, and help you as well."

Ama didn't respond. She just continued nursing Yoofi, or loving him, as she thought, and ignored Leroy's statements.

One evening, Leroy was expecting a friend over for dinner. He didn't want the nursing affairs of his house known to the village. He tried to have Yoofi sit at the table with him. Instead, Yoofi, at Ama's encouragement, went on suckling. Leroy pulled Yoofi forcefully by the arm. The lad screeched for help more than from pain. Ama remained motionless, crying. Leroy forcefully placed Yoofi at the dinner table, ordering him to eat. Yoofi started to cry for Ama. She continued nursing the other boys. Yoofi, feeling frustrated and abandoned, took a handful of food and threw it at Leroy's face. It hit, just as his friend arrived. Leroy moved towards Yoofi, who started to run. On opening the door, the visitor saw the mess on Leroy's face and Yoofi running away from his father. Leroy started in pursuit of Yoofi, but soon gave up, returning to entertain his friend.

Yoofi, being annoyed with his mother for not coming to his defense and fearful that Leroy would punish him, ran to Miss Hene's house where he spent the night. The Tylers were neither told nor suspected anything unusual. Yoofi often came to play with Kwame, sleeping there if it was too late to return home. That was early on Friday evening. After the friend was gone, Ama went to the Tyler's house happy to find Yoofi there. She returned home without saying what had really happened.

Now, on this eventful Friday evening, years later, Ama disclosed the whole incident to her sister and friend.

"We could help each other there, Ama."

"In what way?"

"Why not have dinner with us on Fridays, you, Leroy, and the family. Leave the children with us on Saturdays, and Yoofi will bring them home on Sunday evenings."

"That would be excellent!"

"But it comes with a catch."

"Oh?"

"You do our grocery shopping."

"That's easy enough, Miss Hene. We can do that while we do ours on Saturday."

The families relished it! And so, with Miss Hene's suggestion, it became the custom for the Kendals to visit the Tylers on Friday evenings, their weekly family event.

The pattern the Kendals developed, and not by conscious design, was to take their three boys to Providence Pond before visiting Miss Hene for dinner. Following the meal, the Kendals would lazily spend the rest of the night and morning in their bed. On late Saturday afternoons, they both would saunter to the market and retrieve the provisions which had been pre-packaged for them and the Tylers.

Though still on the lower end of the economic scale, Leroy Kendal had managed to provide a good life for his family. Ama adored him for it and, in return, became the wife he had longed for. Their oldest child, Yoofi, was by then fast approaching his seventh birthday.

One spring Sunday afternoon the following year, as Lev and Miss Hene lazed on the verandah, Nweka, accompanied by Kisi, sauntered across the front lawn of Barton estate. Ama immediately sprang up and hurried across the lawn, hugging her mother and sister and inviting them into the house.

As soon as the visitors were on the veranda, Miss Hene and Lev returned from the kitchen with refreshments.

"How have you all been?" Nweka asked, sipping the lemonade Miss Hene handed to her.

"Good," replied Lev, "and you, Kisi?"

"Happy, happy to see home again!"

"And how are things in Fellowship, Nweka?" Miss Hene asked.

"I do not spend much time there, you know. I travel with Asa, always looking for bodies."

"I hope his search stops here!" Lev remarked.

"It goes on and on," Kisi responded, "and every so often I get one more to care for," she said, smiling.

"That's quite a bit of work for you, Kisi, but where does Asa keep these new bodies?" Miss Hene asked.

"In St. Thomas, of course! That's where I live now." Kisi said.

"We should talk about that," Nweka said, "Or better still, why not come up to see us in Fellowship, Miss Hene, and then we can talk about that kind of thing."

"Okay, I will, Nweka!"

"And you too, Lev. You should come and join us!" Nweka said.

"I will, Nweka, and maybe before Miss Hene does!"

"Wonderful! I can't wait," Nweka said. "Now, where are my grand-babies?" she asked.

"Looking for tamarinds in the back yard, no doubt," Miss Hene said.

"Let me get them," Ama said.

"Better still, I will go and join them," Nweka said.

"We will surprise them!" Kisi said, "I can't wait!"

Soon Nweka and Kisi joined the children. They chatted and ate tamarinds until it was time for Nweka and Kisi to leave. They had to join Asa in Fellowship for still another trip to Panama: again seeking the whereabouts of Headmaster Henry Isaac Love in order to complete Asa's scheme of his grand Family.

Rites for No Body

L ev, not wanting to be away from home for any considerable time, still had additional business to do in Oracabessa. One Friday evening that Spring, as he hurried home, wanting to be there before the Kendals, Lev decided to take the very shortcut Nweka had taken many years prior.

With his focus on reaching home, he steered the horse off the main road and down the hill that passed the pond to take him finally up the incline leading to his home. At a slow gallop, the horse descended the hill and approached the pond. As he neared it, the horse reared on its hind legs as if scared. Lev panicked, and, in a moment, his childhood monster pounded out of the water. Lev leaped from the horse and fell into the water, immediately struck by an epileptic seizure like those he'd had in childhood.

On that very Friday afternoon, Ama and Leroy's family ritually sauntered to the pond for a pre-dinner walk. No one knew how long Lev had been in the water, but on seeing his horse standing on the far side, Leroy became immediately concerned and hastened around the pond. He was alarmed at seeing Lev's body floating face down in the clear, shallow water. Without a moment's delay, Leroy pulled Lev from the water and, with magical insight, got the horse to lie down, so he could strap the limber body across the nag. In a rush he rode up to Barton House. Ama, imagining what must have gone wrong, took the children and followed, saddened and in tears.

Congo, who still reviewed the operation of Miss Hene's estate on Friday evenings, was fast approaching. He saw the commotion concerning Lev's body. Congo scurried his horse. On looking at Lev, Congo shouted, "Quick, let's take the body into the jail."

"The jail?"

"Yes. Lock it there. No time to explain now. And let it lie on its back."

"Okay. Okay, Congo."

"Let Miss Hene know right away. I will get Doctor Singh from the hospital in Port Maria."

Without further delay or hesitation, Congo galloped to the post office.

"A telegram, a telegram!" Congo said as he pushed himself to the head of the line to talk with the Postmistress.

"For whom?"

"It's urgent! No time to waste. Dr. Devinder! Hurry!"

"Yes. The message?"

"Hurry, Lev is dead!"

"Too late."

"No! Do not add that!"

"What? Too late?"

"Yes."

"But it's true."

"Not in this case. At least not yet. Hurry!"

"Okay, okay!"

The Postmistress had been working for five long and patient years when she graduated to the point of sending telegraphs. She had become relatively good at it by then, having to deal with many impatient, impolite, and overly concerned accounts such as Congo's. Therefore, the telegram that busy and tensed Dr. Devinder Singh received late that tiring Friday evening read:

> *"A telegram, a telegram for whom it's urgent. No time to waste, Dr. Devinder! Hurry! Yes, the message, hurry! Lev is dead too late. No. Do not add that, what. Too late! Yes, but it's true. Not in this case, at least not. Yet, hurry! Okay, okay?"*

Poor Dr. Devinder Singh! He was a good man, a clever Sikh physician who knew and did everything in the Port Maria hospital. So short-staffed he was and so dedicated, he sometimes worked as nurse, porter, doctor, and cashier, neglecting most often the latter duty. To heal others, they even said he played patient: self-administering, at times, his own prescriptions, until he became dutifully sick. Staff and patients loved and respected him even more.

Miss Hene's household waited. Late after sunset, it became clear the good Doctor must have been lost in the dark and couldn't find the house. Congo had one of the workers fetch a cart full of ice. The ice Congo ordered was put over Lev's body to slow its deterioration while burial plans were made. Soon after, a servant, at Congo's request, nailed shut the oversized coffin in which the naked body had been placed, surrounded by the packed ice.

Early the following morning, Congo returned to his sister's house to find Miss Hene in the prison cell. He found Miss Hene sitting on a chair, leaning over the coffin, and weeping. He quietly walked over to her, stooped, and without saying much, hugged her.

When her grieving subsided, Congo asked, "Did he come last night?"

"Who, Congo?"

"The Doctor, Miss Hene."

"We don't need him anymore."

"That's what the Postmistress said, too. I hope she sent the telegram."

"You know she will send the telegram. She always does."

"Yes, but should we send another telegram, just in case?"

"We do not need to."

"Why? Don't you think he is dead?"

"No! Gone!"

"Gone, Miss Hene?" Congo looked into the coffin.

"Goodness! He is gone!"

"Where do you think he could have gone?"

"Stepping!"

"By himself?"

"No, he is too young at this."

"So . . . ?"

"Yes . . . !"

"What! Have you been teaching him?"

"Yes! Are you surprised? He asked, and I told."

"So, you think he is out practicing?"

"By himself? No! They might have come for him, though."

"Oh, and Walked him?"

"No, Congo. Not Walked him. You know he has to be initiated before he can be Walked. They must have Stepped him!"

"So he is gone, then, ah?"

"Not just gone, Congo. He is clean gone!"

"Clean gone?"

"Yes, Congo. Are you forgetting? That's how we prepare them for their passing on. Then they can go Stepping. He is clean gone, after a bath and iced down. That's our custom."

"Yes, but I didn't know . . ."

"It seemed he got his bath in the pond; cleaned there and iced here."

"Oh! Clean gone. You are right, Miss Hene."

"I taught him our Family traditions, and it seems Asa thought he was ready."

"So you think Asa came to get him?"

"How else can you explain him clean gone?"

"Did you see Asa?"

"No."

"He would have said something."

"Maybe not."

"I better tell Detective Graham."

"Yes, Congo. Let me see you pull this off. You go and tell the Detective that the dead body you nailed shut in his coffin, then locked in your jail with the keys in your possession, is clean gone, and you are not responsible."

"But it is!"

"*He* is: Stepped. Yes."

"So you agree."

"We agree he is gone. And if you convince Graham the dead body is gone Stepping, you will be but put in an asylum."

"I wouldn't tell him that."

"What then would you report? That Lev, who you informed the hospital is dead, is now missing?"

"Yes, something like that?"

"And now Detective Graham will hold you on suspicion of murder, and, in addition, responsible for providing the body. Is that what you want?"

"It does not have to go that way."

"But it could."

"You know I didn't do that and would never do that!"

"Yes, I know. But do they?"

"So what should we do?"

"We bury the dead."

"You mean give him his last rites?"

"Yes."

"Do you mean last rites for no body?"

"Yes."

"Since you take this so matter-of-fact, Miss Hene, I must ask. Why were you crying so much when I came here?"

"Congo," she looked up at him. "I grieve for you."

"Me? I am not dead."

"But Ulu is seeing to it."

"Ulu? What, is she slowly poisoning me?"

"How did you know?"

"I am asking, Miss Hene!"

"Yes, you asked. But why did you ask that way?"

"Listen, Miss Hene. I laid my trap out for her. I caught her. I married her."

"Is that so, Congo?"

"Yes, and you know it!"

"Yes, I know she married you. And she is leading you, Congo."

"Miss Hene! You make Ulu sound evil. If you think so, you should talk to her."

"Evil? Ulu, evil? No, Congo. Not in the least! She is following her heart. Whose are you following?"

Congo paused for a long while before continuing, "We are happy, Miss Hene. You know that."

"Happy?"

"Yes."

"So where is your Family?"

"There is our daughter, Princess. You know her."

"Yes, of course. I know Princess. But where is your Family?"

"You mean . . . ?"

"Yes, your Kumina Family. The Family Asa brought you here to start. You know, Congo, I am to follow you, to be the Mother. I am still waiting on your lead."

"Yes," he said with some hesitation, "as soon as I am done with a few more things Ulu wants me to do, I will start it."

"You were not brought here to start anything for Ulu."

"Yes, Miss Hene, but I am in it now. I just need some time to clear some things up and get started with Asa's business."

"It should be your business, Congo."

"Yes. I will do it. I just need time."

"So, first things come last with you, ah, Congo?"

"Not so, Miss Hene . . . do you think . . . ?"

"Think what?"

"That's why he Stepped him by himself?"

"You mean Asa?"

"Yes."

"Yes, I do think so."

"Then he must be angry with me!"

"Yes, very much so!"

"And was he so angry he came here and didn't talk to me?"

"Well, maybe with him, first things still come first."

"If he forsakes me, I will die."

"Yes, that is what I told you. You are dying, Congo. And others will replace you."

"Like Lev?"

"Yes, you see he is clean gone. It must be for a reason!"

"I will live, Miss Hene!"

"It's all in your hands, Congo. And you know what to do."

"Well, there is unfinished business here," he said, looking at the empty coffin.

"We need the Doctor."

"I will get him."

"We'll have a funeral on Sunday."

"Tomorrow?"

"Yes."

"The doctor must be here, to give the death certificate."

"We have witnesses and a coffin. Let's have the burial today, then."

"And get the death certificate tomorrow when the doctor comes."

"We will have the site prepared, and the burial will be tonight."

"Yes, let's do that. And invite all we can."

"And no viewing of the body."

"Of course not. They all know Lev. I will nail the coffin shut before I leave."

"Good. And you better set your life straight, Congo. I do not want to grieve any more over you."

"Thank you, Miss Hene. I must go now. I have work to do."

"We will see you with the Doctor tomorrow."

"Yes, tomorrow."

The first part of the plan worked. Congo had his men prepare the burial site. It was close to Lev's favorite seat beneath the trees overlooking Providence Pond. Later that night, Congo, Miss Hene, the Kendals, and all the folk they could find attended the funeral for their beloved, Lev.

Sunday brought the reprieve the families sought. Lev's business was slowly conforming to reality. Good Doctor Devinder Singh came on time. Well, anytime before the bustle of Monday would have been on time. As expected, he came with his wife.

"Have you had the burial as yet?" the Doctor asked politely.

"Yes, Doctor. We had a good funeral last night."

"That is nice to know. It can become a health issue to hold the body too long."

"We understand, Doctor."

"I would have come before, but I apologize. It took me some time to find the home. And thank you for sending the telegram. I see things are improving at the post office."

"We welcome you to our home again, Doctor, and we thank you for being here," Miss Hene said.

"And were you able to get Monsignor Ricardo Silva or the Reverend Bernard Watkins to give a Christian funeral on such short notice? Lev was a Christian, wasn't he?"

"We gave him our Family burial, Doctor."

"But, Lev was a Christian gentleman, I believe."

"So he lived." Congo said.

"And died otherwise?" the Doctor asked.

"Yes, Doctor. He went as a good Family man." Miss Hene said.

"Excellent! Sweet soul, Lev. Good heavens, we will miss him here! May I say a few words on his behalf?" the doctor asked.

"We would be delighted."

A few families accompanied the Doctor and his wife to the funeral site. The small procession gathered about the grave.

"I have known Lev all my life. I birthed him here at his house. I attended to him while he suffered from epilepsy. I thought it was all over. But there was something else. Something that to this day I still do not understand. Anyway, he is now gone. The demons do not attend to him anymore. He is now at rest. Let us pray," the doctor invited.

"Oh, great Lord Krishna. A humble Sikh, your servant and friend, I, Devinder Singh, approach you here to intercede for Lev: a friend, a Christian, and good Family man. I must ask you, great Lord Krishna, to look at your child. Take his hand and give him safe travel to your home. Actually, it's our home, Lord Krishna. We are all your children, and in whatever form we come from your bosom into this world, let us serve you here. And let Lev's service to you, now that it has ended, be acceptable to you. Great Lord Krishna, please hear us today, and grant us your peace and your blessing, those of us still here to serve. Let us know the true value of service, and the sacrifice of our lives to your cause. And if it pleases you, give us the strength to carry on. Accept Lev's spirit and, with love, bring us into communion again, here on this earth. Amen."

"Amen."

"Shouldn't we throw even a little dust?" asked his wife, as they were preparing to leave.

"Yes, yes, that might look good!"

The Doctor stooped and collected a handful of earth. Everyone followed suit. Then he started, slowly sprinkling the earth.

"Dust to dust . . ." The chorus followed and then faded.

The Doctor walked over to Miss Hene, hugged and kissed her. "He is well," he said.

"Yes, he is well," Miss Hene, echoed.

"And here you are, the death certificate. I signed it on Friday, after I read the telegram."

"Thank you, Doctor," Congo replied.

With that, they sauntered back up the hill to Barton House where Ulu provided refreshments.

Part 3: Family Development

(1911 to 1919)

Ulu

By the start of the new century's second decade Ulu's plan had begun to enjoy great progress. Congo had seen to that. Ulu had instructed him to purchase a grand property in Jacks River using the proceeds of the sale of her property in Providence. Set along the main road to the parish's capital, Port Maria, her Jacks River estate was Ulu's greatest dream, now realized. The land was beautiful, flat, with rich moist soil. It made her wondrously happy.

On that land, set back a respectable distance from the road, Congo constructed a large two-story house. It was built of heavy timber and boasted a white cut-stone façade. The roofline was a high cedar shake, and on it stood an antenna, signifying to all that they could listen to what the waves radio had to offer. The Kings had become well connected.

Ulu's plan called for a bee apiary. Congo found the best help and created a colony of Italian bees, consisting of hundreds of boxes. Soon after, he built and staffed a large bakery and then barbeque spaces. These were concrete flats where produce such as pimento, cocoa beans, or chocolate nuts could be sun roasted before storage and sale. Congo bought produce from small farmers, dried it in his barbeque pits, stored it, and sold it to export merchant Laura Wong.

To grow her business without any debt – the only way Ulu would have it – Congo built servant quarters at the rear of their residence. At dawn, while Congo went to manage the large plantations, Ulu roused her house staff, then set out to the bakery. Later in the day she sold baked goods as well as produce such as eggs, chicken, milk, butter, and washing soap out of a shop in front of the house; it was all from her industry. Everyone worked hard, and soon the Kings were wealthy beyond their expectations.

By using the profits of one concern to finance another, the Kings had set a foundation of growth that was sure to boost them into the ranks of the richest families in the parish of St. Mary. With their intensely busy schedules, Ulu and Congo still had time to start a family. Within the third year of their marriage, Ulu had conceived her first and only child, Princess.

It was after the birth of Princess that Congo discovered Ulu's real plan. Ulu wanted to use her great wealth to secure a husband for Princess. With the business running well, she set out to educate Princess and provide the best of everything for her in preparation for marriage. Before her birth, Ulu had already chosen a doctor as husband for her darling Princess.

Despite Congo's amazing vigor, he was beginning to tire, not from his own enterprise alone, but from what was finally expected of him. Within nine years of her marriage, Miss Hene had found herself managing the Barton estate. She was not prepared to do so, but Congo was.

Consequently, Miss Hene needed Congo. Being without experience but wanting to maintain the excellence of her holdings, Miss Hene turned to her willing brother. He had offered Kendal the position as headman of the Barton property, but the man refused it, preferring to concentrate on building his own small estate. It was not only the management of the Barton property that demanded Congo's time at his sister's house. There was also Kwame. He needed a father.

The last thing Congo could do for Lev was to father his son. To lessen his administrative load, Congo, with Miss Hene's blessings, relinquished the management of the Barton jail, which slowly drifted into oblivion. The regulatory function it provided was gradually assumed by police stations from neighboring districts and the talented Detective, Charles Graham.

With his lessened load, Congo, at Ama's request, also spent time with Charm in Free Hill where both she and Laura lived. Many of the farmers with whom he did business also lived in Free Hill. In his travels through the many villages, visiting Charm was easy for him. Moreover, it was pleasant because he dearly loved Charm and thought of her as family. Because of this, too, Laura also got to see more of Congo.

Yoofi, Ama's first son, fast approaching his tenth birthday, also needed

Congo. Her other two sons didn't come under his patronage. Kendal wouldn't allow it. Congo, however, was steadfast with his care and love for Yoofi, and with him, Congo's Family was complete.

His wife, an Amazon, didn't miss him at first. When his absences and split allegiance caught her eye, Ulu saw how that too could advance her plans. What pained her in the beginning became her tool of choice in the end.

Father of the Man

The summer of Yoofi's eleventh year slowly waned, making way for a new and fateful part of his life. Yet Yoofi didn't know it. How could he? With his uncelebrated tenth birthday just passed, Yoofi's life was just beginning to have some smidgen of meaning, bringing with it a horizon of dreams, endless possibilities of pleasure.

Without being told, Yoofi sensed that something was different. He didn't want to nurture his fears or forebodings though; he preferred to accept that the freedom and joy of summer was to be replaced the next day with the equally exciting reopening of school. He, with his younger brothers Dean and Agu, lived that last week of his tenth August in anxiety and high expectations.

Dean, the second child, was returning to school for his second year. His grades had been the best in his class the previous year, and he looked forward to learning everything. For Agu, the largest and youngest of the three brothers, Monday would introduce him to the world of learning. He didn't know what to expect. He was not particularly sharp, but he was unusually agile for his age and size. The fear of starting school bothered him, and he couldn't let go of it. What brought Agu solace was the companionship of his older siblings and his memories of the long recesses, the many games, and new friends his brothers told him about.

It was what he kept dreaming, however, that kept his fear and anxiety high and ever present. His recurring dream was of a teacher who bit off his thumb because he couldn't write the letter "Q." Despite Agu's numerous attempts, the stem of his "Q" kept falling off, then reattaching itself to whichever part of the "O" it pleased. He attempted to erase and reattach it where he had correctly penciled it. Agu couldn't understand what marred his attempts. In his frustration, Agu snarled at the teacher, who threatened to punish him. In response, she bit off his thumb. His dream wouldn't leave him alone. Neither could he refrain from hiding his thumb in his mouth when he awoke.

To drown his brother's angst and develop camaraderie for the ensuing Monday, Yoofi invited Dean and Agu to the pond. The three boys were enthusiastic to go, and Shep wouldn't be left out. They walked down to the pond and, while they undressed to dip in the cooling water, Agu looked at Yoofi and said, "I will race you."

"Yes, but I will win."

"No, you can't."

"Prove it!"

"Let's do it right," said Dean.

"Right?" asked Agu.

"Yes," he said, marking a line in the sand. "We start here, right. Then we run around that tree at the end of the pond. The first to cross this line wins."

"Okay," said Yoofi. "Do you agree?" he asked, looking at Agu.

"Yes. But what will the winner get?" Agu asked.

"If I win," Yoofi said, "I get your pocket knife. If you win, which you will not, you get my kite. Agreed?"

"Agreed," said Agu.

"I will hold the bet," Dean said.

"Okay then," Agu said, handing his knife to Dean. Yoofi did the same and gave Dean his kite.

"Get to your mark," said Dean.

"Yes."

And with that, Agu started before the start signal was given. He reached the tree with Yoofi trailing him, turned and raced full speed toward the finish line. Moments before Agu reached it, Yoofi, with a sudden burst of energy, dashed ahead of his brother. He passed the finish line and bent over, his hands gripping his knees, panting. Agu intentionally bumped Yoofi, sending him face down into the sand.

"What did you do that for?" Yoofi asked angrily.

"Teach you a lesson. And I won anyway!"

"What do you mean you won? I did!"

Agu pushed his older brother. "I won, you heard me!"

"No. You are unfair!"

Agu pushed Yoofi again, making him fall. Yoofi got up, facing him.

"Don't do that again!" he said. "You lost and you know. Poor loser!"

Agu kicked Yoofi. "Shut up, I say! And if you don't, I will tell *my* father you hit me and stole my knife, and you know what he will do to you."

"Leave him alone!" shouted Dean. "He won fair."

"Stay out of this, Dean," Agu yelled. "I'm going to have *my* father teach you a lesson. Thief!"

"What can he do to me? And I have a father, too!"

"Yes, is that so? Why not let *your* father come help you when Leroy is beating you tonight."

"Beat him for what?" Dean asked.

"You stay out of this, Dean! Do you hear me?" Shifting his stare to Yoofi, Agu continued, "I am going to tell my father you stole the knife, then hit me when I tried to take it back from you. You are going to get a whipping tonight, and I will see what your father can do about it."

Yoofi didn't answer. Agu looked at Dean. Dean handed his knife back to Agu and the kite to Yoofi. Agu began to walk back to the house.

"Come on, Dean," Agu called. "Leave that brute by himself."

Dean started to walk behind Agu.

"Come on, Shep," Agu called.

Shep wagged his tail but remained by Yoofi, licking his fingers.

Near the top of the hill, Agu called again for Shep. This time, the dog simply raised its head and curled closer to Yoofi, as if wanting to hug his friend.

The rivalry between Yoofi and Agu had been years in the making. It started in the very bed in which Ama had nursed them, immediately following Agu's birth. At eleven, Yoofi was still Ama's baby and she continued nursing him, despite Leroy's attempts to stop her. Still, Yoofi would have dinner and, if he chose, nurse with the other siblings before falling asleep.

Agu was made in the very image of his father. From his birth, Leroy received him as his child, his baby. With Dean being somewhat indifferent to Leroy, Agu, the more active and outgoing, hadn't only his father's complete love but also his time and attention.

Yoofi, who before the arrival of his siblings had whatever fatherly time Leroy deemed appropriate, had much less now. Nevertheless, that was all Yoofi knew, and he accepted it in full measure. Ama, in the meantime, showered Yoofi with love and attention, making up for whatever Leroy didn't give. The older Yoofi grew, the more Leroy withdrew his meager attention and the more Ama compensated. Although Dean's arrival didn't unbalance that workable equation, Agu's birth did.

What threw the entire affair off kilter was Agu's birth. When the boys played with Leroy, it was clear who had and didn't have his attention. Clearer still was the line of succession. He would toss Agu in the air and ask before catching him, "Who is your father?"

The lad would reply, "You, Daddy!" as if the correct response assured him another coveted toss. The amusement would continue, sometimes including Dean but never Yoofi. He simply sat, trying to decipher the enigma. At times, Ama would snatch him away and nurse him, not because he was hungry or because she had milk. She sat with him and shared his pain. To Leroy, that was his way of making the lad tough. A part of what he called training. In Ama's estimation, it was a cruel neglect. Yoofi, Dean, and Agu saw and played the game. It was the only one they had.

So as his younger siblings returned home, Yoofi sat by the pond thinking, worrying, and questioning what happened in other families. With the exception of his mother, the one he was closest to was Miss Hene. She had always treated him on par with Kwame, maybe ever better at times. Why is my family so different? Is it because of my father or me? Where is my real father, anyway, and why doesn't he return to take care of me? Why did he leave my mother alone and allow Leroy to be my father?

Yoofi didn't understand. He lay in the sand with Shep resting his head on his chest. Yoofi patted and kissed Shep, whom he often considered his best friend. He liked Kwame and Dean. They were nice to him, always fair and loving. It was Agu, four years his junior, whom Yoofi feared. Or was it Leroy, whose wrath Agu could unexpectedly bring to bear on him?

"Come, Shep," he called, abruptly getting to his feet. Yoofi had always wanted to swim the length of the pond. He had secretly challenged himself to accomplish the feat before the end of summer. Summer was almost gone. This was his last chance. He stripped bare and dashed into the pond. Yoofi swam to the farthest end with Shep beside him, then circled to the far side. From there he swam to the head of the pond where the streams flowed, then back again to where he started. Yoofi barely made it, deathly tired and out of breath at the end of the exercise. He managed, though, to pull himself onto the warm sand and rest into a quiet doze. Just passing twilight, Yoofi regained his strength. He and Shep walked home.

He had long forgotten the scuffle, but Agu hadn't. Despite Dean's many attempts at correcting him, Agu twisted the story to his father's liking. The children were aware of Yoofi's stubbornness and open defiance of Leroy. Dean and Agu both understood how, in quiet and subtle ways, Ama's defense of Yoofi seemed like encouragement to him. In the end, if Leroy punished Yoofi, it would be Ama who forsook them in preference to her oldest son, bringing Leroy's curse on her and his liberal kindness on them. It had been a well-rehearsed script, and now, with Yoofi's entrance, the show was about to start.

"You will sit over here, Yoofi," Leroy said to the lad. "And for the last time, I am telling you: keep the dog out of the house." Shep held his head low and his tail still as he walked out the door to his bed under the house. Yoofi took the seat. Before him was the stern Leroy. At each side of the table sat a brother. Yoofi looked at Dean for sympathy. Ama was in her bedroom, awaiting her screaming cue from Yoofi. It was not to come.

"Yoofi."

"Yes, Daddy."

"Not anymore, boy. I am not your daddy. From now on, you call me Mas Leroy. You get that?"

"Yes, Daddy . . . sir. Mas Leroy."

Agu started to laugh, and Yoofi to snivel.

"You better stop that boy, and take it like a man."

"Yes . . . Mas Leroy."

"Good. Agu, where is Scorpion, I told you to get it."

"Here, Daddy." Agu took the heavy, black leather belt and placed it, coiled like an adder, between his father and Yoofi. The hitting-end was splintered and knotted, leaving cut- marks with each stroke. "Teach you right. Teach you not to steal," Agu said, looking at his brother.

"He didn't!" Dean shouted with tears flowing down his face.

"Shut up!" shouted Leroy. Yoofi jerked to a nervous attention. "Now boy, you are ten going on eleven years old. For what you did at the pond, hitting your younger brother, you deserve a lashing. But let me give you a lesson in manhood instead. Maybe it will do you some good. Are you listening to me, boy?"

"Yes, Mas Leroy."

"Good then. You are almost a man. That means you must start taking care of yourself."

Yoofi looked confused. Taking care of myself? The command echoed in his head.

"You look puzzled. But before I go on, you should give me thanks for not punishing you tonight, before your brothers."

"Thank you, Mas Leroy . . . Daddy."

"Not Daddy! Not anymore," Leroy yelled, his hands clutching scorpion.

"Yes, sir. I mean, Mas Leroy."

"Good."

"You still look confused, so let me ask you, Yoofi. You see I am a man, so who takes care of me, here?"

"God, Mas Leroy."

"I mean in this house, boy?"

"Mammy, Mas Leroy."

"Mammy? Do you see her go to work or bring money into the house? See, you are really confused. Think again, boy."

Yoofi sat, thinking.

"Have you figured it out yet, boy?"

"If it's not God, then it must be Mammy. She cooks, cleans before and after you, irons your clothes, and takes care of your bed, and . . ."

"Well, you never mind that."

"Then, Mas Leroy, if it is not God, and it's not Mammy taking care of you, then it must be you, taking care of you, Mas Leroy. But it sure sounds strange to say that."

"Strange or not, it's true. I am the man in the house. That means I provide everything you see here," his hands waved over his head, "from roof to floor, and what you eat and wear. Do you understand now, boy, who takes care of me? I do. And if you are to be a man, you must learn to take care of you and yours. Are you getting it now?"

"Yes, Mas Leroy. But can I tell you something, Mas Leroy?"

"What is it, boy?"

"Well, it is two things, Mas Leroy."

"Quick. What is it, boy? I don't have all night here for you, understand?"

"First, can I go to the toilet?"

"Toilet, at this time. Sit down and be a man. And what is the next?"

"It's not that I don't want to obey you, Mas Leroy. But sometimes 'Daddy' will just slip out by mistake."

"Well, you better not let it happen too often. You hear me, boy?"

"Yes, Mas Leroy."

"All right then. As I was saying, you are almost a man and must start living like a man, feeding and clothing yourself. I have been doing that since you were born. Before, actually. And now it's your time. Am I making myself clear?"

"Yes, Mas Leroy."

"So, starting tomorrow, you will not go to school anymore."

"What!"

"You heard me right, boy."

"Well, my father was the Headmaster, and I deserve to go to school!"

"Yes, Yoofi. He was the Headmaster. But where is he now?"

Ama remained silent in her room, silent and in tears. She remembered the day Henry Love left Providence, and the eyes of dejection and disgrace he'd worn on his face. She remembered, but couldn't decipher their dark foreboding until the present moment. She wished he were here at the table to witness the desolation – the wilderness – befalling his legacy. If only Congo, Miss Hene, Lev, anyone, were there now!

"I still have a father, though."

Leroy laughed. "Sure, Mammy's Bigboy, you still have a father. Just where is he, now?"

Defeated, but not lost, Yoofi bowed his head. But in thinking of Shep, how he too was fatherless but always alert, Yoofi stood upright and in rebellion shouted, "I have a father. You hear me? You hear me!" and broke out into tears. Dean moved to comfort him.

"You leave him alone or get yours, too."

Dean withdrew his hand.

"So, father or not, Headmaster or not, you are out of school."

Yoofi sat motionless.

"Do you hear me, boy?"

"Yes, Mas Leroy," he sobbed.

"Then speak up!"

"Yes, Mas Leroy."

"Starting now. After I am done with you here, you go into the kitchen and wash six of those one-quart rum bottles. You will use them to carry milk. You get that?"

"Yes, Mas Leroy."

"And in the morning, you take your brothers to school and place them in their right classes. Then you run right back here so I can teach you how to milk the cows. After a few days, you will know how to milk and pasture the cows. After that, you bring the milk home, bottle the milk, and carry it to the customers. Do you get that so far, boy?"

"Yes, Mas Leroy."

"Good, now. So you return home from serving the customers and get something to eat." He paused and looked up from the table at Yoofi.

"Yes, Mas Leroy."

"And I didn't say nurse. You get something to eat, then run and find me in the fields. I will have a few things for you to do. Get it?"

"Yes, Mas Leroy."

"Good," he said with a smile.

Yoofi sat more relaxed. His torment was over.

"Now, come kiss me and thank me for being your father and wanting to make something out of you, starting at such a young age."

Yoofi did as he was told, making as scant a contact with Leroy as he could, pretending to enjoy and appreciate his goodness.

"Good boy! I will make something of you yet."

"Thank you, Mas Leroy. And can I ask you something now?"

"Sure, boy. Sure. What is it?"

"Can I go to the toilet now?"

"Yes. Better not stay long. Come back, and take care of the bottles, feed Shep, and get something to eat before going to bed."

"Yes, Mas Leroy."

"And say your prayers before going to sleep."

"Yes, Mas Leroy."

"Good, then."

"And both of you," Leroy said, looking alternately at Dean and Agu, "you have eaten dinner already. Tidy yourselves, say your prayers, and go to sleep."

"Tomorrow is a new day for you. You start school. I am expecting good things from you. So go prepare yourselves for it."

"Yes, Daddy."

The boys left the table. Leroy called to Yoofi, who was about to leave the house and go into the detached kitchen, "You know why I do this for you, Yoofi?"

"Yes, Mas Leroy. The same reason you punish me every time."

"And why is that?"

"Because you love me, Mas Leroy."

"Good! And you never forget that. Okay, boy?"

"Yes, Mas Leroy."

Sleeping Dogs

With the first conflict of the great European war in its second year, the demand for men and materials in the colonies grew. From all corners of the island, boys, some as young as fifteen, were conscripted into the army. Providence was not immune to this thievery. The rakers went through the town leaving drunken boasts of male pride and bitter wails of female sorrow in their wake.

To some, the Kaiser's war also brought commercial opportunity. With his fields properly planted and cared for, Kendal's estate grew profitable. The increased demand from Britain meant higher prices. From his point of view, one shared by his peers, older boys should be taken out of school and hidden on the farms where their labor would fatten farmers' bank accounts.

This was a part of Leroy Kendal's justification for taking twelve-year-old Yoofi out of school. Leroy explained to Ama that, by hiding Yoofi on his farm, he was shielding her from the misery of seeing Yoofi killed in war. He didn't mention that with the younger children at school and Yoofi weaned from his mother's breasts, Leroy would have Ama all for himself again.

Leroy balanced promises to Ama and threats to Yoofi in his solution to the dining table problems. The heavy leather belt was brought out only to scare Yoofi. Leroy also managed to convince Ama that the other boys should sit at the dining table. This should be their first incidental lesson in understanding that the management of the household had rightly shifted to his complete control. Ama conceded that the running of his estate should mirror that of the British royal household.

That night, with Dean and Agu scarcely in bed, Leroy opened the bedroom door to see Ama's hazy eyes, still mourning for Yoofi.

"Oh, Leroy! I love him."

"I know, Ama. I love him, too, but he has to grow up. That war is changing everything quickly, and Yoofi must be prepared for a new world."

"Yes, but . . ." she cried. "There must be another way. And on top of everything, you called him Bigboy. Imagine that, Leroy, right before his brothers, you called him that. You know he is no fool."

"I didn't say he was a fool!"

"So, what were you saying then, Leroy?"

"I do not think Yoofi is stupid. If I thought so, I would call him Quashie. But that boy is no Quashie! All he wants to do is suck breast all day long: stay home and suck breast. That must stop. And if he can't stop it, I will stop him. Just watch me. Just watch me, Ama. After all, he should be ashamed to be still nursing at eleven!"

Leroy used the term "Bigboy" indiscriminately, the demeaning term describing a fortunate fool. That was not how Leroy intended to portray Yoofi. He knew better. Without saying so, Leroy admired Yoofi's cleverness.

Leroy had called Yoofi "Mammy's Bigboy," not "Mammy's boy," adding "Mammy" to underscore the sexual dimension of his target. Leroy wanted to imply that Yoofi imagined himself having an affair with his mother. He knew he couldn't say it openly; the charge would be seen as untruthful and unfair. Moreover, Leroy knew and respected Ama too much even to believe such a thing would happen. Leroy could never imagine nor would he ever think that her affection had any other focus than himself.

Leroy shamed Yoofi for continuing to nurse. He felt that the boy fondled rather than fed, and that Yoofi's deep, unbroken attraction to his mother's breasts robbed him of his wife's pleasure. The mere thought of it increased Leroy's jealousy, sending a nervous chill through him.

Leroy was a farmer and understood men as he understood animals. He witnessed hens, goats, and cows weaning their youngsters. It was a struggle. Yet, the act of separation, a constant female function, always prevailed. He also saw juvenile male dogs or bulls mount their mothers to mate or maybe to practice mating. Never had he seen the mothers reciprocate. Instead they drove the youngsters away. Why was Yoofi still holding on? Why wasn't Ama nudging him away from her breast? Why was competition there for him, for his wife? Calling Yoofi "Mammy's Bigboy" was his last and final kick, ensuring that separation. Yoofi's stare should be pointing elsewhere. It didn't seem to him as though Ama caught the nuance of his meaning. It was clearly a slap at Yoofi and a shout to her: Let Yoofi go!

"I see things differently, Ama. You have been stuck together for too long. This nursing must end, Ama. Now he knows he is a man," Leroy continued.

"But you called him Bigboy!"

"Yes, maybe he heard me, and you, too, Ama. Listen, the children will be in school tomorrow. What do you intend to do, go and nurse them there, too?"

Ama didn't reply. She had made no plans; in fact, she hadn't thought of it.

"I had to discipline the boy, Ama."

"You could be gentler."

"What do you mean? Keep putting it off so he does not have to face up to it?"

"If you would just love him, Leroy."

"I may have saved his life."

"And another thing, Leroy. How could you take away his education?"

"I didn't get an education. Look at me, Ama. His father did. Did that make him more of a man than I am?"

"You always bring him up and compare."

"I am right. Do you agree?"

"What provisions have you made for Yoofi, now he will not have his education?"

"Farming. I will train and teach him all I know."

There was a long, bitter silence. Leroy remained quiet. He had a message for Ama, and wanted to deliver it that night.

"Okay, Leroy." Ama started to sob. "Maybe that's how it was intended, for my baby not to have an education." Before the words could leave her lips she held her head in her hands and cried, "Is this what you intended, Leroy?" Ama cried and cried. "Nweka, could you come back? Congo, will you come back? Where is everybody? Why did you all go and leave me alone?" She cried as Leroy sat by her, waiting to speak. She did not let him.

"I will go to the school in the morning, Leroy, and talk with the teachers. They know who I am."

"Yes, they do know you. They know me, too, Ama. And I spoke to Headmaster Forbes earlier in the month. I told him Yoofi was too sickly to return to school and not to prepare a seat for him."

"Jesus Lord!" Ama said. She suddenly felt lifeless, dead. She fell prostrate on the bed, not able to listen or cry anymore. Leroy sat beside her. He laid his hands on her back, but she didn't feel them. He rubbed her head, but she was unaware of it.

"He will be of great help to you, now, Ama."

She didn't reply. He continued massaging her, thinking that more important than sharing her feelings, her pain. In reality he did not.

"You may ask me why, Ama."

She turned to face him. "Why, Leroy?"

"Well, with the government buying all we can supply for the war, you can make coconut oil to sell in the market and rear pigs from the trash."

Ama remained silent. She fully understood his plan. Yoofi was taken out of school to assist him with the cows in the fields and then her in making coconut oil and caring for pigs. The war effort, as he called it, was his pretext for keeping Yoofi on the farm. Yoofi, the Headmaster's son, her first born, was to be denied an education and made into a workhorse to satisfy Leroy's vision of manhood.

"I know you will be a good wife and obey me, Ama. If you don't, you will come to nothing – wasted, just like Patsy Blue."

She didn't hear him. She had long forgotten that he was there. Her pain and solitude went inside. She lay there, wondering what kind of prison she had been placed in and what it would take to relieve herself of it.

"Would you like wine?" he asked.

"No, Leroy. Nothing at all."

"But it's bedtime. I have to be up early in the morning."

"You will be up."

"But, you, Ama. You still have your nightly duty to perform," he said, stroking her stomach. Maybe a little wine would . . ."

Again, Ama understood. And without waiting for his finished sentence, she quietly started to undress and laid herself bare for him.

The old fellow smiled and sipped the wine he had with him. Knowing that he had conquered the territory, he lay on her and pleased himself.

Maybe that's how it was intended, Ama comforted herself.

Leroy, in the meantime, moaned from victorious relief.

Ama's tortured soul sought reprieve. Her body remained lifeless, imitating death, even as he rolled from her body and snored into oblivion. Ama did not hear, though. The echo of Nweka's question, how do these things happen, played long in her mind.

Divergent Dreams

Leroy ruled the night, but his family found refuge elsewhere. He slept. Ama's mind still worried until, out of energy, it faded, following her body into nourishing sleep.

With the rest of the house quieted and Yoofi quite sure Ama wouldn't nurse him that night, he gently crept out of bed. Taking what food he could find, Yoofi scampered under the house to find his friend, Shep. He would understand.

He had done it before. When Ama's affection couldn't reach him, he would find love where it was constant. He and Shep were about the same age. Leroy, Shep's first master, set out to train the dog. He did. When, however, Yoofi was old enough to crawl and Leroy was out of the house, the Shepherd found Yoofi and they played. Later, when Yoofi could climb, he found Shep's back, where he rode as they played. When Yoofi was sufficiently able to run errands, Shep accompanied him, and they cavorted. As Agu progressively became the central object of Leroy's attention, with Yoofi increasingly slighted, the lad romped with Shep. And lastly, when Lev died, when Congo left Providence, when Miss Hene was out or busy, Yoofi would find Shep and . . . yes, they played just like boys do!

Now everything was lost. Ama's voice in his defense had been quieted. Not only that, Yoofi had become a man. What? Yes, as he entered his twelfth year Yoofi was pronounced a man, and his brothers were taken from him. But Shep was there, under the house, in a bed Yoofi had made for him.

Shep must have known to expect him, for as Yoofi approached, he licked his friend's feet and waited for Yoofi to lie down. He did and Shep put his head on Yoofi's chest. They both fell asleep. Shep slept and Yoofi dreamt.

He had gone to his favorite haunt: the green, sloping meadow behind Miss Hene's house. He went there when he was sad; for the ground had a way of talking to him, of bringing him back to happiness. He would simply lie on the ground and listen. So he did that night in his dream. And the voice he always heard brought a body with it this time: the body of a man in his mid-forties, small framed, with black hair and a narrow brown face. He was well dressed, sporting a brown felt hat and a walking cane. The man didn't speak to him, but played with his cane and glided across the grass to the sound of music, the source of which Yoofi didn't know. The music played, and the stranger danced. He pointed to Yoofi, and the boy got up and danced. It was easy, delightful, and calming. He floated inches off the grass, joining his teacher. It didn't last long. Shep, hearing Yoofi laugh in his sleep, awoke and pawed at him. Yoofi awoke, hugged his friend and went back to sleep. But Yoofi had learned to Dance!

Yoofi was not the only one who needed to dream. Farmer Leroy Kendal, after having securely established sovereignty over his household, almost abruptly glided off into a land of fearsome images.

He found himself manning an old bamboo raft with a double-sided paddle. He didn't ask for and wanted no help. Old, decaying strings held the raft together to Leroy's ignorance and detriment. Leroy stood at the bow while Yoofi sat in the stern. Ama sat facing Yoofi, singing, while Dean and Agu sat on either side of her, grabbing at straws in the passing water.

For no certain reason, the skies blackened as if to rain, with lightning and thunder preceding it. That didn't matter. Leroy led with perfect ease and complete control. He knew the water and, moreover, he was close to home. With the darkening, the pond seemed larger than normal. Or was it that the accustomed shorelines were becoming indiscernible? That aside, Leroy knew he was completely in charge.

Without warning, the strings securing the raft under his feet weakened. The raft started to fall apart. In preventing his foot from sliding through, Leroy tumbled and fell, hitting his head and back hard against the wood. He lost control! Yoofi, seeing what had happened, jumped into the water, repaired the broken string, and with Leroy tied onto the raft, paddled and pulled the sick assembly of sticks to the shore. There, Ama sat by the side of the pond with Leroy's head on her lap, nursing him from both breasts, trying desperately to restore his strength. Dean, and especially Yoofi, jeered at him. Husky, wretched Agu watched in fright.

Disobedient Monday

Not wanting to give much weight to his dream, Leroy arose earlier than normal and, with Yoofi, hurried down the grassy dew-filled path to milk his cows. For Yoofi, things were easy. He felt joy, the source of which he didn't know. Leroy, with full memory of his nightmare, worked faster not to have it completely consume his mind. Despite his efforts, a heavy lump of anxiety followed him.

Leroy's greatest prize was his Red Poll bull which he had bought as a yearling four falls before. From a calf, the animal had grown into a handsome beast that stood over six feet at the shoulders. It had bellowed all night. To make sure it was all right, Leroy walked by the pen where he kept the bull. Yoofi had always heard of the animal but never seen him. As a stud, Bullcow's singular purpose was hidden from the children. Now, Leroy considered it opportune for Yoofi to accompany him, reaffirming his statement that Yoofi had indeed reached manhood. Immediately, Yoofi went into rapture at the sight of the bull. It was not its immense size that caught his attention. It was rather that the animal was in musk and had been bellowing all night in response to the cow from the adjoining farm belonging to yet another farmer. Theirs was a poem of sorts: the cow begging, it seemed, and the bull, tormented that it couldn't give what it naturally should. It bellowed and huffed the ground as it snorted and butted the air. It was in misery. What caught Yoofi's attention was that the animal was aroused and in full display, calling, waiting, wailing! On seeing his master, the bull pranced in the air, kicking at it and the fencing.

Yoofi looked at Leroy.

"My Bullcow," Leroy said. "Fine fellow, just can't wait."

"Bullcow?" Yoofi asked, in tense laughter.

"Yes, Bullcow, Yoofi! That's what I call him, too, Bullcow. Got it?"

"Yes, Mas Leroy!"

"And, do you hear the cow mooing, too?"

"Yes, Mas Leroy."

"That's what she is begging for," Leroy said, as he turned to Yoofi with a smile. "My Bullcow. You see? A bull for the cow, not a steer for the butcher."

"Oh! So why not let him go to the cow, Mas Leroy?"

Leroy held his head back and roared a long, deep laugh. "And I thought you were smart! That's how I make my money, Bigboy. When my bull serves that heifer, the farmer pays me. Getting it, Bigboy?"

"Yes, Mas Leroy."

Leroy, pleased with himself, approached the fence with freshly cut grass in his hands. He threw it in the trough for Bullcow, but the animal flashed his head from side to side and snorted sparks of mucus, filling the air around him.

Still smiling as if he had accomplished a great deed, Leroy looked at Yoofi and said, "One day it will be your turn, Bigboy!" He left the pen where Bullcow was and headed to yet another pen that housed the milk-cows. Leroy, experienced with the cows, soon prepared for milking. As soon as Leroy completed every act, he looked back to Yoofi as if to ask: Did you see that? Got anything to ask?

Yoofi would nod as if to say, piece of cake. They conversed in silence throughout this first and only demonstration.

When the lesson was over, Leroy handed Yoofi the bucket of milk. Yoofi first put a kata – a circular winding of his old crocus bag – on his head. Following that, he lifted the heavy bucket of milk and placed it on top of his kata. Yoofi then started home.

Leroy intended to feed the cows with grass cut the day before and leave them in the pen for the day. He made a mistake, though. Or was it Yoofi? When Yoofi left the pen, he didn't close the gate. That was not part of the lesson. Leroy, believing the gate to be shut, walked off to gather the grass. Seeing the gate open and feeling the taste of freedom, the cows started to run. At first, Leroy ran towards the gate, trying to head them off. It didn't help; it served rather to speed the cows' run down the hill.

He knew where they would go, into the high meadow about a mile away. He reluctantly gave chase and walked after them. He would give them time to eat and settle before taking them back to the pen.

With Leroy clearly out of sight, Yoofi, instead of going directly home, went back to the pen where Bullcow was. He opened the gate and watched as the animal strutted without fear or interruption straight to the penned, mooing cow less than a quarter mile away on the neighboring farm. Yoofi watched as they met, smelling, snorting, submitting, and giving each other permission to touch in turn. Yoofi noticed that Bullcow equally aroused the heifer. He watched her, holding her head low and turning her rear for Bullcow's approval. It didn't take long before Bullcow attempted to mount. The cow quickly turned and circled. Bullcow followed her, snorting, sniffing the air and baring his great, grass-stained teeth to the wind. He tried again, this time holding the cow between his front legs and, in rapid jousts, forced himself in, repeatedly jabbing, jabbing, until exhausted or outdone. He dismounted, smelled her and walked off. Yoofi was still in shock, for he didn't know why his pants felt wet.

Returning to his senses, Yoofi securely placed the milk on the ground and untangled the stranded heifer which had been caught in rope carelessly left on the ground. He then chased Bullcow back into his pen. Strangely enough, Yoofi thought, Bullcow was indifferently submissive, returning to his pen as if he wanted to.

That had been Yoofi's first lesson in sex. For a long time, it would also be his only one.

With the first part of his morning's chores almost done, Yoofi thought of his brothers and his task of walking them to school. He continued home with the warm milk on his head. Upon reaching home, Yoofi filled each quart bottle with milk with the aid of a funnel, then placed the bottles of milk in a bag. On the way to make his deliveries, it suddenly struck Yoofi that Kwame lived in just the opposite direction to his delivery route. Thinking of making life easier for himself, Yoofi hid the milk-bag in the hedging and, instead of making the deliveries as Leroy had instructed, started out with Dean and Agu to school. Yoofi intended to do as he was told. He simply wanted to walk with his brothers to school, then deliver the milk. He cherished the last morsel of that camaraderie.

On his way to the school, Yoofi got Kwame. They had walked to school together the last three years and, in the last two of those years, with Dean. This new year their company changed to include Agu, who had just turned seven but by his size seemed eleven. Shep also went with them, seeming brisker than the boys in the cool morning air. Maybe Shep too had expectations of attending school.

Maybe it was Kwame's company. Maybe it was the presence of his brothers. Maybe it was his shame. Maybe it was all that and more. Whatever it was, Yoofi remained silent. He walked only in spirit, because his heart bled. He hadn't had the opportunity to say good-bye to his school, his teacher, or his old school-friends. His life had a sudden, untested direction for which he was not prepared. School was on his mind. That's where he belonged and wanted to be. How could he disclose to Kwame he wouldn't be in school, but instead had become an errand-boy, a steward for his brothers, a milkman, a farmer, and his mother's main helper as she started her new career as coconut oil maker and pig-keeper? There were no words he could find; neither could he muster the courage to talk if the words were there. He remained quiet.

Kwame must have sensed something, too. Why was Shep so happy? Why was he going to school? What was the poem about Mary? It was about a lamb. Shep, a shepherd, that didn't come close. Something was not right. Yes, Agu was there. That addition was correct. It was Shep that unbalanced the equation, bringing doubt and uneasiness to him.

Soon it didn't matter anymore to any of them. More and more children filled the path leading to the school, and then Shep indeed became their lamb. Yoofi was sure to take his siblings to their seats and, on leaving Agu, make straight to the Headmaster's office.

The new Headmaster was not very new after all. He was the retired Headmaster Forbes, whose old position Henry Love filled. Now the elderly but highly respected Forbes had allowed himself to be recalled from his twelve-year hiatus as an interim replacement for Henry Isaac Love. Shortly after Love's departure, Congo had gone to Headmaster Forbes and entreated him to retake his position. He had been Ama's former teacher.

The door to the Headmaster's office was ajar, and the Headmaster busied himself with more papers than he and his assistants could easily manage.

Yoofi was rather abrupt when he marched into the office and asked, "Where is my seat, Headmaster Forbes?"

"Oh, good morning, Yoofi. I was not expecting to see you here."

"Why not, Headmaster?"

"We do not have a seat for you. You know, our seating is limited and parents must inform us in advance who is coming to school. In that way we can prepare seats for them."

"But before summer recess, my teacher said I was the best in my class and a seat was reserved for me."

"Yes, we reserve seats for our top students, and you certainly were one."

"Well, if my father were here, I would have a seat. He was the Headmaster and you should have a seat for me."

"Your father, Mr. Kendal, was here, Yoofi. He told us you wouldn't be coming back."

"How can he say that? See, I am back, and my real father would have a seat for me."

"Well, see here, Yoofi. Mr. Kendal told me you were sick and, according to what Dr. Devinder Singh advised him, you wouldn't be returning to school."

"What? I didn't see Dr. Devinder all summer. All I did was play!"

"Well, Yoofi, that's what your father said. And based on that, we couldn't waste a seat on you."

"Waste a seat on me, Headmaster Forbes? I am sure my father in your position would have a seat for me."

"Listen, young man. He is not here, you do not have a seat, and you'd better go. It is already busy and there is no time to waste."

"I do not have to go, and you are not a Headmaster, either. My father is!"

"Yoofi! I understand you are upset. Based on what you said, I have the right to cane you. But I will let you off. And if you leave now, I will not tell your father, either."

"My father, my father? You do know my real father! You and that Leroy gang up on me to rob me of my education." His speech slowed as his eyes welled with emotion. "You have no right to steal it from me, you have no right." With that, Yoofi bent over, collapsing on the floor.

The Headmaster, with the aid of his assistant, moved Yoofi to the nurse's office. No one was there to attend him, but after a while Yoofi recovered and, with Shep, returned home.

He didn't forget what Leroy required of him, that he come to the field and work before going home to assist his mother with her oil-making efforts after dinner. Defiantly, and without remorse, Yoofi went home and started to work with his mother. They worked long and hard, yet harmoniously, until it was time for their meal.

"Yoofi, my dear," Ama started at dinner. "I know you want to go to school. I know how bad you feel."

"How can you know, Mammy?"

"I was not allowed to stay in school, either, Yoofi."

"You didn't go to school, Mammy?"

"No, Yoofi. Not much. Bem didn't see any need for it."

"So how did you learn to read, Mammy?"

"Self-taught, mostly. It is possible if you really want to, Yoofi."

The lad didn't reply, and Ama continued, "When I got old enough, I got a job as the janitor at the school, so I could go to the library and read. That's how I met your father. Now things are changing. All Leroy is thinking of is money. Maybe he thinks it's worth something."

"But he shouldn't take me out of school to make me his slave."

"Just do what he says, Yoofi. Do it, no fuss; it gets easier."

"I love to work, Mammy. It's not the work that is bothering me! It is leaving school. I can't live without school, Mammy. I feel like am going to die."

"I know it is hard for you, Yoofi. But you may think of it another way."

"What way, Mammy?"

"That you are getting a chance children of your age don't always get."

"A chance to be out of school, Mammy?" He asked in defeat and disbelief.

"No! Not to be out of school, but to have a special life, Yoofi."

"What special life is that? School is what I want, Mammy!"

"Sometimes, Yoofi, we have to accept just what we get, and not pine for what we want."

"Why don't you back me up, Mammy?" Yoofi looked askance at his mother sitting before him, a cruel veil of doubt and anger shadowing his face.

"Sometimes, Yoofi, fighting is of no use; and you must learn to control your . . ."

"Control what, Mammy? Control what?" he interrupted. And before Ama could respond, Yoofi continued. "Why don't you take my side, Mammy? See? You are just like him. You hate me. You hate me, too!" In helpless despair Yoofi threw himself down on the ground and started to bawl.

"No, Yoofi," Ama said, rubbing his head and back as she knelt to comfort him. "I love you. I love you with all my heart. You hear me, Yoofi?"

"Yes, Mammy," he muffled through his sniffling.

"And you never forget that. Okay, Yoofi. You never forget that Mammy loves you."

"Okay, Mammy," he said, turning to her and drying his face.

"I will always love you, Yoofi, no matter what happens to you!"

"All right, Mammy," he said, standing up to face her.

"Then come over here and give Mammy a hug," Ama said, smiling with her arms opened wide to accept him.

He ran and hopped into her lap and, though he'd just eaten, felt for her breasts. He nursed until he fell asleep. Yoofi slept and Ama thought: Maybe that's how it was intended anyway. Who knows?

She walked him to his bed and went to her work, but Yoofi didn't sleep long. He soon got up, fed Shep, and busied himself with the chores his mother gave.

The afternoon's work between mother and son progressed well. She sang, and he worked. He sang and she worked, until it was time to go for the children at school. Yoofi dreaded the hour.

As he was about to leave, Leroy came in. His day's toil was over and he would wash, have supper, and leave to play dominoes or drink at the *Any Questions*. He would – if there were no unfinished business.

In the past he would have asked Ama to accompany him. Ama would be delighted to be at the *Any Questions*. Now, with Ama busy at her endless tasks and Leroy preoccupied with moneymaking schemes, things had changed. The life that had been good between Leroy and Ama in the beginning gradually degraded into something neither could describe.

In fact, it had not been good since Agu's birth. It was about then that their characters seemed to separate and they became individuals. They descended from the oneness – the unity created by their marriage – to empty, self-serving, thread-worn statements of love. Leroy's desire for control budded and gave rise as it did to an equally strong and abiding indecisiveness on Ama's part. He hated her inability to make clear, vital choices. She abhorred his desire for power and control. Soon, they were not one anymore, but slowly drifted from honey, my dear, love, and mi putus, to simply Leroy and Ama. With the process of crystallization complete, the journey of separation ensued. Her path led her after supper to nursing and reading to the children, while his took him to the tavern for ale and idle discourse.

For now, there was unfinished business, and Leroy meant to bring it to conclusion. He came into the yard with a heavy stick around which he intended to twine his one-chain-long measuring tool. The sight of Yoofi brought back anxious memories of his dream. Leroy, however, focused on what he had to do.

"Yoofi!" he called.

Shep, like his shield, came running ahead of Yoofi.

"Yes, Mas Leroy?"

"So what happened to the milk bottles, Bigboy?"

"Kiss-mi-neck!" Yoofi responded, suddenly scratching the back of his neck in surprise and disbelief. "Lawd mi-gad. Mi figet!"

"Watch your talk, boy! And what'd you forget now, Bigboy?"

"Sorry, Mas Leroy. Mi . . . I forgot the bottles in the hedging," Yoofi stuttered as he struggled with his memory.

" And why were they in the hedging, Bigboy?"

"I left them there, sir."

"So, that's where you leave them, ah?"

"Yes, Mas Leroy. I was going to deliver the milk after I walked Kwame – I mean my brothers – to school."

"And who told you to walk Kwame to school?"

"Mi . . . myself alone, Mas Leroy," Yoofi replied, digging his toes nervously into the ground.

"I see. So, what I tell you to do is not what you do. And what I do not tell you to do is what you do. Ah! I wonder who is the man around here?"

Yoofi didn't reply.

"I guess you don't know the answer to that, now, ah, Bigboy?"

Still the lad didn't reply, but started grinding his teeth in anger and fear.

"Well, Yoofi. I delivered the milk."

The lad remained silent.

"Don't you hear me speaking to you? The least you could do is to thank me."

Still the lad didn't reply.

"So tell me, Bigboy. What is this argument you had with Headmaster Forbes, telling him he must give you a seat?"

"Why ask me if you know?"

"What! What was that you said, Bigboy?"

"I said, go and ask him yourself, you liar! Liar!"

"So . . . me . . . the one who put clothes on your back and a roof over your head since the day you were born . . . me . . . I am now a liar! Is that it? Is that it, Bigboy?" Leroy asked, all the time beating his chest.

"You are a liar, Leroy! Why did you go and tell Headmaster Forbes that I was sick and would not be returning to school? Why?" The lad asked, looking fiercely at Leroy.

"Bigboy! You good for nothing, ungrateful wretch! It looks I have to give your backside a good licking for your own good! Like ol' time people say, 'get into it or lickin' into it.' Is that what you are asking for, Bigboy, a lickin' into it?"

Leroy was panting from anger and fearsome anticipation. "In fact, I tell you what. Don't kneel. Don't even bother to kneel on the cut stones today. I see that is of no use to you. No matter how much it has cut your knees you still will not learn, so don't even bother this time. And don't say anything else to me, either. I won't even bother to listen to that. It seems like my talking to you is of no use. Go get scorpion, let him do the talking, tonight!"

Yoofi didn't move. "Did you hear me, Bigboy! Go get Scorpion. Let him talk to your rhatid backside tonight!"

The lad looked Leroy in his eyes. "You want scorpion, Leroy? You want scorpion? Go get it, yourself!"

"You Bigboy, bastard! What was that you said? And on top of your big lip, you have become a rude-boy. And in my own house? No sir. Not here!" Leroy said, shaking his head violently as his wrath deepened. Leroy grabbed a heavy stick beside him.

He moved toward Yoofi to strike him with the stick. Ama motioned sideways to intercept his path. As Leroy waved the stick backward, his arm hit Ama and she fell. Yoofi rushed to her side and bent over her. She lay still.

"Stupid Fool! See what you did? You better not hurt her!"

Leroy waved again, intending to strike Yoofi. That very moment, Shep pounced on Leroy. Leroy's hat and heavy stick fell in different directions as Shep brought Leroy in a heavy thud to the ground. The animal bared its teeth and growled at Leroy until his master relented.

"Leave him alone, Shep." Yoofi walked to where Leroy lay, and patted his dog.

The dog wagged its tail and remained calm, sitting with its eyes focused on Leroy. Yoofi took Shep and walked to where his mother lay. He raised her and walked her up the steps to the porch.

"And you better not set foot in there tonight," Leroy said to Yoofi.

"No intention to," Yoofi replied, looking back at Leroy.

Just then, Ama turned around and said to Leroy, "All you have to do is love him. Is that so hard, Leroy?"

"Damn disobedient Monday!" Leroy replied and, grabbing his hat, made his way to the tavern.

"I will get Kwame and the children, Mammy."

"Thank you, Yoofi. Supper will be ready when you get back."

"Miss Hene will have supper ready, Mammy."

"That's right. That's right. I almost forgot."

"Thank you, Mammy." And with that, Yoofi and Shep set out to complete their evening rounds.

Laura's Choice

Encouraged by the brisk economic activity of the early war years, Laura set out to enlarge her father's business by dealing with produce, jewelry, and fabrics. In this new enterprise, she became the local wholesaler, receiving merchandise from agents of manufacturers and distributing them to local stores. To accomplish her goal, Laura borrowed heavily from the Bank of England, enlarged her store, and credited new merchandise, thereby risking her seemingly thriving enterprise.

Laura had never fully understood her love affair with Congo. With no formal beginning it did not know how to end. Laura was certain that from the instant she saw Congo she wanted him. The same was no less true for Congo. Maybe what astonished them was the recklessness of its beginning: without word or kind, nothing but a certain look. All they wanted was to be on the other side of the pond, hidden, but not hiding. The passion that brought them together didn't recognize their differences; it transcended them, bonding them into one. Laura was Chinese, Congo African. Didn't they know, or could it be that they didn't care? They felt. That was it! And all they had to do was to take themselves out of sight and let their love flow. It did, and continued, on and off but unabated in desire, long into Congo's marriage to Ulu.

It was not only in love that their relationship excelled. It carried over into business. Congo made sure that Laura was supplied on time with the best produce from the valley. But he did more. His search for new accounts brought him in contact with an old friend and business partner of Laura's father. It was with Ho that Laura's father, Li, had developed the import business. After Li's death, Ho, a full generation younger than Li, moved from Oracabessa to Port Maria. In addition to the jewelry business he had, Ho also opened a restaurant, specializing in seafood. That was how Congo first met him.

His friend's death did not deter Ho from continuing the studies and practices he and Li had pursued over the years. Ho and his mentor had embarked on quests of physical and inner purity by reading, performing, and internalizing the essence of certain eastern rituals and customs. Soon Ho grew humble and astute in the ancient ways.

Congo was at first surprised, maybe even amused, by Ho's appearance. Ho stood only five feet tall and boasted a medium-built frame. His short-cropped black hair flopped around an oval face supporting a large, flat nose. Small, squinting black eyes seemed to dart from under markedly fat lids while wayward teeth pointed away from the excessive overbite of his upper jaw. That was what Congo first saw, a gaping mouth unable to tame its huge upper incisors. What puckered his sun-baked skin, or rendered his beard so long, uneven and sparse, Congo couldn't wager. When Congo first saw the spectacle, he laughed, mistaking Ho for a clown. Ho stood his ground and said: "Happy day for you, sir? May I please be of service to you?" Ho's request was so confident, genuine, and bold, it jolted Congo from his laughter.

"Food, please?" Congo asked.

Congo was soon seated, and in slow degree the affable Ho opened his life before him, encouraging Congo to do likewise. It was not too long before they realized Laura was a common friend, and soon Congo and Ho became friends.

Ho Chen, a generation older than Laura, had made his love interest in Laura known from the time she was a mere teen. Her father encouraged the relationship, but Laura refused. She neither liked Ho's bristly beard nor his protruding gut. She liked his brilliance and easy manner, but rather disliked what brought his pleasing disposition on him. Ho's life, as Laura saw it, was prayer, morning exercise, sea-bath, breakfast, rest, work, dinner, reading, sleep, morning exercise, without end.

Laura thought of Ho as living like a tree: existing, and responding to the seasons without diversion, fearing it should forget its routine. Even so, Laura liked what his life had brought him: a quiet, humble disposition with charm and abundant kindness, free of complaint or denigration. Ritual was her torturer, and she would avoid it at any cost. Sadly for Ho, he came with ritual, forcing Laura to scoff and reject. But Ho, good ol' Ho, was also forgiving and patient.

Congo found an excellent and ready account in Ho Chen. He was astute, unselfish, and foresighted enough, encouraging Congo to open a ledger with him, not large enough to rival Laura's, yet of sufficient life to give Congo's business an alternate leg were Laura's to fail.

Congo didn't understand at first what kept Laura and Ho apart. To him they seemed well suited for each other. He liked both of them and, on understanding Ho's feelings for Laura and her expressed desire to expand her life beyond Congo, invited Laura to dinner at the *Hong Kong Seafood Gardens* in Port Maria. It was not long before Congo's matchmaking efforts no longer needed him. With their new footing, Ho and Laura were awakened to deeper potentials in each other, seeing facets to which more hopeful attachments could be made. Neither Laura nor Congo had reason to disclose the depths of their intimacy to Ho. Nor would Ho have had any interest in it. His new study was Laura; that's all Ho saw, and she encouraged him.

It did not take long for Ho Chen to propose to Laura. He had long ago done it at Li's bequest, and repeatedly afterward to satisfy his own longings. After Laura's first refusal of Ho and her rejection of her father's traditional life style, it became easier for her to dismiss Ho's succeeding invitations of marriage without much thought. The persistent bachelor, however, thought that with the passage of time and the new spark that had developed between them, it had become opportune for him to try again. On this occasion, however, he would elicit the advice of Congo.

The table where Congo and Ho sat, comfortably musing after a sumptuous dinner outside *Hong Kong Seafood Gardens*, gave them a full and undiluted view of the turquoise sea gently foaming up to their feet. The fresh, gentle, sea breeze caressed their satiated bodies, lulling them almost to slumber.

"I have been thinking, Congo, to propose to Laura," Ho started lazily.

"Yes? You may want to tell her, though."

"I know, I know. But I want to try a different approach this time."

"So what's your plan, Ho?"

"To send her a letter."

"A personal approach may be better."

"That's where you come in, Congo. You will have to take the letter to her."

"Me, ah?" Congo asked.

"Yes, what do you think?"

"Anything for you, my friend," Congo teased, patting Ho's shoulder as he spoke.

"I'd like to read it to you."

"Okay. Let me hear it, Ho!"

"It starts off this way: My dear Laura."

"Maybe you should leave off the 'My.' You do not own her."

"Okay, Congo, but let me read the entire thing to you; then you let me know what you think."

"Okay."

"Good then," and Ho read:

Dearest Laura:

I have wanted you to be my wife since the first day I met you. The beauty of your glowing countenance, the black of your large bright eyes, the gently flowing curves of your body compel me to look at you in adoration and praise. You are as beautiful as the starlit heavens, and gentle as the wind. And did I mention your smile? I take it wherever I go. It captivates me, and constantly reminds me of your radiance, your beauty, calling me constantly to you. I want to express this love to you and take from your womb sons to fill the earth with children of your beauty and joy. I have already totally devoted my life to you. You just have to say yes to my proposal, and all that I have is yours. I am yours, truly in devoted love to you, forever."

Ho looked at Congo, who looked back at him smiling. "It's a good offer, Ho."

"So you think it will win her?"

"Maybe not this time."

"You said it's good."

"Yes, but it does not address Laura."

"What, Congo? What do you think she is looking for?"

"Acceptance."

"Not love?"

"That's what it means to her."

"Oh . . ."

"Yes," said Congo, nodding his head. "Laura just wants to know you accept her choices."

"Her choices? Full acceptance, though they are not right?"

"Who is judging?"

"Oh . . . so what do I do?"

"Tell her!"

"This is a letter of proposal, Congo."

"Yes, Ho. So propose to Laura."

"Let's see then. I could write, *Dearest Laura . . .*"

"You said that already."

"Yes, yes," replied Ho as both men laughed.

Ho continued to write:

I didn't understand how important your choices have been to you. I have always sided with your father in supporting our traditional way of life. Though I accept it for myself, I do not anymore hold you responsible for it. Our friend Congo let me see you in a new way, as one needing to live as you choose. We must thank him for that, and for relieving me of my burden of wanting to have you live as I choose. I must accept that there is something other than the traditional. You, Laura, have given me glimpses of that. Of course, you know how I live. My life is an open book. I sometimes feel restricted in following my path, but it has taken us, our people, this far. However, I accept you now as another window, my window. Of course, God must have made you this special contrary way for a reason. And now, I am getting a view of that. So, I must never again ask or expect you to live as I do. In all manners, follow your own heart, as you have allowed me to, never asking for change. I respect your courage and worship your principle, knowing that whatever you choose for us, I will live with joy and comfort in your heart.

Your friend in all humility,
Ho

"Good, Ho. Very good! You have almost got her! But where is the love, Ho? Do you love her?"

"Yes, I have told her so many times before."

"You may want to tell her again!"

"Thank you, Congo." So he rephrased his last line to read:

Your friend, forever with love: all my love and deepest humility,
Ho

Congo took the letter to Laura that very night. She read it and smiled. She read it again and cried.

"Yes," she said. "Tell him yes, whenever he likes."

Later that night, postman Congo rode from Free Hill to Port Maria to complete his dinner engagement with Ho. They celebrated it with cognac.

Tired but satisfied, Congo arrived ready for sleep in Ulu's bedroom early the following morning. For Ulu, however, that was insufficient reason for Congo to slumber.

Sister for a Princess

A brilliant dawn breaking through the lush yellow-green foliage brought golden sunlight to the Kings' breakfast. The table was not set as usual. Ulu had thought long about the changes she wished to usher in, as gentle and unnoticeable as was practical without the least betrayal of her message. That the maids were at first confused didn't bother her, that her dearest Princess didn't quite understand seemed to please her, for it offered more proof that her message would be delivered.

Until the night past, Congo had sat at the head of the table. On that fateful Friday morning, following his late return home, Ulu awoke early and instructed the maids to make the breakfast settings so that Princess sat at the head of the table and her husband and herself at either side of Princess.

Congo came hurriedly to the table, already dressed for business. His intention was to greet his family, then close his business accounts for the week. He thought Ulu would understand. He had been doing that for so long.

"Good morning, Ulu," he said, kissing her where she was seated and then lifting Princess to kiss her.

"Good morning, Pappy," Princess said, full of smiles and admiration.

"Won't you have breakfast with us, Congo?"

"Well, Ulu, it's Friday. You know . . ." he said returning Princess to her seat and kissing her again.

"Yes, Congo. I know. But I need some help around the house."

"Is there a problem with the new servants?"

"No, Congo. Not in the least. They are working out just right."

"So what do you need, then?"

"I need help with Princess. And if you were here more in the days, you could help with her."

"We could play hide and seek, Pappy," the girl offered.

"Yes, Princess. But there is work outside the house, too."

"Work until one or two o'clock in the mornings, Congo?"

He looked at her and stiffened. When his eyes roamed to Princess, he smiled. Ulu watched him. She had placed Princess at the table on purpose. Congo would have preferred if she were not there, since he desired frank and open exchange with his wife.

"Yes. Work and socializing," she continued.

"Sometimes, Ulu, socializing is just as important as work."

"I do not see myself socializing, and all my work is done."

"What is socializing, Pappy?"

"Oh," Congo smiled, looking at his daughter, "it means having friends."

"So, why can't I have friends, Pappy?"

"Of course, you can have friends, Princess."

"But I don't. Mammy says you are too busy for us, and your friends are more important than your family."

"Oh, she said that, ah. Well, Princess, there is another view of that. Your Pappy works all day outside the house, building our business to make sure you can have anything you want. Anything in the whole wide world."

"My business is fine. It's your whereabouts that concerns us, Congo."

"Mammy wants to know where you are at nights, Pappy. Where were you so late, Pappy? I want you to read to me again at nights and tuck me in like you used to do."

"You see, Congo, you have a daughter to raise; and you spend your time socializing and wasting money at it, no doubt good money I make from my business."

"I work, too, Ulu," Congo said in embarrassed tones.

"Yes, you work, running here and there, socializing, and spending money on new clothes and horses. The whole world will soon think we are rich!"

"Ulu, we have worked and created this business. What's wrong if I should enjoy some of the fruits? And what if people think we are rich?"

"It's not what they think, Congo. It's what you do and don't do. Why can't you say honestly where you are at nights?"

"I am with Ho. That's where I spend my time."

"What a thing to say! Ho? Ho!" Ulu laughed. "He does not even talk. No one knows what he thinks. How can you socialize with someone who does not talk?"

In exasperation, Congo became silent. He looked to Princess for help. She leaned on her open palm, looking in her mother's direction, then helplessly at her father.

"It does not seem true, Pappy. Mammy said you would tell her a pack of lies."

"Have your fruit, Princess."

"She's had enough."

The silence and Ulu's bitterness forced Congo to quiet thought. He had been unprepared for her attack. "I do not want to mention names, Congo. But I tell you, it better not be her again."

"Who? Laura?"

"What did you just say? Didn't I tell you not to ever mention her name in this house ever again?" Ulu screamed.

"For goodness sake, Ulu! We do business with her."

"This is not a business discussion!"

"God!"

"Yes, bring God here to clean your guilty conscience."

"Guilty of what, Ulu?"

"What? You just mentioned her! So don't play coy with me, Congo. You know exactly what I mean."

Congo became silent.

"And instead of running to see her night-in, night-out, why not stay with your family and help raise your daughter? She is who you need to spend time with." Ulu reached over and began running her fingers through her daughter's hair. "Mammy loves you, Princess."

"I know, Mammy." Her large eyes turned to her father, who cringed like a trapped animal within his chair.

"You know, Ulu. I must go. I have business to do."

"Yes, every time we try to discuss something, you walk away."

"I am not walking away, Ulu. I have our business to get done."

"My business is all right," she asserted. "It's only Princess that concerns me now."

"Princess? In what way, Ulu?"

"You are not here as a father to her, and God knows I am too busy with the new girls, and my business is growing faster than I can handle it. You know," she said, as if talking to herself, "what Princess really needs is a sister."

"How will that ever happen when you have her in the . . ." He paused, thinking of his daughter and the confusion his question could cause. Congo wanted to accuse Ulu of having Princess sleep in their bed at nights, excluding him and any possibility of a second child.

"Go ahead and say it. Go ahead, you single-minded . . ."

Congo remained calm. He knew he had already lost. All he could now do was end the game and prevent further erosion of his credibility in his daughter's mind.

"I know of someone," he said.

"What someone?"

"Someone to be a sister to Princess."

"Oh, yes. That's what you want, right, Princess? Someone to be a bigger sister to you, while he is away," she said, stressing the he and looking at Congo.

"Yes, Mammy. Can you get me a bigger sister, Pappy?"

"Yes, Princess. I think so."

"What do you have in mind, Congo?"

"Do you remember Esi?"

"Yes, of course, Congo. She was my mother's best friend!"

"Her daughter was the flower girl at Ama's wedding. Do you remember her?"

"Yes. Charm, I think her name was."

"Yes, she is quite grown now, you know. And as a relative . . ."

"She is no relative of mine. She is not a Covey!"

"I meant," Congo tried to correct himself, "Esi and Nweka were almost like sisters."

"Yes, they were close, and . . . well, I better not get into the details now," he said, looking at Princess. "But you know how she is related, don't you?"

"I know what you mean, but I am not related to her. I want to make that clear. So don't bring her here with that expectation. If I accept her, Charm will be a servant like anyone else here. I hope you understand that."

"Oh, Ulu! But Charm has blossomed into one fine girl. She has been out of elementary school now for about three years, and she has not been able to find a good house to go to."

"Well, from what you are saying, she is about eighteen or so. Is that right?"

"Yes, that's about right, Ulu."

"I'll tell you what, Congo. If she is hard working, and will not come here expecting anything because we are somewhat related, then I see no harm in giving her a chance."

"You will not find anyone more suitable, Ulu; and Princess will like her. Won't you, Princess?"

"If you like her, Pappy."

"Good, then. I will go to Free Hills this morning and tell her to get ready. I will bring her back at lunch time."

"I will have a room ready for her."

"And dinner, too?"

"Yes. But I usually like to see the new girls do a full day's work before I feed them. That way they know if I approve of their work."

"Listen, Ulu. The Boydells run a decent home. Charm has been brought up by them, and I give you my word: she will be worth much more than a meal."

"We will see."

With that, Congo kissed Princess, and bade good-bye. "Kiss Mammy, too, Pappy."

"Oh, Princess." Congo bent and kissed Ulu. He turned to leave. Discreetly, Ulu wiped her face and called for her maids.

Princess ran downstairs and waved her father good-bye. Congo looked back to smile at her, then returned to the door, lifted and kissed her. "I love you Princess. I love you, I love you," he said.

"And I love you, too, Pappy. And I miss you every day and every night, too, Pappy."

Congo kissed his daughter again and lowered her feet to the floor, rubbing her head while he smiled pensively, then walked to his waiting horse.

Ulu and Laura

Ulu's anxiety and misgivings about Congo's attachment to Laura loomed as he left the house. She could see nothing except his entry to Laura's bedroom and her imaginings of what must happen there. Ulu had no direct evidence that her suspicions were accurate. She relied on the gossip of her staff, even though she forbade such hearsay.

As she watched him leave, Ulu was drawn to a letter she had received a few months previous from Laura. She retrieved it from a stack of business papers which lay on her desk and read it as if for the first time.

I remember, Ulu, you told me before: all play and no work will make Ulu rich, very rich indeed. I know that in your mind you have turned your work into play, and that soon, if not already, you will become very rich indeed. Do not, however, forget your poor friend Laura who still wishes to invite you to lunch with her any Friday you choose. If you wish, we could talk about work or business, which, I know, you would rather be doing.

Loving you still, Laura.

Ulu read the letter time and time again, asking each time: Is she my friend? Is she really my friend? And if she is my friend, why is Congo spending all his time with her? Why doesn't he spend it at home where he belongs?

It was not only the friendship between Congo and Laura that drove a wedge in their long, relished friendship. Sure, it was an issue, though buried, everyone thought. It was also their ardent work ethic along with their differences over business models.

What Laura inherited from Li, her father, and he from his, was the belief that as the business owner, Laura sat on top of a pyramidal system which imported as many relatives from Hong Kong as were needed to fill every job, even with duplication. She housed and fed her workers, and each morning gave them the same instructions: "You all know what to do. Study the business and work where you fit best. If you do not know what to do, come and talk with me. If I can, I will help you fit in. Work hard. The business needs to be profitable, or we all go back home. Do you want that?" She wouldn't wait for a reply. She knew from the faces of humility and submission at the breakfast table that all understood. "So go do your work or pack you bags. Either way, it's up to you."

With that, she allowed her workers to figure out for themselves what had to be done and how to do it. She didn't participate in the work, but simply watched for the leaders, praised and encouraged every good thing they did, and, as soon as they were ready and capable of moving on their own, financed the new endeavor as part owner. That was how Ho got his start, until he was able to buy out Laura's father and became an independent business entity.

Ulu's method, developed from observing her father, relied on her own fortitude. Ulu was strong and she liked to work. She threw herself into her business, working at anything, taking on the hardest tasks and seeing them through. She was a fighter. She loved the heat and intensity of the bakery: kneading the dough, removing the coals from the huge brick ovens, then, finally, breaking open and tasting of the day's first bread with swift gulps of sweet, milk-drenched coffee.

Opening the bakery long before dawn, Ulu would have steaming batches of fresh rolls to take to the breakfast table, where the aroma called Congo and Princess for quick nibbles. Ulu then readied herself for the store, but only after seeing that the produce was placed to dry and carts of honey and fresh bread taken to shops in other towns. Finally, she would open the next phase of her day in her shop. Before she closed the store each night, Ulu called her crew together, reviewed their work and gave instructions for the coming day. Such work might include taking bananas to the wharf in Oracabessa or coconuts to the copra-processing house. And so it went with Ulu: working, organizing, and managing her affairs with rigid efficiency. It was this fierceness with which she attacked each day, plunging headlong into every job, that brought her servants into order and gave them a keenness for their tasks. They knew her standards, that her rewards, though exact, were fair. Without making personal demands, she controlled her crew.

Ulu, because of her high standards, wouldn't accept inferior quality; and if her example was not followed, dismissal was sure and sudden. In that way, she soon had a good staff, well trained and fully disciplined. So, too, was each worker chosen, trained, and placed in the job that was most appropriate, based on skill and temperament. Salaries were as low as the worker could stand, and promotions were few and slow.

When Ulu saw how well Congo performed on Lev's property, she quickly snapped him up by way of marriage to rivet him to her for life. Just as he had increased Lev's estate, so Ulu thought Congo would make her rich! Yet Congo recognized little of this deceit. He was in love. Ulu fell in love with him only after Princess was born; and now, Ulu's old disdain for him was resurfacing. Moreover, there was Laura.

Their systems of business operation were so opposite that both Laura and Ulu reevaluated their positions and later their friendship. When these friends shared business problems, each found she had little to say to the other. In addition, the rift over the closeness between Congo and Laura seemed destined to doom their friendship.

From Laura's point of view, Congo had nothing to do with the deterioration of the connection between Ulu and her. Both relationships were, in her eyes, independent of each other. She felt a strong bond with Congo and he, her. Additionally they forged a business association that involved Ulu. Were the business to die, she would still want Congo and crave his love. Laura knew that she would still be Ulu's friend.

In the beginning, it was strictly an amorous attraction that pulled Congo and Laura together. During that time, Laura and Ulu remained friends while Ulu married Congo. Later on, a business relationship developed that connected the three together. Unwittingly, the triangle formed, connecting them in business and love. For Ulu, it was the profitability of the business that kept the triad stable. As she pondered the situation, Ulu didn't know if there would be any friendship remaining between them were their commercial interests to fail. It was the financial association between Laura and Congo that had become the hub for Ulu's growth in business. It also kept creditors away from her doors.

Laura was still determined to keep their friendship alive and growing. As young women in business, they had much to protect and prove. They wanted to prove they could win on their own terms. That meant working harder than normal, long nights, and sometimes weekends.

Friday at lunch was the best time for them. Friday lunchtimes were unusually long. The one thing both businesses had in common – an outgrowth of plantation work habits – was that the servants had their longest mealtime on Fridays. It was really lunchtime followed by a siesta, and then preparation for the long, long Friday evening, which in many cases spilled over into Saturday morning market.

Ulu decided to have lunch with Laura in Oracabessa that Friday. She hurriedly gathered her staff, gave them precise instructions, which they must have heard ten thousand times before, told them that a new girl, Charm, would be joining the staff, and what she was expected to do, which was nothing but wash and iron Princess' clothes for church on Sunday.

With that done, Ulu prepared herself for her journey by buggy to lunch with Laura. She had just reached the gate when Congo drove up with Charm.

"Good morning, Aunt Ulu." Congo had taught the girl what to say, and she now parroted with boldness.

"Miss Ulu, to you, child!" she replied, "and the girls will tell you your duties. I will discuss your compensation when I return."

"I thank you, ma'am," Charm said, curtseying.

"And Congo, I will be gone for the morning and afternoon. See that she gets started before you leave."

Congo didn't reply. He simply smiled and waved to her. Ulu drove away and Congo took Charm into the house, offered her a seat and hurried up the stairs.

Princess didn't take long to find the arms of her father. He lifted and kissed her. "Now Princess, you better go down and meet your new sister. Her name is Charm."

Excitedly, Princess raced downstairs to find Charm standing apprehensively at the landing.

"Good morning, Charm," Princess said, taking her by the hand. "Pappy says you are my sister."

"Good morning, Princess. I will be taking care of you."

"Then come on, Charm. Let me show you my room and all the toys Pappy bought for me."

"In a minute, Princess. Let Pappy talk with Charm for a while."

From the great hall which they had just entered, the three walked through the house, Congo showing Charm every room and explaining its use. He then took her into the kitchen and bakery and out onto the barbeque, introducing her to all the other workers as Princess's sister. They returned to the kitchen where he secured some refreshments for the three of them, preferring to eat in the kitchen rather than at the dining table. It didn't take long before the fruits were eaten, and Congo made sure Charm was comfortable before he left the house to continue his weekend business rounds.

Ulu arrived at Laura's just in time to see a buggy driving off in the opposite direction and Laura still waving good-bye to the rising dust. Laura didn't wait for Ulu to leave her carriage before she started hollering in Chinese for help. It came, quickly and politely, taking control of the horse, freeing Ulu to hug Laura as they walked from the road into the house. On seeing Laura, and sensing the enthusiasm she displayed towards her, Ulu's fears died and her old trust returned. Laura called for refreshments, which came courteously into the parlor where they sat, and immediately Laura offered to show Ulu her new building.

It was just completed; a new floor was added on top of the old. It would serve as a wholesale center for fabrics. With the war rapidly approaching its third year and the British factories going at full speed, English marketing teams unloaded as much merchandize on the island as was possible. Their method was to sell on credit. Laura got funding from the Bank of England, enlarged her store, and by using credit stocked her shop with the finest fabric Britain could produce. Things went well for her. Produce supplied by Congo formed the cash flow part of her business. With ever-increasing demand for produce from her customers in Hong Kong, Laura saw the possibility to expand her business. A part of the reason for inviting Ulu to lunch was to firm up her source of produce, on which the rest of her business depended. A part of Ulu's reason for accepting the invitation was to study Laura's business for weaknesses and potential ways of attacking it were the necessity to arise.

Laura and Ulu soon returned from touring the store and sat down to lunch. The women spoke as they did in high school, forgetting their differences. Laura wanted to share more with Ulu. She wanted to let her know how helpful Congo had been to her, especially the previous night. She eagerly desired to show Ulu the ring Ho had just brought to her, her ring of engagement. It was the loveliest thing Laura had seen. In her high school years, Li, at Ho's advice, had imported it from Hong Kong.

It remained for a long time the center of their jewelry display; and when Ho first told Li of his love for Laura and his desire to marry her, the father quickly pointed to the ring that would satisfy Laura's heart. Laura was jubilant with Ho's present. Not because of its beauty or its price, which she knew, but because it came with the understanding that he accepted her, and crowned it with something she loved. How did he know! She now felt truly understood and appreciated. Laura was happy, rejoicing and bursting with eagerness to share the news with her Ulu. Yet a strange whisper of caution bade her be silent. With great restraint and discipline, she obeyed. Laura wanted to keep the secret yet longer to herself, cherishing it until it was time to let it out, like an athlete's great exhale. Until then, her joy would remain hers and hers alone.

During her return home, it soon occurred to Ulu the strange way in which Laura had developed her business. By comparison, hers she saw as robust, standing like a stool on footings of a bakery, farm produce which Congo bought and sold, and her personal farming endeavors. Each she considered independent and survivable without the other. Ulu knew her business was debt free, whereas Laura's was entangled by debt. Now that her business had matured, Ulu didn't any longer see the need for Congo. She could easily replace him with a manager. She already had a daughter. Why was Congo necessary?

Ulu remembered how she had used her old Covey bank accounts to which she didn't add the King name. The Jacks River property, which Congo found, he purchased with her money and in her name alone. So Ulu wanted it, even though they were married. Since Congo didn't object, subsequent land and house purchases – quite a few choice Victorian rooming houses in Port Maria – were all transacted in the Covey name. Congo had bought and rented most of them even without her knowledge, all in Ulu's name. She had grown wealthier than she knew and all her business was on a cash basis. With her position so strong, and Congo's so tenuous, why did she feel so threatened by rumors of Laura and him? Why didn't Congo rush home to her at nights? What did Laura offer him, and vice versa? Her old question – what does she see in him? – was now more pertinent than when she had first asked it at Providence Pond.

This was not so with Laura, as Ulu had just found out. Laura's business was not only partially based on credit, but Ulu was her only produce-supplier. Were Ulu to lose her footing in the produce business, Laura's empire in Oracabessa and perhaps, too, her home in Free Hills, which she had recently expanded into a mansion, would tumble. How precarious, Ulu thought.

Her yard-boys, who had heard her carriage approaching, hurried to the gate to help Ulu descend, and they attended to the horses.

Without much ado, Ulu rushed into the house to see Charm reading to Princess. Expecting rather to see a slothful Charm and not knowing of her penchant for books, the surprised Ulu gasped and lifted her daughter.

"Let's go upstairs," Ulu said, looking at Charm.

"Yes, Miss Ulu."

Again, Ulu was surprised. Charm's Sunday clothing was neatly pressed with matching shoes and handbag placed by them, and the room cleaned and dusted.

"How much did Congo tell you to ask for?"

"Seventeen shillings and sixpence a week, ma'am."

"It will be ten and six, with room and board. And sleep upstairs in the room closest to Princess, so you can keep an eye on her at nights."

"Thank you, Miss Ulu."

"Good, good. Now, go in the kitchen and tell the cook to feed you."

"Thanks, Miss Ulu."

With that, Ulu undressed and went to the store to find the operation running as though she had been there all day. She smiled and returned to the house, where she poured herself a long refreshing drink and wearily sat down.

Soon, the tiresome afternoon drifted into a busy Friday evening, and a heavy shopping activity pulled Ulu back to the store where again she went to the shelves, rearranging the merchandize. Much later that night, she closed the store and took her accustomed hot bath, still with strategies from her meeting with Laura playing in her head.

It was not only for her relaxation that Ulu stayed longer in her bath that night. She knew she had to reward Congo for bringing Charm to her home. Congo had found what Ulu considered the perfect sister for Princess. For that, and not in words, she would reward him.

Congo also knew that. As he passed his daughter's room to go to Ulu's, he noticed Princess was in bed. He got in and awaited Ulu's delicious arrival in her soft, warm bed beside him.

Elements of Attachment

My Dear Ho:

My first recollection of you – at my father's side in our store, in the gardens where you both meditated and exercised, in the rooms where you counted money and discussed business, or at the dinner table when you spoke my name – was of a family friend or uncle. It was much later when my father, Li, referred to you solely as "Brother Ho," that I certainly knew you were much more than his good or only business friend. Living without a mother or any other of my relatives here, I was glad to know you were my uncle.

When Li separated the business and you left our house to live in Port Maria, my father had to disclose to me that he was not sending a family member out of his house. By his business plan, you had to start another venture, but it appeared that I lost my only uncle. That was not the case, as you know quite well, for only a true and genuine friendship bonded you to my father, and no sharing of blood could have bonded you better. Yet to me, you remained my sweet uncle, Ho. And now that you ask me to marry you, a niece must undo her innermost self and make her true estate known. This is hard, perhaps impossible; for even a niece needs her robe of mystery.

If I were to marry you, I must disclose parts of my life that hitherto I regarded as secret. The difficulty in answering you earlier on your proposal of marriage was that I failed to plunge as deeply into my thoughts and feelings as I should have, to discover who I am and what I can bring to you. Now that I have begun that journey, I am closer to a reply, one that should emerge as I write to you.

My pride, Ho, and my concern for my father's estate dictate that I come to you, if ever I do, with self-sufficiency. For that reason, and to protect and increase my father's estate, I have decided to expand the business. That you know. The work is almost done. Merchants are presently stocking the shelves. With the war behind us, with a friend in Ulu, and the steep rise in that sector of my business, I see a bright future. In that regard, I shouldn't be a burden to you. To the contrary, we, if we do, would marry as equals, and I would have proven myself.

Yet, Ho, there is a deeper matter which you must know about. That is my relationship to Congo. Long before he got married, we fell in love and have kept the relationship through his marriage. His wife hates it. In some sense, I do too and would prefer I hadn't fallen into it. Nevertheless, it has given me some insights into my feelings and life that I suppose I was destined to have. I do not know fully why he does it. Perhaps I do know, but find it hard to accept. He has said so many times that he doubts his wife's affection for him. He loves her; that he has confessed. But he has expressed doubts of her sincerity towards him. I do not know why he chooses to live, loving without an equal return. It could simply be that Congo has remained married in the hope that he may yet feel Ulu's passion. Maybe he has never been loved and does not know what to expect. That I do doubt, for he has disclosed and expressed such tenderness and warmth to me, it rather confirms that he does. Still, I find it confusing what he lives for in his marriage. Of course, his daughter binds him to the relationship, but she was born long after the marriage. So after all this time, that aspect of his life is puzzling. But this letter ought to be about us, or at least me.

For me, I love Congo and have always desired him. I have never questioned his sincerity to me but have always accepted him fully. With Congo, I have never asked about tomorrow, neither have I ever doubted his steadfastness. Yet we cannot be married. I sometimes dream of returning to Hong Kong and reuniting with all my family. I know it is a dream. I do not even know if they would accept me. I doubt they would, having not known of me except by scant description and photographs from my father. Not even in my dream can I manage to make our relationship work everywhere. Yet nothing is wrong with it. It has blessed me. I have grown in it, and I do hope Congo has as well. Yet, Ho, I will not be fooled of its acceptability much farther away from my bedroom. Not even my father would have accepted it, I fear. In that, I would have to plunge alone. Should love always be so challenged, Ho? I know, with good cause, you think of me as a rebel. But Ho, I am not a rebel without *reason! Remember me so. I didn't change my father's world, but had to leave a mark on mine. For this I do not seek forgiveness, only understanding, if it may be afforded.*

Ho, it would be easy for me to say I hate. But I cannot do that and love. That is all I feel in my bones – love. And I must not direct it; rather, I must let if flow and encircle where it finds acceptance.

Perhaps I should go back to something mentioned earlier. As a child, Ho, while I learned to love, and you – through your gentleness and caring manner taught me much – you were my uncle. No, you were more than that. You were like the kitten father bought me for my seventh birthday. I loved you like I loved Dove. But when I went to high school and was apart from my father, I rebelled against him and you also. You were so much alike. I couldn't change either of you, your customs and traditions. My father joined the Catholic Church, and he gave much in time and money to it. But at home he practiced the old faith. You know, you prayed with him. Deep down he never changed, and neither have you. All I see with you is tradition and customs. At least you do not go to mass. You are firm, yet, maybe, in some ways, more practical and, therefore, more flexible. But that does not always help. It makes it harder for me to understand you, your motives, desires, and may I say, your love. And yet, you are very accepting. Maybe you have no real belief. Maybe you doubt everything, but you do not even realize it. For that, should I consider you less hypocritical than my father? How should I consider you, Ho? Like the earth, I grew from you. You seem to absorb everything, demanding nothing, and critical of none. What kind of man are you, Ho?

But, there may yet be an answer. I know why you are still my uncle. You have no passion! I mean none for me, Ho. None that will burn me and let me desire you, long for you, and care for none other. That is what I fear. Why don't I feel your flame? Where is your fire? Is your love buried so deeply beneath in fear so as to escape extinction from the wind of my own passion? Be not afraid of me, Ho. Shine, show me your fire!

In high school I had feelings. Not the same playful feeling I had for Dove. They were feelings for boys. My father knew and it almost killed him with fear, for I was impulsive; perhaps I still am. Yet, I didn't know where to place those feelings until I saw Congo. He was everything, and I couldn't deny myself. He has remained everything since then. And now, sincerely, I believe with humility, that you come to me.

Now, that I am beyond my Dove years, I want certainty! A well placed security for my feelings. I need a home with comfort and love. I know I am changing. I grew from Dove to Congo, and perhaps now, with your proposal, you seek to be placed permanently in my life. My father's will made it clear that he offered me to you as your wife. You have honored him in your life, never looking elsewhere. I have rebelled.

My love needs a home, Ho, with a fire in it. Why do you come to me if you have no passion? Why do you come to me out of custom and tradition? Or is it fear?

I cannot get any deeper. I do hope my robe is now gone, and I am naked before you. Yet, I am compelled to ask: how must a rebel undo herself and say yes to her uncle's proposal?

With passion, Ho!

And now, with all questions remaining open, but true enduring faith: Yes! Yes, Ho.

Forever yours,

Laura

Sojourn in Fellowship

M iss Hene had reason enough when she saddled Lev's horse and headed to the district of Fellowship in the parish in Portland. It was a small, isolated village high in the hills overlooking Port Antonio. It was her birthplace.

She yearned for its greenery, the never-ending footpaths up and across undulating terrain. Yet her haunting memories of childhood were not all that propelled her. She missed Lev. In her loss and grief, she felt broken and alone. Miss Hene wanted to know if anything remained of the relationship they had honed. She did not know how to let him go or how to hold onto him. Not just her memory of him, but Lev, her husband. Why didn't Asa leave him in Providence with her? And why had Congo chosen to chase other dreams? Why had the unity she'd worked for in Ama's marriage been so fleeting? So in perplexity, loss, and sorrow, Miss Hene headed for home.

Disappointment and sorrow waited in the empty village. No children greeted her; she saw none of her elders, no friends. Only the broken sign, "Heaven," hung loosely from its nail in the tree. Long ago Asa had placed it there, telling the world what he expected and hoped of his small Family.

Miss Hene surveyed the landscape. She still loved it. That alone welcomed her back home. She dismounted the horse and, removing its saddle and bridle, set it to graze. Regaining her legs, Miss Hene walked about the compound. She went to the large room called Father's House. It had been

Asa's favorite. If Lev were in Fellowship, he would lie there. Father's House was the place where bodies were stored, protected, and cared for.

Quietly, Miss Hene walked into the darkened room. Her appearance did not bother the form that bent over an unusually large box. Miss Hene realized the box was a casket. For whom she did not know.

"Come on in, Miss Hene," a voice called.

"Is that you, Nweka?"

"Yes, Miss Hene. It's me," Nweka said. She faced Miss Hene, who hastened to meet her. Nweka dropped her buffing cloth as they hugged. "I am so glad to see you, Miss Hene. At last you come to visit us!"

"Oh, Nweka! I am so glad to be home. Where is everyone?"

"Gone with Asa. He is gone to St. Thomas to gather more bodies. He wanted to take everyone with him."

"Oh, there must be a Dance there."

"Yes, there is, but even more, Miss Hene: Asa told me I should start preparing for more bodies here. He is growing this Family."

"So is that why they leave you here alone?"

"Yes. Asa told me I would soon get my first body."

"And who would show you how to care for it?"

"You, of course, Miss Hene! Asa said you would be here to show me."

"He did, ah? Well, Nweka. Here I am."

"So where do we start?"

"Right here. But tell me, Nweka, whose is this casket?"

"I do not know, Miss Hene. But since Asa told me to be ready, I had it built," Nweka said, walking towards the coffin.

"Ah! So smooth and beautiful," Miss Hene exclaimed.

"Thank you, Miss Hene. I have been polishing it for days, in and out." Miss Hene examined the coffin. It was mahogany with red, inlaid cedar and pearl ornaments.

"How lovely!" Miss Hene said. "This could easily hold two bodies."

"I thought that would be nice."

"It might be, but that is not how we keep the bodies."

"How do you do it, Miss Hene?"

"In separate compartments."

"That could be lonely."

"Not lonely, Nweka, only separated."

"Why not lonely, Miss Hene?"

"As it says in one of the good books, 'In my Father's House there are many mansions.'"

"Yes, it does say that."

"And each body is a mansion."

"That must indeed be lonely, Miss Hene!"

"The mansions are not lonely, Nweka. They lay there by themselves, but they are capable of anything."

"Of anything?"

"Yes, of any thought or action, as they are in full communication with abundant Light."

"So they can be anything, Miss Hene."

"Why? Yes, Nweka. That's why each is a mansion."

"A mansion in a house . . . how strange!"

"Yes, but each becomes so full and rich when the light comes in we have a special saying for them."

"And what is that, Miss Hene?"

"At that time we say that 'everything is in everything . . . '"

"Yes, and 'everything is complete.' I have often heard Asa say that," Nweka said. The women laughed, acknowledging that they had both shared deeply from Asa's soul.

"Ah! Now I see. But, wouldn't it be nice to share the light with someone you love. I mean really love, Miss Hene?"

"I suppose. But it is not necessary. So we keep the bodies separated, like mansions apart."

"I see," said Nweka, thinking of Esi and how some day they might still be reunited.

"So," started Nweka, "what am I to learn?"

"Nothing you don't already know, Nweka. Just remember that the bodies are like children."

"Yes. But what do they eat?"

Miss Hene went to the cupboard where the food was kept. "It's empty!" she said.

"Yes, Asa took what little there was with him."

"I see. Then let's get ready, and I will show you how to make nectar."

The women went into the kitchen and took a few pails and a crocus bag. They walked into the yard where Miss Hene noticed that her ride was missing. The saddle was still there, but the horse was gone. She had not heard it walk off. In the lateness of the hour, she took the path leading into the logwood grove. She would worry about the horse on their return.

The further the women went up the incline, the more they noticed how the scent of pollen and honey filled the air.

"There, Nweka! There is a comb. Watch me get it." Miss Hene stealthily approached the heavy beehive that hung from a nearby branch.

"It is rich," she called back to Nweka. Gingerly, Miss Hene flexed and loosened her fingers. With a swift, wiping action, Miss Hene swiped the bees from the beadlike honeycomb. Without delay, she quickly collected it in her pail and closed the tight lid. The bees in a madding rush swarmed the branch where their home once hung. Leaving them alone, Miss Hene walked back to meet Nweka. Without saying much, the women ambled down into the valley. Not long after, Miss Hene dipped her hand into the pail and called: "Come Nanny! Come Nanny!"

Soon after her shout, a goat followed by her three kids cautiously approached the women. Miss Hene took another pail from Nweka and, walking over to her goat, let it lick the honey from her hand. That having been done, Miss Hene squatted beside the mother and took its milk. Miss Hene patted the goat, saying "Thanks, Nanny. Thank you." Then she placed a small piece of honeycomb on the grass for the goat. She and her kids soon licked it up, even sharing the comb.

Further down the grassy slope, Miss Hene stopped by her old garden. There she collected the flowers and leaves from many herbs, placing them in the crocus bag. When they had gathered enough, she led Nweka back to Asa's Heaven . . . before it grew darker.

In the kitchen, Miss Hene drained the honey into a large jar. She then laid a portion of the honeycomb on the table. After carefully washing the herbs and flowers, she chopped them and the honeycomb together into a smooth, pasty substance. She then stirred the mixture with the honey.

"Fetch me the milk, Nweka."

"And add it in?"

"Yes, warm like that, blend it in."

"Like so?"

"Yes, just like that. Not too much."

"Okay."

"Good, it looks good, but keep stirring."

"All right. Let me taste it."

"No! No, Nweka, not with the herbs in."

"Why not, Miss Hene?"

"This is food for the saints only."

"You mean the bodies?"

"Yes, the bodies. It is for them alone," Miss Hene said, gazing at Nweka.

"For them only?"

"Yes, Nweka. This is nectar for the saints. It keeps them nourished and, as Asa likes to say, in Heaven."

"So, only the saints can be in Heaven, Miss Hene?"

"We are, too, Nweka. Right now, we are in Heaven," Miss Hene said as she laughed.

"Ah! What can't Asa do!" Nweka exclaimed.

"Well, we have food." Miss Hene said. "Do we have water?"

"Yes, over there." Nweka pointed to the huge red earthenware yabba in the corner. Miss Hene went there, dipped her finger and tasted it.

"Ah! Salt water," she exclaimed.

"That's what Asa asked for."

"Yes, sea water to make salt, Nweka. It is not good for the saints. It makes the skin wrinkle. We keep our saints looking like babies," Miss Hene said as she walked into the kitchen.

"Come with me, Nweka."

Miss Hene took yet two other pails and walked with Nweka to the spring. She dipped one pail into the clear water sparkling in the moonlight, then lifted it to her mouth. She drank and handed the pail to Nweka.

"Here, Nweka. Drink."

"This is home!" Miss Hene said, as Nweka drank. A flood of energy such as she had not felt since she left Fellowship filled her soul. "It is good to be back home, Nweka!" she said, stamping her foot on the grass.

The women filled their buckets with water and, on returning home, noticed that the horse had returned. This time it was attached to a buggy. The women hastened to the kitchen with the water. They went back to see who had brought the horse and buggy. Search, call as much as they wanted: no one replied. They did not see or hear a driver. The horse stood sweaty and nickering for relief.

In the back of the buggy the women found a casket. They soon separated the horse from the buggy and reversed it to the window. Carefully they slid the casket from the buggy where it lay on dried, slippery banana leaves onto the windowsill, then onto a table inside Father's House.

With great anticipation but closed eyes, Miss Hene opened the casket.

"Lev!" Nweka called.

"Shhhh! Quiet," Miss Hene whispered.

Nweka looked up.

"A saint!" Miss Hene said. "The Divine is here."

"How beautiful he looks," Nweka whispered.

Slowly, Miss Hene looked at the eyes that gazed up at her. "My love," she asked, "do you remember me?"

Lev's body gave no sign of earthly life. Yet when Miss Hene bent to kiss it, the body was warm, sweating with a soft breath very slow. She gazed at it in admiration.

"We must care for it," she said to Nweka.

"How, Miss Hene?"

"I will show you. First, we bathe, then feed it, just like a baby."

With that, Miss Hene gingerly removed the swaddled linen in which the body was clothed. With cotton dipped in the cool spring water, she wiped Lev's body gently, slowly removing the dust from his hair, his fingers and feet. Miss Hene held his hands for a long time, even pressing them against her face. The body returned only an eternal stare. Nothing of appreciation, of thankfulness, even recognition graced its handsome face.

"He is gone from me," Miss Hene said, as if asking a question. She did not want to give up seeking Lev's attention or acknowledgement. But the saintly body lay there too absorbed in its eternal rest to re-enter chaos.

Miss Hene fetched clean raiment and dressed the saint.

"With thankfulness and from the breast of the world we now nourish you, Lev," Miss Hene said.

She took the jar of nectar, and with a long wooden spoon she scooped her brew onto Lev's lips. With tender fingers, she parted them even further and placed the delicacy on his tongue. He swallowed it and for a magical moment blinked his eyes. Nweka gasped and held on to Miss Hene. A whip of a smile lit her face. She did not know what it meant or whether or not Miss Hene, busy with returning the lid to the jar, noticed. Nweka did not care. It filled her soul with delight.

Miss Hene, after feeding, cleaned his face and removed all traces of food from the casket. She looked once more at Lev's face and, kissing him as if to say goodbye, closed the casket.

For the first time in her life, Miss Hene cried from inside herself. She had cried before, but for others. This time her tears were for her own condition, which she could not bear. She, who had always given strength and hope, shrank like a helpless lump. Nothing, no thought of joy, no happiness, came to her. Shut off from the Light, she mourned. Neither did anything stop her long solemn wailing. Nweka, not knowing what to do, returned to the clear, crystal pool. There she sat naked watching the moon as she pondered. Lost in her wonder, her mind drifted to the *Any Questions* and her meeting there with Esi decades ago. Any Questions? Any . . . Questions? I wonder: what did St. John have in mind? Wasn't it also named the Sunrise Sunset Tavern? Yes! Sunrise . . . . Sunset? Why? What do they have in common? That little devil! What did he have in mind when he named it so? Could it be he was thinking of now, a time like now . . . of twilight? That's what they have in common: sunrise and sunset. They share twilight. Just like Lev and Esi, too! Yes. Esi is living in twilight! So? So I will let her know. I will name her casket Twilight! That is her home now. I will call it Twilight for her, and Esi will know.

Nweka, feeling some quiet and calm in her mind, slowly arose from the water. Clutching her clothes under her arm, she allowed the warm air to dry her skin as she walked naked back to her home. Memories and her deep longing for Esi quieted her soul.

Child Support

An uneasy peace settled within the Kendal's household. It grew from an unwritten and grudgingly agreed-to understanding that Leroy alone ruled. Nonetheless, there was peace. It first glimmered when farmer Leroy Kendal changed his strategy of control.

Instead of forcing Yoofi, Leroy maintained as much pressure as he could muster on Ama, trying to make her change. He first appealed to her sense of support for him and his bustling business; then he urged her to produce four zinc-pans of coconut oil each week. The capacity of each pan was four gallons. He showed Ama how much money would go to his savings account were she to accomplish her goals. The process was laborious, but when it seemed Ama might object, he tempted her with all the fineries their new wealth could afford her and the new apparel Yoofi would have. Leroy would provide the coconuts in the fields. Ama would transport the oil to market on Saturdays and return the proceeds of the sale to Leroy.

Leroy knew Ama couldn't accomplish the work by herself. Yoofi had refused to work with him on the farm. Leroy had abandoned force as his tool and worked to maintain a truce. Yoofi still had his original chores, first as milkman, and secondly, as escort for his siblings to and from school. These he did with some ease. For the last three years, however, he still struggled hardest with adapting to his new reality of not attending school. That often pained him.

Yoofi, scarcely fifteen years old, quickly learned to take care of the cows. He spoke to and fed the bovines fruits each morning, making pets out of them. He milked while the animals chewed. The cows came to trust him with their calves and never did they run from him as they did from Leroy. Instead, they knew their names and in the pasture followed him as Shep did.

At home Yoofi would do anything to help Ama. Leroy knew that all he had to do was set the goal to spur Ama into action; then her mule would follow. This strategy worked well. Yoofi hauled the coconuts from the fields and husked them in the yard. He broke the nuts, caught the sweet, pale juice, and saved it for sale at the *Any Questions.* With the aid of a small knife, he separated the coconut meat from the shell – a process called shelling. He then made separate stacks for shells and husks for later use as fuel.

Yoofi would hand the latex-filled coconut flesh to Ama. Her task was to grate, and that she did. Ama sat by the fire where she would grate and grate, taking no time off so as not to offend Leroy.

The shredded coconut flesh had to be water-washed two or three times so that its oil-rich milk could be extracted. Ama performed this task. After the milled flesh had been washed and squeezed dry, Yoofi carried it in buckets, one held in each hand, to a large storage bin from which he would later use portions to make pig fodder. On his return to the kitchen, Ama handed the coconut milk to Yoofi. This he boiled in huge iron pots on the fires he maintained. Subsequently, Yoofi skimmed clear oil from the caldrons, leaving a residue of gray, oily custard. Yoofi later mixed this with the processed coconut trash. Together, they would then be added to other kitchen waste and rejected farm produce to feed Leroy's ever-growing litter of pigs.

The pig business was so successful that Leroy became confused about which business was primary. He didn't care which was secondary, though. He had both and knew that they were linked by Ama's industry, which he controlled.

Yoofi found comfort and strength by working with his mother. Since his siblings were at school, he had her for himself at work and play. Play for him now was what came after lunch.

Ama, who sat for long hours in a bent, cringing position as she grated, found great relief at dinnertime. That gave her reason to stretch, change her position, stand, even to temporarily walk out of her self-imposed prison.

She pulverized the coconuts, even denying herself bathroom breaks, in attempting to appease Leroy's crazed ambition and restore order to her house. But dinnertime was her reprieve. She relished it, for it was followed by her afternoon catnaps.

Yoofi also savored the times. For as Ama lay prostrate on her back, her arms stretched above her head, he would lie beside her, cuddling his mother until he fell sleep. There he would remain slumbering until Ama would awake him for the resumption of the afternoon chores. He finished these by fetching his brothers from school and bringing home water for the ensuing day's work.

But there was something that of late was taking a sliver of time between the end of Yoofi's work and his going for his siblings. Whether it was the expression of joy that a day's work had just ended, or simply to escape to a place of peace and inner fulfillment, Yoofi didn't know. What he knew and felt was the urge to dance, and that he did. Ever since he had received by dream his first lesson at dancing, he had privately practiced it. Yoofi feeling strong and confident, he took his dancing public after first showing it to Ama. She rejoiced that Yoofi had found something for himself, an outlet, like school, as she interpreted it. So Yoofi would dance and dance, and the absence of music didn't delay his steps either. He jumped, jumped so high, always landing on time, for Ama would keep the beat with her bobbing head and stamping heels. Yoofi would dance! And when he stopped, he would rush to Ama. She would caress and kiss him, and praise him not just for bringing hope and laughter to her but because her precious Yoofi had found himself.

Despite Ama's joy with Yoofi's dancing, she pondered still who had been his teacher, if he had learned it at the *Any Questions* or if, perchance, Miss Hene had taught him.

In the meantime, Miss Hene returned from Fellowship. Soon after her arrival, she invited Congo to Barton House where she told him all that she had seen. She brought back love from the Family in Portland and the news that Asa still hoped and expected Congo to blaze the path for which he was prepared. Even though it appeared to the Family in Portland that Congo had strayed, Congo still believed he would return to the plan Asa had laid for him.

This news Congo shared in some unhappiness with the apprehensive Ulu, at Jacks River. She began by listening attentively but soon offered only discouragement and spoke disparagingly of his Family. Moreover,

Ulu reminded Congo of his commitments to her, their marriage, Princess, and their growing business. It didn't bother Ulu either to sweeten her statements with hugs and kisses, to talk of his growing share in the profits of the business.

On Boxing Day, Miss Hene and Kwame visited the Kendals. They would, as usual, exchange presents. Instinctively, the children knew which toys belonged to them or, more accurately, which ones they would play with first. Guns, either designed for cowboys or the European theatre, were well received. Firecrackers, bright red fire engines, spitfire airplanes, and balloons followed in that order.

Leroy waited for Miss Hene's visit to distribute the gifts he had bought. He gave the younger boys what they had asked for: trucks, trains, jeeps and, yes, guns, again. He had each child come to him, starting with the youngest. Leroy made his presentation, watching the glee in their faces, remembering how it had been for him. The largest box remained unopened. It was for Yoofi. Neither he nor Ama expected such a huge present.

The box was dressed in red ribbons with Yoofi's name all over it, something not done for the other children. Maybe that was Leroy's way of saying thanks for all the labor Yoofi had contributed. Miss Hene did not know what to make of it. Ama surmised it was a peace offering. It was more than that, much more! With the box finally opened, a large naked doll with the face and torso of a budding teen-age girl fell to the floor! The women looked away in disgust. The younger boys pointed and laughed. Leroy cheered.

It took Yoofi a few seconds to decipher what it was, but he did. Immediately, he lay beside it and the music started. With the softness and ease of a seasoned maestro, Yoofi raised the semi-flaccid form from the floor and started to dance with it. Miss Hene didn't quite understand at first. The music got louder and Yoofi danced. Smiles, then tears, came to Ama's face as her head slowly bobbed. Miss Hene watching, started to stamp her heels, too. Yoofi danced and, with a tormented face, Leroy shouted, "Damn you, Yoofi! Get out!" pointing to the open door. Maybe Yoofi did not hear Leroy, for the music didn't stop. It didn't stop: the music grew louder. Yoofi did what he knew. He danced.

Miss Hene looked ashamedly at Leroy and, taking Kwame by the hand, led him onto the floor and started dancing with him. Soon the other children started to dance, the doll and Yoofi taking center stage. Ama looked at Leroy as if to ask: This dance, please?

Leroy, feeling shame and defeat, grabbed his hat in a warlike gesture and marched out of the room and headed to the *Any Questions,* not remembering it would be closed on Boxing Day.

Before anyone could make full sense of the proceedings, Ama looked around in bewilderment. She felt utterly helpless. Trying to deflect shame and guilt, still attempting to justify the events, Ama asked, "How do you know that's not the way it was intended to be?"

No one cared to respond.

It had been planned that food, drink, and recorded music bought on her honeymoon would continue the revelry later at Miss Hene's house, where the Family and Shep had planned to pass the remainder of the week.

That, however, was not to be. Kwame complained of an aching stomach, and so Miss Hene, Yoofi, and Shep accompanied him home. Yoofi hurried back home with Shep to play with his doll and dance.

Leroy sought comfort in ale and strange, meaningless tales from Puncus St. John.

Masks

Divine was a man with an extraordinarily large and open heart, especially to married men. He had never been married because he never understood the politics of it and, being careful not to cause pain where none existed, thought it best to leave marriage alone. Whenever he dared to ponder the institution, he considered it for the brave, the fool, or folk sufficiently blessed to be both. He made one exception though: marriage as a means for rearing children. In that case, he praised the institution, surmising that only the brave or fool, or those sufficiently blessed to be both would ever dare to raise children without it.

Marriage was not the only thing he considered distasteful. On societal issues Divine took no side so strongly that one could label him by it. When first he crept into Providence, he was referred to as "Hi-man." He lived alone and earned his livelihood by talking about the future and what it held for people, Providence, and the world. This earned him the nickname of Prophet or Prophet St. John. His opinions took the form of stories and were eagerly sought.

When Divine opened the Tavern, he served only vegetarian food and herb in his private smoking room. He allowed his hair to grow and he never shaved. As his life became marked with the learnedness of a Pharisee, he was celebrated kindly as Nazarite St. John. Soon, however, Puncus realized that the locals expected alcoholic beverages to be served at any respectable tavern. He started serving white rum. This didn't do. Most preferred a beer or ale with their meal and then a smoke with dessert: so he added drinks to his menu, still warning against their use. St. John never touched the bottle. For his abstinence and view of the spirits, he was named the Divine. This last name stuck, but the other nicknames never quite faded. He didn't care, but responded to whatever he was called, refusing to be labeled.

Divine never turned away anyone in need. He knew that custom demanded that *Any Questions* should be closed during some holidays. Boxing Day was one such honored holiday at the tavern. On that day, the *Any Questions* was closed, truly closed at the front. For a few regulars who understood the rules – that St. John's home would always be opened to friends – the back door was never closed.

In his rage, Leroy forgot. He returned home. Knowing he couldn't face the merriment inside, he dallied outside where Shep rejected him. Leroy endeavored to teach the dog a final lesson, then returned to the *Any Questions.*

Leroy slowly unlatched the back door and, hesitatingly, moved to his favorite table.

St. John was there, pensive, looking through the window at the golden haze of the moon.

"Is that you, Leroy?"

"Yes, Divine. What a night this has been!"

"Do you mean the moon, Leroy?"

"I mentioned the night, Divine."

"Yes, you did. The moon is nice tonight, though. I have been watching it."

"Damn the moon, Divine. Let me have a double white . . . no rocks."

"You got it, Leroy."

As Leroy guzzled, Divine watched the changing expressions on his face. He saw an ocean of blackness, of unspeakable fear, guilt, and weakness. Divine dared not mention it, for fear of its volatility, especially with the rum. Puncus Divine had seen Leroy at the *Any Questions* many times. In fact, of late, Leroy had become his best customer. His interest, however, was gambling with cards or dominoes; he had become expert at both. Leroy gambled heavily and won big. That night he had peculiar expressions that bothered Divine. Puncus observed in silence, watching the moon, waiting for a flow of words from Leroy. At last it came.

"Damned dog!" he muttered and banged the glass with sufficient noise to get Divine's attention.

"Which dog?"

"Uh! Good question, Divine. There are three of them, and sometimes I do not know which is worse."

"I didn't know you had three dogs, Leroy. Shep is the only one I know of."

"Well, there are two more, and maybe it's better they go nameless."

"Ah. Well, whenever you wish, let me know which one you mean, Leroy."

"Shep. That's the one. Damn untrainable dog."

"What makes you say that, Leroy? I see him going like father and son with Yoofi."

"That's the other one you better not mention, Leroy. I am here to get them all out of my head."

"You mean you have trouble with Yoofi, too, Leroy?"

"Yoofi's got his own troubles, St. John. I go crazy keeping him straight."

"So, why not just let him be?"

"What, so he can grow up to be like . . ."

"You mean me, Leroy."

Leroy didn't reply immediately. Puncus St. John looked at him, then at the moon.

"You can say it if that's what you mean, Leroy. You are safe here. Yoofi cannot hear you from here."

"Damn you, Divine. Don't play games with me."

"What do you want of me, Leroy?"

"I want another drink! Pour me another, will you?"

"Yes, Leroy, but you know I preach against that spirit. It is not good, Leroy."

"You preach against it. I preach against it, too, Divine."

"Yes, you do."

"And you sell and I buy."

"Yes, you are right."

"So what's your question, Divine?"

"No questions, Leroy. You mentioned a dog, and things have been running loose since."

"I did. Yes, and I had to hang it!"

"Hang the dog? God! Which one?"

"The dog, dog! Shep! I hung the dog!"

"You hung the little doggie? My God! Poor little doggie. What will Yoofi do?"

"Never mind Yoofi!"

"Well, the other dog is dead."

Leroy looked at Puncus St. John. "Yes, dead, St. John. It's my dog, and I had to kill it."

"Whatever for, Leroy?"

"I have too many damn disobedient dogs around me."

"So you went and hung one of them?"

"Yes. It's not my fault either, I tell you. I have had that dog since it was a pup. I trained him, fed him, until that Yoofi came along. Then he took the dog over and completely turned it against me."

"In what way, Leroy?"

"Imagine this, St. John. I went to scold Yoofi, teach him a lesson . . . which is a father's duty, right? And Shep attacked me. Me, its master!" Leroy was beating his chest. "The dog attacked me. And besides that, it will not even do what I order it to. You see, that Yoofi is a no good! And the dog is totally ungrateful. So he got his right deserve. Don't you think, Puncus?"

"You hung the dog!"

"I hung the dog. Yes, St. John, I did. And stop repeating that, like it's something bad. It had to be punished for disobedience. It's that simple."

"You hung the dog!"

"Yes, Puncus Divine. Shep is no ordinary dog. Before this, he wouldn't stay home at nights and guard the house. He just kept roaming the streets at nights, looking for bitches, no doubt. I would feed him and ordered him to stay home. Sometimes he would. But if I hid and caught sight of him running out after he thought I was gone, I would grab and beat him and order him to stay and watch the house. After a proper thrashing, he would stay home, at least for a while. You do not know that dog, Puncus, and how Yoofi has just confused him. Just imagine, when I leave here and go home, the dog would still be out, later than me! Or that little rascal would sneak up behind me from wherever he roamed and meet me at the gate as if he was always home. It was of no use trying to train that dog, so I gave up on it, just like I give up on Yoofi."

"You gave up on the dog!"

"Yes, Puncus. I even had Yoofi hold him while I castrated him. I thought that would help, Nazarite, but it was a waste of my time. I thought that would make the dog stay home and do as he was told. But in a few days, the dog was gone again! So this time, I hung him."

"You castrated the dog!"

"Stop saying that, Puncus Divine! It is disgusting."

"And if I don't?"

"Well, if you were my dog, I would teach you a lesson!" Leroy laughed.

"You castrated and hung your dog? I can't believe that, Leroy. And such a nice little puppy!"

"Shep was no pup, Nazarite, and you know it. And don't make is sound so hard, hanging a dog. All I had to do was get a heavy, seven-foot guava stick, place it in the 'Y' of two branches in the grapefruit tree, put a slip knot about the dog's neck, pull the dog by the rope over the stick, and let it hang there. I didn't even have to kill him. And I will never even remove the stick after Yoofi buries the body."

"Why not, Leroy? Why won't you remove the guava stick?"

"I will never remove it, Divine. And I will tell you; Yoofi will not remove it, either."

"Why, Leroy?"

"I have two reasons, Divine. The first is: if Yoofi moves it, I kill him. Second: because each time Yoofi looks at it I want him to remember a lesson on obedience and what might befall him."

"Are you threatening Yoofi, Leroy?"

"No, Puncus Divine! No, not at all. I will leave the stick there as a warning and a lesson to him. He may get the message one day and change. You know what I mean?"

"You know, Leroy, while you drank here, Shep would lie in the back, in the cemetery. He would follow you here, and after you left, Shep would keep his distance but follow you home, Leroy. Did you know that? Sometimes I would even feed Shep and throw him a crocus bag to lie on until you were ready to go home. The dog loved you, Leroy. Shep loved you. And you hang the dog? You castrate and hang the dog?"

There was a long, very long pause in which St. John wanted to question Leroy on his motives, how he thought Yoofi would react, even later in life when he was old and strong enough. He didn't, however, and sought instead to pacify his customer, remaining silent.

"Okay, Puncus, if you say so. But I take it, you do not approve."

"Killing is all right with me, depending on the situation, Leroy. I guess if that's what you are asking about, we kill all the time. There is a war. Well, it's coming to an end anyway, and that's all about killing."

"The war is over there, and as far as I am concerned, it works for me. I am talking about Shep. You must learn to stay with the subject, Puncus."

"Yes, you are right. We are talking about Shep. You hung the dog!"

"I hung the dog. Yes, yes, yes!"

"At night."

"Yes, at night."

"Why not choke it to death during the day?"

"What's the difference, Nazarite?"

"To me or to the dog?"

"What's the matter?"

"Well, to me it does not matter. I am still alive."

"And for the dog?"

"Speaking as a dog, Leroy, I would prefer my owner to strangle me with my face turned to him, in the day."

"Why, Divine?"

"I suppose I would know in the end he didn't really love me. But he could see in my eyes, I still loved him."

"And if there was no love?"

"Then it wouldn't matter, Leroy. That is, if there were not love at all, none on either side, Leroy. But I suppose if I still loved him, he would know, and that is all I would care to show."

Leroy sipped in silence.

"What will you do with the body, Leroy?"

"I will tell Yoofi to bury it."

"Bury your dog?"

"He took him over and turned him against me. They deserve each other. But not only that, Puncus, Yoofi must be taught a lesson. I hope he learns the lesson of obedience from this. And another thing, too: just who is the man in my house?"

"Well, I suppose if there is some doubt, he may . . ."

"May what, St. John?"

"Know who is the man when he buries that dog!"

"I am damn sure he will, and maybe that will save his skin, sooner or later."

"Yes, I have been saying that for so long. Pity it takes this for him to know."

"Yes, St. John. It sure is a pity."

Silence brewed.

"Would you like something to eat, Leroy?"

"No, Puncus. And this talk has been helpful." He looked at the old clock on the wall. He was never certain of the time it kept. The minute hand would fall forward after it indicated the hour and remain at the half past hour until it was seconds from the following hour, then it would spring to life and join the hour hand in striking precisely on time.

"It soon will be morning," Puncus St. John said.

"Good, they must be gone now."

"Who, Leroy?"

"Miss Hene and her flock."

"There is no need to speak of her like that, Leroy."

"What, does she mean something to you, Divine?"

"Not to me in person. No, but we have been talking. She has got something about her. She's a real woman, I tell you, Leroy."

"I just wish I could have had something like that, and not that dog Congo tied me to."

"Well, well. All you speak of tonight are dogs, Leroy."

"Yes, it does seem that way, doesn't it, Puncus? Maybe they fill my days."

"Sad, sad. And look, things could have been otherwise."

"Yes, only if they listened."

"Yes, Leroy. But maybe they did!"

"What's that, Divine?"

"Maybe it's best leaving it alone."

"Okay. But tell me, what have you and Miss Hene been talking about, St. John?"

"We are just talking for now, Leroy, all about Family things."

"You mean Kumina?"

"Yes, that and other things. How did you know?"

"This girl and me, I was supposed to marry her. I belonged to the Family in Galina. She walked out on me after I beat her, beat her badly. Then I left Galina and came here."

"I did hear mention of that, Leroy. But that was long ago. Maybe you should get back in the Family, Leroy."

"I got what I wanted out of it. That's not for me anymore, Divine. You see: a house, land, everything I ever wanted."

"You make that very clear, Leroy."

"The only thing on my mind now, Divine, is to get rid of those damn disobedient dogs, and live in peace. And maybe . . . who knows where Patsy Blue might be right now? She may have learned, after all."

"But you have two boys of your own, Leroy."

"Yes, they are good children. If anything goes wrong with Ama or if she leaves, I will keep them and get someone to care for them."

"Oh, so you have it all *worked out*, it seems to me, Leroy."

"I wouldn't say worked out, St. John, but working on it," Leroy said, draining his glass as he prepared to leave.

"Plan your steps right, Leroy. And if you do it with love, you will have nothing to fear."

"I never fear! Leroy never fears, Divine," he laughed, walking to the back door.

"Good then, Leroy."

He left like a wanderer in the night. Puncus Divine watched him hobble along the road to his house alone under the murky haze of an aging moon. This time Leroy was really alone. There was not the customary distance traced by the lumbering Shep, trailing after his beloved master.

Howling Dogs

The merriment had died in the house by the time Leroy arrived home. Excitement still lingered, however, in Yoofi's heart. Never before had he felt so secure, protected, and wanted. The two women whom he most adored gave him the acceptance he longed for and Yoofi took that and his doll to bed with him. The other siblings were fast asleep then. They had played themselves so tired that sleep was all they could do.

Yoofi heard each of Leroy's footsteps from the moment he unlocked the screeching gate and entered the yard. His steps were not brisk, but followed an unusual course into the house. Yoofi listened. At times, Shep greeted Leroy at the gate, then followed his master up to the door. That didn't happen.

As soon as Leroy was in bed, Yoofi crept out with food to search for his friend in the darkness. He was not in the yard. Yoofi crept under the house and was glad to notice the curled up mass in the bedding. He questioned why Shep didn't wag his tail or even raise his head to greet him. Of course they had slept there together many times. Undaunted, Yoofi crawled to the bedding where Shep lay. He touched Shep and wondered why he felt so cold and still. Yoofi pulled the animal into his lap and, try as he liked, he couldn't awaken the dog. Yoofi felt a rope around the dog's neck. Realizing the animal was dead, he bellowed a howl of despair and death so loud that Ama was soon under the house with him.

She knew instantly what had happened. She knew that Leroy killed Shep. Without delay, she shouted, "Run, Yoofi, run!"

Yoofi came from beneath the building and stood up, defiantly facing the edifice. He wanted to enter it and challenge Leroy. That would have been a grave mistake, for that was exactly what Leroy expected, and he was well prepared to destroy Yoofi in a pretext of self-defense.

"Run, Yoofi, run!" Ama called again, and Yoofi, not fearing Leroy's wrath, walked out of the yard and down toward the pond. The hazy moon guided him to Lev's tomb. Under the pale light, he stripped himself bare and lay on Lev's grave where he cried himself to sleep.

Ama, not knowing what to do, awoke Dean and Agu and took them to Miss Hene's, seeking safer shelter.

The following morning, Yoofi awoke earlier than normal. It was hard for him to sleep late on the cold slab of concrete. He got up and returned to his house. The first thing he saw was the heavy guava stick that had killed Shep still braced in the tree. He walked to it to remove it and cut it into firewood. Not knowing why, he felt restrained and left it there, hoping no one would ever remove it, letting it serve as a permanent reminder to Leroy of his cruelty. He did notice that neither his mother nor his siblings were at the house.

Yoofi's next task was to place Shep's body into a crocus bag and take three extra bags with him, along with a spade and mattock. These he would get from Leroy's work shed.

On Yoofi's returned to the intended gravesite, he stopped by Miss Hene's in search of his mother. Kwame was already awake and had joined the conversation between Ama and Miss Hene. Kwame looked out the window and saw Yoofi with his tools and crocus bags over his shoulder.

"What's Yoofi doing so early all by himself?" Kwame asked the women.

"Isn't he your best friend?" Miss Hene asked. "Why not go and see what he is up to, Kwame?"

Kwame really didn't need his mother's instruction. He had already fled the table.

"Yoofi!" yelled Kwame. "Wait for me!"

Yoofi turned to see Kwame running to meet him.

"What's in your bag, Yoofi, and where are you going?"

"Kwame. You really do not want to know this."

"Tell me anyway. What is it, Yoofi?"

Yoofi removed the yoke from his shoulders and, on exposing the contents on the grass, said, "See. It is Shep!"

"Shep? Shep! He is dead, Yoofi!"

"Yes. That's why I am going to bury him."

"Bury him? Did you talk to Miss Hene about it?"

"No, Kwame. And no need to. Shep is dead, right?"

"Yes, but Miss Hene knows how to bury. She buried my father, you know."

"Yes, she and Uncle Congo. I know all about it."

"So, how come you are burying Shep by himself?"

"He won't be by himself. I will dig a grave beside Lev's grave."

"I tell you, Yoofi. You should ask Miss Hene about it."

"It's all right, Kwame. Do you want to come with me?"

"Yes. But do not put Shep back into that bag. It does not look right. Let me see." Kwame hesitated. "I tell you what, Yoofi. Lay him on the bag. Then you can hold the two corners and go ahead. I will hold the other two corners and follow you."

"Okay, Kwame."

So, the friends carried Shep down the hill and approached the pond.

"Go across, Yoofi."

"He will get wet, Kwame."

"We could hold the bag high."

"Okay."

As the boys neared the far side of the pond, close to the intended grave, a weight greater than any they had ever felt descended on the crocus bag, dragging it and the dog to the bottom of the pond. The boys stumbled and their cargo slipped. In vain they searched for the dog, until, in frustration, they crawled out of the pond to find Shep lying beside Lev's grave.

With astonishment the lads eyed each other, not saying anything, Yoofi started digging the grave. It did not take long in the loose marl to find a suitable depth for Shep. Yoofi started to drag his dog into the grave.

"Not so, Yoofi. Let's put him onto the crocus bag, wrap his body with it and lay him in."

"Okay."

Try as they might, the lads could not move Shep's dead body onto the bag. They gestured, and tried, until at last Yoofi said, "Let's get rope."

The boys hurried from the pond, making sure this time not to walk across it but, instead, to go around the pond and up the hill to Miss Hene's kitchen shed. There they found a suitable rope. They hurried back to the pond, only to find that Shep had gone and the grave was neatly covered with flowers on it. Across the grave, and on top of the flowers, lay the same stick from which Shep had been hung.

The friends looked at each other, then at the grave, and started to run. This time they would make a short cut of the pond, running across the shallows and up the hill into Miss Hene's arms. But before they knew it, down in the pond they fell, entangled with each other.

"Get off of me!" Kwame yelled.

"Let me go!" shouted Yoofi.

"What's bothering you, boys?"

Astonished, the lads looked up to see Miss Hene smiling at them. She took them by their hands and helped them out of the water. In doing so, Miss Hene stumbled and fell into the pond. She stood up, wet and soggy, with her waterlogged hat drooping onto her face.

Feeling somewhat safer, yet embarrassed and nervous, the friends crossed the pond, leaving Miss Hene behind. At least, so they thought.

"I have Leroy's work to do." Yoofi said with sudden urgency.

"Come to the house and get breakfast before you go. It is still early, Yoofi."

With brevity, the boys reached the house to find Miss Hene in the kitchen with Ama, still locked in conversation.

"Mumma Jesus! She is dry!" Kwame cried, as he fainted in a limp heap before them.

Ama bent to lift him up.

"He is learning, Ama. He will soon be all right," Miss Hene said.

"Come, Yoofi," Miss Hene called. "Drink some cerrosy tea before you go again, Yoofi."

"No thanks, Miss Hene. I can't take anything now."

"I understand, Yoofi. We will talk when you get back."

"All right Miss Hene. Okay then. But is Kwame going to be all right?"

"Yes, yes, Yoofi. Just you hurry on and get your chores done. Kwame will be fine."

Looking one last time he saw his mother take her seat again beside Miss Hene. Yoofi eyed Kwame with a long, ponderous gaze, wondering what had happened at the pond and now with Kwame. Yoofi shook his head in amazement and left the house.

His morning's chores still lay ahead of him. These Yoofi decided to do differently. Before, Yoofi took only one bag full of fruits to the cows. That morning, he took three full crocus bags of fruit, one for each milking cow, and another for Bullcow.

His approach to the pen was less casual than usual. He gave the fruits to each cow and, as she ate, he released her calf so it could suckle. Normally, he would milk the cows and distribute the milk to customers. This time he didn't. He watched the calves suckle, smiling as they did. He patted the cows, rubbing them all over. In the meantime, he said good-bye to them.

After the calves were done feeding, Yoofi opened the gates and led the cattle into the high grass where he left them. He then went to the pen in which Bullcow was sequestered and, upon opening the gate, led the wretched bovine out and in pursuit of the cows grazing in the meadows.

Yoofi smiled as he watched Bullcow hurry down the slope. He then followed the path back to Miss Hene's house and knocked on the door. He was glad when it was Kwame and not Miss Hene who opened it for him.

While Yoofi tended his morning duties, the women spoke and cried. Miss Hene devised a plan requesting the Family presence at Barton House where they would discuss Yoofi's future. Yoofi, of course, would remain with Miss Hene until his fate was decided.

With his house abandoned except for his own lonely presence, Leroy dined at the *Any Questions*. There, Puncus dissuaded Leroy from going to Barton House. Strangely, Leroy obeyed.

Mantle of Motherhood

By suppertime that same Friday, everyone from the Kendal household except Leroy had gathered at Barton House. The boys shared perplexing stories about Shep while they remained in Kwame's bedroom. They were not afraid of Miss Hene, but they were not sure what had happened. Not knowing what questions to ask, they stayed away from their mothers.

In the kitchen Miss Hene and Ama talked endlessly while Miss Hene finished her cooking, finally luring the boys. Kwame was the first to creep from the safety of his bedroom.

"I called all of you for dinner, Kwame," Miss Hene said to her son. "Where are the others?"

"In my room, Miss Hene. They want me to bring their dinner to them."

"Ha! I asked all of you to come to dinner."

When Kwame did not respond, Miss Hene continued, "So please go and get your brothers. All right, Kwame?"

"Yes, Miss Hene," the reluctant lad said and left the room.

"Miss Hene!" exclaimed Ama. "When did you call the boys to dinner? We have been here laboring. I did not hear your call."

"I did not call you, Ama. I called the boys."

"I mean, Miss Hene, I did not hear a sound from you."

"They heard and that's enough!"

Soon Kwame, followed by Yoofi, Dean, and Agu, entered the kitchen. They each took their accustomed seats. Yoofi and Agu sat on each side of Ama with Miss Hene sitting between Dean and Kwame at the small, circular wooden table.

Miss Hene brought a steaming bowl of spicy mixed vegetables and set it at the center of the table. She then set loaves of simple warm bread, seasoned coconut oil and hot pickle sauce on the table. An appetizing essence soon filled the air. The boys looked at the food, then up at Miss Hene, and down at the food again. Ama looked at Miss Hene, then at the boys. Miss Hene placed a small amount on her plate, gave thanks, and started eating. Still, that did not break the stalemate. Food did not entice the hungry, it seemed.

"Kwame," Miss Hene summoned, "Let's bring grace to the table and eat."

"But, we are not hungry, Miss Hene."

"And you, Yoofi?"

"Were you at the pond this morning, Miss Hene?" Yoofi asked after some deliberation.

"Yes, of course. I saw you there. Don't you remember?"

Yoofi looked at Kwame, then at Miss Hene, and asked, "But Miss Hene. We left you at the pond dripping wet, came back here, and saw you talking with Aunt Ama. And you were bramble dry!"

"Yes, you did, Yoofi."

"And where is Shep?" Yoofi asked.

"So is that it, why no one is hungry?" Miss Hene asked.

It was Ama who broke the silence. "Miss Hene, when did you leave me in the kitchen and go to the pond?"

"She must be a witch!" Agu said.

"And what did you do to Shep?" Yoofi asked with returning confidence.

"Yes. Tell us, Miss Hene," Dean, siding with Yoofi, asked. "Where is Shep?"

"Shep is where he is," Miss Hene said. "But if I call him, he will come."

"Who are you, Miss Hene?" Dean asked.

Ama looked at her son. Still steeped in her own suffering, she appeared lost, distant from the conversation. She liked the interest the boys showed in Miss Hene's talk; it did not cease to bemuse her.

"Your Mother," Miss Hene said after much hesitation.

"Ama is my mother," Dean protested.

"I am your great Mother, and Ama's Mother, too."

Interrupting the silence, Yoofi asked, "Where did you come from, Miss Hene?"

"Ah! I am from the Great Light, Yoofi. I am here as your Mother. So, like the Light, I can be in many places."

Silence returned to the kitchen.

"All at the same time, Miss Hene?"

"Yes, Yoofi. In our Family that is called Splitting."

"But all of you were here with Ama."

"Yes, Yoofi. It is not my body that Splits. It's what's inside me. It goes where I point it and makes things happen."

The heavy silence returned.

"It was a busy morning for me, Yoofi," Miss Hene laughed. "I helped you at the pond. I spoke to Ama, and I planned a Dance with Puncus," Miss Hene said with great emphasis on the word "Dance."

"A Dance?" Ama asked.

"Yes, Ama?"

"Why, Miss Hene? You know I can hardly even walk."

"Because you are coming into yourself, Ama, and that calls for a Dance."

"Me, Miss Hene?" Ama asked placing her palm over her heart, "Me coming into myself. What do you mean, Miss Hene?"

"You will be going through changes, Ama, big changes. But at the end you will join us in the Light."

The children looked at each other. Kwame looked at Ama wondering what was to become of her. Yoofi motioned as if to protect his mother and asked, "So what kind of Dance is this, Miss Hene?"

"A Kumina Dance, Yoofi. That's the way we danced in your house at Christmas. Do you remember?"

"Yes, Miss Hene, that was nice!"

"Well, that is one of our Family Dances."

Again silence hovered. Ama remained with her curious smile. With calm returning to the table Miss Hene asked, "So should we eat now?"

"You never gave us only green leaves to eat, Miss Hene," Kwame said.

"Yes, Kwame. But today is different. Today we become a Family, and we mark the day with a special meal."

"Why don't you give us meat?" Agu asked.

"Because today is special," Miss Hene said again. "So we give praise."

"I still like meat, Miss Hene," Agu said.

"Yes, you do, Agu. But today we eat only what the Light has nourished – green leaves, grain and fruits – to show we are connected to the earth like plants."

"Cows live on the earth, Miss Hene," Yoofi said.

"Yes, but they are not like plants. Plants are connected to it."

"I like yam and meat with my dinner," Ago inserted.

"Yes, we all like yam. But today we do not eat anything that comes from under the earth either. We eat only what is connected to the soil and gives thanks to the Light."

"Oh! Like leaves, Miss Hene?" Yoofi asked.

"Yes, today we are humble like leaves and give thanks to the Light just like leaves. This shows we are connected to the earth and to the Light."

"So you can be everywhere like the Light, Miss Hene?"

Miss Hene laughed. "Not everywhere, Yoofi, but many places. I can Split and be in many places. So today we become a Family of that Light, never to die."

"Like Shep?" Yoofi asked.

"Yes, like Shep, Yoofi. Shep and I go back a long way. But I am here as Mother."

"As Mother? Asa is your Father!" protested Yoofi.

"Yes, he is my Father. But in another world, I am much older than Asa. And so is Shep. Asa needed help, so we came back to work with him."

"Shep is just a dog, and you know that!" Agu protested.

Miss Hene leaned back in her chair and laughed. Just then, Shep trotted into the kitchen and, with his front paws on Miss Hene's lap, he licked her face."

"You have work to do, Shep," she rebuked the animal while kissing his snout. Shep walked to where Yoofi sat. Yoofi knelt and patted his dog and hugged him. Before Ama could offer him food, Shep moved toward the door and soon disappeared.

Silence brewed.

Kwame thought of asking about his father, but was too nervous to. He looked at Miss Hene.

"Lev has another purpose in another place, Kwame." Miss Hene said.

"Where Asa is?"

"Yes, Kwame, Lev serves where Asa is."

"And you, Miss Hene? How do you serve?" Yoofi asked.

"As your Mother, Yoofi, the Mother of this Family. Have you for-gotten?"

"So, why don't you help Mammy?"

"She has all the help she needs, Yoofi. Ama simply had to finish what she had to do. But that's all over now. After all, she asked for it," Miss Hene laughed.

"Do you mean she does not have to grate any more coconuts, Miss Hene?" Yoofi asked, feeling some joy for his mother.

"That's not mainly what I meant, Yoofi."

"So what did you mean, Miss Hene?" Kwame asked.

"Patience, children. With patience everything will come to light. And, moreover, it's Ama who should be asking," Miss Hene said smiling.

Dean looked at Ama's pondering face, wondering why she did not pick up on Miss Hene's invitation. Maybe, he thought, it was because questions from the table seemed ceaseless.

"And Leroy, Miss Hene?"

"He is lost, Yoofi."

"My father is not lost!" Agu shouted.

"He will be home tonight, Agu. But in another way he is lost, if even for just a while. But still, we must learn from him."

Miss Hene went silent and, focusing her eyes as if in deep contem-plation, continued, "But it is Ulu that makes me sad. She does not even take the time to listen . . . not to me, not Asa, no one!"

"Then why not talk to Congo?" Ama asked.

"I have, Ama," Miss Hene replied. "He hears all right, but he does what Ulu wants. Why? I hope he knows!"

"Can I be like you, Miss Hene?"

"In what way, Yoofi?"

"Well, can I be in many places at once?"

"You can be, Yoofi. But not while you are questioning it."

"Oh!"

"Did you question it when you learned to Dance?"

"No! Of course not, Miss Hene. I like to Dance," Yoofi said.

"Then, when you accept it, you will find yourself Splitting."

"Oh!"

"And, by the way, you should stop Dancing for money at the *Any Questions*, Yoofi."

"But they pay me, Miss Hene."

"I know they pay you, Yoofi. But we do not Dance for money. We Dance to give praise and to express. And Divine knows that. He just allows too many things!"

No one spoke. Miss Hene looked at Ama. She was silent with thought and question.

"And," Miss Hene continued her conversation in a rather absent-minded manner, "Divine is hearing better now. He is laughing at what I am saying."

"He is laughing?" Dean asked.

"Yes. And he says, 'Ama, you will have a good Dance.'"

"Tell him thanks for me, Miss Hene."

"He heard you!"

"Maybe we should eat now," Ama said.

"Yes," said Miss Hene. "Let's just give thanks to the Light, first."

Miss Hene stood up and, gesturing that each hand be held, she connected her small Family. They gave thanks for the understanding of who they were now and were to become.

In silence they ate and pondered.

Yoofi's Smile

Yoofi's night was restless. Early the following bright, sunlit morning, he walked down to the tamarind tree where he liked to muse. It was the place where he'd been taught to Dance in his dream. He had never forgotten that first lesson. He now returned there by himself just to lie on his stomach and pluck leaves of grass as his mind roamed.

He was not sure what bothered him that Saturday morning, or why he wanted to pluck grass blades. Maybe he thought it would sooth his weary, meditative mind.

Yoofi was alarmed when, on reaching the tree, he saw Miss Hene sitting there. She greeted him: "Searching for tamarinds, Yoofi?"

"What are you doing here, Miss Hene!"

"We need to talk about school, Yoofi. So I called you here," she said, offering him a handful of tamarinds.

"School, Miss Hene? This is Saturday. We do not have school today."

"Yes, Yoofi. I know," Miss Hene laughed. "You do not have school anymore."

"Yes. I didn't even remember that. So why do you want to talk to me about school, Miss Hene?"

"Because, Yoofi, Headmaster Forbes is home this morning. And I was just thinking how nice it would be for him to hear your apology."

"What! What, Miss Hene?"

"Your apology to the Headmaster, Yoofi."

"I did not do anything wrong to him."

"Is that so, Yoofi?"

"Yes, Miss Hene. I have not seen Headmaster Forbes since . . ."

"Since . . . ?"

"Oh!" Yoofi paused abruptly.

"Since when, Yoofi?"

"But he . . . he is the one that . . . he took away my . . . He should apologize to *me*, Miss Hene."

Miss Hene did not respond.

"All right, Miss Hene. I see what you mean. I will apologize to him."

"Good for you, Yoofi. You see, I am thinking you may be leaving Providence. And you want to depart with a clean slate. I want to help you do that, so when you are gone you will be at peace with yourself."

"Okay, Miss Hene. I will tell Headmaster Forbes I am sorry for what I said to him."

The lad sat facing Miss Hene, expecting that she would be happy with him. Instead, tears rolled down her face.

"Why are you crying, Miss Hene?"

"Because, Yoofi, I expect so much from you."

"I will apologize to the Headmaster, Miss Hene."

"I know you will, Yoofi. But that is not the end of it."

"What more do you want me to do, Miss Hene?"

"Well, Yoofi, there is Leroy."

"What about him?"

"He has been mean to you, Yoofi."

"Yes, Miss Hene. And all I want to do is forget him and live my life in peace."

"How can you forget him, Yoofi?"

There was a silence. "Every time he comes to my mind I just think of something else, Miss Hene, something else like Providence Pond."

"Oh! And how has that been working out for you, Yoofi?"

"Good, Miss Hene. He doesn't bother me anymore."

"I see. So why didn't you sleep last night, Yoofi?"

"How did you know about that?"

"Who else in this house wakes in the night and dances, Yoofi?"

The silence dragged, and finally Miss Hene watched as tears streamed from Yoofi's eyes. "He did me wrong, Miss Hene."

"I know, Yoofi, and the pain from that wrong is inside you."

"Inside me, Miss Hene?"

"Yes, like a memory. But it wakes up and stings when you do not want to remember or think about it. And, like last night, it did not let you sleep."

Yoofi did not respond.

"Soon your Dancing and your dreams will turn to nightmares, Yoofi!"

Still the lad did not reply.

"I know, Yoofi, that you like the pond. You go there alone sometimes and swim. But have you ever watched the pond on a quiet day, just how the water lies there, like it's smiling at you?"

"Yes, Miss Hene. That's how I would like to be!"

"Good!"

"But nothing hurts the pond, Miss Hene. It does not have a stepfather to bother it!"

"Yes, I know. But in a way it has more."

"What do you mean, Miss Hene?"

"Have you ever thrown a stone in the pond, Yoofi?"

"You know I have, Miss Hene!"

"And what happens when the stone hits the water, Yoofi?"

"The pond ripples and ripples and ripples, Miss Hene."

"And what next?"

"After the rippling it smooths out and is quiet again."

"Ah! You have been watching Providence Pond, Yoofi!" she said, shaking her finger at him.

"What's so strange about that, Miss Hene?"

"Just what you said, Yoofi. Only that I would say, Providence Pond ripples and then *smiles* again."

"So, what's that got to do with Leroy, Miss Hene? And why I should apologize to him?"

"This is not about Leroy, Yoofi. This is all about you."

"So, why not make Leroy apologize to me so I can be happy, Miss Hene?"

"Well, Yoofi, Providence Pond sheds ripples. You can say it shouts or whispers or cries its hurt away every time you throw a stone in. That's how you hurt the pond. But, the pond lets pain ripple out. Do you understand, Yoofi? It does not hold the hurt in."

"Yes, Miss Hene. But how do I ripple out and smile again, Miss Hene?

"First, Yoofi, you let Leroy know that he hurt you. But not the way you did to Headmaster Forbes. Just ripple in a nice way, like we are rippling now. Got it, Yoofi?"

"Yes, Miss Hene. But is that all? Is that all I have to do to let my pain out, Miss Hene?

"Not quite, my Son. There is this, too. Just let Leroy know that deep down in your heart, you have forgiven him for everything, especially for killing Shep."

The mention of the dog's name brought tears to Yoofi's eyes again. Miss Hene moved closer to the lad, embracing him. "I love you, Yoofi," she said, "and I am expecting great things from you."

"I love you, too, Miss Hene."

"Then let's go get breakfast," Miss Hene said, "or do you just prefer the tamarinds instead?"

Yoofi looked at her and laughed. He took the tamarinds from her outstretched hand and placed them in his pants pocket, thinking of sharing them with his brothers. Miss Hene watched him and smiled.

Hand in hand, they walked back to the house to see the other children busy, assisting Ama with breakfast.

Of Kitchens and Bedrooms

The end of the First World War in 1918 left the English workforce devastated and confusion in the little town of Providence. Instead of importing raw materials in abundance, the mother country sought to reestablish and enlarge its workforce by pulling an increasing number of men and women from her colonies.

From this, Providence was not spared. At first it didn't matter. Finally its effect hit home when prices fell. Leroy now had to supply five extra cans of oil in order to make as much money as he had previously.

To maintain or even increase his cash flow, Leroy simply increased Ama's workload. She accepted it without complaint or criticism and absorbed the extra grating to satisfy Leroy.

Yoofi had long ago arranged a grating station and assisted his mother with her portion of work. In the beginning, his novice fingers bled as they accidentally grazed the grating pad. He would cry, he would scream, but he would grate. Yoofi pitched in and with all his strength, he helped his mother.

During this time, Yoofi lived at Miss Hene's and came to the house daily to assist his Ama. Leroy didn't mind. He preferred things that way. They rolled into his dream of having Yoofi do his work without the bother of wrangling with him. After supper Leroy would sometimes sit on the front porch where he smoked his pipe and laughed as Yoofi struggled.

The kitchen sat a few yards away from the main house. It was a long rectangular structure built of raw lumber, placed behind the house and forming a "T" with it. Upon leaving the house from the front door, one had to turn left and follow a gravel path to enter the kitchen. The long side of the kitchen that faced the house was partially opened. One extra large window at the other side was always open, assuring good ventilation. The wood stove that the Kendals inherited from Lev was erected at one narrow end of the kitchen, and a work counter as well as a place for kitchenware was close to it. The floor was made of pure earth that was rammed and beaten until it was dust-free smooth. Additionally, the floor had a slight slope, making it tilt forward. In the unlikely event water should percolate in from the higher grounds at the rear, it would flow and not settle. In lieu of a window, a large opening remained high in the back wall close to the roofline. The vent was to Ama's back as she sat at her workstation facing the stove. Cold air from the hills beyond could then flow unencumbered into the kitchen, fanning the fire and removing excessive smoke from the enclosure. A trench had been dug around the kitchen's sides draining rainwater away. The inverted V-shaped roof was made of bamboo rafters on top of which hung corrugated zinc.

All around the kitchen, except at the entrance, Ama planted daises, roses, hibiscus, and bougainvillea flowers, one or all of which were always in bloom, bringing a sweet fragrance borne on light breezes into the kitchen. At first it had been a joy for her to work in there.

In the beginning, her bedroom was her favorite place in the house. Ama, with Miss Hene's help, had spent days and nights decorating the room, placing many paintings, even some from Congo, on her walls. The bedroom, which stood at the rear of the structure, offered a view of the valley with the pond below and the last glint of the fading sun. It was a large room. There was the mahogany bed with matching chest of drawers.

Except for a large seat for Leroy – the seat where he sat when they were first married, when she would lie on the bed and read poetry to him – the room was sparsely furnished. This left the highly polished cedar floor, which was covered with a warmly decorative woolen rug, always open and ready for eager lovers. Ama was in the habit of placing small bouquets of fresh flowers against the walls each evening and lighting her candles even before the sun has set. She worshiped the place and treated it with reverence. The room brilliantly reflected the harmony and joy of her soul.

As time went on, the kitchen gradually usurped her bedroom, becoming Ama's favorite haunt. She accepted it. Yet the path of that transition was blistered with anguish and finally, defeat.

Ama didn't like her status as merely a worker. Not that she disliked working. To the contrary, she loved being active and had always been a hard worker. Long ago, Ama had volunteered as school custodian when, by her parents' status, she didn't have to. Moreover, she was an excellent housewife, making clothes for her children and, with her skills of embroidery and crochet, she created many beautiful doilies for her furniture and bed linens. Her cooking brought praise from family and friends alike. She loved to serve, and did it with honor and joy.

But the job that Leroy forced upon her seemed to a far degree mechanical and unreal. Moreover, Ama perceived it to be a sterile offering with no immediate or future recompense or satisfaction. It was without any uplifting aspects, but conveyed instead the degrading feeling of a curse. Ama hated it and performed it in the same way one cleans filth, with indifference and scorn. Yet, wanting to avoid Leroy's wrath, she continued with grudged devotion.

Ama had always seen herself as a wife and mother. She had prepared herself to be the best at it. She had gone to the school library, the only one available locally, to read and keep her interests alive. She read what the teachers did; and with her avid reading, she conversed with them easily. It was her openness for ideas and a taste for adventure that first caught the interest of the Headmaster. True, she was unusually beautiful, exotic if you wish, but she didn't come with an empty head. Her ardent desire to be her best at motherhood kept Ama focused on her family. It also prevented her from understanding or easily accepting her new role as worker. She resented it, even pleading hopelessly to Leroy. Yet, things seemed to worsen.

In the past, she had bought oil from the shop or hired a servant to make oil for her. Now she had become the servant. Maybe that was what really bothered her. Leroy no longer accepted Ama as an equal, even though her labor and her property had been joined with his in producing what they had. Leroy saw it differently. He promoted himself as lord of the meager estate. Ama didn't mind his self-promotion. She was comfortable with it. It was how he abused his power that bothered her.

When she first started the work of oil making, Ama fancied that her efforts would help in mending the rift between Leroy and Yoofi. She never intended for Yoofi to disregard Leroy in any way. She wanted peace and a good life for both. Her intentions were sound. She didn't understand, however, how her actions would by both be so misinterpreted.

With a clean healthy kitchen and the wholesome thoughts of assisting her husband with his economic plans, Ama set out to make coconut oil. At first there was a kind of joy to it. Believing that there would be a quick endpoint to her new tasks, Ama plunged into it and Yoofi followed as wholeheartedly.

Ama had in an ad hoc manner carved out a workstation for herself. It was at the far corner of the kitchen, diagonally from the wood-burning stove. In that way, she would be as far as possible from the direct heat at her face and full exposure from the wind flowing down into the kitchen at her back. In her estimation this kept her cool and made her able to work longer hours. Ama chose a simple seat on the ground. Her only support and separation from the earth was a folded crocus bag. Her work stood before her, a large wooden tub – the kind that with the aid of a scrubbing board, women used for the laundry – and a large homemade grater. So there Ama sat, crouching minute after minute, hour after hour: her frail figure cringed and distorted while she baked in front from the fire and cooled from behind by the wind seeping through the wattled walls of her kitchen. There the friend, the wife and mother, the lover, the servant girl sat, grating, grating, grating.

With fresh muscles, her youthful strength, and great zest to defend Yoofi, the job did not appear difficult in the beginning. Despite her initial hatred for the task, Ama found that as she grated, she liked it, for her work pleased Leroy. Leroy in turn, grew happier with Yoofi, who became increasingly contented. Neither entropy nor karma, however, would leave Ama to her wiles for long. In great measure they soon visited her.

What Ama first felt as aches in her arms, back and legs, she explained as lack of exercise and poor muscle coordination. To eradicate the pains, Ama worked harder. She never thought of consulting a doctor. She simply plunged deeper and deeper into her task.

Four years passed, the seasons changed, the winds shifted from hot and dry to cold and damp. The drainage trench around the kitchen and the roof both fell into disrepair. Moisture crept up from the earth beneath her and the winds blew. Never did the fire in the distant corner die; Yoofi kept it blazing hot, bringing more and more oil to purification. Demand for oil increased and so did the workload. Ama grated and grated until her body took on a different form, the appearance of an old hag, shaped now by her task. At first she called for Yoofi to pull her up when she desired to stand, so tight and insensitive her muscles had become. They initially saw this as humorous. When his aid became indispensable, then their moods dulled to sadness. Yet Ama, without nagging, grated. Grating seemed to grow into the fearsome beast in terrible, recurring nightmare, become the sure thing Ama wanted to kill. It became her battle, her obsession, as a traveler on a long unknown road, believing that the turning of one last corner would finally signal home. So Ama grated, hoping to end her travail.

It didn't. The slight slouching in her poise grew into a characteristic stance, and finally it tipped her forward, forcing her to use a walking stick. Yoofi soon figured out what was wrong and, in addition to making her crutches from branches he cut and carved, increased his own grating.

It was not only her work which plagued her. Ama had been blessed with large breasts. In addition, her long years of constant nursing, her habit of never using brassieres, and more often, leaning forward in her work, kept her breasts full of weighty milk and growing. If only she had protected herself more from the raw elements, if only Ama had taken the time to eat and rest, maybe her body would have been able to restore itself. She didn't. Grating was her life, and even when the younger boys stopped nursing; Yoofi persisted, adding more pressure to her frail form. Soon she folded, as her body continued to cripple. In short, Ama's body, for lack of proper attention, had been broken beyond repair.

Leroy didn't like that. Yoofi had left the house, and there were children to care for. Sure Leroy had the money to provide medical treatment for Ama. He was also in position to provide a maid for her. He did neither. Instead, seeing her as used, completely spent, Leroy sought to replace or dispense with Ama. He took care of the boys and himself as best he could and left Ama to fend for herself. He often wished he could make his home life more comfortable for himself.

Now that Yoofi lived with Miss Hene, he began spending more time assisting wherever he could. Yoofi also unwittingly became Miss Hene's sole Kumina student. Because of this, Ama's oil production dwindled. Puncus became less patient with Leroy, and the farmer increasingly became angry and isolated. Ama's reprieve from her hard labor and withdrawal to her bed for comfort and healing, Leroy took as an invitation for sex. When their misunderstanding grew, her sobs turned to screams of pain. This piqued the boys' interest, forcing interrogations. Leroy desisted but changed his frustration into blame or derision, causing Ama even greater pain and confusion.

Ama, having lost her kitchen to ache and her bedroom to scorn, sought love and acceptance from Miss Hene.

For Leroy, it was longer days in the fields and much, much longer nights by himself at the *Any Questions.*

The Mirrored Fire

B y the spring of 1919, the months of heavy toil, loneliness, and despair came home to Ama with renewed vigor, seemingly to stay with her forever. Nothing she could do or think would make the monster go away. Like an unbearable yet invisible weight, it moved from her bedroom, following her to her kitchen as, on that day, instead of Yoofi, Ama made the feeble fire and prepared to boil her day's quotient of oil.

She did not forget any of Leroy's demands. They stood like ghosts taunting her. Neither did Ama forget Yoofi. She wanted him back! She had promised herself that when she gave Leroy this week's toil of oil, she would beg him to let Yoofi return to her, even for the hours he cavorted at the *Any Questions*. Yet she did not. The tedium and lethargy of her despair had teamed to trap Ama into overwhelming exhaustion.

But one day Ama moved: she stumbled back on her grating seat and mechanically leaning forward, took up a piece of coconut, brought it to the grater attempting to grate. Without knowing why, Ama leaned backwards; her legs spread to accommodate the huge tub and with her head leaning against the wall of her kitchen, closed her eyes. Still, the piece of coconut remained clutched between her fingers.

Though she sensed and dreaded her awesome misery, Ama did not know the extent to which her torment had captivated her soul. Yet, her sad companion, the monster that had followed her from her bedroom, finally overpowered her. Succumbing to its wrath, Ama lay back, large warm tears streaming down her face. She had lost control. She could not think. She cried, hurting, hurting, as she lingered in gloom, pleading, "Oh Miss Hene, where are you?" Her monster, unrelenting, held her as she cried herself to a strange sleep.

Ama still heard all the sounds around her, yet she drifted deep into a dream. Miss Hene entered the kitchen. That was not unusual. At times Miss Hene had visited her, and they would sit in the kitchen working together. But now Miss Hene seemed to float through the whittled wall behind the cauldron of cooking oil, holding a very young baby girl in her arm close to her breast. As soon as Miss Hene neared the fire, she placed the baby in a safe corner and gave her something to drink.

Soon after that, Miss Hene added oil-laden coconut shells to the flames. She stoked up a rich bright fire. Ama loved looking at the flames as they danced and warmed her. She watched Miss Hene attend to her boiling pot of oil, finally removing it from the fire. Just before Miss Hene could put on the second pot of coconut milk to boil, the fire flared, reaching the ceiling and nearing her frock.

Ama knew Miss Hene would be in trouble, but as she was about to shout to her, Ama noticed the baby girl. It was the daughter Ama had always wanted. How gentle and lovely she was! Her child came to her in the inferno. At first the baby laughed as if with Ama. Then, as the fire roared and flamed her butter-brown skin, the baby uttered a deathly scream of pain. She hollered for help! "Save her, Miss Hene. Save her!" Ama cried. But, as Miss Hene, busying herself with the oil, did not respond, Ama struggled to life.

Ama did not know what propelled her. But, when in the future she recounted this moment, Ama would always start: "Then I raised my head and opened my eyes . . ." And with one great leap, Ama flung herself into the fire to rescue the child. This she did only to find that her palsied fire had long died. Even the cinders had cooled, and only the warm ash, now covering her face and body, remained.

No one was there, no one but Ama alone.

With a harrowed delight, Ama got to her feet and hobbled to Miss Hene's house as fast as she could. That too was empty. Not Miss Hene, not Kwame, not even her cherished Yoofi was there. In disbelief and despair, Ama fell on the grass in the open sunlight before Congo's cottage. She cried.

Later that day Ama woke in her bedroom to the panting of a dog. As she saw Shep leaving, Ama sighed a deep long sigh and fell back on the pillow where she slept until Yoofi awoke her.

He had just returned with Kwame and the other boys from school. For the first time that day, Ama felt sure of something.

She moved from her bedroom to find that indeed Yoofi was in the house. She ran and hugged him as well as the other boys.

To her further delight, dinner was already cooked and on the table. Ama hurried to the kitchen to see who had cooked the meal for her family. No one was in the kitchen. The only things to reach her eyes were the cans of oil she intended to produce for her week's work. All seven cans of oil had been done.

Ama, as if not seeing the children serving themselves at the table, returned to her bedroom and wondered. In silence and delight, she wept.

Ama and Miss Hene

Ama lived in torment for the next few weeks. She had no explanation for what she had seen. To her it was real. The baby girl for whom she had longed had come to her, and no sooner had it come than it was taken back!

Fear pushed her away from her kitchen and closer to her children. Ama vowed not to return to that frightful place. Instead she walked Dean and Agu first to Miss Hene's to get Kwame. There she had breakfast with the family and, following that, walked the lads along the school road until they were in comfortable large groups of children. That gave her some comfort. In the afternoons when school was over, Ama would leave from Miss Hene's house, meet the children, and join them on their way home.

But it was more than that. Without explanation, Ama had taken partial residence in Miss Hene's house. She still slept in hers at first; but since she would not go into her own kitchen, she and her boys ate at Miss Hene's house, then finally started sleeping there as if it were their own.

Miss Hene loved Ama's company, but she hated her silence. None of Miss Hene's promptings could force Ama's tongue free. It was the burden of Ama's silence that did.

"Miss Hene," Ama finally said one morning, long after she had walked the children to school. "Who are you, Miss Hene?"

"Why Ama! Your sister, of course!"

"That's not what I mean, Miss Hene, and you know it!"

"What do you mean, Ama?"

"I mean about me and the child."

"The child in the fire?"

"Yes! So you do know about it!" Ama said in great relief.

"You in your pain, Ama. I saw it. You were so sad."

"So you were there, Miss Hene? Were you in my kitchen?"

"Did I say I was there, Ama? I saw you and what you did. Awful, isn't it, rolling in ashes? Why on earth would you do that, Ama?"

"Because of the fire."

"What fire?"

"The fire my child was in!"

"What fire, Ama? What baby?"

"The fire that burned the baby you brought, Miss Hene."

"I did not bring you a baby, Ama. And there was no fire!"

"No fire?"

"No, Ama. Is your kitchen burnt?"

"Oh no! Don't make me into a fool, Miss Hene," Ama started to sob.

"A fool. Heavens, no!"

"Then what, Miss Hene? What happened?"

"You were in distress; deep pain and distress. Then you got up and threw yourself in the ashes and started to cry. That's what I saw."

"And why didn't you say something?"

"There was nothing to say. I was not there, Ama."

"You saw me but you were not there! And you were not here, either. Not you, not Yoofi. No one was here. Where were you and Yoofi, Miss Hene?"

"We were in Providence Pond, Ama. We go there from time to time and commune. Yoofi is coming along nicely."

There was a long silence. Ama, still puzzled, did not know what to think or believe. Not wanting to appear more lost or hopeless in her own situation, she started, "And she was such a beautiful child!"

Miss Hene did not respond. From her front verandah where they sat, she saw Leroy approaching her house. He was not happy, not angry, just worried. Uninvited, he came and plopped himself in a chair beside the women. He did not speak and they barely gave him notice.

"That's why I have been here for the last weeks, Miss Hene."

"Why? Because she was a beautiful baby girl?"

"No, Miss Hene! Because she was in the fire."

"Oh, and that's why you have been walking the boys to school?"

"Yes, Miss Hene. I cannot let anything happen to them."

"It's not their time yet, Ama. You needn't worry."

"What do you mean by that, Miss Hene? Is it my time?"

"Not in the least, Ama. We need you here."

"So whose time is it, then? Leroy's?"

"I might be worried but not dying! So leave me out of this!" Leroy said, trying to sit upright.

"We are not talking to you, Leroy!" Ama said. Leroy remained silent.

"So nothing will happen to the boys; and, as I told you, Yoofi is coming along real nicely."

"Well, that is good then."

"Yes, except for the baby girl." Miss Hene said. "I hope she will be okay."

"I need you home, Ama. So, okay or not, you have to come back home, Ama," Leroy said.

"She was so real to me, Miss Hene. I have to find her, and take care of her."

"Find her or not, you have to come back home, Ama," Leroy reasserted.

"It's better for us here, Leroy, and I am happy, too. The children and I are happy here. Isn't it so, Miss Hene?"

"Yes, of course, Ama. All is well."

"Not at your house where you belong, Ama."

"What's not happy there, Leroy?"

"Divine's cooking and company is good, I must say, but you have oil to make. Don't you remember that?"

"Do you need more oil, Leroy?"

"I do. And don't ask like you do not know!"

"Well, if you need oil, Leroy, you better make oil, because I am not going back in that kitchen again."

"What do you mean, Ama?"

"My days in that kitchen are over. And if you want food, you better make that, too!"

"I want oil, Ama. Oil is what Leroy wants. And who is going to feed the pigs? I need the oil and the coconut trash to feed the pigs."

"That's why I said you better make the oil yourself."

There was a long pause.

"And she was so beautiful," Ama said, somewhat absentmindedly.

"Who are you talking about?" Leroy asked.

"My baby girl. Miss Hene brought her to me."

"Not me, Ama."

"You must be losing your mind, Ama! Maybe you need some rest."

"Yes, Leroy. That is exactly what I need. And you know something else I miss, Leroy? The days we spent at Providence Pond, all by ourselves. Are those days gone forever, Leroy?"

Leroy did not respond. He sat in silence. Miss Hene looked at him. He felt that something had gone wrong with Ama. He did not know what it was. He thought of getting her medical aid and of bringing a helper in the house. He did not know how to divulge what he had come to Miss Hene's house to tell Ama.

For the weeks that Ama had been there, Leroy had the foreboding she had run away from him. Leroy did not know why, though. He was delighted Ama had produced so much oil in only a day! He thought of ramping up her schedule. He even calculated how much more he would have earned if Ama could continue producing that quantity of oil. Now that she was missing, he thought of getting help for the children and for himself so Ama could fully devote her time to making oil and feeding swine.

In his customarily abrupt manner, Leroy started, "I have some business in Galina to take care of, Ama, so I will be leaving for a while."

"What kind of business, and when will you go?"

"I am not just going for business, Ama. I want to get some help for you."

"You want to find help for me, Leroy?" Her eyes swelled with tears.

"I want to find a girl to help you with the domestics and take care of the children. I know someone in Galina that will do just fine."

"Oh! Thank you, Leroy. I always knew you loved me."

"I love you, Ama, and want things to work for us. Now that Yoofi is out, we can make it work, just like how it was when we were first married."

"Yes, Leroy. I remember. That's what I would like, too."

"So, let's go home. You can rest and I will get some help for you."

"That's wonderful, Leroy!" Miss Hene said. "Just remember, the help should be for Ama."

"Just as I said, Miss Hene."

And with that, they bade Miss Hene good-bye and walked off the veranda onto the grass.

"And let me know if you ever find that child of yours, Ama," Miss Hene said.

"Okay, Miss Hene. I will," Ama said, leaving.

Yoofi and the other boys watched as Ama looked back, waving at the house. The morning sun had painted a radiant expectation on her face they had never seen before. From their window perch, they watched Ama's slow, seemingly hopeful hobble across the greenery with Leroy at her side. Yoofi gazed with an amazed smile.

Ama's Diary

A ma remained sad and perplexed despite all that was done or promised to her. She did not understand the towering flames that sought
to devour the thing for which she yearned the most, a daughter.
Where was that lost child?

Ama did not know. Overcome and pained by guilt and fear, she
hobbled from bedroom to front yard, around the house and back in,
pondering her loss and what Miss Hene had said to her. Her loneliness
and despair remained until the early afternoon when, avoiding food, she
went into her bedroom and opened the lowest drawer of her bureau. There,
in the far back corner, she had long stored, or maybe hidden, her diary.
Reluctantly and without knowing why, Ama pulled it out and sat on the
floor where she opened the pages.

This was the diary she had kept before she met Headmaster Henry
Isaac Love. Her hands shaking and her stomach in knots, she opened the
pages. A smile came to her face as memories of her youth returned. Just
before she had hidden it, she wanted to glue the pages shut, say goodbye
to that past. Now she was happy she hadn't. Such sweet memories they
brought her. So, lost in the intrigue, Ama turned until she found an old
family picture pasted in the diary.

At first Ama could not decide who she was. But after goggling over
the frame for some time – with guesses and ponderous eliminations
– she finally claimed the beauty that was once hers. Of course she knew.

She remembered the day of the photograph. After leaving church that Sunday the family had traveled to Port Maria and taken pictures in the photographer's office.

Ama remembered the bright lights, and the large black box and the black silk under which the photographer hid just before taking the picture. Of course, she remembered standing in the front row at her mother's right. She still remembered the love her mother felt for her as she wrapped her arm about her shoulder, and just how precious and safe she felt with her father behind her, pressed close to her. How lovely everything was then, and how beautifully she was dressed! Ama gazed at the picture, staring at her face, looking at her siblings, the entire family, and then back at herself. She fell in love with that face and the memories of her youth. Ama was totally lost in devotion to the feelings of the happy, carefree young woman who went to the school library to read poetry and started her own in her diary. Ama's childhood joy flooded her mind and momentarily transfixed her at the height of her beauty and contented life.

How long Ama remained bent over the diary she did not know. But as she returned to life, Ama slowly rose, facing the mirror as she did. On seeing the reflection of her gaunt face and frame, in despair and disbelief, she crumpled back to the floor, losing all consciousness.

Ama did not know what caused the stirring on her veranda, but it brought her back to life. In silence she listened, still with her eyes closed. She heard the brisk walking of a dog and what she surmised to be its wagging tail beating against her bedroom door. Ama opened her eyes to see Shep standing in the open doorway whining with joy to see her. Ama did not know what to do. Happy to see the animal, Ama asked: "Is that you, Shep?" and got up to offer it food.

As Ama got up, the dog walked out of the room onto the veranda. With pain from her stiffened spine, Ama, still eager to offer it food, walked after the dog. Shep went down the stair and started walking in the narrow path leading to Miss Hene's house. What could Ama do? Her joy now turned to curiosity, and she decided to follow the animal. Despite all her efforts Ama could not come in touching distance of the animal. It walked, constantly looking back at her, but never allowing Ama to get too close to it. Yet Ama followed, until the dog walked up the stairs leading to Miss Hene's living room and, if Ama saw right, walked through the closed door and entered the house.

"Asa!" cried Ama, as she opened the door and entered Miss Hene's living room. "What are you doing here?" she asked the old man on the sofa.

"Ama?" called Miss Hene, rushing from her kitchen with flour covering her hands. She had been kneading dough for dumplings. "Why are you shouting like that?"

"I am just happy to see Asa! Why didn't you tell me he was here?" asked Ama facing Miss Hene.

"That who was here?"

"Asa!" said Ama, pointing and looking at the empty sofa.

"Who?" Miss Hene enquired.

"Asa! Asa, our Father, Miss Hene, he was just here. I saw him with my own two eyes!"

"First it was the child, now it's Asa. Soon you will be telling me you saw Shep."

"Don't you play with me, Miss Hene. How did you know about Shep, too?"

"We all know about Shep" Miss Hene laughed. "Listen, Ama, I am busy making soup. Why not come in the kitchen and talk?"

Ama, eager to learn, followed Miss Hene into the kitchen, and sat down. Miss Hene brought her a spoon full of soup. "Taste it for me Ama," Miss Hene said. "Does it need anything?"

"Puhh!" Ama spat out the soup. "Why not ask Puncus to make soup for you?"

Miss Hene laughed, then said, "I just wanted you to know how you look to me now, Ama. You are raw!"

"Don't make fun at me, Miss Hene. You brought this thing on me!"

Miss Hene laughed. "You are getting sensitive, Ama. You are learning to see."

"What do you mean, Miss Hene?"

"Wait a minute, Ama. Let me put some things in this soup and leave it to simmer, ok?"

Ama walked with Miss Hene to the stove and watched her add the dumplings and vegetables to the soup. On her return to the kitchen table, Miss Hene poured wine for herself and Ama. She sipped and Ama followed.

"Oh goodness! Who are you, Miss Hene?"

"Your sister, of course, Ama."

"You know I do not mean that!"

"Yes, Ama, that's what you meant. You are my sister, just years younger," Miss Hene said. Ama looked up at her with a long questioning stare, noting the gray that had come to Miss Hene's braids. "I am here to help you along and anyone else Congo brings into the Family. Do you understand?"

"But I have been in the Family for a while now, Miss Hene."

"Well, if you say so, Ama," Miss Hene laughed, bringing a smile to Ama's face. Miss Hene watched her younger sister intensely. She admired Ama's wizened face that had been prematurely aged by sorrow. Momentarily, it transformed into its youthful charm. "But it does not matter. You are here now, and what's marvelous about you is that you are beginning to see."

"To see what, Miss Hene? I have always had my eyes!"

"You are beginning to see more now, Ama. You saw your child, and now Asa and Shep? That's a lot for a beginner." When Ama did not respond, Miss Hene continued. "That can be confusing at first, but, just give it time. You will soon be seeing clearly, Ama, and things will not seem so confused then."

"So what's next, Miss Hene?"

"Nothing. But in fact, everything, Ama. Just walk with your eyes open. That's all."

Ama remained silent. At first her body felt calm, quiet, and cold. Then soon again a warm, comforting feeling flooded it. It was the same feeling she had as she looked at her youthful picture. Miss Hene touched Ama's hand. "I am your Sister, Ama. Welcome to our Family."

Ama did not respond. She finished her wine and walked out of the house.

"Where are you going, Ama?"

"Down to the pond."

"Be back for dinner!"

"Yes!" Ama shouted back and walked to the pond.

There she stood remembering the body and the pond of her youth. Enchanted by joy and devoid of pain, Ama stripped bare and waded into the clear sparking water, forgetting food or drink. From that day when Lev had his fete, she had not returned to the water. She would not forsake it any longer. She stayed there by herself, musing until long after dinnertime.

Later, Miss Hene, after feeding the children, joined Ama. They stayed by the water and watched the slow moon as it mounted the heavens from the far horizon. For a moment it seemed to pause as if centering itself close, just over the pond, sharing the solemn instant with sisters. The women talked, disclosing everything, becoming one.

By then, Ama felt like a child. The women walked to Miss Hene's home and Ama, with hardly any strength left, threw herself onto the floor of one of the guest bedrooms. There she slept until the following morning. She dreamt long, soothing dreams of Yoofi, Shep, and her child, but never, never of Leroy. Not once did he soil her blissful slumber.

Rex Covey

Ulu took complete control of her household. She was no tyrant, but she ruled without gentleness or love. Ulu's home, her life, her connubial relationship – all except her attachment with Princess – were a part of her business. Business gave her life meaning, consuming her creative energy.

Congo couldn't understand why he remained an outsider. He had done all Ulu requested. His efforts had made her wealthy, and still she expected more. In the beginning, Ulu gave Congo what she deemed he needed from her . . . her body.

True, Congo and Laura had each other. That, in their eyes, was a different concern. They loved each other, entertained and played together. Yet when they parted, they knew that the attachment they desired with a life partner lay with someone else. Who developed the rules of relationships anyway? They had often posed that question.

The responsibility was with the parties in love. Marriage, however, came with rules from age-old books and times that may not even have existed. Such books! Laura thought of them. Marriage she described as a trap, implying but not guaranteeing security. Especially, it did not assure love.

Yet, as much as Congo enjoyed Laura's company, at the depth of his heart he wanted Ulu's admiration. She was home to him, mother, and family! He wanted her when his labor was over. He wanted her attention, her praise, and her love. Sensing that, Ulu withheld them, except when it pleased her.

Ulu's plan for Princess was so devised. Ulu had always dreamed of marrying into the elite. She had education, ambition and good looks. Class was her barrier, or so she surmised. If only Bem, her father, had been rich! If only we lived in the city and not in Providence, if only . . . It was always her situation that she pondered, never her own character!

Having found Congo a hard working yet selfless, unambitious fool, Ulu ensnared him for wealth and progeny. Now Ulu wanted a daughter through whom she could live her own misbegotten ambition.

Now that Congo had fulfilled what Ulu saw as his life's mission, her duty was to force him out of her bedroom, out of the marriage, and finally out of her life.

Ulu had gotten an oath from Congo to end his relationship with Laura; then she asked her trusted house servants to spy on him.

After the oath, Ulu often let Princess sleep with her, while Congo stayed in the guest room. Congo couldn't decipher how to pose the question of sleeping rights – and spoke only to Ulu alone about it. She rebuked him for not understanding mother-daughter bonding.

Congo, knowing more about how to give than grunt, relented. Ulu didn't mind. Her only concern was that he might turn his attention to Charm. But she had guarded that nest as well. Ulu painted Congo as the devil's first son who at all cost should be shunned. Ulu's gospel was unnecessary. Congo had far too much respect for his daughter. In that, Ulu had misjudged him. Nonetheless, her messages to the child, like storms out of season, went on unabated.

With full disclosure to Ho, and with his complete understanding, Congo began spending more and more time with Laura. He avoided sleeping in her house, preferring to return home each night. He would, however, eat with Ho at the *Hong Kong Seafood Gardens*. From there, Congo took dinner back to Laura's home, where they chatted while she ate.

Initially, Congo did not understand the full significance of the oath he had pledged to Ulu. He did not foresee all its consequences that were to chart the deepest change in his life.

It didn't take long for a servant to inform Ulu when Congo visited Laura. One particular night Congo rode Ulu's horse to Laura's house since his had been lame. The use of her ride vexed Ulu. She decided to spring the trap she had set. As the night aged, Ulu saddled another horse and rode in silence to Laura's house. She hitched her horse to the one she rode, forcing Congo to walk home. He did, and found Ulu's horse tied to the front door.

Ulu now had the proof she needed; Congo knew. He had broken his oath to her and so fell into Ulu's trap. He didn't know all that it meant. Princess permanently replaced him.

Nothing was ever said about the incident. Never did Ulu confront or ask him about it. Yet it remained with Ulu as her chastising fire for Congo whenever she desired.

Ulu spent much of the following weeks in deep and sincere correspondence with Rex Covey, her brother in New York.

The Gathering

At Miss Hene's request, Puncus St. John sat in her living room with Ama and Yoofi, awaiting Congo's arrival. Ama had been staying there, allowing the tumult at her home to quiet. Yoofi had been staying there for his safety. Congo's presence had been requested to help in finding a solution to Yoofi's problems. He was sure to attend, for he loved Yoofi and would do anything to help Ama.

Puncus was asked to attend simply because Miss Hene was fond of him, and he, no less, liked her company. He sat beside her on a couch facing the front door with Ama beside Miss Hene and Yoofi at the far end of the couch.

"I wonder why things happen the way they do?" Miss Hene asked. "It seemed like things should have worked right for you and Leroy, Ama. It's such a pity they haven't."

Ama was about to reply when the canter of Congo's horse prevented her. Yoofi abruptly ran to the door shouting, "Uncle Congo, Uncle Congo, glad you are here!"

Congo took him by the hand and they walked into the living room.

"Something to drink, Congo?" Miss Hene asked.

"Brandy would be good, thank you. And how is everyone?" he asked.

"We are not serving drinks tonight since Puncus is here, Congo. He preaches against it, you know."

"Yes, yes, and sells it by the cart load."

"And he is not smoking, either," Miss Hene responded. "Since he promised not to smoke, I promised not to serve wine."

"So it's lemonade then," Congo said.

"Oh! There is plenty of that here," Ama replied, filling his glass.

"We are really glad to see you, Congo," Miss Hene continued. "I know you have to get back home tonight, so maybe Ama will tell you what has been happening at the house and see if you can help."

"Oh, Miss Hene!" Ama said. "It's better if you tell it."

"We would rather listen to you, Ama, since it's your story."

"It's simple," Yoofi said. "Mas Leroy might kill me."

"No, no. He would never do such a thing," Congo said.

"Well, he hanged Shep. I do not trust him anymore," Yoofi replied.

"Is that so, Ama?" asked Congo, turning his focus on her.

Ama didn't reply. Her head drooped to her stomach and she turned her eyes to look at Congo.

"We believe so, Congo," Miss Hene confirmed. "And it's not safe for Yoofi to stay here or in Providence any more. So we were wondering if you could find Yoofi work and lodging? Yoofi is a fine worker, and very intelligent."

"You needn't remind me, Miss Hene. We have so much work at Jacks River, we would be delighted in having him. You know, the produce business is really strong now, and with Ulu having contracts with all the farmers to buy their crops, there is a lot of drying and bagging to do. Yoofi would be more than welcome there."

"When could I start, Uncle Congo?"

"If you are ready, it could be this evening, Yoofi. You just need to come back with me."

"Thank you, Uncle Congo. I will go and pack."

"Good, Yoofi. Let's leave as soon as we can." With that, Yoofi began walking from the room to pack a small brown grip for his journey.

"Here, Yoofi," Miss Hene called. "Take this jug of lemonade into the room where your brothers are. They may need something to drink."

"Okay, Miss Hene," Yoofi said, as he took the jug and walked to serve the other boys.

"Fine chap, that Yoofi!" Congo said, looking at Ama as soon as Yoofi had disappeared down the hall. "And now, Ama, you have something to say. I would love to hear it."

"Oh Congo! Just take good care of him for me, and show him a little love."

"You know I will, Ama."

"Yes, Congo."

"You are very quiet there, Puncus," Congo said. "Do you have anything to say on the matter?" Puncus moved as if coming out of a sleep.

"Yes, in fact, I may have."

"We would love to hear it," Miss Hene said. "Your opinions are welcome here, you know."

"Yes, of course. But I'll tell you by way of a story."

"If it is short and spicy," Congo said with mirth. "We still have to ride back home tonight."

"Well, there are two parts to it, Congo. One part has to do with how nature works, how rain falls and trees grow, the natural side of things . . ."

"We more or less understand that, Puncus."

"That's what I thought, Miss Hene. That you wanted a more general, a more human side to the reply."

"Ama's side, her story, is what we are interested in," Congo said.

"Then Ama, please give us a day-by-day account of your marriage so we can answer the question."

"Oh Puncus! I wouldn't know where to begin," Ama said.

"So, you see then, Congo, I must tell you the little story, and this is the other part of it." Puncus looked at Congo laughing, and he started: "It's the one about the old wife and the house of six windows."

"We are waiting, Puncus," Miss Hene said.

"You see," Puncus started, "this wife lived in that house with her husband forever— she and that old house, neither capable of death. Early in their marriage, it so happened, she would open a window at random and, on looking out, would fix her eyes on an object of delight. The wife would then call her husband, stand behind him and point until he was sure what it was that entertained her. Each time, her request was the same."

"'If you get it for me, I would be so happy.'"

"And in the beginning he would reply, 'That's what you said last time.'"

"'Yes, I did. And when you got it for me, it did make me happy, and I made you happy too, didn't I?'"

"'Yes,' he replied."

"'So, do you want to be happy, love?'"

"'Yes.'"

"'Then make me happy!'"

"So off the husband would go to fetch the object of his wife's joy, and as promised, she brought him pleasures unceasing.

"Soon, however, the only thing the wife had to do was choose her window and look and, without argument, her husband fetched the object of her desire. So, they learned to live happily for a long, long time. But one day, as the husband journeyed, he fell into a ditch and died. Then the wife's joy turned into sorrow. She cried and nailed her windows shut, forever. She remained unhappy."

"So what happened, St. John?" Yoofi asked. He had not too long before rejoined the group and like the others, listened attentively.

"No one knows, Yoofi. The window remained shut: remember?"

"We should, Puncus!" remarked Miss Hene. "What on earth is the moral of your story?"

"It has no moral."

"So why tell it?"

"You asked the question."

"What question, Puncus?" Miss Hene asked with some irritation.

"You asked and I quote: 'I wonder why things happen the way they do?' That was your question; do you remember asking it?"

"So what does that have to do with anything, especially this story you told us?"

"Well, Miss Hene. Your body is like that old house and your soul like the wife, your senses like the windows, and so on. If you accept that, then you must agree that your soul, by using its senses, finds what it thinks will bring it comfort and beckons the will, in this case the husband, to go in search of it. And the story of this world, the war just ending and the ones to come, yes, even the happenings in Ama's house, are nothing more than the story of that wife wanting to be pleased. That's how things happen. We selfishly do what we think will make us happy, Miss Hene, and in so doing, things happen: all kinds of things! With all the pain and sadness around us, it might not look so. But, believe me, Miss Hene, we all started just like that maiden, looking for happiness."

There was silence for a while.

"Puncus St. John, I do not know why you think of these things, and I do not know why I paint, either. But let me say, painting gives me solace. That I know. So I suppose, if silly stories are what your maiden sends you for . . . then I accept them," Congo said.

"Thank you, Congo."

"But who asked you to answer my question, Puncus?" Miss Hene asked. "This is not the *Any Questions*, you know."

"I know, Miss Hene. I travel with it. Moreover, you asked."

"Yes. I did, of course! But that's because not knowing the answer dissatisfied me."

"Now, that is all gone. You will have to come up with another question, Miss Hene."

"Oh! And why is that? So you can tell another story, and leave me with nothing to ponder?" This time she laughed, removing the stress from Divine's face.

"I didn't think of it that way, Miss Hene. You see, I always thought questions were asked to be . . ."

"So you see, Puncus, some questions are better left unanswered," Miss Hene corrected him.

"Or better still, left unasked," Puncus said.

"Well, it is not the same . . ."

"If ever you looked, Miss Hene," Congo said, "you would see you have found your match."

"Do you mean in that Puncus Divine over there?"

"The very one, Miss Hene. And since we have a long journey ahead of us," Congo continued, "we had better get started."

"There is another little thing to talk about, Congo," Puncus said.

"And what is that, Puncus?"

"Tell him, Miss Hene," Divine said.

"We must call a Dance, Congo."

"A Dance? For whom?"

"Can't you tell, Congo? It's for our new Sister!"

"Ama?"

"Yes!"

Congo jumped from his chair and started to dance.

"Not here, Congo," Divine corrected "At the *Any Questions*, two Saturday nights from now. Come prepared and tell all you can."

"Good! Excellent!" Congo said, walking toward Ama. He took her by the hand so she could stand and walk to his Sister. Ama leaned down to the seated Miss Hene, kissing her repeatedly on her forehead."

"Well done, Ama!" Miss Hene said, "We have work ahead. But I can see, Ama is ready for a new path."

Ama took a seat next to her, not knowing what Miss Hene really meant. Yet she was happy that something was going to be done in her honor.

"You have a long journey ahead of you, too . . ."

A sharp, angry knock on the door interrupted Miss Hene. "I love you, Ama," a voice sounding like a demand stated. "I love you, Ama, and it's time you come home."

"Goodness! Is that you, Leroy?" Ama asked, perking up.

"I am here for you, Ama. Who else do you think it could be? Come on home, Ama. I love you."

"Don't go! Don't go, Mammy," shouted Yoofi.

"It's between your mother and me, Yoofi."

"In a minute, Leroy. I will be there! Did you all hear that?" Ama asked rising to her feet. "Did you all hear that? Leroy loves me!" And clutching her cane, she hobbled to the door, holding herself up as high as she could.

"So, you came for me, Leroy?" Ama asked as she approached the door.

"I am here to take you back home, where you belong, Ama."

"Don't go, Mammy!"

"It's okay," Miss Hene said. "It's quite all right, Yoofi. She has made a decision!"

Ama prepared to step onto the lanai and meet Leroy at the front door, but then she turned to face the room. She had something to say.

"Oh, Yoofi! Be good to yourself. Be kind. Work hard. Show love to everyone, all the time. And behave yourself so your Mammy can be proud of you. Give my love to your Aunt Ulu, and tell her I love her, even though I have not been to see her since she left here. Tell her and little Princess I love them."

"Yes, Mammy. I will do just as you say. And show everyone I know how to behave, especially Aunt Ulu."

"Good, son. Let your mammy be proud of you. And Congo: please take good care of Yoofi for me."

"I will, Ama, I will!"

"And see that he stays out of trouble, and show him some love, and tell Ulu the same for me. But this is not right, you know. Who is going to teach him about life and women and things like that?" Ama started to cry. "He is not really ready to go, you know, he is not really ready. But Congo, you will have to tell him. Anyway, Congo, tell Ulu he is a good boy and will do whatever she wants. All she has to do is love him, and that's not hard. Really, it's not too hard. Good-bye Yoofi. I love you, my son. Come hug your mammy before you leave."

Yoofi ran to the door and hugged his mother. He kissed her and wondered if he would ever see her again. He hugged her once more and sobbed loudly. As he released her, Ama turned to go. She addressed the room: "How do you know that this was not intended all along? How do you know, Puncus? Maybe if you accept everything as the way it should be, then maybe you would not have to answer so many hard questions. And maybe, we would not have to ask so many questions either!"

She stood there for a while, wiping her eyes, and then walked away into the darkness with Leroy. He rode, and with her stick, she walked by his side, both of them talking, all the way back home.

Meanwhile, as Congo motioned to go, Yoofi hastened back to the room where Kwame and his brothers were. He looked at Agu, who only four years previously he had walked to school on Agu's first day. Agu had grown taller than he, though he still wore his baby face. Dean and Kwame had grown proud of Yoofi. Often they spoke of him with sadness. Now the two boys lay sideways on the bed, looking up at each other now and again but without speaking knowing the other was thinking of Yoofi. Agu sat on the bed leaning against the wall as he played with his pocketknife.

Yoofi, not knowing where to start, bade farewell. "I am sixteen now. That is because three months ago, in June, was my birthday." Yoofi paused as if searching for his next word. He felt just as sad as he felt compelled to speak. "That means I am a man now . . ." he continued. "You know . . . and I must leave home to make a living. I do not know what that means! And what is a man anyway . . . I mean, really . . . What is a man?" The boys looked puzzled at Yoofi as he continued. "But Uncle Congo is here to get me. I think things will be okay. I love him, but I do not know Aunt Ulu. I do not think she is like Miss Hene, and you know how nice she is."

Yoofi looked and saw Dean sniveling, but continued. "You don't have to cry, Dean. I am going to miss you, and the Pond. There is no place on earth I love like Providence Pond. It has never said 'no' to me, no matter what I did. I do not understand how it killed Uncle Lev. I do not believe it killed him. It could have killed us so many times. I do not even know what I am saying. But, maybe, I am scared."

Yoofi had placed his dancing doll beside his small suitcase. The suitcase measured about eighteen inches long and scarcely a foot wide and certainly less than six inches deep. His entire fortune until then, except his doll and kite, were in it. He intended to take them along, too. Yoofi wanted to leave, but didn't know what to do with the doll. He had danced with it almost every night since he got it, and certainly made it his constant pillow. Now what was he to do with it? He thought of giving it to Dean or Kwame, but he had never seen them dance. Agu certainly would have nothing to do with it. He loved the doll, like he had loved Shep. Without knowing what to do, he pressed it against his body, kissed it, and placed it in a corner.

"Take care of it, please," he asked, looking at Kwame who didn't reply. "And don't let him hurt Mammy. You must not let him hurt her, or I do not know what I will do. I may not know what I am saying; do not let him hurt her. And Agu, you better make sure of that." He left the room in tears.

Congo had already said his parting salutation and gone to get a horse for Yoofi, who had just reentered the living room where Miss Hene and Puncus awaited him.

"I love you, Miss Hene, and you too, Puncus. You look good together." They laughed, and he walked up to both of them, taking their hands.

"Am I going to be all right?" he asked.

The adults looked at each other and then at Yoofi.

"In everything, just do the best you can, and you will be all right," Puncus said.

"Is that what being a man means, Puncus?"

"Yes, That's a part of it. And to state your mind without causing unnecessary pain, and always, always do whatever good you can, expecting no reward."

"Is that it?"

"And maybe this, too, Son: Listen," said Miss Hene.

"To what?"

"We must listen to everything," Miss Hene replied. But mostly to silence, Yoofi."

"And especially to women, Boy. You better listen to women," Puncus added.

"Thank you, Puncus."

With that, Yoofi ran from the house to find Congo holding the ride he had prepared for him. They mounted and headed to Jacks River.

Quietness brewed over the living room in which Miss Hene and

Puncus sat. He was thinking of her; she was thinking of Lev. He stood between them. Miss Hene had gone in search of Lev. She had not found the companionship she missed. What she did find, however, was herself! Miss Hene went to Fellowship forlorn and returned with her old self.

Puncus had grown fond of Miss Hene and wanted to live with her, but he feared she might want him to ask for something else, marriage. He was certain she loved him, and his adoration for her was sure and absolute. He, however, couldn't find a comfortable way to express his feelings. He knew the words and had more than ample opportunity, but he didn't get the sense from Miss Hene that he would be accepted. Miss Hene found ways of creating tension, uneasiness, and situations that cautioned him not to spout his love when she might be open to it but not ready for its acceptance. Lev, and to a lesser extent Kwame, stood between them.

"We didn't mean to ridicule your ideas, Puncus. I think, rather, they were well thought out," Miss Hene said, breaking the long silence. He was stretched out on the couch when she returned from the kitchen, so she lifted his head and rested it on her lap, then sat looking down into the tender, loving eyes of her friend a generation older than she was. She wondered for a moment how Puncus had managed to bridge the gap in years, appearing as youthful and as energetic as Lev had been.

"I understand, Miss Hene, and I do not hold that against you, but it's the whole situation that is uncomfortable. We should be able to express love rather than skepticism."

"Yes, that's what love is for, Puncus," she laughed, "to be expressed."

"But something comes in our way, and I know what it is."

"We both know, Puncus. It's Lev. We have spoken about that before."

"Sure, and you have all the proof he is gone. You needn't crave his return."

"In that you are right, Puncus, I should let it go. But then there is Kwame."

"I'll take care of the lad, Miss Hene."

"I am sure you will. But I have never been sure what to tell him about Lev. We know the truth and he deserves to know it, too. And how can I tell him and then, in the same breath, tell him I am to marry you?"

"Tricky! That's a tricky one," Puncus laughed. "But tell me, is that a question or just something for you to ponder?"

"It's a question, silly."

"So just tell him the truth," Puncus said.

He felt somewhat embarrassed by his statement. Puncus heard it as implying that in some way, either by her concealment of Lev's fate from Kwame or by not disclosing the nature of their attachment, Miss Hene was being less than honest. Yet he trusted her and believed in her integrity. Silence brewed until St. John found a solution.

He started, "But the truth has to be something he can understand now. And even if he does, he may not be able to fully deal with it. We can tell him what's best for him now, the truth, and another truth later, when he is capable of it. I hope that does not sound confusing to you."

"Not really. But it's tricky, as you say, telling truths that are opposites, without turning them into lies," Miss Hene responded.

"Yes, just separated in time," Puncus said.

"I understand, and what a blessing time can be!" Miss Hene said.

"Yes, especially so when we do not understand what it is."

"You know, Puncus, you are right in that."

"Thank you, Miss Hene. But if I may add, it always is a blessing: it creates wrinkles in our lives and brings out different truths, and makes otherwise unacceptable situations palatable."

"So opposing truths may not be lies then, ah?"

"Right! They do not have to be."

"Well then, Puncus, in that way we may have a solution with Kwame. I know he loves you; and if you have half the regard for him that you have for Yoofi, I know we will be all right," Miss Hene said. She gazed at the man resting on her lap, and recognized what she felt for him, despite not knowing what, if anything, they agreed on.

Puncus, whose eyes had been closed while he spoke, opened them to find Miss Hene leaning to kiss him. He accepted her lips and reached his long slender arms to her shoulders.

"I know how to make breakfast, too, you know," Miss Hene said, raising her head.

"And I, too, know how to wash dishes," Puncus replied.

"Good then," she said, and walked him toward her bedroom. "The boys need to sleep."

"And so do we," he laughed as hand in hand they strolled down the hall.

The children played late, as they usually did. They did not know how to speak about Yoofi and his departure. Dean thought of it as Yoofi's death.

If they failed to talk of their brother, it would seem as if Yoofi had died. On the other hand, if they spoke of him, the pain they buried might return. Moreover, what about the questions Yoofi had put to them? How would we ever find answers to them? Dean wondered.

In silence, the boys quieted from their play and fell asleep in each other's arms.

The following morning, breakfast was served with as much ease and comfort.

A Simple Sketch

Congo, at Ulu's prompting, had spent the past week prospecting. As the demand for spice increased, Congo was sent further and further from home in search of new pimento plantations. His sojourn took him from the borders of Portland to the farthest regions of St. Ann. He traveled on horseback. Congo was not familiar with most of the places he went, but his affable nature soon won him easy friends and comfortable lodgings with the farmers who signed on to do business with him.

During his travels, Congo and Ulu communicated through telegrams. It was one of her telegrams that made him know Miss Hene desired his counsel. One reason Congo started to travel was to escape Ulu's niggling. Ulu had never forgiven Congo for having betrayed her in his affair with Laura. She sought revenge.

Congo, instead of returning home directly, went to Miss Hene's house. From there, he took Yoofi and started the journey to Jacks River.

"Uncle Congo," Yoofi started as they rode side by side under the brightness of a full moon.

"Yes, Yoofi. Is there something you want to ask?"

"Yes," Yoofi replied with more hesitation. "What is a man?"

"A man, Yoofi? Do you mean any man?"

"Yes, Uncle Congo, any man. What is a man?"

"Well, why do you ask, Yoofi?"

"Mas Leroy says I am a man, and I should be responsible for myself."

"Ah! He does? So, tell me, Yoofi. How old are you now?"

"Sixteen."

"Goodness! You have some growing to do, Yoofi."

"Before I am a man?"

"Yes, I fear so."

"So how will I know when I am a man?"

"I suppose by the way people respond to you. I do not know if there are any clear signs, Yoofi."

"I wonder what sign Mas Leroy saw in me?"

"He may not have seen anything in particular. But he may have had his own motive for saying you are a man."

There was silence. Yoofi knew that Leroy had long wanted him to stop nursing. Yoofi guessed correctly that Leroy didn't understand or trust the relationship between him and his mother. He knew Leroy hated him. Maybe, he considered, it was his fault. He had been stubborn, insolent, and unmanageable. It must have been his mistakes, his behavior, which gave Leroy the motive to prematurely call him a man. The horses stepped briskly, making the only sound. Maybe they were talking, too, Yoofi pondered.

"But I would still like to know, Uncle Congo. What is a man?"

"I suppose, Yoofi, you could look at it this way. The world consists of different types of people. So I suppose a man is someone who knows how to live, or at least get along with every type of person."

Yoofi reflected on Leroy. That made him feel as though he had failed a major test. He had failed completely to live harmoniously with Leroy.

"But that takes time, Yoofi. Years and years of living. And, even then, the best of us, man or woman, fails sometimes."

"But people look up to you, Uncle Congo. They think you are a man."

"So they think that, ah?" Congo laughed.

"Yes, people admire you. I hear what they say about you. To them, you are a man. How do you do it, Uncle Congo?"

"I try to live an open life, Yoofi. I keep no secrets about how I live. I make few promises, and keep as many of them as are possible. If something prevents me from keeping a promise, I let the person know, and find a way to make up for it."

"Is that all?"

"No. I suppose you could say there is more than that. I try to show respect without expecting any. And if I can be kind, if I can find something to give: I am happy."

"You make it sound simple, Uncle Congo."

"Life should be simple, Yoofi. When I find it too hard, I mean impossibly hard, I know I am going in the wrong direction and quickly turn around. I like difficulty. I like a hard day; it makes me sweat and I like that. But there is a difference, Yoofi, between something that is challenging and a thing that is impossible. I suppose the trick – and this goes back to experience – is knowing the difference. So as I said, Yoofi, there is a lot of road ahead of you."

"So if I live long, you are saying, I become a man?"

"Not quite, but that is a part of it, Yoofi. Another part of it is giving yourself a purpose, a reason to live. Some folks call that a goal. It can be looked at like our journey home. We are riding for a purpose. If we get on the wrong road, we get help and change our path. That is a big part of being a man, Yoofi. Getting help, admitting mistakes, rectifying the damages of the past and changing. I suppose some would call that humility. Really, it's just living. And if you do not make your mistakes hound you, but grow from them, that is also a part of being a man."

"Now, you make it all complicated, Uncle Congo."

"Just remember this, Yoofi. There is a little voice inside that talks to you. That is what I should have told you about at first, maybe. That is all that matters."

"What, Uncle Congo? That it talks? Because I hear it all the time."

"No, Yoofi." Congo replied laughing, as he glanced admiringly at the lad. "Life is complete only when we listen to it. If we truly listen and follow it, then living is easy, and the things I told you about will all fall in place. But first, we must learn to be silent: silent and listening!"

"But sometimes it's confusing, or sometimes it tells me things that get me into trouble."

"When you hear two voices, you should listen some more, till one of them goes away. Do not fight, just listen, then follow through. And as for getting you into trouble, Yoofi, that's what will almost always happen if you listen correctly, even if you don't realize it at first. So I suppose I should also mention courage, just enough to do as you hear."

"What, Uncle Congo? I do not want to get into trouble."

"No, Yoofi. None of us want to. But sometimes trouble is exactly what we need! I know I did say life should be easy. But trouble, if it is for the right reason, is good. And that is the kind of trouble you really want."

"So listen to that voice. Is that it?"

"Yes, Yoofi. Simply listen and be obedient to it."

"Now, that's much easier."

"Of course it is. Remember, Yoofi. Life must be easy!"

"I thank you, Uncle Congo. Whew! I feel relieved!"

"Well, there is one more thing, Yoofi."

"Something else, Uncle Congo?"

"I always find something to do for me, just for me and no one else."

"What is that for you, Uncle Congo?"

"For me, that is painting. I do it all the while, whether I have paper or not. I keep on sketching, drawing and redrawing things in my head, then on paper. When I am satisfied with my paintings, I give them away. Whether or not folks like what I do, it does not matter. Of course, I would prefer if they got some pleasure from it. But for me, the pleasure is in the sketching of it. So when the drawing is done, I am happy. I may not like it either, but that does not matter. I had pleasure in doing it. That is everything, making the sketches. And no matter how it comes out, no one can take that pleasure from me. And when I am done with one, I go on to the next, and so on.

"I Dance, Uncle Congo. And that's how it makes me feel, too."

"Very good, Yoofi. I have heard that. And Dance as much as you can. It will do good for you some day."

"Thank you, Uncle Congo."

They rode on in silence. Yoofi pondered what Congo had told him.

"Perhaps, Yoofi, I should tell you these things, too. I always have something much bigger than me to believe in. For me, that is Kumina. You already know that. When everything on earth fails, when all seems lost, I have that to hold on to. And for day-to-day living, I always have someone here, older, wiser, and so on, to look up to."

"And who do you look up to, Uncle Congo?"

"For me, that is Asa King, of course! He is the greatest man I know and the reason is that he always shows me a bigger world."

"Can I look up to you, Uncle Congo?"

"Why, yes! Of course, Yoofi, you can. But please remember. I make a lot of mistakes. Or should I say, get into a lot of trouble? So I change courses quite often. If you can understand that, Yoofi, you can look up to me."

"That's all right, Uncle Congo. Just let me know what you are doing."

"I will, Yoofi. As soon as I know."

They laughed and looked admiringly at each other in the bright moonlight.

"Thank you, Uncle Congo. I believe now, I can be a man."

Congo leaned back in his saddle and laughed. "Of course, Yoofi. You are right on time, but remember, you have a lot of road ahead of you."

It was quite late when Congo, accompanied by Yoofi, arrived home. Congo lit a candle as he entered the house and began showing Yoofi to his bedroom. For that, they had to go upstairs, since that was where all the bedrooms were. Congo intended Yoofi to have the guest bedroom. To Congo's surprise, a man was in the bed. Congo closed the door and slowly walked to his room. Princess was in his bed beside Ulu. Further down the hall was another empty room. When Congo went there it was filled with suitcases and unopened boxes. He didn't know what had happened, but he surmised they belonged to the visitor. Charm occupied her room. Princess's room was unoccupied. Congo beckoned Yoofi to follow him. They would share Princess's room that night.

Before going to bed, Congo pointed out the washroom to Yoofi. He asked him to bathe and put on his best clothes in the morning to meet Ulu and the rest of the family.

Displaced Assignments

When Congo was finally called to breakfast the following morning, he roused the well-groomed Yoofi from the chair where they were waiting in conversation and, placing his arm about the lad's shoulder, escorted him to breakfast.

To Congo's great surprise, the unknown visitor sat at the head of the table. This was Congo's accustomed position. Ulu, standing behind her seat at the foot of the table, beckoned Congo to sit across from Princess and Charm. Ulu didn't know of Yoofi's arrival, but nevertheless, pointed him to the seat next to Congo and facing Charm. Yoofi's eyes went straight to hers, and, exchanging anxious little blushing smiles, they lowered their heads. Charm, by Ulu's orders, ate with the family, not to accentuate any blood ties with her or to reward Charm for her good work, but purely to serve Princess.

The maids nervously busied themselves with frequent trips to the table, wanting to know when to commence the service. Having seated everyone and finally taking her seat, Ulu signaled for the beginning course of fresh cut fruit.

Congo eyed the stranger, then looked at Ulu, awaiting her introduction. When it didn't come, Congo reached out his hand and said, "Good morning, my name is Congo; and who, may I ask, are you?"

"Rex Covey, Congo. I thought you knew!"

Congo smiled. He had heard of the name, and knew that Rex lived

331

in New York, but hadn't the slightest hint what he looked like or that he would be visiting.

"Ah! You are the brother I have heard so much about. Nice meeting you, Rex," Congo continued, rising to embrace his brother-in-law. "And this is Yoofi. Stand, Yoofi, and say good morning to your Uncle, Rex."

"Good morning, Uncle Rex, and you too, Aunt Ulu, and Princess. Mammy sends you her love and says she will come to see you soon," Yoofi said, standing. He held his head down, as if shy or simply afraid of the strange, quizzical eyes darting at him.

"Good morning, Yoofi," Ulu replied. With cheerfully returned greeting, the lad reclaimed his seat.

"And the young lady before you is Charm. She is the stewardess for Princess, your cousin," Congo said.

"Kiss-me-neck! Lawd mi-gaud she pretty!" Yoofi exclaimed, bowing his head in embarrassment. He was surprised and dismayed by what he had just said.

"You say that because you do not . . ." Charm was about to rebuke him.

"What's that you said, Yoofi? You better pay more attention to your cousin," Ulu interrupted Charm. "You will be much better off that way!" Ulu dabbed her lips with her napkin and neatly set it on her lap.

"Yes, Aunt Ulu. Sorry, Miss Charm."

Charm looked at him with equal pity and disdain. She was glad for not having had the opportunity to complete the insult she intended to throw in his face.

"Charm is your . . ." Congo was about to explain to Yoofi.

"And learn to think before you speak, Yoofi!" Ulu interrupted Congo.

"Yes, Aunt Ulu."

"What you said was very impolite! Don't let me hear that country-bumpkin talk from you ever again. Do you understand?"

"Yes, Aunt Ulu. I will behave myself from now on, ma'am."

"Good!"

To change the conversation and save Yoofi from more unnecessary scolding, Congo turned to Rex and asked, "So tell us about yourself, and your trip, Rex. Was it easy to find us here?"

"About me? Well, I doubt there is anything you have not heard as yet."

"He attended college in New York."

"Ah! And what was your discipline, Rex?"

"What a quaint way to ask it! I studied philosophy, theology, and ethics."

"And what was your degree in?"

"I didn't apply for a degree. I simply studied."

"I understand."

"What do you understand, Congo? Have you been to college?"

"No. But . . . Well . . ."

"I can tell you," Rex smiled. "I really couldn't make up my mind what to settle on. But I have all the education I need. I have been there for over seven years."

"You couldn't make up your mind?"

"No. And it was not really necessary. Based on our plans, a degree wouldn't really make a difference," Ulu chimed in.

"And what, may I ask, are those plans?"

"Rex is here to take over the Covey family-business," Ulu responded.

"Yes," confirmed Rex. "I spent the last few days looking over your records and going into the fields with Ulu, seeing what you have been doing."

"And he has struck up a remarkable friendship with Detective Graham, I should also add," Ulu said.

"Just a boyhood reconnection, Ulu. You know that," Rex said with a smile.

"Yes, but this time it's business, Rex. I hope you remember that."

"Of course, Ulu! Business always comes first here," Rex said, looking up at Ulu as if to ask for her silence concerning Graham.

"So, Rex . . . what do you think?" Congo asked, breaking the ensuing silence.

"To tell the truth, Congo, the house here is run really well. I must lift off my hat to Ulu, seeing she does it by herself."

The maids removed the used fruit dishes, replacing them with eggs, toast, cereals, ham, an assortment of drinks and hot bread. Yoofi watched as the service punctuated the flow of the conversation, giving him time to eye Charm.

"This situation out in the fields, your verbal contracts with the farmers, their setting the prices and you simply agreeing with them, what appears to be your friendly unbusinesslike tone – and what it means to us – your entire approach is striking, to say the least."

"And to say the most?"

"Disgusting. Totally undesirable!"

There was a pause. Congo looked at Ulu for support. She and Rex eyed each other with nodding smiles. The trap she'd laid for Congo was sprung. He stopped eating, staring pensively at the table. This was the moment Ulu had waited for. Congo had hurt her.

It started at the picnic at the pond years ago when, instead of chasing her, Congo had chased her friend, Laura. He hurt her when he continued the relationship with Laura, choosing to spend his time with her, and now, more recently, with Laura or Ho. It hurt her how sometimes, instead of placing all her money in the bank, he bought lavish clothes for himself. He overpaid for the produce and undersold it to his lover. She hated her dependency on him. She'd hated it from the very first. She hated him for encouraging the relationship between Ama and Headmaster Love. He should have had the foresight to discontinue it and lead Henry Love to her. She hated that, with Henry gone, this son of a bizarre Kumina King renamed her through marriage. It was a fall in her social class from which she never considered herself recovered. She hated his artistic talent, how he labored over it, dedicated his time to it and not to her. She hated that she was never taken to the center of his life. She hated her dependency on Congo: that her only child, her wonderful Princess, came through him. She hated that aspect of Providence that brought and stuck them together, not only legally on earth, but maybe forever though their progeny. She hated it, and wished day and night that she could relieve herself of him. She loathed him!

"What exactly I have always been saying! See, Congo! Thank goodness, there is someone else in this world who agrees with me!" Ulu said.

"I agree with you on most things, Ulu; and I have served our business."

"My business, Congo. This is a Covey business."

"We had better talk in private, Ulu, both of us, thrashing this out."

"In private! In private? Did you disgrace me in private? Did you take that loathsome bitch in private? Did you once consider my feelings? Or did you flaunt your sinful life in public before me? Why is public not good for you now, Congo?"

"It is good for me, Ulu. But not everything you mention concerns everyone here."

"Well, it does now! This is the Covey business; and if you want to live here any longer, you will show Rex what you do, all the new and old customers, everything! He will take over from here."

"I don't mind showing you everything, Rex," Congo said with the faintest smile he could muster.

"You don't mind? You will, Congo! You will show him everything, if you know what is good for you."

"Could you really explain what you mean by that, Ulu?"

"What I told you before: this is the Covey business. And if you want anything out of it, you better do what I say!"

"Our business, Ulu. We are married."

"Married! Where did you sleep last night? Let that serve to tell you how well we are married. And from now on, you better find another place to sleep."

"I can sleep anywhere, Ulu."

"Yes! And I know you will, too. Anywhere, and between any legs that are open for you. You should be ashamed of yourself, admitting to your daughter you can so easily find someone to sleep with."

"This is going too far, Ulu. I have business to attend to."

"It has just started, Congo. And you have no business to attend to, anymore. Rex took over while you were gone. I ordered the farmers, all whom I know, to work only with Rex. You will show him the rest of the farmers I do not know. Laura will buy only from Rex. And as for Ho, he will not get any produce from me. Who is he anyway?"

"Well, at least, I need money to . . ."

"That's all you ever want from us, our money. Money, money, money! It's such a good thing I didn't put you on any of my bank accounts! Rex is in charge. I added his name to all my papers. And don't bother going to the renters in Port Maria. They will not hand over the rent to you anymore, either. I want you to understand; Rex is now the man of this house."

"So, Ulu, if you want me to leave, we should split the estate as man and wife."

"What man? Yes, if you were a man! Everything is in my name, Congo. And you have taken more from the business to flirt with your friends than you are worth. You ask for a split. What is there to split? You took yours already and squandered it."

"Such a shame," Rex said. "How did you manage to stoop so low, man?"

Congo didn't reply. He slowly surveyed the table. No one was eating.

Princess sat crying, and Charm did whatever she could to comfort her. Princess loved her father. She wanted him to stay. But she also wanted her mother to be happy.

Yoofi sat in confusion. He didn't know what to do. What is Congo, if not a man? Yoofi pondered.

Congo looked at Rex. "I brought Yoofi here to help with the pimento. He is strong and hard working. I am sure you can find things for him to do."

Ulu looked at Yoofi. "You can stay. We will try you out. But if you are anything like that uncle of yours, you will have to leave right away." Ulu paused, with her eyes fixed on the lad.

"I can work."

"I can work, who?"

"Sorry, Aunt Ulu," Yoofi repented. "I can work, Aunt Ulu," he corrected himself.

"And you better!"

"Did Congo tell you how much to charge me?"

"No, Aunt Ulu."

"For the first three months you get nothing except room and board. You are here to learn. And you'd better be thankful I have the heart to bother with you. Rex will train you. I do not want you playing with Princess and teaching her your bad, country-bumpkin habits. I am trying to make a lady out of her."

"Yes, Aunt Ulu."

"You will sleep in the servant's house, and never, never again up here. Do you understand me?"

"Yes, Aunt Ulu."

"Congo will take you to your room. And no playing with the servants. You seem mannish, bit too tallawah for my taste! You have the gall calling the young woman 'pretty' to my face. You better mind your own business from here on. And if you have anything good to say, say it about Princess. She is your cousin."

"Yes, Aunt Ulu," Yoofi managed to mutter.

"And five shilling a week for you, after your training, if I decide to keep you."

"Yes, Aunt Ulu."

"He is worth at least fifteen shillings a week, Ulu," Congo protested.

"See! That is exactly what I mean!" Rex responded. "The boy has nothing. Ulu is trying to help him and you are making it harder for her to do so. Think, Congo. Yoofi is the only one that can lose here!"

"Yes, that may be so, but still he is worth it!"

"Congo, you are not in a position to pay, so you are not in a position to decide," Ulu said.

"Take Yoofi to his bunk in the servant's cottage, and let's talk when you get back," Rex said. "I'll show you how business is done."

Congo looked at Princess and Charm and managed a little smile. Placing his arm around Yoofi's shoulder, Congo walked with the lad from the table. They retrieved Yoofi's little brown grip from the room where he and Yoofi had slept and walked outside to a small, cobwebbed room. Congo sat for a while with the lad. They didn't talk much. Congo pointed to the corner of the room and asked Yoofi to choose a bunk. He did, and soon Congo lay on his back across the other bed, his head resting in his open palms. Congo peered through the window, his gaze slowly concentrating on a distant yet undetermined object. He stared, as Yoofi took the old broom from the corner and started removing the cobwebs. Then slowly he unpacked his clothes, carefully laying them in the upper drawer of the aged bureau.

Congo didn't know how long he remained prostrate, gazing. He stayed in the room until Yoofi seemed comfortable, at least comfortable enough to sit.

"I will look over your shoulder from time to time, Yoofi."

"I know, Uncle Congo."

"Soon I must leave. I will move my office to Barton House."

"Your office, Uncle Congo?" laughed Yoofi. He was well aware that Congo kept all the information about his operation in his head.

"Yes, Yoofi," he replied, raising himself from the bed. "I will operate from Miss Hene's. So if you need me, don't hesitate. Ride a horse there and wait until I return."

"Okay, Uncle Congo."

"I will be talking to your Uncle Rex. After that, I will ride out to see some business partners. In about a week I will be at Miss Hene's."

"It's all right, Uncle Congo. I will be fine."

"Well, okay then," Congo remarked absent-mindedly and moved to the door.

"By the way, Yoofi. What do you intend to do in your spare time?"

"Spare time, Uncle Congo?"

"Yes, your own time, when you do not have things to do for your Aunt Ulu."

"Oh! I didn't know that word, Uncle Congo."

"Well, what do you plan to do then?"

"I never thought about it, Uncle Congo."

"I know the Detective. His name is Charles Graham. He is quite a friendly man. I will arrange for you to attend classes at the police academy in the evenings with the new recruits and exercise in the gym with them."

"Go to school?" Yoofi asked in great surprise.

"Yes, Yoofi. It will not be regular school. You must be over eighteen years old to be registered. I know you are only sixteen, but I will get you in, if you are interested."

"Yes, yes! Uncle Congo. And please remember to tell Mammy for me. Tell her I am going to school again!"

"Yes, Yoofi. I believe the exercise and associating with progressive men in the constabulary will be of great help to you."

"I really thank you, Uncle Congo. Thank you. Thank you!"

"I must leave now, Yoofi."

"I am going to miss you, Uncle Congo."

"I will be back soon, Yoofi. I know you will get lonely and sad when you think of Providence. But I will come back to see you as soon as I can."

"Thank you," the lad said, restraining his tears.

"Very soon, I will take you to Port Maria and show you around. Till then, good-bye, Yoofi."

The lad moved toward Congo and hugged him. Without looking back, Congo released him and hastened to talk with Rex.

Shining Mountain

Rex was already downstairs in the large, mahogany-paneled living room. Its walls were rich with Congo's drawings. The stamp Headmaster Love had put on his work gave it lasting meaning for Ulu. Rex removed the pipe from his mouth, mainly playing with the Cuban flavor and smoke which soon filled the room.

"Get us coffee, Congo, and let's talk. I can't wait to get your opinions on life."

"It's not easy to hold an opinion of life now, Rex. I have just been fired," he smiled.

"Come on, come on old chap. That will soon wear off, and life goes on, you know."

"Yes, but as you see, it's quite strange how these things happen. Between yesterday and now, I have gone from rich to poor without doing anything different, except to work harder. How on earth do these things happen?"

"Well, in your specific case, it seems to be thoughtlessness. And, since you ask, a bit of selfishness on your side. After all, this is a family business, you know. And you can't expect Ulu simply to hand it over to you. Can you, Congo?"

"No. Not at all, Rex."

"Well, there is your answer. But if you meant the larger question of how things happen, that is quite another matter."

"What do you mean, Rex?"

"I mean nothing more than this, Congo. All kinds of things are possible. Everything, actually. There is certainly enough energy around for that. But this leads to many kinds of possibilities. So you can easily see, the world is not entirely predictable. Neither can it have a single purpose."

"That's certainly a curious view, Rex."

"You may say so if you like, Congo. But . . . if I may continue . . ."

"Please do, Rex."

"Well then," Rex said smiling, "some of these events may be fortunate for you. I suppose you would call them blessings or miracles, you being of a religious persuasion."

"Well . . . ?"

"Let's say the same conditions lead to an opposite set of results. If you do not like how those events affect your life, you say you have bad luck. Maybe that's what you are saying now," Rex said in a roaring burst of laughter.

"I didn't say I have bad luck, Rex. I simply asked a question. But you may not be right, anyway."

"How can that be?"

"Well, Rex, you left out will power. I can will things, and they happen."

"Will things, like the weather?"

"I am talking about things in my life, Rex. I plan, dream, and will things, and they happen."

"You make yourself sound like God," Rex laughed. "So stupid! So tell me, Congo, did you will your present situation on yourself?"

"Of course not! Ulu did. She planned it. It was her will, her dream, and you know that quite well."

"So what happened to your will?"

"Let's put it this way: Ulu prevailed. I willed other things. She willed this. I suppose one cannot cover all aspects of life at once."

"Nonsense, nonsense! And you know that. Your own negligence, your own selfishness, your sloth led to your downfall. You must at least admit that."

"The thing I must admit, Rex, is that I am now willing to rethink my life and will things differently."

"You may at least admit, Bongo-man, that you failed. But you know, Congo, there is still something of a curiosity about you."

"And what is that, Rex?"

"Your name, Bongo-man. Your name!"

"My name? What's curious about that?"

"Actually, Congo. It is the M that starts your name that I find intrigu-ing. Master M. Congo King! Now, what on earth is that miserable 'M' for?"

Congo thought for a while. Do I have something to hide? Why should I tell him? "The M is for Manjaro," Congo finally ventured. He was unaccustomed to the sound of his own name, but he was glad to say it out loud rather than hide it from Rex.

"Manjaro? Master Manjaro Congo King! Quite an expression!"

"It is my name, Rex."

"And do you know where the Manjaro comes from or what it means, Mr. Bongo-man?"

Congo stood dumbfounded for a while. He had never asked that question of Asa. He simply accepted his name, but finding Manjaro long and meaningless, simply used "M." instead of the entire word. "Strange. I do not."

"Maybe I can shed some light on it. Manjaro seems to be derived from the word Kilimanjaro . . . any knowledge of what that is, old chap?"

"No at all, Rex."

"So you don't even know what your own name means? Tsk, tsk, tsk," Rex sucked his teeth. "Maybe a little enlightenment even this late in your life may help. What do you say, country boy?"

"That may also be useful, Rex."

"Well, Congo, Kilimanjaro is the highest mountain in Africa. In fact, Congo, in the Swahili tongue your name means *Shining Mountain*. I believe that's what you were willed to be. But you, a shining mountain? You are so ignoble, insolent, and incomplete . . . you make an absolute mockery of mankind!"

"I suppose you are right, Rex," Congo said, more weary than con-vinced.

"This I am leading to, Congo. You must stop the incomplete pro-cesses in your life. And if, as you said, you want to start over, then begin by accepting responsibility for your situation and not blaming my sister for what has happened."

"I suppose you are right, but do you really understand what I was asking; how this really happened between Ulu and me? I did not expect all of this, Rex. Maybe that's what you learned in college, but that was not what I asked about.

"Yes, I understand, and soon you will. Soon you will understand fully what Ulu really means."

"I understand her quite well, Rex. And I choose to call this a blessing! You may label it whatever you like."

"Whatever! But you needn't be so obstinate. At least, admit that you are a loser. And what about my coffee, anyway?"

"Before I leave, Rex. I have a suggestion. Why not try things out for a while, learn on your own, and then ask me whatever you like, later on. I will be at Barton House. Ulu knows how to find me."

"Don't change the conversation, Congo! And let me add, yours is not the best attitude for someone in your position. You may need my help sometime, and imagine, you are so stubborn! Or is it your false pride, or your broken manhood? You wouldn't learn good service and bring me even a cup of coffee. How do you expect to succeed? I could still put in a good word for you with Ulu, you know."

"Let's leave the coffee alone for a while, Rex. And yes, I may be strong-willed. But I offer my help to you here, in my way. Just give the suggestion a try. I will be available later to answer whatever questions you have."

"On second thought, Congo, you may have a point. This will give me an opportunity to see your errors first hand and create a brand new plan from ground up, rather than patching yours here and there."

Congo laughed and turned to go, "We'll have coffee later, Rex. I still have a full day ahead."

He left the building, walked to the store, and beckoned to Ulu. She left the counter and came to see what he wanted.

"Ulu?" he asked. That was his way to get her out of the store. He could talk privately with her, away from the servants.

"Yes, Congo."

"There must be a better way for us to settle things."

"Better for whom, Congo?"

"Both of us."

"What do you want, Congo?"

"For now, traveling money."

"You spent all that's yours already."

"Well, Ulu, at least pay me for last week's work?"

"What do you think you deserve when you were out having fun with *my* money?"

"Please, Ulu. Let's not fight."

She looked away from him. Let me pay him off and let him go, she thought.

"How much?"

"Five guineas."

"What! Five guineas!"

"Yes, five guineas, Ulu."

She went into the store, opened the till, and brought out the money.

"Here, take it and go. And don't come back here. You are not a Covey!"

"I know, Ulu. But until your dying day, you will be a King. You do not know us, Ulu."

"And I do not care to know you anymore. So you better go!"

"Yes, Ulu. I will go and do Asa King's business. I will go build my Family. You will see, Ulu, I will find a way!"

"Yes, go to your Asa King and his God-forsaken business. But you better not dare set foot back on Covey property."

"Are you threatening me, Ulu?"

"What is there to threaten? No, Congo. There is no threat here. You are done for. Why did you really believe I married you? When you and that penniless Asa King sat at our breakfast table telling us your stupid ways, I devised a plan for you. Do you see my plan now? How wise are you and your Kumina god? Tell me, Congo. Tell me!"

"I will when I get back."

"Well, you come back here and you will see!"

"See what, Ulu?"

"What? See what? So help me, God. If you set one foot back here on Covey property, I will go straight to Detective Graham and tell him what you did to Lev. You remember Lev Tyler, don't you? And if you don't, you should not believe for a moment that I forgot about him. He was my best friend! You hear me, Congo? My best friend, and you and your demonic Kumina Family killed him. You better just go! Leave now! Go back to where you came from and don't you ever come back!" she said as she broke out crying.

Rex heard the commotion and joined them. He came closer to Ulu and, placing a comforting arm about her shoulders while he looked scornfully at Congo, said, "Old chap!" Then, after kissing Ulu's cheeks, he repeated: "Old chap." He patted Congo on the shoulder. "It seems you are up the creek without a paddle again, aren't you, man?"

When Congo didn't reply, Rex continued, "How on earth did you get yourself in such a pickle in these short years? I'll bet it had to do with not keeping your eyes focused on Ulu's business, or by not being accustomed to this lifestyle. Haven't you been playing out of your league? Now, you have the lesson of a lifetime. Just go on! Get on with it, old chap! Don't keep your Kumina Family waiting on our account," Rex ended with a roar of laughter.

With that, Congo mounted his ride.

"You know, Congo, you do remind me of someone from the Bible."

"Who is that, Rex?"

"Jonah. Do you know that disobedient fellow?"

"Do you mean, Rex, the Jonah who swallowed the big fish and had to spit it back out, because it almost choked him to death?" Congo asked with a sarcastic twist of the old tale.

"You are so daft!"

"What he means, Rex, is that you ate the big fish," Ulu explained, "in taking over the Covey enterprise. It will choke you to death!"

Rex looked up at Congo. "Get out! Get out, you damn scoundrel!" he repeated, pointing Congo to the road. "Just go on and leave our ship in safety!"

Congo looked at Rex, then paused. He quickly dismounted and rushed back into the house, to Princess's bedroom.

"Princess! Princess! Where are you, my Princess?"

"In here, Pappy."

Princess liked playing hide and seek when Congo was about to leave the house. She knew he would go to look for her. She didn't this time, though, for fear of not being found.

"I love you, Princess!"

"I love you, too, Pappy."

He took off his hat, sat on her bed with her in his lap and started to read to her. It didn't take long before Princess dozed off into her midday nap.

He laid her on her bed with the window above her head open. The gentle breeze wafted the smell of Cuban smoke into the room. He wished it were not so. But knowing the odor would soon dissipate, he kissed his daughter and departed.

As Congo moved away from Princess his mind turned immediately to Ama. At first he did not know why, but he felt Ama's strong presence, almost overpowering about him. It was a troubled, desperate visit, calling, pressing on him for help. Congo almost turned to go to Providence, but deferred and assured himself and Ama, or at least her presence, that he would soon be with her in Providence. For now, there were more urgent matters at hand.

When it seemed to him that Ama had reached a place of peaceful understanding, Congo, with steely resolve, quickened his pace into the ensuing day.

Master Congo and Detective Graham

Congo's mind turned next to Oracabessa and Laura. There he thought he would find comfort and a space from which to see and then recreate his future. Congo would have gone there directly, but he had to see Detective Graham. He remembered the promise he had made to Yoofi.

Detective Graham was a staunch Catholic. That was how Congo met him, at Sunday Mass. However, Congo also loved the Anglican homilies, which Ulu, with quiet insincerity, encouraged him to attend.

Ulu had once remarked that it would be better for them to fish from either bank of the religious river, for by doing so, at least one of them might get to heaven. Congo had replied that the river was the same from either bank. That strengthened Ulu's position since, being embarrassed to be in church with her husband, she urged him to attend the Catholic services.

Monsignor Ricardo Silva, a stout friendly man, engaged Congo and the Detective in conversation following each service. The affable Congo could not resist inviting both men to his home for brunch on Sundays when the Reverend Bernard Watkins, Ulu's guest, would certainly be there. An awkward but true friendship had sprung from these early meetings.

Unknown to Congo, the friendship between Rex and the Detective had grown remarkably strong. The relationship started at brunch in Ulu's presence, but it matured in the bars and restaurants of Port Maria where the men played. To gain acceptance, Rex was unusually forthcoming in offering information that concerned Congo for the Detective.

Congo encountered Graham on horseback that very Monday morning as he traveled to Oracabessa.

"Hello, Graham," Congo called as he slowed.

"Nice to see you, Congo. Seems you are in a hurry this morning."

"Yes, Graham. I must be in Oracabessa before noon. But I thought I would chat with you for a while."

"Certainly. What about, Congo?"

"A favor, Graham. I need to ask you a favor. Then I must be going."

"And what is it, Congo?"

"It concerns Yoofi, my sister's son."

"Well, what about the lad, Congo?"

"You see, Graham, my nephew Yoofi is living with us. I would love if you could allow him to attend classes at the academy and exercise with the men."

"How old is he, Congo?"

"Sixteen."

"Sixteen! He is just out of elementary school, ah?"

"Yes, Detective . . . it's the graduating age."

"Green! He's very green, Congo."

"Yes, Graham, but he is willing. And it would be a great favor to me."

"Give me some time. I will work it out, Congo."

"Thank you, Graham. Now I may be away on business, but you can let Ulu know your decision."

"Okay, I will."

"Thank you again, Detective," Congo said. He nudged his horse closer to Graham's for a departing handshake. Although Congo sensed cold insincerity in the Detective's hand, he allowed it to pass, blaming it instead on his own uncertain mind and some innocent preoccupation of the Detective's.

He rode along, lulled by his reverie of Laura's love and her gentle comfort that would soon calm his soul.

Give–away Man

Congo rode steadily into Oracabessa, thinking only of Laura. He had left one world behind, and only another realm, one in which Laura ruled, filled him with joy.

He didn't quite know what to say to Laura. Surely he loved her. But he also still cared for his wife. It didn't matter that Ulu's love hadn't been fully manifested, that he knew not where it flowed. He loved and still hoped for its fruition . . . that it would someday find him. Moreover, how could he give up his daughter? He adored Princess and would do anything for her comfort. In any case, there he was, deeply loving Laura, grieving that his wife had always hated and used him.

He didn't know what Princess had made of the conversation at the breakfast table. Congo wished it hadn't happened. He surmised Rex was right. He had been blind and irresponsible. Was he the ever-trusting fool? How did her deceit go unnoticed? Ulu's attack was a total surprise. The swift, efficient follow-through by Rex prevented Congo from creating a good defense, let alone a counterattack. Congo was left wounded and thoroughly saddened.

That it happened at all, Congo considered unfortunate. That it occurred in public, he considered sinful. Yet he didn't blame Ulu. Neither was he angry that she behaved the way she did about the money they had earned. Disappointed, dismayed, hurt, and awakened to treachery and lies, yes. But Congo was not angry.

Congo dressed well, and most often in excess. There was a splash of flamboyance in him. He worked hard and considered his appearance a part of his persona. He didn't understand how to do business otherwise. Was he a squanderer? Congo considered not. He enjoyed the results of his toil and liked to share them.

Distraught, he traveled to see Laura, thinking of Princess and how he could remedy what had happened and still maintain her trust. Ulu's concern about Princess's future bothered him. Ulu wanted to use their wealth to buy or trap an unsuspecting husband for Princess. Why should a parent be so overly concerned about the future of an offspring? He thought it sufficient to provide for and protect the child, to point out acceptable choices. But to provide wealth to pass from one generation to another, he considered preposterous. Yet that was his wife's desire for Princess. She would never toil, only consume and command. It struck him that he had been used, and for a scheme he despised. His mind grew heavy. It would have weighted him down to despair and sadness were it not for his dreams of Laura and her deep, comforting love.

Upon seeing Congo, Laura left her counter and met him in front. She took him upstairs to show him her completed building. She walked him everywhere, displaying new and exotic merchandise.

Finally, they reached her bedroom, where Laura rested when late work prevented her return to Free Hill. They no sooner sat on the bed than they were clutched in each other's arms and in the throes of lovemaking. Their thirst for each other was not easily quenched; and even upon a respite, they were still locked together body and soul. Laura began to talk. It was what she liked most about making love, that they remained joined long after the vigor died. It pleased her that Congo remained, studying her eyes, searching for her concerns or joy, understanding her moods without speech. At those times Congo became more open and transparent.

"Why are you so sad, Congo?"

It took him a while before answering. He hadn't been in that bed with her before. It was a lovely room high above the road. From one set of windows, the hills climbed into majestic sun-baked greenery; and from the other, the broad sea lay like an azure blanket, touched with billows of roving, white foam. He watched the birds stretch their wings, sailing silently, as if supported from the bright blue skies above. He caught a wisp of warm, clean sea breeze. It is lovely, he thought, lying here with my Laura. How did she know I was sad? Am I sad for me? Is it for Ulu or me? Sad?

But what is Ulu doing here? She never came here with me before, never! Sad? I must be sad for Laura! What must I tell her? Why am I sad?

"It's not so easy to tell, Laura. But I'll tell you what's on my mind, and you tell me what's making me sad," he laughed.

Laura smiled, and Congo told her. He told her about Rex replacing him. He told her of his removal from Jacks River. He said he was going to develop a business of his own, then do as Asa King had requested of him. He wanted to be self-supporting, to be able to give to his Princess and to live as he had grown accustomed. He assured Laura that her business with Ulu would continue under Rex's leadership and that she should refer all questions to Rex or Ulu. He told Laura about his love for Princess, something he hadn't before disclosed to anyone save himself and his daughter. He had kept it silent in his heart, loving her and doing whatever he could for her, but never divulging the deep intensity of his feeling. Congo spoke and spoke. He scarcely gave Laura a chance to talk or even smile as he moved from subject to subject, talking about his nephew, Yoofi, and the difficulties there. He went on and on, like the rolling sea, encouraged by Laura, the wind behind him. At length, when Congo had no more to say, he looked at her and the tears in her eyes.

"Thank you," he said.

Laura remained pensive.

"I didn't know why I was sad. I didn't even know I was sad, Laura." Still she said nothing. They lay together, side by side, still attached.

"I need a give-away man," Laura said, finally.

"A what?"

"You! A give-away man."

"Well, what for?"

"I spoke to the priest about marrying Ho, and he said since my father is dead, I need someone to give me away. Stupid idea. I already gave myself away to Ho when I told him yes!"

"Oh! Goodness. Congrats! It is nice to know you will marry Ho. That will make him very happy."

"Yes. And you will be my give-away-man, so I can marry him."

"I will, Laura. Anything for you."

"But after that, I don't want to see you again, Congo. Never in this way again! Do you understand that?"

Congo smiled, and nestled closer to her. She could still feel his pulsations. She closed her eyes, in anticipation for his pleasure. He was slow and tender, filling her, as she liked him to. They stayed locked, loving, smiling at each other, loving still.

"You didn't say you will miss me, Congo."

"I won't miss you, Laura. You will always be with me."

"As always?"

"Yes, always. I will love you."

"But, I will never see you like this again, Congo. I will turn to Ho, and stay with him, only, forever."

What connective tissue brought it home Congo did not know. But the memory of the great birds in his dream years earlier, when he had first arrived in Providence, flooded his mind with intensity and new meaning. The feeling of letting go of the birds of that dream and falling helplessly rushed forcefully to his mind. "Oh God!" he said and went silent.

Congo didn't reply. He understood that his relationship with Laura would change. They didn't know how they came together. They never once tried to explain it, just accepted and enjoyed it, one forbidden bite after another. Without understanding its foundation, they had built a magnificent edifice of love, one they honored and celebrated each time they met or merely thought of each other.

They had often said to each other that if on that first day when they met at Providence Pond, they had tried to connect with words, even the simplest, they would have been thrown hopelessly apart! It was trust in the unspoken language of the heart that bonded them. The language still resounded as they lay, tied to each other. Now, it was the language of words that would split them apart forever. Yet it had to be that way.

"Now I must plan my wedding."

"The give-away man will do that."

"You will, Congo?"

"Anything for you, Laura. But tell me, which of the priests have you been talking to?"

"He is not really my priest. He is my friend, Monsignor Ricardo Silva."

"Ah, I know the Monsignor quite well. We talk quite often, you know."

"And what about, may I ask?" Laura asked teasingly.

"We talk about spiritual matters, Laura. He wants Ulu and me to leave the Anglican Church and attend mass."

"You would like that, Congo. He is a good man."

"No doubt. But I have other plans of my own; and so we talk."

"I see. Well . . ."

"In fact," Congo interrupted, "I should be talking to you and Ho together, too, on the same matter, as soon as the wedding is over."

"That's good for you to think of us in that way, Congo. That will be fine. But there is something else bothering me, too, Congo, and you have not asked about it," Laura said.

"Yes, I should have. What is it, Laura?"

"You see all this merchandize? I took it on consignment. Now that the war is over, the merchants want me to pay cash for everything. I asked them to take back the stock, and they refuse. And there is another thing, Congo: the bank increased the note rate. They agreed to one rate while I built the store. Now that it is completed, they want to lend the money at a higher rate. They are after me, and I do not know what to do."

"Well, you still have the produce business."

"Yes. I will ask Ulu to send me more. That is the only hope I have."

"She will, Laura, she will. Rex told me he will expand the business. So be assured, you will be all right."

She believed him. Li trusted his business to her. Now, Laura wanted it to grow in honor of her father's wish. She had to believe Congo.

Congo suggested Laura tell her creditors that he, her new general manager, be consulted instead of her on all her business. He planned to shield her from them, giving her time to repair the ailing business. Laura, liking Congo's proposal, sank further in his arms. They slept.

Finally, Laura and Congo stood up, embraced, fell back on the bed, then struggled to rise and stay away from it and each other. That was their first lesson. Soon they left Laura's bedroom for the very last time and looked back fondly, yet with parting sadness. They entered the dining area, where Laura called for tea. They sipped, watched the sea without speaking anymore. Soon Laura handed Congo his hat and walked him downstairs, out of the store, and to his horse.

Laura returned to her bedroom and cried.

Having unburdened himself in front to Laura in Oracabessa, Congo headed straight to see Ho in Port Maria. He learned that after having lunch and his afternoon exercise, Ho had gone for a swim. Congo walked down to the beach, sat on the sand, and waited for Ho to emerge from the water. Ho walked up to him and, still out of breath, sat beside Congo.

"Congratulations!"

"Thank you."

"When is the date?"

"I do not know."

"Best if you set it now."

"A month from today then, on Saturday."

"Good."

"Why, Congo?"

"I am doing the planning for Laura," Congo explained, and they spoke of having the reception at Providence Pond.

"What will you do now?"

"I have to go into St. Ann."

"I meant about Laura."

"Oh! Do you mean . . ."

"Yes, about you and her."

"Oh, she will not have anything to do with me anymore."

"Yes, but I asked about you, Congo. What will you do?"

"I will be your friend and hers, if you still want me to. But I will do what I would expect you to."

"And that is . . ."

"Be respectful of and, if needed, protect or defend your estate. That is my word."

The men sat in silence for a while before Congo began inviting Ho to start a separate line of the produce business. Ho soon understood that Laura's side of the business with Ulu would go unaffected, and possibly grow. All the new accounts that Congo had recently developed in St. Ann would pass to Ho. When Ho began to explain that starting a produce business was too sudden for him, that he didn't have the barbeques or storage facilities, Congo suggested he could teach him the business and have the barbeques built.

"But for doing that," Congo said, "I would like a special arrangement with you."

"In what way?"

"I get the building we need, all the pimento you can sell. That is my side."

"And mine?" Ho asked.

"You sell all you can. We clear all the expenses and split the profits 50-50. What do you say, Ho?"

"No problems, Congo."

"Then it's done."

"No. I mean . . . don't you want a contract, one from my lawyer?"

"I have a contract. We shook on it, right?"

"Yes. That's enough for me."

The men stood up, shook hands again, and embraced. They had formed a new partnership.

Almost running away, Congo said. "If I am not here, I will be in Providence or on the road. In any case, you will hear from me."

"On the road, Congo?"

"Yes. Why?"

"I have something for Laura. Could you please give it to her?"

"Oh, yes. I will be going through Oracabessa anyway."

Ho removed a letter he had carried with him for some time. Its edges had been crusted red and the face soiled from the excessive handling and the time it had spent in his left shirt pocket, the only remaining one the old shirt had. Ho knew the post office would deliver his letter. He preferred, however, to give it to Laura himself. He had hesitated, waiting for the right moment. Now, Congo conveniently became his personal mailman.

"Thank you, Congo."

"Don't mention it!"

"This means a lot to me, Congo. I have been wanting to deliver it for some time."

"I mean that, Ho. Don't mention it. But I have no intention of opening a mail service business as well."

"Oh, I see," Ho said and chanted off into laughter. Congo soon joined him.

"Ho," Congo said, seriousness suddenly replacing laughter, "you must meet Asa King. He is my spiritual leader."

"Asa King? Where is he?"

"Portland. I will let you know when."

"Okay, my friend. Now, go, and make us profitable!"

Congo, who had had his horse fed and watered as he spoke, was traveling again. His plan was to visit all the farmers in St. Mary, let them know of the change in leadership of Ulu's business, then ride into St. Ann, hoping to enlarge his contacts.

It didn't take long before the word spread. Congo had offered the farmers a slightly higher price than they could get at the government cooperative. At the same time, he would collect the produce at their farms, erasing their transportation costs. In a few weeks, he would have a cache of produce in St. Ann – a parish more productive in pimento than St. Mary – much more than he had for all his old labor there.

Congo might have stumbled onto something!

Part 4: Family Reunion

(1920 to 1921)

Idolatry

Yoofi didn't understand at first the fire into which he had fallen. Neither was there anyone to save him. He and others along with him were destined to burn.

Ama spoke to him of love and Congo of dreams. He fully understood neither until his eyes met the young, alluring Charm. At first she didn't see him as any more than a brash, backwards country-boy with an undisciplined mouth. She dismissed him, forgetting his banal remark at the breakfast table. Charm, with her female instincts heightening, cast a protective net about Princess and herself. She would not let Yoofi break through. In fact, Charm would have completely shielded Princess from the ruffian had Ulu not reaffirmed that Yoofi and Princess were cousins. Nonetheless, she was diligent in her care of the little girl who had become her friend and sister. Being in a house of adult servants, the mutual need for sisterhood developed between them. Yoofi was still a stranger to that kind of relationship.

Was it her beauty and gentleness, or her seeming innocence and coy smile that first transfixed him? Poor Yoofi didn't know. His deep and secret preoccupation with Charm, his inquisitive desire to know her planted a single seed in his heart. Love. Yoofi at once wanted to possess and to give to her. Offering what or presenting how he did not know. He hadn't a thing save his Dance and a remark he dared not utter again. But he had a penchant for hard work, and that would be his sacrifice.

Yoofi remembered his first sight of Charm: how her appearance, her appeal transported him to a realm of imagination and mystery. He knew women: his mother, Miss Hene, teachers, both at home and school. He had seen drawings Congo made, creatures of immense splendor and delicacy. That was the extent of his contact and knowledge of women. Nothing in his past had prepared him for what sat before him that morning. It was not she alone who had conspired to mesmerize him, for at sixteen Yoofi understood that childhood was behind him. He had no words for what was happening to him, yet he knew he was changing. Indiscernible tufts of hair had graced his chin and, disguise it as he might, his voice had failed him enough times to assure him he should talk only when he definitely had to.

Charm sat with her back to the sun. The light streamed down the silvery foliage behind her, through the large beveled glass windows at her shoulders. She seemed a goddess, wrapped in golden light with her honeyed face framed in soft, tender curls of long black hair. On looking at her, his old life went into suspension, and he knew then he would live for her.

Without thought of himself, Yoofi plunged into the tedious work his aunt had laid out for him. For Charm, he would do anything! At first it was a test to him. Ulu endeavored to know of what Yoofi was capable. Starting at less than fair labor for a youth and seeing the rapidity and completion with which he did his tasks, Ulu gradually increased his workload until it reached and passed the level of any man in her service. It didn't matter. Without complaint or bitterness, Yoofi dived into his work and, believing Charm to be watching him, devoured all that his aunt laid out before him. He constantly impressed the Charm he carried in his head. His fantasies delighted him.

Within six weeks of his arrival at the Jacks River estate, Yoofi had completely won the attention of all the workers and, most importantly, his Aunt Ulu. Yoofi's room was always immaculate. His clothes, home tailored by Ama, didn't bear the stamp of modernity. In fact, they were made with his future in mind, grossly oversized. Nonetheless, Yoofi always ironed them, making him appear large but tidy. In his spare time and without being asked, he attended to his aunt's horse. He made sure the steed was properly fed and watered and, early each morning, whether or not his aunt would travel, he still brushed and talked with her mount.

Soon Detective Charles Graham informed Ulu of Yoofi's acceptance into their night study and athletic program. Initially, Ulu, not knowing of Congo's petition on Yoofi's behalf, was alarmed. On thinking how his time at school would distract Yoofi from doing her work and considering further that she had to advance him his school fees – an amount exceeding sixty shillings for the year, Ulu became frightfully saddened. As Graham assured Ulu of Yoofi's sharpness on the verbal tests and the enthusiasm he had displayed, her fears were allayed. Yet Ulu wondered if investing what she considered a fortune on the education of a pupil with unknown capabilities was good for either of them. However, time passed and Yoofi repeatedly proved himself to his aunt. That and continued visits from Graham at Congo's urging finally convinced Ulu King that Yoofi had more than deserved the opportunity to improve himself. She finally made him an advance on his wages so that he could pay the entrance fee and start attending classes. Yoofi was ecstatic!

He soon loved his lessons and threw himself into them, devoting every moment of his spare time to his studies. Moreover, his aunt trusted him with a horse he could ride to school. His industrious ways, in and out of the classroom, his friendly nature and competitive spirit, soon endeared him to his teachers. At first he was best at athletics, where his strength, his Dancing, and his low center of gravity made him best at wrestling. Boxing came slower. He moved easily, but didn't know he had to punch back to win. That soon changed, and, although he was younger by far than any in his class, he nevertheless outdid his competitors in athletics. Seeing his willingness to work, the instructors spent extra time with him on arithmetic and especially reading. It was not easy for Yoofi, but soon he was reading almost at class level and thought about writing a letter to Charm.

At the academy, Yoofi learned that Congo was frequenting there during the days. He understood that Congo, Graham, and some of the senior officers were close friends. A meeting was arranged for Yoofi and Congo on the Saturday following his first exam, on which Yoofi excelled.

From the academy, Congo took Yoofi to the barber and then on the promised trip into Port Maria. Yoofi had been there before on foot to sell coconut oil. Never before had he been there as a tourist. Congo took him into the best stores. He bought him fine clothes; a beautiful comb and brush set, and advised the youth always to leave the house looking his best. On learning that Ulu had not yet started to pay him, Congo gave Yoofi pocket money and, to top the day's excursion, treated Yoofi to dinner at the *Hong Kong Seafood Gardens*. As they ate, Congo told Yoofi to take a seat at the front of the class and to volunteer an answer to any question asked, whether or not he knew the correct answer. The enthusiasm, he told the youth, is what would get him noticed. If he were wrong, the instructor would have the opportunity to show off his superior knowledge in making the correction. On the other hand, if the reply was correct, the instructor would take the credit as a good teacher, but Yoofi would get his notice.

With his new sharp look, his own horse, and in attendance of school, his self esteem and pride increased. This greatly impressed his aunt, who now made it a point to bring his meals to him in his room. She preferred to do that rather than invite the lad into the great house. If Rex were not there, she might have chanced it. Ulu thought that bringing Yoofi into the house would be a mark that he was progressing too rapidly. She saw how that might signal a premature reward: make him unnecessarily proud, gain him unwanted attention, and finally hurt his progress. Moreover, Ulu could hold that out before him as the goal he still had to achieve. For Rex, servants and masters must be separated. In that way, the servants would have the greatest respect and esteem for their masters, wanting more and more to please them through labor and diligence.

Ulu took Yoofi's meals to him each day. She laid the tray out on his table and spoke to him as he ate. She didn't eat with him, either. Never did she take Princess there, nor did she ever ask a servant to take his meals to him. Ulu, for her own reasons, brought food to Yoofi three times a day. Maybe, he thought, she wanted to spy on him. That, however, was far from Ulu's mind. Ulu simply wanted to show her appreciation for Yoofi's work and bond with him. Through Yoofi, Ulu saw a positive side of Ama, and this brought her hope that something good might still come of her poor sister. Ulu was amazed at Yoofi's resemblance to his father. She still thought fondly of Henry and, at times, wished his return. Yoofi didn't know, and he was never told. Ulu was constantly surprised that Ama's son had talent. She didn't want to admit it. Maybe she wanted to tell him, even be a mother to him. Ulu didn't know why she did it; she simply wanted to be close to Yoofi, but never in her house!

Even though Ulu brought his food, her first visits were about money. With his six-week apprenticeship long since completed, his aunt explained that his training at the police academy had cost over sixty shillings and he could consider her first loan to him paid. Yoofi was so happy to be in attendance at the academy, and, since he had never before been compensated for his labor, he didn't understand nor did he see the need for his aunt's explanations. Nevertheless, she had it all on paper. She explained that the books he needed were the same ones had she used in elementary school so she would loan them to him, even though they were intended for Princess. If, however, Yoofi was cautioned, he lost or destroyed the books, he would have to replace them from the money he earned.

One day, as Yoofi ate dinner and they spoke, Ulu watched how her nephew's eyes stalked her breasts. He looked at her bosom, smiled, and looked at her eyes. Without knowing it, Yoofi was begging. He would have given anything to sit closer to her. His aunt, after studying his curious motion for a while, told him to sit up in his chair. In a strong yet non-rebuking voice, she asked him to look at her face while they spoke. She told him that women loved to be admired, but they hated staring eyes. Yoofi didn't understand what she was saying. He was not even aware of his actions, so native they were to him. Yet without remorse or rebellion, he followed her instructions and looked into her face, watching her soft eyes accept his.

Soon Yoofi was invited to attend church with her family and sit with them in the same pew. Rex didn't mind that either. He saw nothing wrong with doing some good on Sundays. Mondays, however, would be different! Moreover, Rex had never presented Yoofi as a relative, but rather a servant who had shown interest in bettering himself. Thus he deserved to be in church. It was also his first attempt at missionary work. As time went on, Ulu, Rex, and Princess became more comfortable with Yoofi. They spoke often of his diligence and scholastic improvements. Gradually, Yoofi gained the proper notice and, occasionally, was asked to have Sunday supper with the family in the great house.

This delighted the young man. Not that the food was any different or better. His Aunt Ulu's food was well prepared and presented. In fact, she would take him meals from the dining table and not from what was prepared for the servants. In that, Ulu was adamant. She had to make clear the distinction between Yoofi and the rest of the servants. In the same way, his separation from the servants and her immediate family could not be misunderstood.

It was not sitting at the same table with Rex or his aunt that pleased Yoofi. It was sitting across the table from Charm that filled his soul with joy. He had given his studying and labor to her. Now she gave her radiance to him. He accepted it with great gratitude and inner satisfaction. She became his dream, the sole object of his passion. Yet he had to bear it in silence, for Yoofi couldn't trust his voice. Not yet, at least. Moreover, he still had no voice for the devotion he felt. Neither had he an audience. In silence he rustled in his flames, worshiping his new but truest idol, Charm.

Laura's Letter

My dearest love:
I do not write much, and speak even less. This, I suppose you already understand. You know me mostly as a businessman; but were it not for the efforts of my loyal friends and family, all would have been lost already. Ho does not take business too seriously, either. But that leaves me time for what I like and follow, without which my life would be dreary. I must hasten to tell you that of all the things I do cherish and follow, of all of them, you only, sweet Laura, completely fill my cup.

However, in humility, I must thank all who struggle here with me, for it is their labor that makes me look favorable to many, perhaps including you, Laura. But above everything else, it is their time at work that allows me truly to love, or maybe I should say to follow all in this world that I do truly adore.

I told my family all I know and feel about you. I poured out my heart to them and asked them to write this letter to you. And when even my family, knowing my plight, has delayed in writing Laura's letter, I have decided to write to you myself and let you see first hand, what horrible thoughts come from below – deep below, inside of me. My essence, I fear, is much unlike the sweet, distilled perfume of your soul!

I love to exercise and meditate, for in these preoccupations away from business, I am free to take you with me wherever I go.

In the beginning, I didn't understand why I thought of you or why your light so filled my soul. I remained perplexed, not knowing why your very being *relieved my fears and brought me such joy. Li – long before I understood what I felt – whispered to me that though my love for you seem as his was for your mother, your tender years separated us. You, Laura, he explained, were not ready. Your journey hadn't yet begun; and it would be unwise for him to put you then with me in actual marriage. So, I have waited and waited, always considering you, my bliss, gone from me forever.*

Yet, understanding my desire for you, Li married us, in spirit. It was a sacred bond, with the understanding that I wait until you were ready. Ready for what exactly, he didn't say. I have been ready and waiting for you all through your rebellious years, and still I wait.

Now, though, I understand your father: the fruit must give of itself. Still, however, I have tarried. And therein lies what perhaps you see as my sloth, my dalliance, or even an indifference to life. This, I believe, is what you look at in anguish and dismay, wishing perhaps that, for my own good, my soul might have been otherwise constituted. This you see as my passionless life.

So my dear Laura, you asked me about passion. I hope one day life will give me the opportunity to express what I feel for you rather than having me explain on paper all I have long thought about you. Even while you were too young to understand, still untouched by love and unable to grasp the depth of my commitment to you, I loved you nevertheless.

For now, let me take care of the rest of today and write you more another day. I know what to say and what I feel for you, but words at this time fail me in how to say it. Some day, believe me, my love, I will show you real passion. I know, for I have willed it so. You only wait and see!

Congo will hand you this unfinished letter. Please, accept it from your family friend.

With all my love,

Ho

Cold Rain Falling

Manjaro Congo King did all he could not to be caught in the cold December rain as he returned from his marketing forays in St. Ann to Providence. He had planned to stop in Galina but bet on getting into Port Maria before the weather broke. His bet was wrong. Miles before he reached Port Maria the showers, cold and heavy, pelted him. From his horse he watched it, the strong winds rocking trees and heaping the high waves against the rocks. It was still early in the afternoon, and Congo thought it wise to keep riding and not get bogged down on the lonely stretch of road separating him from Port Maria and shelter.

Strangely enough, the storm was ferocious but short; and within an hour Congo had ridden past it. Upon reaching Port Maria he headed to the *Hong Kong Seafood Gardens* restaurant. There he was led to his favorite table; but on learning that Ho was out, he walked into the bar where the Detective drank.

"It's cold out!" Congo announced as he rubbed his palms together, approaching Graham.

"Yes, quite windy, too."

"Lot of rain in Galina. It seems I rode through it. No rain here."

"Not a drop," said the Detective, signaling to the waiter. "And what would you like, Congo?"

"Fish tea. That will do it, thank you," Congo said, addressing the waiter.

Graham continued sipping his gin. "Good fellow, that nephew of yours, Congo. He is doing quite well in school. I went to your home to tell you, but Rex informed me you might not be living there anymore."

The "might" of the Detective's statement confused Congo somewhat, for he did not know just how much Graham understood about the recent ruckus in his house or if the Detective was only being polite or coy. Nevertheless, Graham's comment awakened Congo's curiosity. If ever a game was started, Congo was ready to play.

"Thank you, Graham. But maybe Rex knows something I don't," Congo said with a teasing grin.

"It's none of my business where you live, Congo, but I need to know . . . just in case."

"In case of what, Detective?"

"Just in case you are needed for questioning. Something nasty is brewing, Congo. You may need to know."

"I see. You will find me in Providence, Detective."

"That's good to know, Congo."

"And before I forget, Detective, let me say now that we are planning a Dance there next Thursday night. I would love for you to attend."

"That's the Thursday following Ash Wednesday?"

"Yes, Detective."

"A secular event during the holy time?"

"This is not a bailo dance, Detective. It's more like a kikongo, sacred."

"I see. Where will the Dance be, Congo?"

"In Providence, at the *Any Questions*."

"I have heard of it before. Tell me, Congo, who runs that place?"

"Puncus Divine."

"That's a familiar name as well, Congo. Let me see . . . was he that chap that was thrown out of high school in Galina some thirty-five" – the Detective paused, scratching his chin – "well let me see, maybe even forty years ago?"

"If you put it that way, Graham. The very one!"

"That's good, Congo. Things are coming together, slowly, but they certainly are! I do remember the young Puncus St. John. I had just made the rank of Detective then . . . and quite young myself . . . scarcely twenty-three. That was a part of my very first case. Divine had some entanglement with the Kumina group in Galina."

Congo remained silent. Is Graham working me for information? Congo questioned himself.

"So, are you looking for some police protection at the Dance?" Graham asked, breaking the silence.

"No. Nothing of the sort, Detective! This is a Family Dance," Congo added, studying the Detective's puzzled face.

"A Family Dance, ah?"

"Yes, Detective. For Ama, my Sister."

"So Ama, is that her name? Is she married?"

"Yes, to Leroy Kendal. I though you knew, Detective."

"To whom, did you say?"

"Why, Detective? Leroy Kendal."

"Ah! Did you know he is under suspicion?"

"Whatever for, Detective?"

Detective Graham rehashed the case, including the mysteriously disappeared Zadie Blue, about thirty-five years pending, against Leroy. "I did not know where he went. Mind you, he has done nothing wrong. But I can assure you, if something like that comes up again in Providence, we must look at Leroy, very carefully."

"I assure you, Detective, Leroy has done nothing wrong. He farms alongside Lev's property, and there has not been stealing or wrongdoing in Providence."

"Lev! Can you believe? He just died like that!"

"Yes, Detective. Just like that."

"Did you know him well?"

"Yes, of course. He was married to my other Sister, Miss Hene."

"And I suppose you buried him. Right?"

"Yes, of course, with help from Puncus and Leroy."

"So you all gave him a good burial, ah?"

"Yes, Detective. Lev got a really good Family burial. But say, Detective, are you suspicious of something?" Congo asked. He looked askance at the Detective, a man by far his senior, who seemed intent on solving this apparently ancient case at the cost of their young but growing friendship.

"Oh, no, Congo! But you never know. Just one question leading into another, and tidbits I pick up here and there. Sometimes I do not know when I slide into my Detective work. I must tell you, Congo. I am under suspicion for Zadie's disappearance too. Did you know?"

"No, Detective. But who would turn you in?"

Both men laughed. The Detective asked, "So what is this Dance about, Congo?"

"Ama. She is going to be a newborn. She just joined the Family."

"You know, Congo, you are a decent man as far as I can tell. We even attend the same church! Why on earth do you want to have anything to do with the Kumina cult?"

"I must tell you this, Graham. I am the Kumina Master of Providence."

"What!"

"Yes, Detective. And, as you say, I am a decent man."

"You had better keep it that way, Congo." Graham laughed.

"Why not come to the Dance and see for yourself how we celebrate, Graham?"

"I will, Congo. I will go to your Dance. Why not? You come to my church!"

"Nice of you to accept, Graham."

"You are welcome, Congo."

"The theme of our Dance is love. And this year our focus is Baptist Minister Paul Bogle. We are celebrating his spirit of love."

"Bogle died in disgrace, Congo. But I must say, there was something sincere about him, and maybe that should not go unnoticed."

"Thank you, Detective. I am glad you see something good in us."

"Not in Kumina, Congo, that is still to be proven."

"That was some distance we traveled there, Graham." Congo said, "I thought for a moment you were going to accuse me of something wrong."

"No, not enough to go on at this time. But, I must tell you, Congo, I have been talking to Rex, and he's digging in through the past. He promised me he will have something soon!"

"Rex! Rex, of all persons, ah? I wonder what he has to gain from that?"

"Maybe he is just an ethical man, Congo."

"I see. Then let's encourage his dig."

"Yes, we should!"

"You are a friend, Graham, and I wish I could chat longer with you. But I have to go now."

"Enjoy your ride, Congo," Graham said as Congo signaled his horse.

"And remember the Dance, Detective. It's time you learn to jump," Congo said, laughing.

"I will be there, Congo."

"And let the Monsignor know. He might find it entertaining."

"Yes, Congo. Monsignor Silva would especially like that. He is the worldly kind, you know," Graham said laughing. "And you know something else?" he asked after a moment's reflection.

"What, Graham?"

"So might our friend Reverend Watkins, too. For totally different reasons, he may be curious enough to attend. So I will let them both know about the Dance when I see them next."

"Nice of you, Graham," Congo said, shaking hands with Graham who had accompanied him to the door. Congo walked outside, filling his lungs with the clean, moist air. He soon mounted his horse and pointed it toward Providence.

"Have a good night," the men said in unison as they parted.

Congo was indeed happily surprised to see that there was no more cold rain falling.

Eagles

Ulu had what she wanted. Congo left without incident and Rex took complete control. Rex had planned for his new position even while he was in New York. On his way home, he had traveled to Texas where he bought various cowboy outfits, and he made these his working clothes in Jacks River.

Within hours of Congo's departure, Rex placed signs at the post office, notifying all farmers that he wanted a meeting with them. Rex called the assembly a week after the notice was given. The meeting would be held in the town hall. Food and music would be provided.

The gathering was well attended, and the socializing that followed lasted much longer than was expected. Rex introduced himself as the boy who had left Providence to study in New York. He had now returned to run the family business, and all further transactions should be with him. He passed out contracts that he read for them and asked that they be signed and returned to him. The contracts formally replaced Congo with Rex. Additionally:

> Rex would have exclusive rights to their produce.
> The price would be five percent less than the government price.
> Pickup would be at their premises.
> Payment would be thirty days after pick-up.

Congo had paid on the spot, above the government's price, and there was no pick-up charge.

The farmers didn't like the changes but signed the contracts. They asked why Congo had left the business but got no answer. Rex scarcely knew who they were. However, Congo was no longer competing with Rex. The government was. Rex knew that the farmers would choose him over the government, whose system was more remote and less personal.

With victory over the farmers, Rex moved to his next target: Laura. He knew from Ulu the precarious nature of Laura's business. Ulu's plan was based partly on business but more on revenge. Laura had tampered with her interest in Congo from the day of the party at Providence Pond. It was now time to get even. Ulu knew of Laura's insolvency. She knew that the produce was the only viable part of her business. If she set a policy of continuously raising prices on Laura, it would force Laura to either continue trading at a much lower margin or compel her to turn over the business to Ulu. That, really, was what Ulu wanted. Her revenge would be to leave Laura a strangled beggar.

It was not long before Rex presented his contract to Laura. It was done face to face. First, it offered Laura all the produce she could ever hope for but with a progressive pricing schedule. The contract called for her immediate signature. Laura, upon reading the contract, realized she had been trapped. What was she to do?

Laura immediately left her store and went to Jacks River to meet with Ulu. Their business was based on an old and trusted friendship. Maybe her brother didn't understand that. There must have been a mistake.

"Oh, Laura, believe me, I have lost control of the business to Rex. He came back from New York and completely took over. He didn't like the way Congo ran the business. What I can do, Laura, is to talk with Rex on your behalf. He may listen to me. In any case, the first price increase is still three months away. So, go ahead, Laura, sign the contract and leave it with me. Rex will bring the amended contract to you."

Laura, realizing she hadn't a choice, and without reason to doubt Ulu, signed the contract.

"I am depending on you, Ulu," Laura whispered in her departing embrace.

"Say hello to Congo for me," Ulu said.

"Congo!" Laura exclaimed, looking back. "Is Congo here? May I see him?"

"At your house, in your bed, maybe. But certainly not here!"

"Ulu! That's unfair."

"He has been in your bed before."

"It's over now. Do you hear me? It's over."

"Yes, I do hear you. And that's been said before. Do *you* hear *me*?"

"Stop it, Ulu, that's insulting!"

"Then don't even say another word to me. Don't even say hello to me again. From now on, just get your produce from Congo."

"Please, Ulu. Don't do this. I beg you!"

"You beg me? You beg me! You made me stoop to you from the day you met Congo. You stole him from me, tampered with my life, and played him like a flute while you broke every promise you made to me. Did you know, Laura, it was I who rode to your house and took my horse so Congo was forced to walk home from your filthy, wet bed . . . from yours to the decent house I keep, to my daughter and me? Did you know, Laura, I slept comfortlessly that night? Do you know the torment, the pain that his daughter felt not having her father here, Laura, because of you? And you beg? Is that enough, Laura, that you beg?"

Again Laura was caught off guard.

"Tell me, Ulu, what do you want from me? You say I have wronged you. What can I do to make it up to you?"

"What do I want from you? What? Nothing, Laura, nothing!"

"Don't punish me like that, Ulu. Please, tell me. How can I make it up to you?"

"It's almost over, Laura. And until now, I have needed nothing from you that I haven't lived without. I hope when this is finally over, you will say the same of me and find a way to do the same."

"You hated me even in our friendship! You hated me all along, isn't that true?"

"You destroyed our friendship."

"And now you destroy my business?"

"What did you say? You; you destroyed it, Laura! But I will pick up the pieces – yours and mine – and make things work, somehow. I have a daughter to care for."

"You mean my piece of business, you will pick that up, too?"

"Yes, Laura. In the end, I will pick up the pieces," Ulu said with a slow deliberate voice. It had lost its fire of a few days prior when she had railed at Congo.

Laura turned and left. Her last glance revealed her frightened eyes.

Ulu's eyes were cold and dead. For how long, Laura didn't know. Maybe that was her mistake, never to have really studied her friend's eyes before. Laura couldn't muster the energy to cry. She rode home not knowing how. She was beyond feelings; only the thought of putting her broken pieces back together consumed her mind.

Ulu finally exhaled, rejoicing in her victory.

Uncaring Church Mouse

The special attention Ulu paid to Yoofi, along with the grooming and smart new clothes Congo bought him, soon made everyone take special notice of him. That was not all. Yoofi was remarkably handsome. It took time to show, for it had been hidden beneath his crude farm manners and ill styled, homemade clothes. That had all gone now. What he didn't learn from his aunt, he gleaned from the officers at the police academy. His gold glistened, and Charm noticed it.

It was not only his appearance that had improved. He could drill. That he did at the academy with guns and at home with a makeshift rifle he fashioned from wood. His drill steps, the precision timing, and his alertness, he combined with his Dancing to move with increased grace and elegance when he practiced at home. He still loved Dancing; and when the opportunity arose, he did it by himself. He would Dance before dinner. He would Dance after dinner. Yoofi Danced, and folks secretly watched. Yoofi saw them looking, heard them talking, and it didn't matter. Yoofi Danced!

At first Charm disliked him, saw nothing good in him. She even wondered why Yoofi, a family member, was not allowed into his aunt's house. Was he orphaned? What was it that was wrong with him? As far as Charm knew, he was a perfect stranger.

But the sun's eclipse was only for a moment, and soon the splendor of its disk shown fully for Charm. Soon she felt its glow. But her instruction from Ulu was to stay away from him. Yoofi distanced himself from Charm for fear of the consequences of closeness.

Perhaps it would have been better if Ulu had brought them together with proper explanations for, in such a small space, the pair couldn't escape each other forever. Fate would have its way despite conventions.

Ulu held her bedroom as though it were sacred to her. It started with Congo, his best paintings and the best he could find. Inch-by-inch his artistic hand had transformed her bedroom into a temple.

From the second story, it looked out on high bamboos lining the river on the opposite side of the road. On the far side of the river, orange and banana fields filled the valley. Looking north, the ocean spread out like a thin blue veil.

The room itself was large, with a dark, stained-cedar floor below a vaulted ceiling. The leaded glass windows framed flowering gardens, brimming with birds, water lilies, and fruited trees. It was romantic: heavenly! So possessive of it was Ulu that she kept it for herself, forbidding any servant from entering her temple, even to care for it.

Maybe Charm didn't remember she was a servant. Perhaps she was simply disobedient or curious. Whatever it was, Charm wanted to find out, but not by herself, what lay beyond Ulu's bedroom doors. If her beauty had not died, if Yoofi still had any interest in her past, if he was too shy to spend time with her, then Ulu's bedroom would unlock his mysterious mouth and let his river of gold pour out to her. She wanted him there, to unlock his and Ulu's secret at once. Of course, if her indulgence were discovered, it would be Yoofi's fault, and Charm would be absolved.

So one Sunday when all others were on furlough or else at church, a mysterious mouse chanced down the hall and into Ulu's bedroom. Yoofi, Charm knew, might have been dancing, of course, by himself. How silly! From the balcony at the rear of the house, Charm yelled for help. Yoofi had just knotted his tie and adjusted his coat in preparation for church when the distress call boomed.

As if on command, Yoofi dropped his Bible and rushed upstairs. Charm stood at Ulu's slightly opened bedroom door with her hand over her mouth, gasping and pointing under the bed, shouting in hysterics, "Mouse, mouse!"

Without delay, Yoofi got on his hands and knees and crawled underneath the bed from one side to the next, then stood facing Charm. She entered the room and closed the door behind her.

"I do not see it."

"It's gone then! You must have scared the poor thing away."

"Scared it? It scared you!"

Charm dropped her hands from her face. Her honey-colored skin was flushed with excitement, not from the mouse, but on seeing Yoofi so close to her. Before the background of greenery and vibrant paintings, Yoofi stood in the elegance of his new, ash-gray suit.

Charm was dressed in a simple yellow and red striped frock. It was buttoned in front from the low circular cut at the base of her neck to the hem, or so it should have been. As she spoke, Charm moved her hands across her face and bosom, making him follow every movement of her thin, beautiful frame. Yoofi adjusted his view and interest. Charm threw herself on the bed, without taking her stare from him.

Yoofi, as if frightened by Charm's partially exposed body, pulled back.

"Why are you so scared of the bed?" she asked.

"Because you are afraid of the mouse."

"Stop that kind of silly talk and lie beside me."

"We are not supposed to," he said, removing his jacket and, with tiny steps, he moved timidly toward the bed. "You are pretty," he said, as he got closer to her.

"Is that all you can say, Country Boy?"

"I . . . I wanted to tell you that before."

"You can tell me now, right here," she said, gently tapping the bed. She rolled over to meet him as he sat beside her.

"Are you going to leave your shoes on?" Charm asked.

"I do not have to," he said, kicking his shoes off.

"You can touch me, Yoofi."

He touched her shoulder, and immediately saw the curves of her breasts. His heart fluttered and he stammered, "You . . . you are nicer than you looked."

Charm pretended not to hear him. "You ever kissed a girl, Yoofi?" she asked.

"You ask too many questions!"

"You mean you are so old and never kissed a girl?"

He leaned over and kissed the delicate skin of her chest, lingering there to enjoy her fragrance. "See there, I kissed you."

"Not so."

Yoofi reached beneath the unbuttoned bodice of her dress and, removing her breasts, he started to suckle.

"Not so, Country Boy. Not so!"

Yoofi jumped from the bed.

"Not so, either," she grinned at him.

"Like how, then, Charm?"

"You have to come over here, Country, so I can show you."

Yoofi moved back onto the bed beside her. "See, like so," Charm said, gently touching her lips to his and removing them as soon as she did.

"Like so?"

"Yes, just like so. Now you do that."

Yoofi snuggled beside her and tried to kiss her, smothering her lips with his. Charm turned her face away. "Not like that," she said.

"How then?"

"Like so," she said, kissing his cheek and forehead. He followed her, kissing her cheeks before returning to her lips.

"Not like so . . . you should talk, Yoofi!"

"Kiss and talk, Charm?"

"Yes! Don't you have something to tell me, Yoofi?"

"You are pretty, Charm."

"And what else?"

"And beautiful," he said, gently kissing her smiling lips.

"And what else, Yoofi?"

"And I love you, Charm."

She gently kissed his lips, opening hers as she did. "And what else, Yoofi?"

"I love you Charm, only you, not anyone else."

She turned and guided his hand toward her breasts.

"Do you like these, Yoofi?"

"Yes!" Then he moved to kiss her bosom. Charm rolled on her back and looked at him sideways.

"They can be yours, Yoofi, if you can say the right things."

"You are the most beautiful girl in the world and I will love only you, Charm."

Charm reached over and unfastened his pants, touching him all over.

He moved to kiss her and she responded. Yoofi unbuttoned the rest of her dress and sat up, looking at her beautiful form. Yoofi hurriedly undressed, and lay on top of her. Charm resisted but kissed him, again and again, long, slow, delicious kisses. She wanted the moment to last forever. She had realized her dream of having him.

Yoofi's first lesson on sex came to his head like a maddening storm. Suddenly, he became his mentor, Bullcow, and plunged into her. In a moment it was over. Yoofi, without saying anything, got up to leave, looking back at his clothes he had so rapidly removed.

"Where are you going, Yoofi?"

"To church, Charm."

"We can have it right here. Come back and lie with me." Charm said, submersing her dissatisfaction beneath a calm and captivating voice. "Come back to heaven!"

With missionary zeal, Yoofi returned his clothes to the floor and rushed back on the bed. Charm began kissing him again. Yoofi eased on top of her.

"Slowly! Slowly, Yoofi," she coaxed him. "We have time."

And he stayed with her, rolling, rocking with the rhythm of the bed and the hum of the blissful sea leading them. They swayed in each other's arms, sweating, talking, smiling, salting their kisses with joyful tears until, with unexpected suddenness, Charm plunged her fingers in his skin and slowly, relenting to quieted ecstasy, sighed. Finally, in sweet sojourn, she gave as she had promised, a peaceful taste of paradise.

With their eyes trailing the intricate sky above them, they fell asleep, and Ulu's bed didn't care who its blessed occupants were. Neither did the poor little church-mouse.

The Light of Darkness

Victory came to Ulu earlier and with greater ease than she had anticipated. In less than a year, her plan to displace Congo and install Rex as the head of her business, of monopolizing the produce business in St. Mary and establishing an enterprise without peer had all been achieved. It was only the close of the second decade of that century, a comparatively short time indeed . . . but Ulu had done it! Her accomplishments made her happy. Her next step was to lay a path for Princess's life so that she could marry with status, winning the class of husband that Ulu did not or could not have. Yet, she would make it right for Princess.

That, however, would be a long process and was not the idea which immediately occupied her. Rex had suggested that every major achievement should be celebrated. Rex, too, had something to celebrate. Hitherto, his hands were untested in business. Surely, he had studied it, and from history he knew of the ascension and demise of empires. He knew that any enterprise could last only so long, that permanence, like life, was an illusion. Like birthdays, successes must be praised and celebrated, if for nothing else, to bring more!

The idea of increase caught Ulu's attention. To her, celebration meant a few hours more of sleep or an extra serving of dessert or visiting a friend to secretively compare successes in her unannounced game. To Ulu, success was a private matter honored with a fleeting moment. Good planning and hard work – that alone guaranteed victory! Ulu, against her strong intuition but wanting to please her brother, interpreted Rex's pronouncement as a law of success and, like free fall, gravitated to obey it by announcing a victory party.

Rex, however, had an additional, more sinister agenda. Yoofi's eyes were not the only ones that noticed Charm's beauty. Rex saw it as well and had laid out a long and well disguised path to taste her sweetness. That was his real reason for suggesting the victory celebration.

At the top of her game, Ulu still had much to gain; but, on the other hand, there was much to lose! Princess was her only child. She knew that the wealth around her would soon attract a suitor of her liking. Ulu had already decided that Princess's groom would be a doctor. Although Princess had not even yet shadowed her early teen years, Ulu had long decided her husband had to be of the right stature, complexion, and manner. If he were, she would sanction a marriage and immediately establish a private office for them. Princess would manage the office. They and her grand-children would live in a most exclusive country estate, with servants and whatever else they needed. Ulu spent days and nights on her dream. The spendthrift, Congo, was gone. Rex, an apparent stasher like her, would produce the abundance she sought. So simple!

Yes, simple. Above all, Ulu now had to protect what she had earned. Her mind, like a caged beast, roamed the corners of her estate, looking, looking for leaks and patching them. Whatever the cost, Princess' future would be guaranteed.

Ulu didn't understand the apparent silence between Yoofi and Charm. She saw – or did she only imagine – flashes of attraction, or possibly romance. As Ulu traced Charm's development, she saw her early anger and impatience with the country bumpkin turn into indifference and then to casual interest and curious smiles. And what about her eagerness to watch him Dance and her inquiries about his lateness from class? Charm would ask to carry his food to him, to take his laundry to his room, and to have Yoofi repair something in her room. Maybe there was something about it after all, but Ulu was not sure. It didn't help to put Charm in the clear when, on taking his dinner to him one evening, Ulu found Princess's hair-comb in Yoofi's room. That was easily explained, of course, by Yoofi. He had found it and he was about to ask his aunt to whom it might belong. On another occasion, Charm's shoes were found in Yoofi's room. Charm explained that Yoofi had offered to take them to the shoemaker to have them repaired.

Ulu didn't believe the explanations but hadn't sufficient reason to think otherwise. To Yoofi, Ulu's advice was not to hold anyone else's property in his possession. She cautioned Charm to request help directly from either her or Rex. Ulu aimed to keep Charm and Yoofi separated. They had both grown central to the operation of her business, intelligent, capable and not knowing their true financial worth. Neither did they know who they really were. Above all, that had to be kept hidden.

Unknown to Ulu, the relationship between Charm and Yoofi had grown into a flowering romance. The young man, seeing his mother in Charm, had fallen deeply in love with her. So deeply she had fallen in love with Yoofi, Charm left reminders of her presence with him. Her comb and shoes were clear signs to the other girls not to turn their heads to her beloved, and to Yoofi, to see and think of her only. Watching the closeness between Charm and Ulu and also between Charm and Yoofi, the other girls kept their distance, fearing that even mentioning the lovers in their gossip would lead to their dismissal.

It was not only the relationship between Ulu and Charm that kept the other girls from Yoofi. There was also Charm's interaction with Rex. That triangular relationship between Ulu, Rex, and Charm elevated the latter from a mere servant status, making her appear as Princess's older sister. This gave Charm certain leverage which she was sure to use.

Inadvertently, through Charm, those relationships brought Yoofi into Ulu's household, and above the reach of the other girls.

Innocently at first, that interaction between Rex and Charm stemmed from something more primal: Charm's care and closeness to Princess. In his attempt to bond to his niece and to enjoy the country he had left in his youth, Rex spent much time picnicking on the farm or on the warm sand of the beach by pure water, doing nothing . . . nothing, save enjoying the wealth that had been provided him. Rex took Princess everywhere he went. He also took Charm.

Charm saw this as a way to extend her care for Princess outside the house. Also, Rex would not be unnecessarily burdened by his niece as he cavorted. In any case, Princess was her charge.

Ulu's suspicion said differently: Charm wanted closeness to Rex, but not for love. No! He couldn't love her, a servant girl! Neither had Charm the ambition to seek his love. But Charm saw his wealth, as Ulu suspected. And Ulu's battle in that arena was how to satisfy Rex's need for closeness with Princess without upsetting the delicate balance already established between Princess and Charm.

So with Laura's business subdued and surrendered into hers, Ulu now had a household of strong, independent, and largely unspoken wills to manage. That alone now was her current charge, as she saw it. How now would Ulu fare?

Charm, with eyes focused on Yoofi, didn't understand what, if anything else, Rex really wanted from her. Ulu had treated Charm like a daughter. It was certainly not out of kindness nor because she was a child of her mother's closest friend, Esi. Ulu saw value in Charm. With her, Princess was happy. Moreover, Charm's intelligence, her love of reading – reading to Princess while Ulu, and at times even Rex, listened, bonded them together like family.

Charm easily extended to Rex the closeness and trust that existed between the three females, serving and trusting him as though he were an uncle. To her, maybe only to her, Rex was kind and outgoing. True, Rex was kind and attentive to his sister and niece, but guardedly so. But to Charm, Rex was unabashedly open, enticing her in. He greatly appreciated her knowledge of everything local and her willingness to explain the things he had long forgotten. When it was time for him to go to Port Maria or into St. Ann's Bay, Charm was there to show him the stores and assist him in picking out the keenest values. Coming from the well-established Boydell family, Charm knew her way around. It greatly helped Rex.

On the beach, in the water, on the hiking trails, in the stores or restaurants, Charm was with him. His "thank yous" soon came attached with a touch or a friendly smack. Charm hadn't any romantic inclinations for him. She liked the admiration of the older, richer man, the brother of her boss! Rex did much boasting to Charm about America and his days on campus, interesting stories that seemed endless. As they spoke, exchanging stories and opinions, the barriers between them, the natural fear, subsided. Touching came frequently without praise, but with certain anticipation on Rex's side. It was then that Charm grew suspicious.

What could she do? When her gestures suggested she was unhappy with his gradual, yet persistent approach, he entreated Charm for whatever fancied her, making sure, however, to lay the money on the counter. So Charm had receipts for her purchases, making her a confident owner of her novelties. With this manipulation and in many other ways, Rex subtly made his advances.

As time passed, the sham became the accepted. What once seemed to be Rex's strange, even unwelcomed approach changed into overt generosity. Never had Rex directly asked anything special or extraordinary of the prey. Soon Charm relaxed, and gifts and praises flooded her. What could she do, especially when only good had been expressed?

Yet Charm was bothered. Why was Rex so snappy with Yoofi? Why did Rex keep such a distance from Yoofi and bid her to do the same? And why would Rex be either mum about Yoofi or otherwise speak negatively of him? What misfortune had Yoofi brought to Rex, Charm often wondered. She tried to find out. Rex, however, responded with ridicule, suggesting either that the answer was too obvious or that Yoofi was too innately subhuman to deserve civilized discussion.

Unlike Ulu, Rex was keenly aware of Yoofi's obsession with Charm, but less so of hers with Yoofi. Rex didn't know whether it was love or lust. But whatever it was, Yoofi's fascination with Charm rivaled his and he wanted it quelled. Rex's way of making it wane was to shower Charm with time, gifts, and attention while devaluating Yoofi. At Sunday's supper Rex corrected the lad's speech, criticized his posture and his preference for using fingers instead of cutlery, and posed arithmetic problems he knew were too advanced for the lad. In his presence, Yoofi was always on the defensive, apologetic, and tense. Ulu sided with Rex, seeing opportunities for Yoofi, whereas Charm felt shame and helplessness in her inability to defend Yoofi.

Rex tried in vain to take Charm out with him alone. He also failed to arrange a time when he and Charm would be alone in the house. Months passed and he gave, smiled, and signaled in every way to Charm without Ulu seeing that he was ready to collect on his investments. All attempts failed except his last. Rex would have his victory party! He at once had sold to Ulu the idea of celebrating her victory over Laura and her rise in power and prestige! Ulu bought it. What Ulu didn't know and had not even vaguely suspected – what indeed she had paid for by giving the party – was Rex's anticipated victory over Charm that very night!

After weeks of patient planning, the Friday night of the party arrived. Since it was the last Friday of the year, it was dubbed Rex's Christmas Party! Ulu provided the food, even bought the services of musicians. All of the dignitaries and their families were invited. Above all, Ulu saw the party as an opportunity to display her Princess. Doctors and the upper level staff, prosperous farmers, headmasters, teachers, Detective Charles Graham and his staff were all invited. From her church, Ulu invited her pastor and the upper echelon, all of whom were sure to be present. It was to be a well-attended party. Yoofi, in service, would also be there.

Ulu employed him as her caterer, but really Yoofi was invited to entertain with his dancing. Yoofi, however, needed a quick revision of who he was and the etiquette expected. For that, Ulu told Yoofi, if he were asked who he was, to say he was a distant relative of his Uncle Congo, who had brought him there to attend the police academy. He shouldn't talk to the guests; simply ask what they wanted, see to their satisfaction, then disappear until signaled again.

With all that had gone on between them, Ulu nevertheless invited Laura to the party. She had billed it neither in haughtiness nor with the high presumption of a victory party, but rather as Rex's belated homecoming fete.

Charm had to be there. Princess was Ulu's centerpiece, and since Princess was always on Ulu's stage, Charm shared her spotlight.

Unexpectedly to Ulu, Laura came. With great fanfare and pretentiousness, Ulu welcomed her with kisses and greetings of former years. Laura came not to be her guest. She hadn't seen Congo since he had agreed to be her give-away-man and wedding planner.

Congo had busied himself with his new endeavors, taken time to meet with Laura's creditors, keeping them at bay while still making plans for the wedding. Laura had promised her hand in marriage to Ho. Out of superstition, however, Laura avoided seeing Ho, depending on Congo to be their go-between. Laura came in search of Congo to enquire about the status of her affairs. Sadly for her, Congo was absent. After confidently butterflying from guest to guest, displaying her shimmering silk of gold and blue – proudly robed in the traditional evening gown inherited from her grandmother – Laura soon retired, leaving the celebration for lonely contemplation.

On leaving, she met Monsignor Ricardo Silva, greeted him with a handshake and then a hug and kiss. He had christened her before he became a prelate, and now that she looked toward marriage, he was to perform that service as well. She released him and looked with reserve and question into his deep brown eyes, as if questioning the status of her marriage plans. Monsignor Silva looked back at her, still smiling at the fondness of her embrace, but with homespun assurance. Laura knew at once that her fears were unfounded – her marriage was still to be. His eyes followed her as she hurried from the room. What the Monsignor wanted to tell Laura was that he had been talking with Congo and all was well. Perhaps, he thought, she knew.

Laura's departure made life a trifle less anxious for Ulu and Rex, who had invited Laura but had not expected her company. After all, Laura had been newly relegated to servitude.

Not wanting to signal his interest or absorption in Laura, the aged Monsignor slowly turned and joined Rex, who was in conversation with the Anglican minister, Reverend Bernard Watkins, and the Detective, Charles Graham. The spiritual leaders had been rivals for the King family. Graham liked that their current interest excluded him. He sipped gin, amused by Rex's prospects of escaping the spiritual snares awaiting him.

The Coveys had been Anglicans for as long as anyone could remember. That arrangement was easy and convenient, for an Anglican church had long been established near Providence that lacked a Roman Catholic counterpart. Now that Ulu had moved to Jacks River where there were both, Monsignor Silva visited the Kings often. He carried first his message of concern and help with their business and then an inquiry about the soundness of their salvation. Ulu needed friends and desired to add an air of respectability to her . . . so she encouraged him. In fact, she entertained him and took business counsel from him. Ulu never told him, but she had no intention of changing faiths.

The entire back yard was turned into a buffet area. The cooks prepared all manner of meats, salads, and drinks. At dusk and after feasting, the guests were ushered indoors where the dancing began. The first floor was built with entertainment in mind. It consisted of an entrance parlor, library, and formal dining room. The rest of the space was a wide-open area and, with its furniture removed, was ideal for dancing. The musicians played a mixture of mento, calypso, and a few well-known Louisiana classics.

As Rex sipped red wine, the men of cloth and the Detective drank gin. Monsignor Silva had just asked a probing question. When Rex didn't answer, the clergyman repeated, "So, Rex, what do you consider will be the fate of your soul?"

"It depends on the life he lives," responded Reverend Watkins, wanting to shield his parishioner from the baited question.

"And there are no known indictments against that soul either," the Detective added.

"My soul?" Rex questioned. "Like you, it will die and, maybe, go to hell or heaven."

"Like me, you will die, but I will live forever in heaven," said the Monsignor.

"If . . . if you repent, that is," said the Reverend.

"Well, isn't there grace, purgatory, and your prayers for me, Reverend?" the Monsignor asked, laughing. "But if I believe, and partake of the sacraments, then I am certain to live again. I will live forever."

"Yes, because of grace there will be a resurrection. And those who die in Christ, as the Book says, will rise with him," replied Watkins.

"A resurrection of the dead?" Rex asked.

"A well known but unproven idea," added Detective Graham.

"Yes, there will be a resurrection!" repeated Reverend Watkins.

"Just as sure as there is death," Monsignor Silva added.

"Why do you say death is sure, Monsignor?" Graham asked.

"Everything we know has a birth and a death, Detective. You know that."

"Yes, Monsignor. Officially, I know that. But then there is the case of Zadie. Do you remember her?"

"Do you mean that Zadie Blue from Galina?" Reverend Watkins asked.

"Yes, the very one."

"Well, that simply means you have work to do, Detective, to finally account for her true parents and also her death," Monsignor Silva said.

"Yes," added Reverend Watkins, "your incomplete work does not mean she was not born or didn't die."

The Detective remained silent. Zadie Blue's unknown whereabouts had stained his otherwise brilliant record. He, the first child of African parentage to hold that prestigious position of Detective, had done an outstanding job. He was aloof, determined, and zealously pursued his cases. Zadie, however, baffled him. Not only he but the whole community was at a loss to explain her coming and going. Not knowing what else to do with it, they assigned it to Detective Charles Graham.

Feeling embarrassment at his personal failure, for not having brought closure to his case – especially since he had been romantically involved with Zadie, and her disappearance had also been by gossip attributed to him – Graham remained quiet, listening to the rest of the conversation, sipping his gin. It was not that Detective Charles Graham felt rebuke or remorse from Watkins's statement. It was his own incompetence that irked him. Was it the sorrow of a lost love or the mystery surrounding Zadie that had been given new life to stalk and pain him forever? Yet there was hope. Leroy and Rex had become his silent partners. There was hope.

"So I ask you, Rex, what is the state of your soul?" Monsignor Silva repeated, as if to trap Rex.

"I do not know. But of one thing I am sure. I will live out the full potential of my life. I will not live fearing death or resurrection, if there are any such things!"

"Even if that full potential includes sin?"

"Yes, Monsignor, even if it does!" Rex responded, holding his red wine to the light, and laughing as its warmth flamed his body. "What I do know, Monsignor," he continued, "is that you – society I mean – may need to control my instincts, my lusts if you please, with the promise of certain damnation unless I conform. I will not live with fear. I have a life force. I was born with it. I will not tame it or deny it. That's what I am responsible for: to live, to let it out, and not to worry about whether I will be resurrected or not. And let's suppose I do get resurrected: what body will I have, anyway?"

The men sipped their drinks, and the music played. Ulu would have preferred Rex to be less conversational and take center stage, moving the party along with him.

"You speak with a carnal mind, Rex. But be sure to give some thought to the care of your soul," Silva replied.

"Yes, Monsignor, I will . . . when I die. Then I will let my spirit figure out what it has to do. It will go to the realm of the spirit. Right, Reverends?"

"Yes, I imagine so, depending on what you mean and how you live here."

"Well, let the spirit solve the problems of the spirit then; and we can live, really live, now, without guilt or fear that we are alive!"

The men laughed. "He is yours," Monsignor Silva said, looking at Reverend Watkins.

"Yes, we have work to do here," he said, sipping his gin and turning the conversation to laughter.

When no one seemed to understand that dancing was all right, Yoofi moved on to the floor and began to dance. Soon Ulu joined him. Then the rest of the flock rushed onto the floor. The party had begun! Ulu still had time to keep her eyes on her guests, on Princess and her young admirers. Rex found Charm and held on to her as if he possessed her. Yoofi would have loved to touch her. Being the dancer he was, he had no lack of partners, especially the older women. They loved his light, gentle moves; and the husbands didn't care, since it gave them reason to seek out younger partners.

When Yoofi was not busy dancing and seemed to want to approach Charm, Ulu gave him the task of serving drinks or entertaining Princess. With all that, Yoofi's face radiated delight. Ulu didn't know why. She didn't know that Rex's curiosity with Charm had raised her value to Yoofi, and, in that, his desire for her increased. Ulu watched.

At the height of a calypso piece, just as Yoofi had moved with Charm onto the floor, Rex requested the dance from her. Smiling, Yoofi gave him preference. After a few steps of the dance, Rex slowed as if something was wrong. He whispered to Charm to go upstairs to his room and fetch his cigars, that he was not sure where they were, but that she should look until she found them.

Simple enough! With calm and confidence, Charm climbed the old, sturdy staircase. Not long after, Rex left the room and walked into the front yard. The music played. Rex walked from the front of the house to the rear and went upstairs from the back staircase. He quietly joined Charm in his bedroom. When she didn't produce his cigars, which were in the breast pocket of his jacket, he joined her in search of them. Exasperated from dancing and her fruitless searching, Charm reclined on the bed while he searched. Rex read Charm's repose as his invitation. With the swiftness and precision of a cat, Rex sprang on her, pinning her to the bed. In fright and confusion, her deer-like eyes affixed to his large, cruel stare, Charm lay unresisting. He ripped her underwear, and in a moment, Rex knelt above her. He was poised!

With instincts like a hawk, Ulu sent Yoofi to fetch Charm with the message that Princess was crying and needed her. Unaware, Yoofi hurried upstairs, opening one door after another until he entered Rex's room. Yoofi saw in low lights the dreaded deed that was about to unfold. With great calm he said, "Uncle Rex, if I may be excused, Aunt Ulu says Princess needs Charm."

For the three of them, the music ceased and the party was momentarily over. For a moment there was silence, and a deepening feeling of death. Rex's long unspoken desire had found its expression in Charm, and he trumpeted above all; and yet there was silence, a long eloquent silence entombed in this immediate stillness. There the trio remained frozen, immersed in the light of that terrifying darkness calling them to face what they had all feared.

After what seemed an eternity, Yoofi, deadened by his pain, left the room. Charm was next to follow. Yoofi, in his bewilderment, his sorrow, was unaware of her presence, even her whisper of help. In slow, shameful degrees, and burdened by guilt, the lovers reentered the ballroom.

Slowly, in proud, stoic opulence, Rex descended the stairs, adjusting his tie, with the smoke from his Cuban cigar curling about his head, making hellish mockery of his presumed innocence. He mingled with the guests as though nothing had happened. And indeed, nothing had. His attempt had missed its mark, leaving his plans in shambles. He rejoined the company of Monsignor Silva, the Reverend Bernard Watkins, and Detective Charles Graham. Nothing really could have happened!

Yoofi, Rex justified to himself, had seen nothing in the dark. The young naive Charm, as he intended to so cast her, still had much to learn. Indeed, she hadn't yet understood the frightening game of the big bad wolf! It was only a game; and if she didn't know that by then, why was she fit to train his niece?

Not fit? Then why keep her employed? If her subsequent behavior gave him pretext, Rex would discharge her. Without his letter of recommendation, what would her fate be? Charm had better grow up fast! Rex glanced momentarily at Charm with insinuations of stupidity. She looked away from him with a worrisome grimace of scorn and contempt. To Ulu, Rex's smile conveyed the message: conniving, untrustworthy servants must go!

Yoofi, still in defeat and shock, watched his aunt's face. Gentle, understanding eyes received him. Ulu escorted Yoofi aside; and there, in a quiet corner, Yoofi buried his head in her bosom and wept.

From the darkness, the cunning smiles and painful eyes seen in her ballroom, Ulu understood everything. She now saw what she had long avoided.

Dumbstruck, but not in total defeat, Yoofi returned to serve his aunt's victory party. What the bruised lad found instead was love and comfort from his empathizing Aunt Ulu. Finally, she might have found a way to connect to him in earnest. Perhaps it was simply just her time to cry also.

Despite all, the revelry continued. Rex and Ulu, having separately found their own relief and comfort, rejoined the dancing.

Later, much later that night, the guests watched as Miss Hene, led by Shep, sauntered down the quiet, light-flooded staircase, slowly through the ballroom, and out of the house.

"Miss Hene, Miss Hene! Shep? . . . Shep!" shouted Yoofi walking after him, unfreezing the room. Shep paused and looked back. Wagging his tail the dog trotted to rejoin Miss Hene. The wall at the side of the house remained intact, even as Miss Hene and Shep had just exited through it.

Silence, stillness, and strange, frightened feelings filled the room. Miss Hene? What was Miss Hene doing there? And Shep! Who would have invited a dog? Rex wondered. Where had they come from? What had they been doing there? His thoughts ran.

With the music stopped, the guests looked dazed at each other. It was a short yet deep, questing stare of intrigued disbelief. Monsignor Silva and Reverend Watkins looked over their drinks at each other and smiled while shaking their heads in denial.

Ulu signaled the musicians to continue playing. Sipping their drinks and making fun of what they decided did not happen, the merriment returned. From that point, the festivity moved to a frantic pace, with the musicians playing louder and the dancers growing more intense.

Finally, exhaustion set in and, one by one, the guests whispered adieu to their hosts, for then Rex had joined Ulu at the door. He, too, wanted the party to be over.

With Ulu tired from preparing for the party and from too much entertaining and wine, with Yoofi back in his cottage and Princess securely sleeping in her mother's bed, Rex was sure to pounce upon the unsuspecting Charm and finish what he had started before Yoofi interrupted.

This time, however, Rex found Charm just how he wanted her, naked, warm and full of sweet enticements. He was quietly surprised at how easily she gave herself to him, just how placid, delicate and delicious she was. In her, his dreams were fulfilled until, cloyed with delight and spent of energy, he lay in blissful slumber.

To plan, Rex arose early the following morning. He wanted to see Charm's delightful face as she awoke from her bed. For a moment, he looked lustfully at her sensuous form under the covers before walking to the window where he slowly pulled the curtains to let the golden sunlight flood the bedroom, bringing out her glory!

Rex returned to the bedside and, standing before Charm as she slept, gently removed the sheets from her. To his wonderment, a pile of snow-white bones lay before him. He saw no face, no eyes, but heard only crackling, teasing laughter.

Suddenly, Rex realized that while he schemed and played, Miss Hene, even Shep, must also have been at work!

Naked and in fright, Rex dashed from the room and ran downstairs. Just then Yoofi, hand in-hand with Charm, entered the hall that they intended to clean.

"Good morning, Unc . . . Unc . . ." the amazed Yoofi managed to say.

Rex, not knowing what to do, shouted, "It's not me!" As fast as he could, he ran back upstairs, only to find his bedroom door locked. Confused, he bolted into Ulu's bedroom and dashed under her bed.

Luckily for Ulu, she still slumbered. Princess, though, was awakened by the commotion. She wondered why her Uncle Rex, looking so amazingly strange, wanted to play hide and seek so early in the morning. Only her Pappy ever did that. Not caring to know, however, Princess closed her eyes and snuggled close to her mother.

Later, dressed in one of Ulu's robes, Rex finally made his way into the kitchen and poured himself some coffee. His day was just beginning.

Confrontation

The following Sunday did not find Rex in a much better mood. He was perplexed. So too were the congregations of Reverend Watkins and Monsignor Silva. While there was no wide agreement on the form of the woman at the party, that of the dog was obvious. Ulu felt certain that uninvited figure belonged to Miss Hene. Some did not see it. There were others with a frontal view of the being, who testified she wore a light blue gown and a shawl for a hat. Others, seeing her rear, witnessed a pink frock and a wide, feathered, straw hat. When there could not be any definite consensus on the woman's appearance, the conversation descended to the dog, whom everyone described in exactly the same detail. The only disagreement was on whether or not the dog did indeed look back with loving eyes to Yoofi as if at a friend.

To their congregations Watkins and Silva did what they could to comfort or explain the bizarre incident at Ulu's party. When at last they were confronted with the spectacle of a dog who left footprints behind and seemingly walked through heavy masonry, they both pleaded ignorance and promised to provide answers at a later time.

Rex's bewilderment was mixed with anxiety. He could not understand the deep pleasure those crackling, white bones had brought him. How could that have been? Rex was sure he had made love with Charm. Neither could he explain how or why Charm had slipped away from him that very night to Yoofi, that poor, inexperienced lad not nearly his equal.

What bothered him most was that he could not mention any of this at brunch that Sunday.

Ulu had no answers and Rex was not prepared to divulge the embarrassing information. They both sat on the same side of the table. Detective Graham and Monsignor Silva faced them. With Congo's absence, Ulu asked the Reverend Watkins to take his seat as if to remind her where the spiritual head of her family lay.

The Reverend Watkins started with prayer; then the meal was brought to a side table. Ulu sent the maids away and closed the dining room doors.

"I suppose," started Watkins, "that you know nothing of this, Ulu."

"Nothing more than you, Reverend. And I wanted to ask you to explain what we all saw."

"Visions of hell, no doubt," Watkins said. "It reminds me of hell house in Providence. And the sooner we get all this behind us the better for us."

"Do you think Yoofi has anything to do with this?" the Detective asked.

"He is just a child, Detective," the Monsignor replied.

"Why are you afraid to say it's Congo?" Rex asked.

"He was not there when it happened," Watkins said.

"That may not mean much," Rex said. "You must go after him, Detective!"

"For doing what?" Graham asked.

"What about disturbing the peace?"

"God forbid!" the Monsignor said. "The dog made us all laugh."

"He is making a mockery out of us. This is Congo's revenge, and it must not go unanswered, Detective," Rex said.

"Aren't you giving Congo more power than he really has?" Silva asked.

"We know who and what he claims to be. We know that the cult is illegal. We have missing bodies, two, in fact. Those of Zadie Blue and Lev. We have cause to go after him."

"I fully support your point, Rex," Watkins said. "What is your position on this, Silva?"

"I am a bit curious and skeptical at the same time. Nevertheless, I am approaching this with an open mind. I must admit that I am thrown by the presence of the dog. At the one end it could be a fluke; on the other it could be real. But real events can be repeated; and I have never, never before seen a dog walk through a wall. So what do we have? Something supernatural?"

"If you would make up your mind you would know, Silva," Watkins said.

"I will be damned if I am going to let my faith interfere with my curiosity!"

"Monsignor, if I did not really know you, I would wager that you have some dealings with the Kumina thing!" Watkins said.

"Well, I am glad that we know each other, Watkins. But aren't you a trifle curious about this?" the Monsignor asked.

"For me this is a closed case, Silva. My mind is made up. We go after them and in the name of God, stamp them out!" the Anglican reverend responded.

The mood at the table became restive. But the Reverend Watkins was not through. "And you, Detective, where do you stand?"

"I want proof. Something tangible."

"I stand with my pastor and Rex," Ulu said. "The law has long decided this is bad. What more proof do we need?"

Eyes centered on the Detective. "The Dance is only a few weeks away. This I promise: I will follow things closely."

"You are hedging, Detective," Rex said. "We lost our closest family friend, Lev, to this cult."

"You have no proof, Rex."

"Well, I will tell you this. If proof is what you want, I will get it, Detective."

"Are you holding something from us, Rex?" Watkins asked.

"You know I am on your side! But if the Detective is unable to get proof to close this case, then so help me God," Rex said banging his fist on the table, "I will get him proof!"

"It's all right, Rex," Ulu said, patting her brother on the shoulder.

"Good then," Watkins said, "and we will have something to give my congregation. Won't we, Monsignor?"

"Yes, of course! Will you be at the Walk, Watkins?"

"I am not sure."

"I would not miss it for my life," Silva said "and I invite you to accompany me, Watkins."

"Won't you miss Mass by going there, Silva?"

"Ah! I didn't think of it that way. I suppose my entire parish will be there! The news has gotten out, you know. And you know how curious my congregation is, don't you?"

"Yes, I suppose so," Silva said, "but I wonder . . . why is he having his Kumina Dance during Easter?"

"It's a carryover from slavery, Silva." Rex responded. "Many of the African – I mean slave-rituals – had to be practiced on the Christian holidays. That's the only free time the slaves had, well . . . some of them at least. Others still had to buggy the masters to and from church and attend to house chores as well. But the field slaves, they had the holidays free. But you know this, don't you, Watkins?"

"Yes, of course! And that adds another dimension to this event," Monsignor Silva said. "All the better for us to be there, Watkins."

"Duty binds me to be there," Graham said. "And as witnesses, not only to your congregation, but for a court, and maybe the world at large, it would be nice if both of you were there."

"I see your point," Watkins said.

"Good then," Silva said. "We have our sides staked out, and all we have to do is wait a few weeks and keep the dog away," he laughed.

With repose setting over the table, they ended their meal.

A Gift of Time

Having passed his first fifteen months of service at his aunt's house, Yoofi requested a weekend off to return home. Ulu and Rex gladly obliged.

Rex had even mentioned, though not seriously, that he too should take time off from his busy workload and visit the old country. His sister Ama still lived there. He hadn't seen her since he had left for New York many years previously. The thought of meeting Miss Hene, however, irked him sufficiently for him to quickly drop the idea.

In preparation for his visit home, Yoofi went into Port Maria and spent all the money he had saved buying presents for his mother, his brothers, and Miss Hene. He didn't forget Leroy, but it bothered him as to what would make an appropriate gift. He asked Ulu and she suggested a hat. A hat! Yoofi hadn't thought that high up of Leroy. Shoes, socks, a belt, even a tie, but a hat never had occurred to him. Trusting in his aunt's judgment, Yoofi bought Leroy the finest felt hat he could find. It was a tan color variation with a peacock's feather on the right side of the brim.

The storekeeper told Yoofi that the feather was removable, so that the same hat could be used for festive occasions or for more somber times. Yoofi was learning! He snapped up the hat and, in the women's department, bought the finest essence and a brush and comb set for his mother. He had missed her so much. He trembled just in packing the things for her. What would she say? Would she like them? Did she miss him, and did she still like him? It was such a strange time for Yoofi. For him, growing up was so heartrending. When would it ever be over? Yoofi often asked.

His aunt helped him to pack. Yoofi wished Charm would! How had she been? Ulu hadn't spoken to him, Rex, or Charm about the incident at the party. The darkness of Rex's room on the very night of the party had enlightened Charm, giving her a lesson for her age and, Ulu supposed, Yoofi and Rex as well. Yet, the uneasiness remained.

Ulu couldn't easily spank Rex or embarrass him, dampening his enthusiasm. On the contrary, she desired his success. Ulu thought it unfair to confront Rex without also discussing the matter with Charm and Yoofi.

Ulu thought of the possibilities. Yoofi, might, if only to release his pain, tell her what he saw. On the other hand, to protect Charm he might not. He might simply say he didn't know what he saw. Certainly he hadn't seen Charm; he just heard her woe and the anxious rustle of her garments. Maybe he was not certain it was she, for whoever occupied the bed stayed buried beneath the shadows. Small though it was, there was a tinge of doubt. Rex could have denied the entire thing ever happened, and Charm couldn't deliver direct proof.

What Ulu needed for clarity was Rex's confession. If he did confess, Ulu would be faced with a dilemma. Should she discharge Charm? But why? Her brother would be at fault. She would have to send him away as well. Ulu couldn't. Unlike Congo, Rex was a part owner and would prevail! Ulu couldn't risk another family brawl. Much too much would be at stake. For one, it would signal to Congo the full incompetence from which he had been severed. Moreover, if Congo had to return to settle a family dispute, he might demand his rightful part or more of the enterprise. Ulu had no clean options.

But time, great Mother Time, seemed to work for Ulu. Rex's arrogance slowly weathered and smoothed, like limestone against the tide. He now would ask instead of demand and smile where before he frowned.

Charm remained exceptionally beautiful, but a touch of humility and graciousness seemed to have replaced her youthful self-confidence and flaunting. Her change rendered Charm more desirable, as though she had changed dresses or personalities in the midst of a cocktail party, bringing revived attention to an accepted elegance.

Though he couldn't name it, Yoofi needed what Ulu had, time: time to process the tremulous events of his last six months and gain renewed perspective.

So preoccupied he was, his sojourn home came much quicker than he imagined. When he stopped at Providence Pond to gaze at it again, Yoofi realized that he had left home with a tiny suitcase and was returning with two, each of which was many times larger than his original. Life had truly changed for him!

Yoofi arrived home late that Friday evening. It was another Friday just like the one when he had left Providence. As if they knew he would be there, an entire party was at Miss Hene's home.

Since Yoofi's departure, Ama and Leroy's life had returned to the friendly casualness of former years; and Ama's happiness, though not her health, had fully returned. The Family was delighted to see him, including Miss Hene, Puncus St. John, the boys of his childhood; and still a new face, Patsy Blue's, was introduced.

The presents were opened, and everyone was delighted with what they received. Puncus got a new set of handkerchiefs which Yoofi had intended for himself. Ama would share some of the used yet still nice things Ulu had sent for her with Patsy. Everyone seemed happy, especially Ama. Yoofi was asked to use the guest room at Miss Hene's; with Patsy working as a live-in maid, all the rooms at his mother's home were fully occupied.

Without much hesitation, Yoofi asked for Shep. Immediately, however, he recalled the dog's demise and his more recent mysterious circumstance. Yoofi soon wiped his face with the open palm of his hands and, sighing, said, "Well, he must be about, someplace."

Puncus, laughing at Yoofi's seeming confusion, promised a party at Providence Pond the following day, after which Yoofi would leave again for Jacks River.

Brilliant sunshine greeted the ensuing Saturday, the picnic day. Unexpectedly, Congo showed up.

Since his dismissal from Ulu's business, he had moved to the cottage where he first stayed. It was not that Miss Hene didn't plead with him to share the house with her. It was not that she blamed him for what had happened. It was not that they had fallen out, nor that Puncus St. John, his impending brother-in-law, was spending so much time there. It was simply that Congo needed clarity. For that, he considered his reclusive life in the cottage best.

Congo was delighted to see Yoofi and immediately enquired about Princess, Charm, and Ulu. He was pleased to know Rex had been successful in controlling the business. The news that Laura had come to Rex's party in search of him, he found bothersome. Congo saw it as his negligence with Laura's business that had brought her again into the witch's trap in search of him. Why hadn't he gone to see her, instead?

Yet Congo mingled well with the crowd. He spent an unusually long time talking with Leroy and Puncus St. John. He and Puncus seemed to be in confrontation with Leroy, with long pleadings and explanations, and still there was discord. At the end of their conversation, the three men surprisingly shook hands, then embraced and kissed each other, as if entering an ancient, secret pact. Congo must have made Kumina converts, Miss Hene thought.

During his time off, Yoofi thought relentlessly. He needed a way to settle his mind. He wanted so much to talk to Miss Hene, his mother, and Puncus St. John. He did make gestures of speaking, and they responded, all with smiles and joy of seeing the gentleman into whom he had been transformed. Their delight and appreciation of him prevented the young man from airing his soul. So desperately he wanted to mention Charm, the beauty that had ripped his soul apart. So much he wanted to allow himself to express what had happened to him, how he loved her, what she meant to him. Most of all he wanted to talk of his Uncle Rex. What seemed like more pressing issues constantly usurped his.

On his return to work at Jacks River, Yoofi found a subdued and somber tone in his aunt's home. Rex had taken Princess to Kingston with him for a vacation and, with nothing much to do, Charm was either too restive or pensive to entertain him.

The change Rex made – a change from weekly to monthly cycles – enabled him the time off. Ulu's attitude toward Yoofi had grown relaxed. She finally invited him to share dinner with her and Charm.

Even though the closeness gave them opportunity to talk, neither Yoofi nor Charm embraced it. Shame, doubt, and uncertainty clouded their relationship. Since the first time they made love on that fateful Sunday, they had secretly worked out a scheme of meeting. They had become open and sufficiently at ease to comfortably verbalize their feelings toward each other. They were in love, had grown proud of each other, and, were it not for fear, would have announced it to the world. Indeed they thought of doing so.

Now that neither knew the state of affairs – Yoofi not knowing the nature and extent of the relationship between Charm and Rex, and she not knowing the extent of his pain – they had lost the comfortable communication between them. Neither knew what to think or feel. They avoided looking at each other and slowly drifted apart.

Ulu witnessed the coldness that was overshadowing them. It froze the warmth of their passion to silence and polite gestures. It also signaled a deeper relationship, the strength or future of which Ulu didn't know. Yet, its past and present sat before her, a thing of such deep implication it couldn't be avoided. That certainly was something to be discussed, to question. Ulu thought it best to let it die, if indeed dying was its current experience. Why resurrect the dead, unless one intends the thing to live forever? Ulu chose to leave it alone, sleeping or dying.

The crack Rex's lust and indiscretion had made in the family slowly widened as it separated them. Ulu was not unthankful for the forces that moved them apart. They restored respectability and hope to her house and, with that, her regard for family. Never did she want to throw Charm out or abandon her nephew. Still, her responsibility was beyond them. Ulu had a daughter and a dream for her. She had that, and her position and prestige in Jacks River, to contemplate. Time had certainly been good to her, and Ulu was thankful.

Ho's Passion

C ongo was not in the habit of discussing his problems with anyone. He tried to live an open life; but when he faced personal failures, he sank deep within himself for answers, keeping his innermost feelings hidden. He treated his failed marriage in the same manner. He lived at his sister's cottage more as a guest, due to his excessive traveling. Although he told Miss Hene of Ulu's decision, he didn't disclose the bitterness it had caused in him or his plans of reconciliation.

His first interest was in becoming financially viable. His second was in getting to the job Asa King had laid out for him. Upon achieving that, he would do what he could concerning his business interests with Ulu. The one thing he was determined to keep alive was his relationship with his daughter. He did not believe that his marriage was over. He certainly wanted to revive it. Most of all, he wanted to be with his daughter. He could not live in the same house with Rex, yet he kept thinking of Ulu and Princess.

With the weekend behind him, he saddled his horse and headed toward Oracabessa. He had not seen Laura in months and wanted to reconfirm to her that the plans for her wedding were progressing well. Miss Hene would give him the use of Providence Pond for the reception, while Puncus St. John catered. The marriage was to be the following weekend at St Andrew's. Monsignor Ricardo Silva had recently given Congo his assurance that the plans were in order.

On reaching Laura's business Monday morning, Congo saw that things were not normal. The store had not opened for business. What a contrast to the last time Laura greeted him outside and whisked him to her upstairs parlor! He went to the rear of the building, where some of her servants lived. They told him Laura hadn't been at the store since the previous Wednesday, that she had been crying and threatening to take her life.

Congo heard about the contracts Rex had the farmers sign. Congo wondered if Rex was so brazen as to place the same offer before Laura. He went inside the store and, from there, into her office. The contract from Rex lay miserably crumpled on her desk.

Congo hurried to Free Hill to see Laura. Her hungry, forlorn cat met him at the door. Congo gave it water and food. With the cat fully absorbed in eating, Congo entered Laura's living room. It was dark and smelled of mold. Congo's astonishment turned to apprehension. He went into her bedroom. Congo saw the mangled body lying on the cold tile floor. She was scantily dressed with cut marks on the wrists, blood on her face and body, with empty bottles of white rum around her.

Congo stooped over Laura. She didn't seem to be breathing. Neither could he detect a pulse. Congo lifted her limp body as he would a baby's. He gently placed her body in her carriage and attached the horses. He raced to the hospital.

Dr. Devinder was on duty. Congo left her on the gurney just past the entrance and gave hurried instructions that she be taken to a private emergency room. Soon after, Congo hastily left the hospital. He wanted to let Ho know what had happened.

On his way to see Ho, Congo stopped at the police station and announced that an investigation of her house might be necessary. He didn't suspect foul play; nevertheless, he wanted the police to know what had happened.

Congo greeted Ho's staff as he always had and walked into Ho's office. The first thing he saw was Ho's unfinished letter to Laura. It was the follow-up letter he had promised her. Congo read the lines:

Laura, you asked me about passion. I hope one day life will give me the opportunity to show you, rather than to explain to you all that I have felt about you, even when you were too young to understand.

Congo didn't understand. From its date, Congo knew Ho had started the letter months before. What had prevented Ho from completing the letter and delivering it? Congo didn't know; maybe he would never understand.

Congo returned to the kitchen where he enquired for Ho. The beach, they said. He hurried there.

"Where is she?"

"At the hospital."

"How is she?"

"Not good."

"What do you think happened?"

"It seems like attempted suicide"

"Suicide?"

"Yes."

"Why?"

"Her problem."

"Her problem is not suicide. That will be my problem if she dies!"

"You will have no problems if you die, Ho."

"Don't change the topic!"

"It seems, I mean, Laura had too many problems, Ho," Congo smiled as he looked askance at Ho with narrowing eyes.

"Like what? What problems, Congo?"

"Her property is in foreclosure, creditors demanding pay."

"Is that all?"

"No! Rex took over her business and wants her to disclose her Hong Kong connections!"

"Is that all?"

"She tried to kill herself."

"You said that already."

"Well, that's all."

"Is that all you come to tell me, Congo? Problems, problems?"

"Well, you asked!"

"I know. But do you have anything else to say? No solutions? You have no solutions, Congo?"

"No, Ho. I told you that already."

"Well, don't stand there useless without a solution!"

"It's marriage, Ho. You have to marry her."

"That's all set."

"So?"

"It's passion, Congo! That's the solution. Passion!"

And with that, Ho started to run through the woods towards the hospital.

"You need a horse and . . . and get dressed, Ho!"

"Keep your horse, keep your clothes. I have a solution!" Ho shouted.

He continued running until he reached the hospital.

Congo went back to Ho's room and placed some clothes in a large suitcase which he carried to the hospital.

Police Detective Charles Graham was already at the front desk making inquiry for Laura's room. He wanted to take a statement from her.

Ho, dressed in almost nothing, raced past the entrance where the Detective stood and down the hall to the emergency room where Li had died. Detective Graham, mistaking Ho for a lunatic, hurried after him. In the room Ho had already placed himself on the bed beside Laura, hugging her in relief that she had gained consciousness.

Laura wasn't dying. She simply hadn't eaten for days and was sleeping off a drunken slumber. She had not tried suicide but had taken a drunken fall, cutting her arms in a few places. Now she had recovered, eaten, and was in good spirits.

"Let's go on the honeymoon, now, my love."

"Honeymoon?" asked the Detective. "Who are you?"

"Ho, Detective. It is me!"

"Ho, you better put some clothes on."

"I couldn't get him to," said Congo, entering the room.

Monsignor Silva, who had a habit of visiting the hospital on Monday mornings, followed. "And what is this I hear about a honeymoon?"

"The marriage is set for this weekend."

"We better do it now, if they are ready for their honeymoon," Congo said.

"So long as Laura agrees," Ho said.

"Yes, we are all here," she said.

And with that, the Doctor said, looking at Monsignor Silva, "This is my hospital. I should officiate."

"I have been contracted to," smiled Monsignor Silva.

"When should I kiss the bride?" Ho asked.

"After you say the 'I do,'" the Doctor replied.

"I do," Ho said, and slid under the cover with Laura "And you can do the paperwork in your office, when you leave."

Congo placed the address of the hotel where he had made reservations for Ho and Laura on the bedside table and, with the rest of the men, left the room.

"Passion, Laura. Show me!" For the first time in his almost sixty years, Ho, burning with more fire than he could contain, made love to his dear Laura.

Monsignor Silva, Doctor Devinder, the Reverend Bernard Watkins, who had just arrived, Detective Charles Graham, and Congo King stood in the cramped office preparing the marriage papers for Ho and Laura. Between Congo and the Doctor, they had all the information they needed.

Of the five of them, Detective Graham was the least familiar with Ho. He was not pleased with this man who had entered the hospital undressed and in a manner that could have caused harm to patient and staff alike. He wanted to caution Ho about his behavior.

With the paper work done, Monsignor Silva looked at the men and told them that some kind of ceremony was appropriate. So with the Detective's need to talk to Ho, and the Reverend's desire for ritual, the men entered the room to see Ho lying on his back in a radiant, yet relaxed smile.

"It was good," he said. "Sorry I took so long. I hope you gentlemen do not mind."

"Ho," asked the Monsignor, "do you take Laura to be your lawful wife until death do you part?"

"And you, Laura, do you take Ho to be your lawful husband?"

"Of course, she does. She is my wife!"

"Then you may kiss the bride."

"I just did! Do you think I wouldn't?"

"We'd better leave," suggested Congo.

"Yes, we'd better," agreed the Detective. "Can anyone here vouch for him?"

"I can, Detective," said Congo. "He is a good man."

"Strange might be better," said the Reverend.

"Strange to the point of craziness," suggested the Detective.

"I wouldn't take it quite that far," said the Doctor.

"I will be dropping in on him quite soon," said the Detective Graham.

"You do that, Detective. What you will find is a heart of gold."

"Well, if there is nothing else now . . ." Graham added, tipping his hat.

"Gentlemen," said Congo, "please remember we have a function in Providence to attend."

"Yes, yes," nodded the Doctor.

"Thanks for reminding us, Congo. We certainly will be attending."

"And, thank you all for helping out at such short notice."

"We are always on duty here," said the Doctor, bringing laughter to the group.

With that, the men shook hands and departed.

Congo was about to step out of the hospital when Detective Charles Graham shouted: "Congo, Congo, I have been waiting to see you."

"What on earth about, Graham?"

"You know, Congo. I have known you for some time and have believed you to be honest and decent. But I have here in my possession a letter from Rex. Your brother-in-law, I believe?"

"Yes, he is my brother-in-law, Graham."

"The letter I hold as evidence implicates you in the disappearance of one Lev Tyler, and the whereabouts of his body. Did you know Lev Tyler?"

"Of course, Detective. He also is my brother-in-law. I told you that already."

"Good then! I must tell you that this letter raises some questions I must look into."

"I understand."

"I just wanted you to know."

"I am willing to assist in whatever way I can."

"Thank you, Congo. I knew I could depend on you."

"Welcome, Detective."

The men tipped their hats to each other as they bade adieu.

"Remember the Dance at Providence, Detective."

"I will, Congo."

"The Walk in Providence will clarify everything for you, Detective."

"It will, ah?"

"Yes, Detective. It will."

With that, the men saluted each other and parted.

Ponderous Ulu

Through time and Ulu's silence Rex felt distanced from the fiasco of the victory party. He sought to appease Ulu and took his celebration elsewhere. He provided her with an ample time to reflect. Ulu, still in awe of her younger brother's rapid though possibly soiled success, gave him whatever his trip required: her money and her blessing. She also gave him Princess.

It was to Ulu's surprise that on the next Friday, a sultry, rain-drenched afternoon, she looked across the counter of her store and saw Princess standing beside Miss Hene and Shep. As the road cleared, Miss Hene and Princess disembarked from the bus, the same bus that years ago had brought Ulu home in style on her return from New York. They came across the street in the pouring rain, Shep following closely behind them. On seeing Princess, Ulu dropped the money she had been counting and hastened out to meet her daughter.

Miss Hene still held Princess' hand. Ulu reached down and picked up Princess, as if snatching her from danger. Eager to get into the house, Ulu started to run with Princess and hollered, "Come on in, Miss Hene, and leave the dog outside."

When Ulu heard no reply, not even footsteps following her, she turned to grab Miss Hene's hand and rush her out of the rain. What had happened? Ulu did not know. Still holding Princess by the hand and with her free hand formed into a visor, Ulu looked for Miss Hene. She peered across the street and then up and down its length, in every direction possible. Ulu, not seeing the least indication of Miss Hene or Shep, not even their footprints, said, "Thank you anyway!" and ran inside her house with Princess.

The young girl shivered with cold and hunger. As her mother lifted her, Princess sobbed, asking, "Where is my Pappy?" Ulu wiped the rain from her daughter's face and again Princess cried, "I want my Pappy." Ulu, still comforting the child, rushed her upstairs.

Hurriedly, Ulu sent for Charm and together they removed Princess' wet clothes from her trembling body, dried and powdered her skin, dressed her in her favorite bed clothes, provided soup for her, then laid her in bed. Not long after, Princess, worn but cozy, dozed.

As Charm gathered Princess' wet, dirty clothes, she found a letter still sealed and addressed to Ulu. Without delay, Charm took the letter to her, who by then was seated herself at a writing desk in Rex's room. She busied herself with papers on his desk, looking for messages or letters he might have sent. Like a flash of light in the dark, it dawned on Ulu that she hadn't heard from Rex since his departure three weeks prior.

On seeing Charm, Ulu put away the papers and took the letter. It was in a simple brown envelope. Ulu didn't want to open it in Charm's presence. She gave the girl a dismissive look, and Charm left the room, closing the door behind her. Ulu read:

> *Thanks for the lovely vacation, Ulu. Now, you are on your own.*
> *Yours always,*
> *Rex*

Ulu didn't know what to make of the note. The phrase "lovely vacation" couldn't leave her mind. Never had they spoken of a vacation except for his recent trip to Kingston. What did he mean? Ulu didn't understand. Where was he?

Ulu replaced the letter in the envelope and started going through his mail. She had left the operation of the business to Rex, fully trusting his judgment and intentions. Ulu had, therefore, never checked the books, receipts, or his letters. She wouldn't have done that unless she were specially asked. Now she was compelled to.

And so she checked. Note by note, receipt by receipt, Rex's hideous practices became clearer to her. His frequent trips to Port Maria were to wager, and it seemed he was not good at it. He had racked up a large gambling debt. It also seemed he was in the habit of entertaining what Ulu imagined to be ladies, since he had many hotel bills and meals for two or three persons. Ulu at first wondered if that included Princess and Charm; but, on further reflection, she realized the bills were for hotel rooms when her household was fast asleep. Ulu could have easily forgot and forgiven that, but most bothersome were her bank statements. They all showed zero balances. In short, Rex had taken all he could and, to disguise his leaving the country, took Princess with him in pretense of going Kingston. After fully enjoying himself there, he put his niece on the bus, paid the conductor for her delivery, and took a ship back to New York. Ulu was devastated. She crashed onto the desk and cried.

It was not long after that when Ulu looked out of the bedroom window and saw cart after cart returning from Oracabessa filled with produce. What on earth were they doing? Was the world spinning backwards? Under Yoofi's leadership, the carts had been loaded with dried pimento and sent to Laura, who rejected them along with all the other shipments from Rex under the new contract.

Perhaps it was his youthful forgetfulness. Maybe it was because of his preoccupation with the new, strenuous currents of his life. For whatever reason, Yoofi now had to do what was ominously apparent to him, what he should have long ago done. He informed Ulu that Laura had earlier closed the produce section of her business and had so informed Rex.

On their last week of honeymooning, Laura and Ho redrew their business plans. Ho agreed to dismiss all of Laura's debts; taking the produce business under the portfolio he and Congo had created. Ho would continue running the restaurant and Laura the jewelry trade, which she combined with haberdashery. It was a good plan for them, but not for Ulu's business. Laura had been her only customer.

Rex, knowing he had the advantage, had locked himself in long-term contracts with the farmers for their produce, whereas Laura was not bound to buy from him. It didn't take long for produce to pile up and start to rot in Ulu's ill-prepared storehouse. Burdened with secret desperation, Rex had gone to Laura and begged her to buy. Her simple response was "please go." Rex didn't inform Ulu of that. He surmised Ulu could do nothing about the situation and took his vacation in silence.

Later that day, farmers came to Ulu's house demanding payment for produce Rex had promised to pay for at the end of the month. Not having enough money on hand, Ulu hurried into Port Maria to collect rent. That had been a great source of revenue to her. Her houses lay empty. Rex had evicted the renters in the hope of getting higher rents from new contracts. His unrealized dreams left the houses empty and Ulu in deep exasperation.

All the ready cash Ulu had was in her store from the proceeds of the current day's transactions. It would not be until late Saturday night that she might have enough sales to pay the farmers. Ulu was by no means broke. Nonetheless, she felt raped. Luckily for her, the farmers agreed to wait until Monday for payment.

She didn't know what to do. She worked late that night, thinking, thinking, asking what could be done. When she was broken by despair and exhaustion, Ulu dragged herself to her church. There she prayed. Later, Ulu returned home and fell asleep beside Princess.

Charm was not in the house.

Charming Aunts

Early the following morning, a Saturday of drizzle, lightning, and thunder, Ulu awoke to find Princess having breakfast. Charm had quietly gone to Princess's room, removed her, and started caring for her. Ulu was sad. She was angry. She didn't quite know what to do. She asked for Yoofi and found he was still asleep. She didn't want him but needed to know his whereabouts. She wanted no more surprises. She was glad to know Princess, even though she had traveled in such inclement weather, was more frightened and shocked from the ordeal than sick.

After Charm's care and attention, Princess's confidence slowly returned, and she drifted from Charm to spend whatever time she could with her mother. Ulu had always been kind and attentive to her. Princess knew her mother loved her. She also knew her mother would soon busy herself with customers. Ulu spent as much time as she could with Princess. After she went to work, she would look in on her daughter as often as she could, even running from the store with her apron still on, to see Princess.

Later that very day, Ulu returned to the table to find Princess tugging herself away from Charm. She wanted to sit on her mother's lap.

"Come, my Princess. Tell Mammy what has happened to you."

"Uncle Rex took me to the circus and bought me ice-cream and candy, Mammy."

"And how are you this morning, my Princess?"

"Fine, Mammy," she said sniveling.

Ulu kissed her daughter, who soon pulled herself from her. Charm followed Princess, but Ulu called her back.

"Nice rain, Charm. Do you like the rain?"

"Yes, ma'am, it makes me cozy."

"I see. So where were you last night when I came in, Charm?"

"When you came in, ma'am?"

"Yes, Charm, when I came in. You were not with Princess, or in your bed."

"I know, ma'am."

"Listen, Charm, I do not have time for games. You better tell me right away, or else!"

"Or else what, ma'am?"

"You will not like the consequences. I am not a happy person this morning, Charm, and would hate to be rash with you for no reason of your own."

"All right, ma'am. I will tell you."

"So?" Ulu implored.

"I went to tell Yoofi."

"Tell Yoofi what? That Princess came back? Yoofi must have known from yesterday and, moreover, you could have waited until this morning to tell him!" Ulu said, reaching for a plausible explanation.

"Yes, ma'am. But that was not all."

"Don't test my patience, Charm!"

"Okay then, ma'am. I had to tell him first. I am pregnant."

"What did you say, Charm?"

"I am pregnant, ma'am."

"That Rex! If I get my hands on him, I will kill him. Kill him, you hear me!"

"Yes, ma'am. I know. But he didn't do it."

"Who then, Charm?"

"The belly belongs to your nephew, ma'am."

"What did you say? Who? To Yoofi?"

"Yes, ma'am. Like I said, its belongs to *your nephew*."

Ulu bit her lip. She flinched and thought, how do these things happen! She was angry. She could have hit Charm or Yoofi and not cared. What would she do? Ulu was ready to attack.

"Did you say my nephew, Charm?" Ulu asked in a raised voice.

"Yes, ma'am."

"Well, Charm. You could easily have said 'your nephew.'"

"I don't understand you, ma'am?"

"What don't you understand? Yoofi is your nephew as well as he is mine!"

"No, ma'am. You are not pulling that one on me. Yoofi is *your* nephew!"

"Listen, Charm," Ulu said with quiet firmness. "Yoofi is your nephew as well."

"My Lord! And nobody told me!"

"I warned you, time and time again, not to have anything to do with him."

"You did, ma'am, but you didn't tell me why. And I asked him about his relatives. He is a King, and his mother's name is Ama King. The only other King I know is Congo King and I have heard about Asa his father. It looks like you married your brother, or maybe your cousin, ma'am. Yoofi is no nephew of mine!"

"Yes, that's what the papers will say. Congo is a King and so is Yoofi's mother. But I know otherwise."

"Is that so, ma'am? What can you tell me about marrying your brother, Congo King?"

"What on earth are you asking? Listen, Charm. The Kings are not from around here. They are from Portland. Your mother, Esi, was a good friend to my mother when they were young. Your father, Vijay Boydell, had a baby with my mother, Nweka, when they were quite young. That is my sister, Ama King."

"Ama King? She should be Ama Boydell!"

"Yes, Charm, she should. But things didn't work that way."

"So, you want to tell me that Nweka gave bun to Vijay Boydell and then jacket to Congo or was it to Asa King?"

"Watch your language, young lady! Speak properly. Despite everything, this is still a Covey house."

"Sorry, ma'am," Charm said, her head bowed low in shame and confusion. To avoid appearing totally defeated, Charm mustered, " I just wanted to ask, ma'am, if your sister had been conceived illegitimately with Mr. Boydell and then passed on as Congo's or Asa King's daughter. I mean, ma'am," Charm asked with great curiosity, "how did she become Ama King?"

"We will let it go this once," Ulu said, staring at Charm as she ground her teeth. A sudden warmth flooded Ulu's soul as she looked at Charm. With a long, deep breath, she sighed and then continued. "No. It is not that simple," Ulu said as she took Charm to Asa's first visit and the incident at Providence Pond almost half a century before. Ulu carefully outlined the steps whereby Ama became a King. Charm sat in awe. She didn't know what to think.

"I know this is hard for you, Charm."

"Very hard, ma'am. What should I do?"

"This is a hard time for us all, Charm. I will go and see Miss Hene today. She has to know!"

"You will get sick if you travel in the rain, ma'am."

"Nonetheless, I must go. You take care of Princess."

"Yes, ma'am."

"And you have no reason to talk to Yoofi about this until we know what to do, right?"

"Right, ma'am. I will stay away from him till you return."

"Good. Just make sure Princess is all right."

"Yes, ma'am."

With that, Ulu left the table and prepared for her trip to Providence.

Potpourri

The *Any Questions* sat on the convex side of a great arc of road leading through Providence. The tavern itself showed hardly any signs of its transformation. It had been built at the end of Providence so it stood out of the way. Perhaps that was the very reason the old church failed.

Puncus St. John had not changed the building much. The old edifice still maintained its wooden, rectangular form and high roofline covered with corrugated tin. Paint had not yet touched its walls, inside or out, nor had the rostrum been removed. In fact, that was where the musicians played. And there, too, was where Puncus and sometimes Yoofi joined them in Dance.

The tavern sat back some fifty yards or so from the unpaved road. A small track of bare earth led from the road through the lush, well-kept grass to the tavern. The visitor needed to climb three wooden steps to enter the tavern from its long side through a set of unfinished double doors. It was as simple as could be. The land behind the tavern sloped up to timber-packed woods, far, far into the hills.

A single road led to the *Any Questions*. One branch of it veered to the northeast and, after leaving the deep arch which seemed to define the tavern, curved toward the southwest. It was on this branch of the road that the Monsignor and the Reverend Watkins traveled to the *Any Questions*.

They traveled together, thinking and talking of what they might expect. Sure, the Monsignor from his days in Galina knew of Asa King and the Kumina Family there. He had not paid it much attention since it did not interfere with his work and the group had been peaceful and remote. On that appointed Thursday night, however, the Monsignor walked with an open, eager mind touched by cautious expectation of just what might lie ahead.

The Reverend Watkins, whose parish included Fellowship, also knew about the maligned Kumina cult, but most of his knowledge was from newspapers. It was a great delight and surprise for Watkins when his comrade agreed to attend the Kumina Dance at the *Any Questions*. The Reverend's private desire was to learn more . . . to unearth whatever harmful information he could to discredit Congo and assist the Detective in driving the Kumina movement out of Providence. What would he find?

For Detective Graham, traveling on the opposite branch of the road, the concerns were different. He had lost his fiancée Zadie Blue to this mystical movement under blue-sky conditions. Her loss still baffled him. He still sought clues to Zadie's disappearance. For that reason, he did not travel alone. A few officers rode with him. Like the Reverends, they were not distinguished by their official clothing.

To Doctor Devinder Singh and his wife, and Ho and Laura, the Kumina movement was not new. The Doctor had been asked by the authorities to examine baby Zadie. She had no pupils in her large gray eyes, but otherwise she was quite normal. The Doctor, having spoken to Asa and other Family members and understanding that Zadie was well cared for, happily informed the police that Zadie was in good hands. The Doctor and his wife quietly attended many Family meetings in Galina and were taken to be members although they did not renounce their native faith. Ho and Laura attended out of curiosity and their respect for Congo. They were glad to be there.

Congo King could not understand his lonely preoccupation as he toiled with Miss Hene and St. John in readying the *Any Questions* for the Dance. He had not disclosed the sadness he felt after Ulu embarrassed and dismissed him from their home. His subsequent conversation with the Detective had disquieted him even further, even though he did not show it. Graham, whose church he attended, and whom he had entertained so often at his house, treated him as though he were a suspect. Congo could not exclude the possibility of Ulu's complicity, but he thought Rex more likely to expose him and the Family.

Congo toiled to put the pieces together. He tried to remember the dream he had had long ago – the dream in which two great, mothering birds let him loose in mid air to find himself – as he first slept in the room Lev had given him. Now that it was his abode again, he wished he could so dream again. He was not that lucky. This lack of memory tormented him.

Miss Hene watched her brother's toil and how he evaded her. As she approached, he would engage Puncus in meaningless conversations. Puncus watched with mirth, wondering which would first relent, the fox or the hound! It did not matter to him. Time, he knew, would yield the truth!

Miss Hene had made the clothes for the musicians, Ama, and herself many days before the Dance. The full-length robes were simple, a rough, white cotton, without much embroidery or other decorations.

Ama, for all the excitement that filled her, could still not decipher why she had suddenly become center stage. Never in her life had she been the yolk of anything. Nweka had described the thrill of being chosen as a beauty queen, and she had something to show for it! Ama's greatest joy, the highest point in her life, had been meeting Headmaster Love in her school library! In her mind she had become the queen of his school. At the height of her joy, Ama understood her mother's elation. What now was to become of her? Why was she seated in the center of the yard of the *Any Questions* to be Danced to? That was Ama's concern, and her fear was to what level would it make her again fall.

With the sun fading and the drumming started, Puncus St. John knew it was he that had to face the waiting throng on the front lawn of the *Any Questions*. The crowd was not large, less than two hundred. Most of Providence Pond was there, along with whoever else heard of the Dance.

Puncus looked at the gas lamps that formed the border of the group. Ama sat in the middle. From the steps leading into the *Any Questions*, Puncus saw the men of the cloth and the Detective. With an inward smile, Puncus remembered escaping what he considered their tyranny. He eyed the gathering for Leroy. He was not there. Why Leroy was absent, Puncus did not know. He looked again at Ama and Miss Hene sitting beside her and began:

"My dear friends, and those of you that are here for the first time, friends in the future, I hope, thank you for being here. This Thursday night, in the Year of our Lord 1921, just following on the heels of Ash Wednesday, is like any other night at the *Any Questions* . . . except you do not pay when you leave this time, and the food is much better. I must say thanks to Miss Hene and Master Congo. They had something to do with that. The only other thing I want to say is: for those who are ready, let your journey start now; and don't let it ever stop! Oh, there is one more thing I should tell you: From Ash Wednesday to Easter morning, this is the Kumina Spring Festivities."

Having said that, Puncus beckoned Congo. Congo had been sitting in the darkness of the building, not knowing how to make his appearance.

"Master Congo will say a few words to you," Puncus said, and again he signaled to Congo.

Intense fear cut into Congo's stomach. He stood, then bent over, unable to move. In the depth of his pain, the memory of the dream returned. His falling flashed before him. But what remained and burned in his mind was the image of the wizard first looking at him in laughter – loud mocking laughter – and then, finally, his terrible transformation from his magical self into Congo, upon what once seemed a steep, impossible hill.

With Puncus's hand leading him out of the dark interior of the building, Congo reached the steps and faced the crowd.

"Sometimes all that one has left is fear," Congo started. "When everything is taken from us and we still must go on, all we have is fear. But if we confront it, what we will find is love. Yes, love and peace. That's what I have now. I could tell you about my loss, but maybe that concerns too many and is too private to disclose here.

"This is what I can tell you, as I should have almost twenty years ago: I am a Kumina Master. Asa, my father, whom some of you know from your connections in Galina or Fellowship, brought Miss Hene and me here to Providence to start a Family. In my own way, I lived a Kumina life. To some, that was not expected of me. It was in a quarrel with my brother-in-law, Rex Covey, that I realized how my life differed from what was intended. You see, Brethren, I was running, afraid of who I was . . . what I was called to be. So I hid. Rex saw that! He called me 'Jonah.' Of all the folk in your Bible, Jonah is the one I detest the most. And he called me 'Jonah!' Well, Rex, you are not here. But I want to thank you for stirring things up in my mind.

"The other thing I must tell you is that, unknown to me, my sister Miss Hene got things started here. She did what I was supposed to do and started a Kumina Family. It takes women to do that, I suppose . . . give birth to things! So, I want to thank her, too, for the reason we are here.

"But none of this would have happened if my dear sister, Ama, had not listened to the voices calling on her to see her way to the Kumina doctrine. That is the reason we are Dancing for Ama tonight. In Ama, we see a great victory! Our Family is coming to life. Would you please stand, Sister Ama?" Congo asked, pointing in her direction.

Confident, but with some discomfort, Ama arose to a great applause. Miss Hene stepped beside her and held up Ama's hand, which waved a red handkerchief.

"Friends, dear friends," Congo called as Ama's toast waned, "but dear friends, Ama is not the only one whom we celebrate tonight. First of all, let us recall the spirit of Baptist Minister Paul Bogle and his sacrifice of love. Also, let us not forget the good folk who have touched our lives but have crossed over before us. Therefore, let us also Dance for Lev, Bem, Esi, Henry, and Aren. Let us also not forget Nweka and Kisi, members of our Family who now serve in Portland and St. Thomas. They may be gone, but let their memory linger with us as we fold Ama into our Kumina Family.

"In her younger days, Ama would come here to the *Any Questions* and eat with you. Since her marriage – and excuse me . . . if any of you see Leroy out there, tell him to stop running and come on home – yes, since her marriage, Ama has been tied to home and business. That has taken her from you.

"It also took her away from herself. My dear Ama fell. But she arose from her pit and, with Miss Hene's help, found a better Family and a better tomorrow, I hope.

"What Ama now has is a new life. She has been born – so to speak – into the Kumina Family and to honor on this special day. We are Dancing for her.

"I know I have said too much already, but let me add this: All the Kumina Families will meet at Providence Pond for our Easter Dance. I have been talking with Asa about this. All of you are invited. Most of you here do not know who Asa is. This is not the time to explain. But if you like what you see and feel here tonight, ask about Asa and the big Family Walk here at the *Any Questions*. Good St. John will tell you all about that.

"Enough said.

"Again, thank you all for showing up, and enjoy the Dance."

He waved and turned to go. Before he entered the building, he changed his mind and returned to the steps. "By the way, if you like the Dance, please join in."

The tension in the crowd turned to laughter as Congo pointed to Puncus and his musicians. Immediately the drumming started. Puncus, Congo, and Yoofi, who had been seated with Congo in the building, walked out onto the grass and joined Miss Hene. They started the Dancing.

It did not take long for those leaning against the fence to join in, singing and dancing. Ama could not Dance. Yet, she delighted in the movement and gaiety around her. Ama watched the old Headmaster Forbes bobbing and moving as if he intended to get close to Yoofi.

The music, the long, apparently endless drumming, changed seamlessly from one rhythmic theme to another. At times it was fast, and at other times slower. With shifting amplitude each new cadence mesmerized, elevating the soul. Ama truly enjoyed it, the peaceful transition the gracious melodies brought.

Yoofi, not noticing the Headmaster, danced his way toward the meal table. The aroma drew others to the food, which was laid out in buffet style. Soon the party was in full swing, and it lasted for hours.

"Excellent Dancing, Yoofi!" Headmaster Forbes shouted as he approached the dining dancer. Yoofi, smiling, stood up and faced him. With outstretched hands, Forbes folded Yoofi into his arms. "I have been noticing you, Yoofi. You are such a wonderful dancer."

"Thank you, Headmaster."

"So tell me. Where did you learn to Jump, Yoofi? I do not remember teaching you to Dance at school?"

"Learn, Headmaster?"

"Yes, Yoofi. Who taught you to Dance?"

The lad thought for a while and finally reconnected to his boyhood dream on the green lawn behind Miss Hene's house some five years previously. Yoofi, as well as he could, described the man who had first Danced with him.

"What! That's none other than Vijay Boydell!" the surprised Headmaster said. "He lived here as a young man. I know him very well. But he died long before you were born, Yoofi. How could he teach you to Dance?"

"Well, Headmaster, it was in the air. He was Dancing in the air and I floated up and Danced with him."

"I see," said the Headmaster, "I see," he repeated, nodding his head. He turned to go, unable to find a proper response to Yoofi's answer.

"Well, Yoofi," he said, "Just keep Dancing!"

"I will, Headmaster."

Headmaster Forbes had walked a few steps when Yoofi called, "I am sorry, Headmaster."

"And what for, Yoofi?" the Headmaster asked, looking back at the lad.

"For shouting at you and calling you an old fool, Headmaster."

"You didn't have to shout it, Yoofi."

"That's not what I mean, Headmaster. It is for calling you an old fool that I am apologizing about."

"But that's as true as your Dancing, Yoofi! At your age I was a young fool. Now look at me – just an old fool," the Headmaster said. Turning, he embraced his old student. He held Yoofi tightly in his arms. "I know you didn't mean it, Yoofi. In your position, I might have said even worse."

"I really thank you, Headmaster," Yoofi said as soon as Forbes released him. They shook hands, and Yoofi watched as the Headmaster ambled toward the center of the crowd, where Ama and Miss Hene had just finished their meal. Forbes held out his hand for Hiss Hene. With a prompt, ready smile, Miss Hene got up and joined the Headmaster in the secular bailo that the music had just signaled.

Yoofi drew near, watching the couple leading that part of the Dance. Soon Congo joined them, and the trio circled around Ama as they Danced, bringing joyous attention and admiration to her. The Dance was slow at first with the base drums carrying the rhythm. Every so often the bamboo flutes would soar high over the drums with breathless, melodious syncopations.

The sweaty, gray-haired Headmaster pranced and bobbed as if he knew onlookers expected still another kind of lesson from him – one rooted in old, Kumina movements. Heads in the audience watched him, Congo, and the elegant Miss Hene whirling in joyous Dance for Ama. The ground rocked, as spectators turned dancers followed the moves Congo, Miss Hene, and Forbes displayed. Devinder Singh and his wife, as well as Laura and Ho were not slow to learn Congo's new moves and, remembering their own sacred dances, added fresh steps to the merriment of the party.

Enthralled by the music and now absent of pain, Ama stood to her full height, Dancing first with her walking stick, then discarding it to shuffle towards the Headmaster, engaging him in slow, seductive steps. With hands held high, they were face-to-face, bodies touching, bumping as the tempo of the drumming moved them higher and higher to rhythmic ecstasy. It was lovely, moving Yoofi to tears, as Ama seemed to grow from one stage of joy to yet a higher. How long the music played like that, no one was sure; but just as smoothly as it had changed, the music started to wane with the rapid tempo fading. The Headmaster, having escorted Ama back to her seat, sat by her as they joked about her Dance.

Yoofi, still twirling, thought of Leroy and wondered why on this special night he was absent from the *Any Questions*, that holy place from which Leroy's life seemed to derive its very sustenance. Yoofi scanned the yard for Leroy, but he was not there. He also wanted to make amends to his stepfather. Ama, Congo, Miss Hene, and Puncus watched from a distance. The group beckoned to Yoofi that they were ready to leave. As soon as he joined them, they left the *Any Questions*.

It was early the following morning when the music died and the last of the faithful crept home.

Leroy's Hook

D rained from the bailo but still excited by its prospects, the denizens of Providence, singly or in small clusters, kept walking away from the *Any Questions* until all that remained were the Detective and the men of the cloth. Neither Monsignor Silva nor the Reverend Watkins left each other's company throughout the event. They stood huddled in a corner of the yard, observing and talking. Slowly Graham drifted toward them.

"What an astonishing performance!" Reverend Bernard Watkins exclaimed.

"Yes, indeed it was," replied the Detective. "In one night I have found all that has been hidden from me for years!"

"And what is that?" Monsignor Silva asked.

"I have found out who and where they all are. Astonishing indeed!" Graham said, happy that he had found the spiritual home of the secret Kumina Family and its central residence, Congo M. King.

"Strange, strange indeed," replied Watkins. "I was referring to the Dance, Detective."

"That, too, was good," Graham replied, laughing.

"That may well be so, Graham. But do you intend to prosecute? That's the issue!" Watkins replied.

"Not quite, Reverend. We need firm evidence. We need irrefutable proof. We need a body. That's what we need, gentlemen."

"Well, you have your case, Detective. There is certainly no spirituality here – just an open, irreverent cult. Did you see that Dancing? It's more like devil worship, if you ask me," Reverend Bernard Watkins said.

"That's an opinion, and not a crime, Reverend."

"But they call themselves a religion," Watkins added.

"And that is not a crime, either," Graham said.

"So what on earth is so spectacular about tonight, Graham?" Watkins asked.

"Listen, gentlemen. I am still on Zadie Blue's case. As you both know, when I resolve it, I will be promoted. Now, tsk, tsk, tsk. Someone here knows something."

"Maybe Puncus knows," said Watkins. "Do you remember he ran away from Galina?"

"Running by itself does not prove anything," Graham said.

"So what are you left with, Graham?" the Monsignor asked.

"I have Leroy. Do you notice that he is not here?"

"Yes, indeed. And why is that, Detective?"

"Well, Monsignor," Graham said, "That's because Leroy is the hook. He is my confidant. That's why. Leroy has agreed to tell me whatever I need to know about the Kumina Family, and especially about Master Congo King."

"Yes? That is quite surprising. I would imagine that on Ama's big night Leroy would be here. Why the sudden switch for Leroy, Detective?" Watkins asked.

"You see, Reverend, Leroy is not so much a part of this Family as you might expect."

"What do you mean, Graham?" The Monsignor asked.

"You see, about a month ago, I met Leroy in Galina. He was there looking for Patsy Blue. Leroy disclosed to me that he got all he ever wanted from the Kumina Family, and he is on his way out."

"I see," Silva said, petting his chin. "And what was that . . . what was it that Leroy wanted, Graham?"

"Oh! This goes back a long way, Gentlemen. But . . . Congo wanted Leroy to marry Ama after Headmaster Henry Love got her pregnant and ran away from Providence to Panama."

"My God!" said, Watkins. "Was that why Love left so suddenly?"

"Yes . . . that was it! Despite whatever else you may have heard."

"So what were you saying now about Leroy and Congo?" Silva asked.

"Yes, yes." Graham said. " According to Leroy, Congo agreed to have Ama sign over her land to him, Leroy, if he would marry Ama. Leroy did marry Ama. So now . . . Ama's land legally belongs to Leroy. Moreover, Leroy, with Congo's help, built his house on what was Ama's land. So, in effect, Ama has nothing; not the land, not the house. Nothing!" the Detective ended laughing.

"What a travesty!" Monsignor Silva replied.

"So is life, Gentlemen," the Detective said. "And now that Leroy has what he wanted, he plans to dump Ama, sell the property, and go back to his former lover, Patsy Blue, in Galina. And let me add . . . that too is not a crime, Reverend," the Detective laughed.

"Is that so?" Silva asked.

"Yes, quite so. And Leroy wanted me to help him find Patsy Blue, his former woman."

"I see. So did you, Graham?"

"Yes! I did, Reverend. I helped reconnect him with Patsy Blue, and he will let me know what's really going on here. Not only that. Rex hates Congo and booted him out of Jacks River. That's why Congo is back here, pretending to be a Kumina Master."

"So Leroy is not a suspect, anymore?" Watkins asked.

"Certainly not. He is on our side now."

"I see where you are leading, Graham," the Monsignor said.

"Rex promised he will let me know what's going on in Jacks River. Then he can permanently get rid of Congo, whom he suspects of stealing from the Covey business."

"Amazing!"

"I have Congo and the rest of the Family all penned up. On the surface, nothing will change. But one more mistake on their part, and I will have the evidence I need. Rex, Ulu, and Leroy will provide that!"

"Good job, Detective," Watkins said.

"Thank you, Reverend," Graham said, "and with this thing wrapped up, I will get my promotion! After these ten long years, I finally see the unraveling of Lev's puzzle!" the Detective ended with a glow of delight.

"I would prefer," Monsignor Silva said, in slow, deliberate tones, "to proceed with a more cautious, open mind and not be too hasty in judging or condemning this whole Kumina thing."

"A more open mind for what purpose?" Graham asked.

"To learn Kumina beliefs and practices. They may have something to offer us."

"Offer who?" Reverend Watkins asked.

"All of us, you may never know," the Monsignor said.

"What they have offered is a series of missing bodies wherever they go. What they have to offer now is evidence, proof, something I can take to court."

"Yes," said Watkins. "You have enough to work on there, Detective. Just keep us informed, and we will let you know what we hear."

"Yes. We will work together and kill this evil thing right here in the ant hill!" Graham said.

"Agreed!" said Watkins and, with that, they too left the *Any Questions*.

"See you at Mass on Sunday, Graham," the Monsignor called.

"Yes, and after that, at Rex's house for brunch!" Graham said, as he rode off in the darkness.

Aunts and Uncles

Miss Hene couldn't have imagined nor was she prepared for the misery Ulu, unannounced, brought to Barton house. She arrived late that Saturday night – in the same week as Ash Wednesday – wet and shivering. Miss Hene couldn't tell whether her sister-in-law had been crying or if her eyes were red solely from worry. Nevertheless, she opened her house to her, gave Ulu her favorite room, towels to dry herself, clean warm clothes to wear, and her favorite drink, red wine. The wine was served to her in her room with dinner.

Ulu ate, but she was remembering a line from the letter Miss Hene had written to her years ago. Even when she went to bed the lines *"And with all my heart, I wish to God you could find love tonight, Ulu, if only for the night"* remained with Ulu, centering her mind on love, comforting her as she fell asleep.

Late the following morning, Ulu and Miss Hene met at breakfast. Normally, Puncus St. John and the Kendals would have been her guests. That morning, however, the Kendals would be absent. Maybe it was the rain that kept them away.

Miss Hene was glad to see Ulu. She wanted to talk to her about Congo, to gather from her what had torn them apart. Congo was not a recluse, but he was not in the habit of explaining his life and deep hurts to anyone, not even his sister. Miss Hene, respecting that, hadn't probed; and Congo hadn't yet divulged. So, things remained that way, suspended, creating a block in their relationship. Miss Hene hated that but preferred fate for time to thaw what had lain frozen between them.

"Miss Hene," Ulu said, looking up from her coffee, "I do not know where to start. But I have problems."

"Yes, I imagine so. You know, Congo has been living in the cottage again."

"Yes, I guessed so."

"You mean you do not know for sure?"

"No, Miss Hene. I do not know for sure. I have been mean to him."

"You must have been. When Congo is not talking, and only paints and paints, you know something is wrong."

"So has he been painting again?"

"Yes, that's all he does here. But he is not ready to show or talk about it yet."

"Oh, I wish that was my problem," Ulu smiled.

"Well, it's yours, too, if Congo is not talking." Miss Hene said.

Ulu nodded her head. "I brought Rex into the business and told Congo to leave."

"You did what?"

"Yes, I did. And things worked for a while. But Rex . . . Rex still has the same mind he had as a child. He has not grown a bit. He is such a disappointment, Miss Hene. To cut a long story short, he stole every penny he could get his hands on and fled to New York, leaving behind many hotel and gambling debts."

"What else happened, Ulu?"

"Well, it's more than that. I threw Congo out with only the clothes he had on. I threw him out because I thought he was a spendthrift . . . dressing like a peacock and spending all his time with Laura. Now I regret doing that."

"I am sure he'll understand."

"And the business he built for all the time we were married, Rex destroyed it in less than a year. I cannot understand it, Miss Hene." Ulu spoke with a steady stream of tears dripping onto her blouse. "Everything is in shambles, Miss Hene. Everything!"

"So what would you like to see happen, Ulu?"

"I want Congo back."

"Why, Ulu?"

"To start over," she cried.

"I am sure he would love to hear that, Ulu. You should tell him."

"No! You tell him."

"I do not need him, Ulu."

"But I cannot face him, Miss Hene."

At that moment, Puncus St. John walked in. He had prepared lunch for Miss Hene. It was her favorite, cowpea soup with pumpkin. He laid it on the table, nodded to the women, and proceeded to serve them. Ulu didn't wait for Miss Hene. She started to eat, looking at Puncus and nodding thanks to him.

"What brought you here, in the rain, Ulu?" Puncus asked as soon as he was seated.

"Too much to discuss, Puncus. It's between Congo and me. Have you seen him?"

"Yes, I prepared the wedding feast for him last weekend at the pond."

"And you didn't tell me he got married, Miss Hene?"

"Not him, Ulu. Laura!"

"That wicked woman! She took him away from me," and Ulu started crying again.

"No, Ulu." Puncus said. "Laura got married to Ho."

"Ho? Ho whom she detests?"

"Yes, you should have seen how much in love they were at the reception. They were happy, dancing, playing. I didn't know that Ho could be so much fun."

Ulu started hitting the spoon against her bowl. "Where is Congo now?"

"He should be here; this is Sunday morning. He likes to start the week out from here. But you would never know he's here."

"Please tell him to come and see me, Puncus, when you see him again. Will you?"

"Sure, Ulu. That's an easy enough message to deliver."

"Why are you still so perturbed, Ulu?" Miss Hene asked. She had watched the joy which momentarily filled her face quickly fade into a mask of sorrow.

Before she could reply, the Kendals arrived. They, too, brought food. Theirs was laid out on the table beside the soup.

Ama walked with less pain; yet she still crouched. With Leroy's help she went to kiss her sister. They took their seats, serving themselves and eating.

"Where is Yoofi, Aunt Ulu?" Kwame asked.

Ulu struggled for a reply.

"Yes, where is my boy?" Ama asked. "Has he been good to you, Ulu?"

Still Ulu couldn't reply.

"Is something the matter with Yoofi, Ulu?" Miss Hene asked.

"Do you know . . ." Ulu started.

"Know what?" Ama asked, her head springing from its bowed position.

"Charm?"

"Charm who?"

"Charm Boydell. She was the flower girl at your wedding."

"Yes, you do not have to explain that."

"Well."

"Well what, Ulu?"

"I hired her to care for Princess."

"Yes, Congo told us."

"So what?" Puncus laughed. "Yoofi gave her a baby?"

"Great Mother!" Ama grunted.

"What!" exclaimed Miss Hene.

"Puncus is right," said Ulu.

"How could you, Ulu?" Miss Hene protested.

"How could I what, Miss Hene? I didn't do it!"

"For that, you would have to be a goddess, Ulu!" Puncus laughed.

"Shut up, Puncus." Miss Hene said and, looking at Ulu, she asked, "Who else knows?"

"All of us here, as well as Charm and Yoofi," Ulu answered, looking at the children.

The children looked at each other confusedly. What did it mean? Was Yoofi going to be a father? Where was he going to live with his wife? They were concerned.

"Have you spoken to Yoofi, Ulu?"

"No, I thought I would talk with you first, Miss Hene."

"You know, they could stay here, till we figure out what to do."

"It's better if they stay with you, Ulu," Puncus said.

"I can't take the embarrassment."

"They need work, and you have it," Puncus said.

"I cannot have Princess know of it."

"So they can stay here," Miss Hene repeated.

"And do what?" Leroy asked.

"Well, Yoofi could work and dance at the *Any Questions*."

"Yes, and Charm could help out here."

"And what would happen to Princess?" Ulu asked.

"Oh!" exclaimed Ama.

"Maybe it's better if Charm stays with Princess till the baby is due, or until she can't work anymore," Miss Hene said.

"Yes, I suppose she should," agreed Puncus.

"That's only one part of it," Ulu said.

"What is the other?"

"Charm is his aunt," Ama said.

"What! Bigboy jooked his aunt? That little devil! I always thought he would do something like that!" Leroy said.

"Beat the brute, Daddy," said Agu, bouncing to life in his chair. "Whip the little devil and teach him a lesson, Daddy."

"Be kind! Both of you," Miss Hene scolded. She looked at Agu with a punishing grimace. Agu looked at Leroy, then at his mother, before bowing his head.

"Don't bring that up again, Leroy." Puncus said.

"But that is the problem now, Puncus. What to do with that Bigboy!" Leroy said.

"His name is Yoofi! And all we have to do is love him. That is not a problem," Ama said.

"We have to save face," Ulu said.

"And let her carry the baby, or get rid of it?" Leroy asked.

"Get rid of my grandchild? Never!" Ama protested.

"I was only trying to understand Ulu," Leroy said, trying to correct himself.

"Well, you better not talk like that anymore!" Ama said.

"Okay," Leroy said.

"I was about to ask," Ulu said, "who are the relations now?"

"Yes, the child cannot come into this world confused." Miss Hene said.

"Well, what will the baby call me?" Ulu asked.

"Aunt! Aren't you his grandaunt, Ulu?" Miss Hene said.

"Yes. And by that, I suppose the child will call Ama Aunt, too," Ulu asked.

"My grandchild, calling me Aunt?"

"Or," Leroy said. "Ama could become Nana. Nana Ama, it even sounds good. You could get the title of Grandmother of Providence, Ama."

"Maybe. Maybe that could work," said Puncus.

"That would mean I must call Ama grandmother, too!" remarked Ulu.

"You and the rest of us, Ulu," Leroy said.

"Maybe, Ama, you are not ripe enough to be our Nana as yet," Miss Hene said.

"Or active enough," Ama said. "It's hard to be Nana," she continued.

"But Aunt might be better," Miss Hene said.

"Yes. It even has a ring to it," claimed Puncus. "You could be my Aunt Ama anytime, Ama."

"But," remarked Puncus, "if Ama is going to be Aunt, then who will be our Uncle? We must have a balance?"

Silence once again fell on the group. Eyes quickly bounced from Leroy to Puncus, who had turned glum after plunging the table into solitude.

"Who will be Uncle?" Miss Hene finally asked. "Puncus Divine? You with nothing to do and with a mouthful to say to every question asked? Did you ask who would be our Uncle?"

"Yes, Miss Hene." Puncus replied, only just realizing the trap into which he had fallen. "That question needs an answer, now."

"Well, Uncle Puncus St. John Divine? How is that for your answer?"

The table bounded with laughter; and Puncus, not knowing what to say, simply raised his hands above his head and said, "Here am I."

Ending the laughter Miss Hene said, "So, it's agreed then. And you will be our Aunt Ama, from here on."

"Yes, I like that," said Ama.

Ama, remembering Henry Love, muttered, "And don't forget, this baby will have a father. A real father this time!"

"Remember, Ama. You will be our Aunt, Ama. Aunt for Yoofi, Aunt for Charm and the baby: Aunt for all of us," Miss Hene said.

"And what will I call you, now, Mammy?" Dean, her second, asked. Ama looked at Miss Hene.

"She is your Aunt Ama, and for you, too, Kwame, and Agu."

"So you will be the great Aunt for everyone. Eh, Ama?" Puncus asked.

"Well, thank you, Puncus," Ama replied.

"What an honor! You must feel proud of yourself," Puncus smiled.

"Mammy is now my Aunt," said Agu, breaking the lull. "All because of Yoofi. Don't let him get away with it, Daddy. You should whip Bigboy!" Agu protested.

"Leave it to me, Agu," Leroy whispered, comforting his son.

Silence brewed at the table. Yoofi and his exploits had suddenly changed the family relationships. The family accommodated him as much as it could.

While they talked, Congo had come into the house. Standing on the porch, he saw the group and overheard their conversation. At its conclusion, one he agreed to, he left the porch and went to his cottage. He soon returned, letting himself in and bringing a larger version of the painting he had done of Ulu taking her morning bath at Providence Pond. He set the picture in front of Ulu, then turned and left the house.

Ulu bounded from her chair, bypassing the painting, and followed Congo across the lawn to his cottage.

"Take wine and food for them, Puncus," Miss Hene said.

It didn't take long for forgiveness and reconciliation to govern their conversation. Ulu didn't speak of Laura. Neither did he speak of business. Led by love, only love, they spoke of themselves, their past and future.

The following Monday morning, Ulu and Congo returned to Jacks River, to the anxious arms of Princess.

Parents at Breakfast

Even though Ulu would have preferred him to rigorously resume his business dealings at once, Congo went in search of Yoofi and Charm. He brought them into the house and sat them down at the kitchen table.

With Ulu soon joining them, they listened as Yoofi tried to say how sorry he was for disappointing them, for bringing embarrassment on their household. Charm was also sorrowful for what had happened.

"Yoofi, my son, and you, too, my daughter," Congo started, "I am at fault. I brought you both into our home but didn't take the time to talk to you about that aspect of your life which now seems like a misery for all of us." Congo paused for a while, shaking his head as if searching for what to say. Finally, he continued, "And I was not the parent you deserved, either. I failed you, and I am sorry."

Yoofi looked at Charm and fumbled for her hand under the table. Charm cast a timid smile across the table, but did not look at Yoofi.

"It is not important to me that as aunt and nephew you decide to have children. That is none of my concern. What bothers me is that I didn't talk to you about your lives, your family history. It is a disgrace to me that I didn't let you know about yourselves and allow you to make whatever decisions you like."

"It's all right, Uncle Congo," Yoofi said. "You have been good enough to us, already."

"Thank you, Yoofi," Congo said, "Just bear with me here for a while; there is something I am getting to," Congo continued.

"Ok, Uncle Congo," Charm said.

"It is not my intention to apologize for you." Congo continued. "If indeed, you think you have done wrong, you can sort that out for yourselves. Should you so continue as man and wife, as you have by your own deeds made yourselves? I do not know. I too have been in a relationship at which some would scoff. I do understand there is a kind of glue beyond our comprehension that binds people together, sometimes even in relationships we abhor. It may or may not be of our own doing. One may say we are bound to each other, at least for a time, so we may be teachers and students at once."

Congo paused momentarily as he noticed Ulu sobbing. Her hands lay lifeless on the table. Congo wrapped his hands about hers and kissed her cheek. Ulu squeezed his hands and managed a pensive smile.

"Some may say it is that glue which our will should overcome if we are to set ourselves free and live an ethical life, even a moral life. I say, maybe not! Perhaps it is that very experience we must have if we are to be complete and find our authentic selves. Even if by means outside of the norm."

As Congo spoke, holding his head bent, he glanced up to see a solemn look overshadowing the table. He seemed rather surprised, for he intended to cause just the opposite effect. "Are you getting my meaning?" he asked, looking at Charm with a crisp smile.

"Yes, Uncle Congo," she blushed, looking askance at Ulu.

"Well, to get back to what I was saying," Congo continued, "I do not believe in anarchy, and convention is not without its flaws, either. My own life has been a lesson for me, too. It allows me to understand why, if you choose to continue your lives as you started. It would be with my full support. So long as it is not forced upon you."

"I thank you, Uncle Congo," Yoofi said. Charm edged closer to him.

Congo, nodding his acknowledgment to Yoofi and Charm, continued: "Now that it has happened, I cannot send you away from here like sinners out into the world. That wouldn't be wise or fair of me. In fact, if I forsake you now and leave you to fend for yourselves, I would be committing a crime worse than the first, of withholding the information you needed."

"Quite so," Ulu whispered, smoothing the wrinkles in the table-cloth.

Congo smiled at Ulu and continued, "So what can I do? First I must tell you, Charm, that I do love you. And you, Yoofi, nonetheless. You are my family and I will hold you to me and bind us together, no matter what may come between us. Yoofi, I am still your Uncle, if you still want to think of me as such. And Charm, now, now that you have put yourself with Yoofi as his wife, you are my niece.

"So, what shall we tell the world? Shall we tell them it's none of their business? Should we look straight ahead when they snicker at us? Shall we bury our heads in shame as outcasts? I do not know. Am I proud of what has happened here? No. Am I happy for it? No. Does it make us any less a family, or you and Yoofi any less as people? No. And yet we have done something unusual. In some circles it might be called sinful. In others it may be cause for laughter and ridicule. Will they be wrong when they look away from us with scorn and contempt? Maybe not."

"I am not afraid of them. Right, Charm?"

Charm nodded and brought their hands on top of the table. "We are in love, Uncle Congo. That's all I care about now, that and the baby," Charm said.

"Yes," said Ulu, "that's all that really matters now."

Yoofi looked at her, warmth flooding his stomach. He struggled to hold back tears.

"But," continued Congo, "now, I cannot care about all that. We will respond to every situation as it arises. The one thing I must say, we will respond as a Family. Your failure in this is mine, but your victory in it is ours.

"So I say, do not be dismayed nor be proud. Life has given you a hand, and it's how you play it out, not what the hand is, that will be your measure. I do not condone what I have done, and I here, now, repent from so doing. You will have to decide how you handle your side. In whatever you do, guilt and shame or forgiveness and joy, I do with you. But I know my choice. I will live with joy, and let this be a lesson to me on how to carry a strange load.

"It wasn't my plan to preach to you. In fact I didn't plan this at all. I intended rather to sit with you and ask what you intend to do. But as I formulated the question, it occurred to me that there was an element of judgment and punishment in it. I would rather not put that on anyone, let alone you. Your state, I suppose, must be frightening to you. I am glad you didn't run away, Yoofi. Men in your situation tend to do that.

Charm, I am glad to see you still find a way to talk with Yoofi. This must be very hard on you.

"Nevertheless, you must take action. Until such time, Yoofi, I would like you to bring your belongings into this house and take your Uncle Rex's old room. Charm, I suppose you may want to stay where you are. Princess is not the only one who needs you now," he smiled.

"Thank you, Uncle Congo," Yoofi said, unable to restrain his tears. "Thank you, too, Aunt Ulu."

Ulu smiled, not knowing quite what to say. She reached across the table and touched Charm's hand. Yoofi and Congo joined in and, for a moment, there was silence.

Still in a pensive mood, Congo placed his hands in his pants pocket and stretched himself as he remained on the chair. "Ulu," he said, looking at her, "would you like to say something?" She didn't respond immediately. Congo looked at her, slightly turning his head for their eyes to meet, then repeated his question.

"Yoofi, Charm: your uncle has put this in an entirely different light for me. I am not sure where to start. Charm, please, for Princess's sake, be discreet." Charm didn't respond. She could only nod at what Ulu had said.

There was silence for a while. Then Ulu started, "The Family discussed the whole affair yesterday. Yoofi, Puncus says you can come and work at *Any Questions*. I am not sending you away. It is your choice, as your uncle has said. Charm, you may stay here for as long as you like. But you must know, Miss Hene will deliver the baby for you. And you can let Aunt Ama raise the baby for you. That would free your hands for whatever you decide to do."

"Thank you, Ulu," Congo said. "Now you know as much as we do. Let us know your decisions when you make them."

The young couple sat for a while. They reflected in the silence on what they had heard. As if awakening from a long slumber, Charm and then Yoofi slowly twisted and turned in their seats and meekly stood up. Yoofi didn't know what to do. He stepped closer to Charm and, with his hands about her waist, kissed her cheek. She looked at him and smiled.

"Thank you for making me keep the baby," Charm said, looking at her uncle.

"And for your advice, Aunt Ulu," Yoofi said.

"Thank you very much for listening," Congo said. "And Yoofi, please tell the maids they may start serving."

"Certainly, Uncle Congo."

"And Charm, please tell Princess her parents would like her company at breakfast."

"Yes, Uncle Congo."

Into the Light

Congo spent the rest of that Monday visiting his old friends and business acquaintances. To each of them he apologized for his absence, explained that Rex had returned to New York, and assured them that he and Ulu were in the process of reconciling. He requested their bills, then promptly paid them with money from back rents he had recently collected. With that, they gladly offered to help in transporting their pimento in storage to the drying barbeques in Port Maria. A few of them also assisted Yoofi in drying the pimento.

Now Yoofi had to shuttle between Jacks River and Port Maria to get the drying and bagging done. Luckily for him, the rains ceased; and with the brilliant sun and steady sea breeze, the grains dried rapidly.

In addition to working with the farmers, Congo also visited Laura's store in Oracabessa, saw that the bills were paid, and that the operation was in good stead.

It was late that Monday night when he returned to Jacks River. On his arrival, Ulu roused herself from bed and served him dinner. In fact, she hadn't yet eaten. Ulu had spent the day in nervous anticipation, searching for a way to complete her reconciliation with Congo.

The night they spent at Providence, Ulu had passed in tears. She didn't know why she was crying, but Ulu cried unceasingly, and nothing Congo did consoled her. She cried and cried, as if emptying pools of bitterness.

At the cottage in Barton House, there was not a bed. Congo had given his old divan to a servant and chose instead to sleep on a pile of crocus bags thrown loosely on the floor.

When Ulu had followed him to the cottage, it was the first time she had entered it. However, the door couldn't have been fully opened before Ulu rushed in and threw herself on the floor – on the old crocus bags Congo placed there – kicked off her shoes and cried.

Congo put her head in his lap, stroked her hair, kissed her cheek, massaged her body, and still she cried. Not knowing what to do, Congo listened to her until they fell asleep.

They had scarcely talked on the trip from Providence to Jacks River. The couple simply traveled together with Congo inquiring now and again whether or not she was all right. Ulu would say yes, and so they traveled home.

There was a difference in the house when Congo returned that Monday night. Ulu was dressed in an evening gown. She made herself especially attractive for him. Initially, Congo was surprised. He had never seen Ulu like that before. She was always tidy, dressed well, but for business or church. Her relaxed, almost sensuous manner startled him. Moreover, there were flowers all over the house. He complimented Ulu on her new look and thanked her for the flowers. She was quick to tell him that Princess, with Charm's help, had picked the flowers from the garden and adorned the house for him.

But Ulu had done more. She pulled him into a small room that was adjacent to their bedroom and sat him down before a small circular wooden table. The table was placed close to a window, with two chairs in close proximity to each other. A large bouquet sat on the table.

"Do you like it, Congo?"

"Yes, it is a lovely arrangement."

"I would like us to have our meal here. What do you think?"

"That would be wonderful!"

"Have you had dinner, Congo?"

"No. I had a late lunch, though."

"Good. Then, maybe, we can have dinner together."

"I would be delighted, Ulu."

Congo was still in surprise at the change in Ulu. He did not quite know what to make of it. He looked at her. "How was your day, Ulu?"

She didn't reply. Suddenly her happy face became tearful. Congo shuffled closer to her and took her hands.

"No, no!" she sobbed. "There is something I must say, but I do not know where to start. I don't even know what it is I want to say, just that something is on my mind and I have to get it off."

"I can listen."

"Congo, when you spoke at breakfast this morning, I didn't realize until just then who you were. When you invoked Laura's name, and disclosed your feelings about your relationship with her, I felt like a child. You made me feel humble and, at the same time made me start examining my life. I am proud of you, Congo; but, at the same time, I feel a bit childish. Can I be as bad a woman as I feel I am? I know you cannot answer me, Congo. I just do not know what to think or feel. This is painful for me.

"I didn't go into the bakery or the store today. I spent a little time with Princess and then, because I didn't want her to see me crying so much, I asked Charm to take her into the garden.

"I spent all day in the house, crying, thinking, and asking myself just who I am. I went back, all the way back to my childhood, and saw how I was brought up, like a queen. Bem made me feel special and better than everyone else, except maybe Rex."

"Maybe Bem should take some responsibility in that, if he were here, Ulu," Congo suggested.

"That's a kind thing to say, Congo, but it was not Bem's fault for treating me special. Maybe he loved me, and that was his way of showing it."

"Maybe you are right, Ulu."

"The fault is all mine, for letting it go to my head. Pride and conceit ruled my early life. And I doubt they are all gone now. Are they gone, Congo? I do not know how to live with them ruling me, and I want to change."

"You will know when those things are gone from your life, Ulu. You will know because you will be able to look back at yourself and laugh at who you were."

There was a pause in the conversation, and Ulu seemed to be reflecting more and hurting less. "You know, Congo," she said after the pause, "I really believed I was better, better than anyone else, until Rex – I am sorry, until I – brought this shameful thing on me. Now I know I am just like anyone else. This is sad. I want to be like you, Congo. Just imagine the people I have hurt, just imagine."

"The best thing you can do for the folks you have hurt, Ulu, is to be more like them. Just go anywhere in the village: talk with them, eat with . . ."

"I must admit this to you, Congo; I didn't marry you out of love."

Ulu interrupted, hastening to dump her misery.

"I see," Congo said with a quick, grim smile.

"Maybe you can say I was selfish."

"I didn't say that. But tell me, Ulu. Why did you marry me?"

"I saw what you did for Lev, Congo. I knew if I made you think I was in love with you, you would marry me and make me rich. Imagine! I did marry you, and you did make me rich. And what sickness was it that came over me? Just as I saw how rich I was, and that I didn't need you anymore, I thought of getting rid of you. What kind of sickness ruled me? Was it greed or selfishness? Imagine, I told you to leave, leave your daughter and all you worked for. And you did! Why didn't you resist? Why didn't you fight back, Congo?"

Congo was about to respond; but Ulu burst out crying, and he sought to comfort her. "No! Do not answer, Congo, and do not touch me. I do not deserve anything good. I just want to die!" Ulu sobbed.

Congo wanted to touch her and let her know he had forgiven her.

"I do not deserve comfort, Congo. I feel I should die and hide from the world. I just want you to know I am sorry for how I treated you. All I wanted was to be rich and get a husband, and a doctor for Princess to marry. That's all I wanted."

Congo looked at her in pity, but Ulu wouldn't be touched.

"I am trying, Congo. I will be a wife to you and a mother to Princess. But I need help."

"Love, Ulu, is all we need."

"But, I fear, Congo, I do not know how. How do I love somebody? How do I love you and Princess?"

"Should I answer, Ulu?"

"Yes, Congo. Why do you think I asked you?"

"Sometimes I find it helpful, Ulu, to laugh at myself when the situation requires it. So I say kind things to me, often. I refrain from self-condemnation and, instead, am quick to forgive myself. Now I can praise every little success I have, teach myself to give and take, and reward myself when I do something right."

"That sounds like conceit and self love, Congo!"

"Yes, it sounds that way; but that's where I started. After a time, I found that I was treating Miss Hene better; and then Asa, whom I hated; and then, then finally, it became a way of life. So I do not think about it anymore; I just attend to me."

"You make it sound so easy! Look what I have been through. How can I treat myself good after all this?"

"Yes, Ulu. When I look at what you have been through, I see a lesson of a lifetime. I wish it had happened to me!"

"You are crazy, Congo, asking for trouble!" Ulu said wiping her face and smiling.

"Just keep smiling, Ulu, and leave Princess, if she so cares, to ponder about a husband on her own."

Ulu pushed Congo on his shoulder. "Were you always like this?" she asked.

"No, only when I am hungry," Congo said laughing.

"Then dinner is served, sir." Ulu said.

"Thank you, Ulu."

She moved from the table to fetch the food. Congo followed her and embraced her from behind. At first Ulu twitched, then accepting his embrace, turned to face him. Their lips met and, kissing their way to the bedroom, they tumbled down on the bed.

Princess awakened them late the following morning.

Family Business

That Sunday morning, Congo explained to Ulu that he had business to do in Providence the following weekend. A part of it, he told her, included Princess, since it was time for their daughter to know her relatives in Providence. The other reason for his visit was to finalize the plans for the Family Walk.

Ulu and Reverend Watkins, following their old custom, had already made plans for Palm Sunday. Ulu and Princess were both central to those activities. Yet Ulu quickly agreed with Congo that, indeed, Princess should visit Providence. She enquired about Asa and apologized to Congo saying she could not accompany him but that she would be with him at the Walk.

For all her new devotion to her husband, Ulu's mind was elsewhere that morning. Having packed Princess for what seemed to be a lifetime away from her, Ulu then bade goodbye and set out to start her day.

By the time Congo reached Providence the rest of the Family – all except Leroy – were already at Miss Hene's waiting for him. Yet it was Princess to whom their attention first turned. The boys gawked at her nice city clothes while the adults admired her urbane manners.

"Do you know the pond?" Kwame finally asked Princess.

"I fear I do not," she replied.

"Would you like to see it?" Dean asked.

"Yes, of course! But will I get wet?"

"Wet? Yes. That's why we go there," replied Kwame.

"Let's take her there, Dean," Kwame said and started out of the house."

"Wait for me!" Princess said, rapidly undressing herself and running naked after the boys. Soon she passed them, screaming, running along the path just as they did.

"She is Afia's daughter!" Ama said.

"Yes, I know what you mean," Puncus added.

"Speaking of Afia – Nweka, I mean," Congo said, "she sends greetings to you all. I was in Portland, hoping to talk with Asa and tell him of our progress here, but he was not there."

"How is Nweka?" Ama asked.

"She is as good as can be. Kisi said that Asa went Stepping."

"Did she know where to?"

"Panama, she guessed."

"What would he be doing there?" Puncus asked.

"Heaven alone knows," Congo said. But after a moment's reflection he added; "You know, Asa's visit might have something to do with Headmaster Henry Isaac Love after all – it just might. But I did leave word about our Walk. Nweka assured me she would let Asa know about it as soon as he returned."

"That is good news, Congo," Puncus said.

"We still need at least one who will Walk for us," Miss Hene added.

"Did you mean, Congo, you planned the Walk without even having our first body?" Puncus asked.

"How do these things happen?" Ama asked, throwing her open hands in the air.

"Sometimes, Aunt Ama, the chicken comes before the egg. Other times the egg comes first," Congo said.

"Yes, that's true," Miss Hene said. "When things go around and around," she continued, mapping out a circle with her hand, "it doesn't matter how they start. We just have to keep them going."

"Getting our first body is exactly what I went to see Asa about. That and the fact that I told everyone who I was. We never operated out in the open before."

"Then they better get accustomed to it," Puncus said. "We just need to make sure we do what is right."

"And follow our faith," Miss Hene added.

"Yes, of course," Congo said. "But we still need a Walker."

"Does anyone know where Leroy is?" Puncus asked.

"He and Patsy went to Galina," Ama said.

"He just keeps running around like that," Puncus remarked.

"Strange how they stick together," Miss Hene observed. After a pause, she asked, "Do you think Leroy could do a good Walk?"

The silence returned. "I have often asked the same thing," Puncus said.

"There is only one way to find out."

"How, Congo?"

"If," Congo hesitated with a solemn look on his face. "If Leroy should become a saint, Ama."

"That's a good suggestion, Congo," Puncus said.

"And who would assist him?"

There was another pause.

"Yoofi?"

"What are you all talking about, Puncus?" Ama asked.

"Sainthood, Aunt Ama," Puncus replied.

"The Detective has both eyes open now."

"Yes, Congo. But I wish he could really see," Puncus said.

"Will anyone protect Yoofi?" Ama asked.

"We will, of course," Miss Hene responded.

Just then Shep walked into the house and lay by Ama's feet. She put her hand down and patted his head. The dog licked her fingers.

"Which house will we use?" Miss Hene asked.

"Nweka's!" Congo replied.

"Yes, of course. No one uses it," Puncus added.

"Which one?" Ama asked. "The main one or the hell house?"

"Both," Congo said. "We need both for our guests."

"Excellent idea! It has such a nice view overlooking the pond. But Nweka's house must need a good bit of fixing up."

"I will get that done, Miss Hene," Congo said.

"Remember to leave the outside just as it is."

"Okay, Puncus."

"Will there be a lot of people?" Ama asked.

"If the food is free, all of Providence," Puncus said.

"And if it is good?" Miss Hene asked.

"Then they will come from as far as Portland," Congo replied.

"So we will plan big then," Puncus said.

"Yes," said Congo, "and you better let Aunt Ama and Miss Hene do the cooking this time, Puncus."

"If Miss Hene is cooking, I will be glad to help," Ama said, sensing her own fear of fire, a fear derived from that horrific image of her burning child in the flaming kitchen. The memory had not since left her.

"Good, then," said Congo. "Fellowship will join us."

With that the meeting adjourned. Ama did not quite know what was to follow. At first she felt uncomfortable, knowing that Leroy would be promoted to sainthood. What had he done to deserve that rare tribute? Ama was unsure. New to Kumina beliefs and practices, she remained puzzled. If being a saint would transform Leroy's heart to that of a loving father, Ama's thoughts ran, then he might finally love Yoofi. In that case, Ama mused, how grand to see Yoofi assisting Leroy in his very first Walk!

"You didn't tell us about Ulu," Ama said, breaking the silence. "How is our Sister?"

"Oh, she couldn't be better, and life between us is wonderful!"

"Is that so, Congo?" Miss Hene asked.

"Yes, of course. How else would I be able to bring Princess here?"

"That's such a nice thing to hear, Congo," Puncus said. "And if Miss Hene does not mind my saying so," he paused and looked at her confirming nod, "your sister and I are getting married."

"When, Miss Hene?" Ama asked, startled at the news of the impending marriage.

"On the night of the Walk!"

"And you didn't tell your Aunt, Miss Hene?"

"I am sorry, Aunt Ama. But now is just as good a time as any," Miss Hene said, smiling.

"So it will be a double Walk, then!" Congo exclaimed

"We will wrap everything into one," Miss Hene said.

"So it's all worked out then," Congo said.

"Yes, it is!"

"I know you have to take Princess back," Miss Hene said, "so let me go get her, Congo."

"Thank you, Miss Hene."

"You are welcome, Congo." As Miss Hene turned to leave, she looked back and said, "Walk with me, Puncus."

They neatly folded Princess's clothes and sauntered down to the pond.

Puncus asked, "Do you think, Miss Hene, that we should have enlightened Ama further concerning Leroy's progress?"

"No, not at all, Puncus! You know quite well that new converts tend to take these things to heart."

"Yes, yes," Puncus agreed. "Why risk vexing Ama's spirit, now that she is coming along so nicely?"

"You know, Puncus," Miss Hene said, smiling askance at him, "sometimes you ask the most extraordinary questions!"

"I have been loved for less than that," Puncus said, reaching for her hand as they ambled down to Providence Pond where Miss Hene prepared Princess for her homeward journey.

Everything went well until Leroy came home that evening and Ama jubilantly told him he was going to be honored as the first Saint of Providence Pond.

Leroy grimaced. He knew exactly what that meant.

Learning that the Walk was some weeks off, Leroy sent an urgent message to Detective Graham, letting him know of the plans at Providence Pond.

The news pleased the Detective, for it brought him closer to the evidence he sought.

Playing Shadows

Having found solace, though not complete peace, in her renewed affection with Congo, Ulu's mind drifted to Laura. Why Laura was on her mind she couldn't say, at least not at first.

In the privacy of the room Ulu had prepared, she and Congo had made their simple, late breakfast of fruit, hot rolls, and honey. They discussed their plans for the day. It was something they had never done before. In the past Ulu had given instructions which Congo followed. This transformation startled him, but he didn't question her affection. He encouraged it, wanting to please her even more than he had previously.

Yet Ulu was unsatisfied. Laura was on her mind. Despite the risk of rejection, Ulu decided to visit her old friend. She found her by the sea at Oracabessa. Laura had adapted Ho's habit of exercising after lunch, walking the beach in solitude to refresh her mind.

Laura sat on the sand with her feet in the water. A shadow crossed her line of vision. She lifted her head, squinting in disbelief. Restraining her joy at seeing her old friend, Laura made space for Ulu on the open expanse.

"I wanted to talk with you, Laura," Ulu started.

Laura silently smiled.

"I don't know exactly how to start, Laura, or even if you want to talk with me."

"It has been hard for me, too, Ulu."

"Yes, I imagine."

"I don't entirely blame you. I take it that Rex put you up to hurting me. And maybe I am at fault, too."

"You at fault, Laura? No, not you; and not Rex either. I did it all."

The sun cast their shadows on the water where they danced, changing from one silly form to another. Ulu watched the shadows.

"You, Ulu! Did you plan this whole thing?"

"Yes, Laura. I did."

"I find it hard to believe you!"

"Why is that so? I find what I have done hard to live with."

"Why, Ulu? Because if you can do such a thing, what must I be capable of?"

"Husband stealing!"

"Please don't say that, Ulu."

"Well, maybe I shouldn't."

"Then don't!"

"I didn't say that to hurt you, Laura. I did that already. I tried to destroy your business. I came here to make peace with you and to ease my mind."

"Then make peace and don't stir up more trouble."

"I do not know how to do that. But I do want to get through this."

"What 'this?' If you did me wrong, and you want to admit it and say you are sorry, then say so. But do not accuse me of stealing your husband and expect things to be better."

"Well, maybe I didn't mean it that way, Laura."

"Say what you mean, Ulu."

"I want to talk about you and Congo."

"What about Congo and me?"

"I didn't understand what you saw in him, why he spent all his time with you, and why he couldn't let you go!"

"What I saw in him? You asked what I saw in him? I didn't analyze him, Ulu. I accepted him. To this day, I do not know all of what made me cling to him at Providence Pond. On that day, he was my first love! Do you know that? I loved Congo then, and you hated him. Do you remember that?"

"Yes, Laura, I remember that. But my feelings were not clear then, and he had an interest in me."

"I loved him then, and gave myself to him. Do you know what that means, Ulu?"

"I don't know what it means to you, Laura."

"Well, let me tell you. I made myself a present to him. I was his in mind, soul, and body."

"That's more than I can do."

"When you love, Ulu, giving is easy."

Ulu started to cry. She didn't sob, but her tears were heavy, rolling, stopping, and finally speeding down her cheeks.

"Well, it's not what I saw in Congo. It's what and how I gave and how he responded. He has always treated me with respect, love, and appreciation. I didn't expect that much in life. And we never talked about our love. That's strange. We never doubted, never questioned, just shared."

"No wonder he couldn't break away."

"Yes, it was hard on me, too. We spent hours on end, and mostly not in ways one might think. Most of it was simply talking, dreaming together, until we became like one. That was my mistake. I just let myself go, blending in with him. And he made it so easy!"

Ulu wanted to ask whether or not Congo had ever mentioned her. What if Laura responded in the affirmative? She would then have to probe. Would Laura surrender to her? On the other hand, if their conversation didn't include her, should Ulu consider it that she had been unimportant to them? Either way, she saw herself holding a losing hand. She left it to wondering.

"So, Laura. You claim you had him before me. And from what you just said, it seems you were not only his first but also his real wife. Now, are you still?"

"Not in the same way, Ulu. I have Ho to fall in love with now, and Congo respects us."

"You married Ho without loving him?"

"It will happen, Ulu. It's just his outside that's crazy, Ulu. He is absolutely wonderful. It would honor me to bear his children."

Silence fell between them. Were it not for the murmur of the sea, all would have been absolutely quiet.

"I am sorry to hurt you, Laura."

"Well, a part of it is my fault, too, Ulu. But this has been good for me. At least, that's what Ho keeps telling me."

The women laughed, remembering moments of their old friendship.

"I love you, Laura. And I must say you have started me on a new lesson here," Ulu said with a giggle.

"It's a lesson for both of us, Ulu. We just have to let it grow."

Ulu looked at Laura whose face glowed in the sunlight. Laura seemed at once sincere, principled, and kind. "Thank you, Laura."

"No, Ulu. We all have Providence Pond to thank. I do not know how these things happen or why. It must be that each of us carries all the seeds of life in us. But how we make some sprout and grow, why we kill others even before they bud or while blooming, I do not know. But whatever it is, this I can tell you: we sure can learn a lot from them. And as far as it goes with Congo and myself, Ulu, I let that seed grow, so I am responsible."

"You are so wise, Laura. I am glad to have you as a friend."

"Yes, we have a lot to look forward to, Ulu."

"But it would be good if we could do something together again, Laura."

"What can we do, Ulu? You have a bakery and I sell cloth and jewelry."

"So how is that working out?"

"Slowly, Ulu, very slow. Now that the war is over, everyone wants to wear readymade clothes."

"Yes, that is the fashion now. So why not give it to them?"

"I can't sew, Ulu. And I do not want to learn now."

"You wouldn't have to. I know a few good tailors whom we could hire."

"That's too much work."

"If you have the space, I could make it work."

"Well, there is the old produce house by the store."

"Let me have it, Laura. And I know just the person to head it up for us."

"Who is that?"

"Charm. You know Charm. She is a wonderful woman. She could take the orders and work with the customers."

"The people don't want homemade clothes, Ulu. They want clothes with a label."

"We have one: 'LU' apparel."

"For you and me?"

"Yes."

"So why not 'LUV' clothing?"

"The 'V' for victory?"

"Yes!"

"That's good, Laura. You know, Charm will have her baby soon. By then, I will have the sewing room ready and the tailors hired."

"Did you say Charm is having a baby?"

"Yes, Yoofi is the father. They are making plans to marry."

"Wonderful! But I think Ho needs Yoofi as his supervisor."

"Well, he has been making other plans, but we will see. I don't see why he wouldn't take it. After all, it would place him close to Charm."

"But, Ulu. If you give up Charm, who will take care of Princess?"

"I will, Laura. I think that's long overdue."

"And your work, in your business, Ulu?"

"Oh, I am sure Congo will find suitable workers to replace me. I want to spend all my time with my family now, Laura."

"You seem like a changed woman, Ulu."

"I suppose you had something to do with it, Laura."

"Maybe. But certainly Ho, Congo, and everyone else as well," Laura said, smiling.

The two women stood up. Laura started, and Ulu followed her, casting sand at the shadows still dancing on the water. They soon looked at each other with childlike smiles. After a long, long hug, they walked back to the store.

Shortly afterwards, Ulu bade farewell to Laura and headed home.

Children Dreaming

As soon as Ulu returned from her visit to Laura, she called Yoofi and Charm to the dinner table in the kitchen. She told them of her discussion with Laura and asked if they would consider the new plan. She also wanted to know if they had made up their minds about marrying.

Charm told Ulu that they had decided to think about it separately, then meet for a final decision. They needed more time.

Time came and went. The following Wednesday was a beautiful afternoon, with pure golden light filtering across the treetops. Charm and Yoofi went to the hill behind the house. Though the hill was not particularly lofty, neither of them had ever climbed it. Both wanted to. Hand in hand, Yoofi and Charm climbed the hill, each bound to accomplish their common goal.

At the top a panorama opened with vast meadows extending for miles around them. It at once alarmed and stimulated them to realize how the house where they lived fit in with all else around. As they looked farther out toward the horizon, they could see the sun falling behind curtains of distant foliage as flocks of snow-white birds streamed across the sky.

"I will soon have a name for the baby," said Charm, as they walked hand in hand on the flat of the hill.

"How can you have a name and you do not know if it will be girl or a boy?"

"Oh, it's a girl all right," replied Charm. "That's what I have been hoping for."

"Ah! Me, too," replied Yoofi, "and I hope the second will be a boy."

"Yes, I knew you would say that. But what will we want for a third?"

"A boy again," suggested Yoofi.

"A girl, just like we started with."

"Well, twins then. Lets go for twins."

"Twins? You can't be serious!"

"Twins are good."

"You have them then!" laughed Charm.

The couple walked on in silence for a while.

"But where will we live?" Charm asked.

"First, I will become a tailor and have my own shop."

"A tailor?"

"Yes, first class. Mammy will show me what she knows, and then I'll find the best tailor and finish up with him."

"I thought you wanted to be a police officer."

"No. I do not like that. But don't misunderstand me. They helped me quite a bit. In three months I will graduate with a certificate that will allow me to join the constabulary, or the army, or get a government job. I like the drilling; it helps me to dance better. And the bright nice uniforms. But I do not want that kind of work."

"It is good that you know what you want, Yoofi, but you seem to put so much into it. I watch you do the drills by yourself, and you study so much."

"I do like the drills. Now our team drills with long, heavy sticks. Next they will give us the guns to drill with. I like that, stick fighting, wrestling, and karate. But I do not want to do that for the rest of my life, Charm. Plus, when I become a tailor, we will be close together all day. Won't that be nice?"

"Yes, Yoofi. But Uncle Congo will be disappointed in you."

"No, Charm. I told him already, and he said it was up to me to choose my profession. He only wanted to make sure I finished my education first."

"Oh! So you really want to become a tailor."

"Yes, Charm. Aunt Ulu's idea is good. What do you think of it?"

"I like it all right. We could work together: you in the back, making clothes and putting labels on them, and me working at the desk. You know, you are right. We could work hard. We could have our own store and our own home."

"Yes, now you see what I mean."

"Yes, Yoofi. But now I mean, after the baby is born, where will we live?"

"The baby could stay with Mammy in Providence. We could stay in the cottage at Miss Hene's on the weekends when we come to be with the baby. During the week, we could stay with Aunt Ulu."

"Do you think Aunt Ulu would let us stay with her?"

"Well, either there, or we could rent a place near the business."

"Yes, that would be better."

"So I will ask Uncle Congo to rent us one of his houses in Oracabessa, and we can live there during the week."

"That would be nice."

"So everything is set then," said Yoofi, turning to kiss Charm.

"Not altogether, Yoofi."

"What did we leave out?"

"The marriage, Yoofi. The marriage."

He paused. Ho and Laura's reception crossed his mind. He thought of Providence Pond and the hours he had spent there. They were the best days of his life. He thought of Shep and Lev and felt only joy.

"At Providence Pond," he shouted.

"Yes, I would like that."

"We could get married and have the ceremony there."

"Yes, and Aunt Ulu will make the cake for us!"

"Yes, it will be the best wedding in the world, and I will invite every-one we know."

"You make me happy, Yoofi."

He turned, facing her fully, kissed her, and said, "I love you, Charm." He held her close to him.

"You know," Yoofi said, "Mammy may not remember you, and Miss Hene and the rest do not know you."

"Yes."

"Wouldn't it be nice if you could come with me to Providence this weekend? You would meet everyone."

"I would love that, Yoofi. When should we leave?"

"Friday! Let's finish our work early and leave on Friday afternoon.

We will take the shortcut by the pond, stop by Miss Hene's, and then go to see Mammy. Everyone will be glad to see you. They will make you happy, Charm."

"Okay, Yoofi," Charm said, hugging him again.

"I love you, Charm," Yoofi said, holding her face between the palms of his hands and looking fully into her eyes. "I love you and the baby and, no matter what happens, I want you to remember that, Charm."

They held each other for a while, not saying more. Charm started to tear and then, managing a meager smile, said, "It's getting late. We should go back for supper."

"Yes, and tell Aunt Ulu and Uncle Congo the news!"

They rushed down the hill to share their happiness.

The Joy of Patsy Blue

Farmer Leroy Kendal had first asked Patsy Blue to help with the children and then later with Ama. From his earlier relationship with her, Leroy came to adore her good, forgiving nature. The more Leroy thought of hiring a helper, the more Patsy's kind ways stood before him. Leroy remembered their torment when Patsy shared his house and considered an offer of employment as his way of making amends. After their separation, Leroy drifted into Providence while Patsy entrenched herself more deeply in the Kumina movement at Galina.

Patsy lingered on the question of closeness to the woman who had replaced her in Leroy's life. Many years had passed, however, since they had fought, since he had beaten her, and she had left him. Patsy wondered if Leroy had changed. She had long forgiven him for his cruelty and had, in fact, forgotten him as a lover. She now thought of Leroy, instead, simply as an old friend.

Of late, Leroy haunted his old taverns in Galina and left word of his need for help with his desperate family and his desire to reconnect with Patsy. Detective Graham soon assisted in finding Patsy Blue for Leroy.

His constant pleading, his crying for help, not for himself but for his children and his sick wife, soon struck Patsy as something she should do, if not for Leroy, then certainly for the sick and weak. Leroy's cries had also come at a time when Patsy had grown less able to find work and to provide for herself.

Leroy was sure he needed Patsy's help. He was not sure if he needed more from her. At the start of her employment with the Kendals, of which Ama and Miss Hene approved, Patsy came to the house only to wash and iron the clothes and care for the children. She returned home each evening. After some time, seeking companionship for herself while Leroy drank at the *Any Questions* and to reduce Patsy's excessive and unnecessary travel, Ama suggested that Patsy sleep on an extra bed in the boys' room. At first Leroy didn't like the idea, but, seeing the benefits, he agreed.

In the meantime, Ama had moved her sewing to the small utility room adjoining the living room. There she would crochet, mend torn clothing, and do things for the house. She loved the room for its privacy and isolation from the flow of traffic in and out of the main house.

Ama's health was not steady. For long intervals, maybe months on end, she was well enough to move about by herself, even without the aid of crutches or walking sticks. At other times, she would be so paralyzed and clutched by pain, she couldn't move and had to be lifted from place to place. Leroy had the doctor visit her periodically. Apart from saying what was wrong – that her arthritis was worsening – Doctor Singh increased her dosage of painkillers, which further upset her stomach.

Many home remedies were tried. Diets of seaweed, diets of fish, eating chalk or limestone, and lots of sunshine were recommended. It was never clear how much of each or which combination was best, so many were tried. Nothing worked, except excessive sunshine and soft breeze, which made Ama contented. Leroy kept his distance from her. He had long ceased to look to her for gratification. He grew to treat Ama as an invalid and thought of her with pity.

Added to this, Dean and Agu despised Ama. Although they couldn't clearly say why, they knew it concerned Yoofi. Dean, her middle child, had been weaned early for Agu's sake. What really happened was that Yoofi fought to keep a breast he considered his. Agu's rapid growth demanded constant food. He was larger and more aggressive than the gentler Dean and so easily maintained ownership of the other breast. Dean was left feeling abandoned. With that originated an early resentment for his mother. He had never, without knowing why, forgiven Ama for rejecting him. Agu grew with the feeling that Ama loved Yoofi over him and hadn't forgiven his mother for not treating him or Dean with the same love she showed Yoofi. They understood that Ama loved Yoofi because he was her first child, and so they were doomed to a lower rank of love and consideration.

With her health failing and, with it, her usefulness, the children grew closer to Miss Hene. As their dependence on Ama waned, they thought less and less of her. Ama's work in the deserted utility room was soon seen as her self-isolation, the prison she deserved; and the children rarely visited her there. In her lonely room, Ama hummed and worked as her pain allowed her, escaping the rejection of her husband and children. There, Ama would have been totally dejected were it not for the care and love of Patsy Blue.

Over time, Leroy complained to Ama – and this was his only complaint of her – that her constant crying from pain at night kept him awake. To alleviate Leroy's lack of sleep, Ama began spending increasing time on the cot in the utility room. Soon it became her bedroom.

Ama asked Patsy to move more and more of the things from her former bedroom to the utility room. Her brush and comb, her clothing, old letters, slowly filled one carton after another until the move was complete. Leroy was happy!

At first Patsy kept a safe emotional distance from both Ama and Leroy. She did whatever she could not to rekindle the love she once had for Leroy. She also thought Ama might have reason to distrust her. Patsy was happy to do her work, not mingling unnecessarily. After a while, after working long periods with Ama, taking food to her, taking her to get sun, or making her bed, a relationship sprang up between the women. As they traded stories, they developed respect and a deepening appreciation for each other.

Patsy Blue had even confided to Ama that, since the mysterious disappearance of her sister, Zadie, she had never found anyone with whom she had felt so comfortable. That made Ama especially happy since, to her, Patsy Blue's friendship had replaced the companionship she had once shared with Yoofi. Ironically, Patsy Blue was the only friend Ama had in her house.

Time went on and Patsy visited the *Any Questions* after work. Before leaving the house, she first made sure the boys had their homework done, Ama had been fed and was comfortable; and, finally, the boys were in bed. Patsy Blue then prettied herself and sauntered to the tavern, where she expected to be called upon by some of the eligible men of Providence.

At the tavern, Patsy and Leroy kept their distance. That was easy since Byah, the rumba box and fife musician, had already signed for her. Patsy loved him and he understood it. Knowing that he might want to visit her at work, complicating the delicate balance there, she declined his proffer of love, asking for time to consider. She would sit with the younger men, dance when asked, or otherwise talk with some of the women. Leroy played cards or gambled. They led separate lives in the house and at the tavern.

Where life differed at first was on their way home. It would be expected that, since they returned to the same house, they would walk together. There were times when Byah offered to walk her home, but Patsy rejected, preferring to walk with Leroy and not wanting him to think she would bring men onto his property. She had once learned how territorial Leroy was and did everything not to arouse his ire. Many of Patsy's prospective pursuers understood and, though they danced or dined with her, refrained from accompanying Patsy home. This left the way clear for Leroy.

For months Leroy had walked home with Patsy, keeping his hands and mind disciplined. He did so because, when the tavern closed, the still lively crowd followed them past Leroy's house. Jealous, suspicious eyes watched.

Time moved and, with it, sentiments. So, after a while, gazes subsided; any decorum the stares had established and maintained gave way to temptation and lust. As soon as he entered his property on the long path to the house, his attitude towards Patsy Blue changed. So, too, did hers towards him. She offered her hand and he couldn't refuse. As he accepted it, feeling her warm, familiar touch, memories of her pleasure flooded his mind. In the darkness, on the safety of his property, they embraced and found each other again.

In the beginning it was only a kiss, with Patsy freeing herself and running toward the house, or else pushing him back when his hands strayed and her defenses weakened. Leroy, who had tried to kill his sexual energy with alcohol and gambling, soon found a sweeter solution.

Leroy gave Patsy money for expenses at the tavern. At first Patsy refused. But for how long could such a pure temptation remain untouched? Some would say Patsy Blue slid; but because of that, she had more fun than anyone at the tavern, fun that cost her nothing! Patsy ate less and drank more, and Puncus St. John preached. He questioned, complained, and then warned; but the spirits did not care!

One night when Patsy had had more than she should, not that she was drunk, but enough to destroy her inhibition, Leroy led her to his bed. He laid her down and she slept. He didn't touch her inappropriately, nor did he make any requests of her. He simply laid her there and she slept.

During the night, when Patsy realized where she was, she made the correction to her usual bed.

After that night, Leroy frequently sent Patsy to his bedroom to fetch or do things for him. This he did until Ama and the boys became familiar with Patsy's access to his bedroom. On occasion, he spoke to her in there, first with the door opened and after a while, with the door closed. The inquisitive boys might burst in on him, but Leroy would welcome that. He wanted to show that everything was kept in order, even with the door closed. In the past, Leroy had forbidden Patsy from entering it and had spoken of it as Ama's bedroom. Patsy would have entered the room only if requested by Ama.

After months, it became known that Ama's room was no longer forbidden to Patsy. In fact, even Ama took it for granted that Patsy had work or some rightful access to her bedroom, though not into her bed. Ama had no reason to question Leroy or Patsy's behavior. Neither did Puncus St. John, nor the boys, nor any of the town's folk.

Time had been good for Leroy and he knew it. So, with everyone's blessing or blindness, he not only led Patsy into Ama's bedroom at night but into Ama's bed. They loved; and the boys loved having their room back, with all of Patsy Blue's things moved permanently into Ama's bedroom. Leroy had taken Patsy Blue for his common law wife. Ama knew.

Once it had been Ama's cry of pain that prevented the house from sleeping at nights. Now it was Patsy's long moans of joy that awakened it. The children didn't know why Patsy's joy sounded the same as their mother's cry of pain. Neither did they know how to ask. Ama knew, but she didn't ask. She couldn't!

Now Ama should have had another kind of pain, but strangely, she did not. Patsy's pleasure was now linked to hers, for in the mornings, it brought her companionship, help, and love: the only love Ama knew in her own house.

This Ama thought of as the joy of Patsy Blue.

Stepping Rage

Yoofi and Charm, trusting in time to bring their fateful Friday to them – the Good Friday when the couple would travel to Providence so that Yoofi could introduce Charm – waited, and waited. Finally that appointed Friday afternoon came when Yoofi and Charm kissed their Aunt Ulu and Princess and bade them farewell. He would return to Jacks River following the Walk in Providence on Saturday.

Ulu, with the presents of openness and appreciation that had recently been given to her, packed clothing and toys for her nephews and her new Aunt, Ama. She even wrote the words "To my sweet Aunt Ama" on the package that was intended for her sister. In addition, Ulu made her horse available to Charm. Yoofi rode one of Congo's stallions.

It was a happy time for the couple. The feelings they'd had on the hill surrounded by the golden sunset remained with them. Everything seemed so right as they headed down the slope to Providence Pond with Yoofi showing Charm where Shep and Lev, his dear uncle, had been buried. Not wanting to lose time, he hastened up the other side of the embankment and made his way, unannounced, into Miss Hene's parlor.

Miss Hene greeted them with smiles and refreshments and quickly showed them their room. Kwame took the suitcases to the bedroom while Miss Hene, still hugging and kissing the new arrivals, told Yoofi to go and see Ama, then come back with Puncus St. John and the rest of the family for dinner. Miss Hene liked having her Family with her.

With Kwame handling the horses for Yoofi and Charm, the lovers walked across the meadow to Ama's house. It surprised Yoofi how small it looked. On reaching the steps to the doorway, Yoofi lifted Charm and took her up the stairs into the living room.

His first view was the opened door to the utility room where Ama sat. He brought Charm to her feet and, holding her hand, quickly walked towards his mother. Immediately, and as if she had never been sick, Ama leaped to her feet and hugged Yoofi. She recognized Charm and remarked how closely she resembled Esi, her mother. With her legs beginning to fail her, Ama sat back on the cot. Charm sat beside her.

Yoofi soon recognized that the utility room had now become Ama's bedroom. He was terribly surprised and hurt by what he saw, but didn't understand what had transpired to convert that dejected space.

Wanting to find out, he quietly left Ama and Charm chatting. First he peeked into his old bedroom to find Kwame and Agu locked in a game of arm wrestling. Yoofi smiled with amusement and delight, then silently closed the door unnoticed, leaving their game intact.

Next, Yoofi opened his mother's former bedroom door. There he saw Patsy Blue dressed only in her underwear, arising from her afternoon nap. Yoofi was at once startled and angry. He surmised what had changed in his absence.

"Who are you and what are you doing here?" he asked Patsy angrily.

"I am Leroy's . . ." Patsy said, struggling to remove the sleep from her lips.

"Leroy's what! This is my mother's bedroom. You can't stay here." Having said that, Yoofi started throwing Patsy Blue's belongings out of the room.

Just then Agu, who had been playing with Dean and Kwame, sprinted out of the house to the *Any Questions* tavern. He ran the short distance and, upon running up the steps, yelled through the door: "Daddy, Daddy! Bigboy is throwing Patsy out!"

"What? What the hell . . . !" And grabbing his hat, the very one with the tall feather that Yoofi had given him on his previous visit, Leroy rushed out of the tavern to his house.

"Walk, Leroy. Walk!" Puncus St. John shouted at the enraged Leroy.

Charm, frightened by the rapidly unfolding events, sat quietly by Ama's side, not knowing what to do. She shuddered to share in the commotion. Ama held her close, as if waiting to explain.

It didn't take long for Leroy to judge what had happened. Most of Patsy's things were already on the front porch; and Yoofi, as furious as he had ever been, was throwing her remaining suitcase out. It hit Leroy and bounded off the porch onto the ground, littering it with her delicate clothing.

"Pick it up, Bigboy. Pick it up!"

"Yoofi Isaac King is my name, Leroy!"

"Yoofi Isaac King?" Leroy leaned back and laughed. "Pick it up, Bigboy."

"You pick it up and get her out of here, Leroy. This is my mother's house. I will not allow you to degrade it any longer."

The commotion had brought the household onto the porch.

"Pick it up, Auntie-man," Leroy provoked. "I knew you would do something like this one day." Leroy pointed at Charm's pregnancy. "Pick it up, Bigboy! You should be ashamed of yourself."

"Shut up and get your trash out of here!"

"What did you say? What did you say!"

"I said: get out of here!" Yoofi said, pointing to the gate.

"That did it, Bigboy. That did it. I am going to teach you a lesson now, Bullcow. One last lesson, you Auntie-man, one last time!"

With that, Leroy went to his room, pulled out his cow whip, and returned to the porch. He clapped it in the air, aiming at Yoofi's head; and Yoofi bobbed beneath its rasping sting. Seeing the cloud of dust it made, Yoofi backed off from the porch and onto the grass. Leroy followed. Yoofi reversed until he was beneath the old lemon tree. Suddenly, Yoofi remembered the heavy guava stick from which Leroy had hanged Shep.

Soon after the fiasco of Shep's burial, Yoofi had returned to Shep's grave, if for nothing else, to verify the whereabouts of the guava stick which last he had seen lying there. Just as it had originally appeared, the stick had mysteriously vanished. On his return home, Yoofi discovered that the very stick, bruised from the entangled rope, was still in the lemon tree, unmoved. The stick had remained there as a reminder of yet another of his lessons. Now, like his savior, it beaconed to Yoofi.

Yoofi pulled the heavy guava stick free and faced Leroy, who swung the whip, hitting Yoofi across the chest and back. Yoofi grimaced and cowered as the cutting blows pained him. On his next swing, Yoofi caught the tail of the whip with the stick and pulled Leroy closer to him, freeing Leroy's weapon as he did.

Leroy lost his balance. Yoofi angrily swung the weighty stick, grazing Leroy's head, flying the feathered felt into the air. Leroy quickly jumped backwards. As he did, he first flung his hands up over his head, then with helpless, goggling eyes, clutched his throat in pain. Something must have grabbed him from behind, Ama thought. What could it be?

It did not matter. As Yoofi moved to strike a fatal blow, Leroy, succumbing to the pain in his throat, foamed, and fell.

Leroy never moved again. Not once did his body twitch. His life's rich, red, blood oozed from his nose and nostrils, drenching the ground where he lay. Leroy was dead.

So, too, were the dreams Yoofi and Charm had brought with them.

In less than a minute – but what seemed like an eternity to onlookers – it was all over. No one who witnessed it understood or believed what had happened.

It took some time before Yoofi came to his senses. Looking up vacantly, he saw Charm in Ama's arms. He used to be there.

Patsy, still undressed, in confusion and shock, looked at Yoofi. Was he the same Yoofi Ama spoke of with such faithful pride?

"Go to Miss Hene, Yoofi."

"I can't leave you, Mammy."

"Go!" Ama shouted at him.

"All right, Mammy," Yoofi said, walking towards Miss Hene's house.

"She will know what to do," Ama shouted.

Agu, believing that Yoofi would get away this time with murder, ran down the road to the post office. He sent a telegram to Detective Charles Graham. The telegram simply said:

Yoofi killed Leroy who is walking.

Dean lay by his still father's body and wept.

Shep trotted down the path leading to the house. He howled and howled over Leroy's dead body, then licked Dean's face before standing between the lad and the prostrate body. Soon Dean stood up and, drying his face, walked towards the women.

Shep ran to Miss Hene's. She kissed and soon dispatched him to Jacks River.

With Yoofi gone, Ama looked at the lifeless corpse before her and murmured to herself: "You could just as easily have loved him. Would that have been so hard?"

Not long after, Agu raced back. Still frightened and angry, he announced the sending of his telegram. He stood outside Ama's bedroom door trembling in the seeming boldness with which fear had smitten him.

Ama gently beckoned the still troubled child into the narrow, anxiety-filled utility room. Dean, Charm, and Patsy Blue, still partially nude, had already clustered on Ama's tiny bed. Agu came into the bedroom and, closing the door behind him, leaned against it as if unsure what to do.

Charm, with a sweet, sisterly smile and uncertain assuredness, left Ama's comforting side on which she had leaned and walked toward Agu. She gently held his hand and brought him to Ama's open arms. He sat in her lap as Charm nestled in her former position. Brooding, partly grimacing, Patsy Blue sat on the floor facing Ama. Bracing herself against the wall, she took Dean in her lap.

With the fading beams of the aging sun filtering through the closed window onto Ama's face and the wall behind her, Patsy looked up to Ama, not sure what question to ask. Soon Patsy's stare found a quiet corner of the room. Ama began: "My children, I am happy for you, and for him, too." She seemed to be looking through the closed door at Leroy's body. "He may be gone from us, but that does not make us weaker, for we are now one: first time together, but one! And now Yoofi is gone, too." Ama could no longer restrain her tears. "From the time since both Leroy and Yoofi came to me until now, this is the first time that I do not know really where they are . . . they are both gone! But my children," Ama spoke through her tears, holding out her hands across the narrow room to Patsy who eagerly joined hands with her, "My children, this must make our lives better. This we must believe. It is only a blessing we do not yet understand."

Dean, clinging to his mother, cried and cried even more as Yoofi's fate, the gravity of that awful evening, and his Ama's sentiments sank deeper in his mind. He felt lost, worried, and alone.

In that wretched, woe-begotten room, the five huddled, as if kindling for the revival fire of a nascent family. For this and her son's safe passage, Ama passionately wept and prayed.

Yoofi, in the meantime, had not gone far when an aged voice sounding like that of his grandmother, Nweka, whispered, "Step, Yoofi!"

At the same time, Yoofi felt someone holding his hand.

"What . . . what did you say?" he asked, looking around in bewilderment but seeing no one.

"Step, Yoofi. Step!
Stepping, Stepping.
Keep on Stepping.
Stepping, Stepping,
Always looking.
Stepping, Stepping
Stepping ahead.

For those whom he loved, Yoofi had always found obeying easy. He Stepped.

"Where are you taking me, Nweka?"

"We are going to Fellowship, Yoofi. But there is something I must tell you."

"What is it, Nweka?"

"You see, Yoofi, I love you very much."

"I know that, Nweka."

"Good, but I have something to tell you."

"Okay. What is it, Nweka?"

"You must know, Yoofi, that I dearly love Aunt Ama, even though she may not think so."

"She knows that, Nweka."

"Yes, that makes me happy, but I have something else to tell you, Yoofi."

"What is that, Nweka?"

"We must thank you for sending Leroy out!"

"For sending him out? What do you mean, Nweka? I killed him!"

"No, Yoofi. This is what I must tell you. You only made it possible for him to leave. You may not know this, Yoofi. But, Leroy intended to sell Aunt Ama's land, leave Providence, and take Patsy and the children with him to Galina. He had to be stopped!"

"So why did you get me into all this trouble with the Detective because of that bad man, Nweka?"

"Leroy did mean things for a reason. He was not bad, Yoofi. "

"What reason on earth could make him so mean, Nweka?"

"It was his love for Ama that made Leroy turn himself into a devil and come in to save Ama."

"I do not understand you, Nweka."

"Leroy was mean so he could help Ama. Aunt Ama was too comfortable to grow. Leroy had to nudge her. That's why he came in and married her."

"So if he was good, why did I have to kill him?"

"I didn't say Leroy was good, Yoofi."

"So what are you saying Nweka?"

"That, most of all, Leroy was forgetful."

"What do you mean, Nweka?"

"Leroy forgot what his true purpose was, Yoofi. He became his role. He fell in love with it and what it could bring him. In that way, he became lost: on a wrong path. But not anymore."

Yoofi pondered this for a long moment. Then, breaking the silence, he asked, "So what am I going to do now, Nweka?"

"Help Agu, Yoofi. That is your job!"

"Help Agu? He hates me, Nweka!"

"I know. But that's why!"

When Yoofi did not respond, Nweka said, "Is there anything else you would like to know, Yoofi?"

"No, thank you, Nweka," Yoofi said, taking time to digest what he had heard while disguising his appetite for more.

"Good, son. Good! Now . . . we go into Fellowship to help with the preparations. The big Dance is tomorrow night."

"But I can't go, Nweka!"

"Yes, you must go. That's why I am here to get you."

"But the Detective . . ."

"Just help where you can, Yoofi. I didn't say my work is over," Nweka continued, pointing to her home in Fellowship.

"We are almost home now, Yoofi," she said. "Your Aunt Kisi will see to your comfort."

Someone must have repaired the welcome sign that said "Heaven."

Flowing Congo

About sunset that evening, as Congo, Ulu and Princess sat in their living room listening to music from Radio Havana, Shep raced in. Congo quickly removed Princess from his lap where she sat. Princess reached to pet the dog as it went straight to Congo. Congo sat up.

"What's he doing here!" Ulu remarked pointing.

"Who? Shep?" Princess asked.

"Yes, don't you touch it!"

"It's okay, Ulu," Congo said.

"To touch that thing?"

"Yes, Mammy. Shep is Miss Hene's dog. I played with him at Barton House."

"Shep has been the Family dog forever, Ulu," Congo said.

"What is he doing here?" Ulu repeated.

"Let's see," Congo said, clasping the dog's face in his palms and looking directly into its eyes. "We have trouble," Congo reported. "Urgent business." He turned to Ulu while Princess petted Shep.

"Ulu," he said, lowering the volume of the radio, "Tomorrow is the Walk."

"Yes, Congo. I know."

"There is trouble in Providence. I must leave now!"

"Should I go with you, Congo?"

"No, Ulu. But, please do this. Take Princess to Laura's house. She and Ho will go to the Dance. Stay there and travel with them to Providence. And when you leave, Ulu, don't lock the doors. I believe Detective Graham will come here looking . . . he is searching for proof, so let him have the house."

"I love you, Congo, and I will do anything for us. But please tell me," Ulu looked apprehensively at her husband, "is there a body in this house? Is that why Shep is here?"

"A body in this house? How honorable that would be! Of course not, Ulu! If that were the case, I would long ago have told you."

"Well, then," Ulu sighed, looking more kindly at Shep. Slowly, Ulu placed her hand over her heart and in a slow, reverent tone whispered, "What a lovely Shepherd!"

"Where will you be, Pappy?" Princess asked, as Shep wagged his tail and licked Ulu's hand. Ulu in turn patted the dog's head.

"First, I will go to Providence and help out there. Following that, I will travel to Fellowship. There I will discuss the situation with Asa and Nweka and decide what to do."

Finally, Shep looked up at Congo and moved toward the door.

"Good bye, Shep," Princess said, waving at the dog. "Good bye."

"I will soon be with you, Shep," Congo said.

"Oh! I hope the situation in Providence is not as serious as you are taking it," Ulu said. "Would you like me to follow you there, Congo?"

"Thank you, very much," Congo replied, holding Ulu's hand. "The situation is serious enough. But you and Princess will be all right with Miss Hene. I must go by myself this time."

With that, Congo hugged both Ulu and Princess and walked toward the door. "Please give my regards to Ho and Laura," he said, looking back.

"We will."

Congo readied his nag and, with Shep running beside him, galloped into Providence. The work there had already been done.

Miss Hene had collected Leroy's body. With help from Puncus St. John, Charm, Patsy Blue, and her nephews, Miss Hene placed Leroy's body on the same bed in the Barton House jail where Lev's body had been laid about a decade before.

The blood in the front yard had been left to soak into the soil and not washed away. Later, the spot was covered with fresh earth, on which no one would ever walk. A short prayer was said over the spot, and the rest of the Family, including Puncus and Byah, went to Miss Hene's house. Doctor Devinder Singh was requested. Why? Charm did not know.

The night was spent in solitude. No one ate, no one slept. Puncus St. John bathed and blessed the body with his prayers, then left it in peace.

Congo thanked the Family for its vigilance and, without delay, traveled to Fellowship.

Silence hovered over Fellowship at Congo's arrival. Supper had already been eaten, and the contingents from St. Thomas were in bed. Asa, Nweka, and Kisi, who had just seen Yoofi to his bed, sat in Father's room talking.

"Welcome home, Master Congo," Asa said, springing to his feet as soon as Congo entered the room. Nweka and Kisi stood up and hugged him.

"Would you like supper, Congo?"

"Water! I hope you have water from that old spring."

"Yes, of course," Kisi said, bringing a jugful for him.

"Thank you, Kisi."

"So is Providence ready, Congo?"

"Yes, Asa. We have a vibrant Family. I rode by the pond on my way here, and I can tell you all is fine, down to the last detail."

"Good, Congo."

"There is just one hitch, Asa."

"What?" Kisi asked.

"Detective Graham."

"Oh!"

"So what will you do?"

"Face him squarely."

"There may be another approach," Asa suggested.

"And what is that?" Congo asked.

"He should be sent away!" Nweka said.

"Sent where?"

"To Hell House! That's where he belongs."

"For what sin?" Kisi asked.

"Poor vision!" Asa explained.

"Who will do that?" Kisi asked.

"Ulu," said Congo. "She certainly knows how to send a man's soul to Hell."

Asa laughingly said, "I saw your travail, Congo."

"Thank you, Asa, but who will accompany him?" Congo asked, sharing the humor with Asa.

"His beloved, of course!" Nweka responded.

"Yes, she is the best to accompany him."

"And, how will he be guided in Hell?" Kisi asked.

"By his experience," Congo responded.

"How long will he stay in Hell, Asa?" Kisi asked.

"That depends on the Detective," Congo said. "When he is ready, he will see again."

"Yes, that's right." Asa added.

"So is everything settled then?" Nweka asked.

"By tomorrow this time, we will be Dancing," Congo said. "For now, let's get our rest."

The Family bade each other adieu and went to bed.

They all slept, but Yoofi wrote. Not knowing his fate, he composed a letter to Detective Graham.

Early the following morning, Congo awoke for his stroll. He liked going into the hills, if only to breathe. He did not get far from the compound when he heard: "Hello, Congo! Wait for me."

He looked around to find that Nweka was behind him.

"Early to rise. Ah, Congo?"

"Yes, Nweka. And so are you. Care to walk with me?"

"Why, yes, Congo." He waited until Nweka caught up with him.

"So what got you up so early, Nweka?"

"Well, Congo, I am not in a habit of disclosing myself. But since you are now the leader in Providence and I, too, am changing – even in my old age – I must tell you, Congo, I want to return home." Nweka smiled as she spoke, and held Congo's hand.

"Home to where, Nweka?"

"Providence Pond, of course, Congo."

"And who will take over from you here?"

"I have chosen Kisi."

"I see!"

"Kisi will be a fine Mother, Congo!"

"I have no reason to doubt you, Nweka, but why the sudden urge to return home?"

"Sudden?" Nweka said with a loud burst of laughter. "Sudden! That's the story of my life. But, Congo, I have been thinking."

"You will have to tell me what you are thinking if you want me to know, Nweka."

"You know, Congo, when I look back at my life, I can see that it always has been driven by a simple dare . . . just one after another, I mean. Some would say I am curious, or adventurous, but I always took that dare!"

"And what would you say, Nweka?"

"I am an old woman now, Congo. I have done more than I set out to do. With Asa, I have traveled to places I never knew existed. But after all this, there is only one place I want to be now."

"I know you are going to tell me that's home."

"Yes, Congo. I want to go back home, to the starting point, to rest."

"What a thought!"

"And I must say, Congo, I have one more dare left in me – to go back to Providence Pond and know life on the other side."

Congo had never before heard Nweka disclose so much of herself. He was taken aback by her openness and honesty. Yet he felt something was lacking. "Is that all, Nweka?"

"Okay," she replied smiling, "It's not only me, Congo. I really want to be with my friends again."

"I see."

"You may not know, Congo, but we were good friends then, like Family. Bem, Esi, Aren – the old Providence Family. And I miss them, Congo, even more now that I care for Lev and the others."

"That's quite understandable, Nweka."

"And my old house still stands! I want to share it with them. It will be a home for all of us again."

Congo stood still and Nweka turned to face him. They had just come to the crest of the hill overlooking plains that tapered down to the sea. Silken clouds touched by delicate slivers of red hovered, promising everything.

"Congo!" Nweka said as if calling him back from a dream. "I want to return home and be with my Family again!"

"And this Family, Nweka?"

"For me, Congo, Kumina will stand forever, surrounding my little Family. I just want to be with them again. Do you understand that, Congo?"

"Yes, Nweka, and thank you for sharing your dream with me. And it will be all right, so long as going back home is what you want."

He looked at her to see that Nweka was crying. Congo held her firmly in his arms until she said, "We have a Walk tonight, Congo."

"Yes," he replied, "Let's go and get ready."

They hastened down the hill and roused the rest of the house from its slumber.

Detective Charles Graham

Armed with the letter he had received from Rex and the telegram with its clear and distinct message from Agu Kendal, Detective Charles Graham gathered as many men as he could muster from all the stations and mounted an early morning assault on Barton House. Even though the telegram specifically said, "Yoofi has killed Leroy," the Detective considered Congo King his primary suspect.

It was under the auspices of the Kumina Family that his cherished fiancée, Zadie, had mysteriously disappeared. Lev had been a full-fledged Kumina follower and living in a Family house with Miss Hene as Mother when he quietly vanished. And what about Congo's rapid ascent to wealth? Was that done with the power of necromancy under the guise of the Kumina cult?

What is Kumina, anyway? Why don't they ever explain themselves? And, maybe it is wise to ask, were those bodies sacrificed to this unknown Kumina fellow, Asa . . . Is he their god? What if Leroy was sacrificed instead of murdered? Why is it always relegated to the shadows of the backwoods estates, away from the light of public scrutiny? Why? Why all the secrecy? For personal and official reasons, Detective Charles Graham had to know.

Under the cover of dawn, the men had already quietly entered Congo's cottage looking for him. The Kings' house at Jacks River had already been searched. Finding it vacant, with nothing incriminating, the Detective was sure Congo was in Providence.

When the search of the cottage proved fruitless, Charles Graham had some of his men circle Barton House while he and a few others knocked on the front door mercilessly with their batons.

"We greet you, Detective. Please come in," Miss Hene said. "How are you?"

"Fine, thank you, Miss Hene."

"Have a seat. And the officers there with you, please make yourselves comfortable. We would love to serve you breakfast."

No sooner had the men entered the room than Puncus St. John brought them coffee. Byah was not far behind with milk and sugar. The men accepted the service, noting St. John's long and seemingly undisciplined hair.

"Who is that other gentleman there?" the Detective asked.

"Byah, Detective. He plays with us at the *Any Questions.*"

"Let him speak for himself."

"He will not talk, Detective," Puncus said.

"How can that be?"

"Because he doesn't hear, Detective."

"Puncus!" the Detective said, "this is an official visit. We came here to question both you and Congo about the disappearance of Lev Tyler and Leroy Kendal. Do you understand?"

"Yes, Detective."

"So what is Byah doing here?"

"Just visiting."

"Go home," the Detective said, pointing at Byah. "We will talk separately to you if needs be."

Puncus pointed, and Byah took his leave.

As Byah left, the Detective looked at his host and said, "I am sorry, but this is an official visit, Miss Hene. Do you understand?"

"We welcome any visit of yours, Detective."

"I got this telegram," he said, showing Miss Hene the telegram from Agu.

"Did you see Yoofi kill Leroy, Miss Hene?"

"No. I certainly did not, Detective."

"Okay. So where is Yoofi now? I would like to talk with him."

"He is not here, Detective. Search if you like."

"Have you seen him? Do you know of his whereabouts?"

"No, Detective. But, I suppose he may have Stepped ahead."

"Where to, Miss Hene?"

"We do not know, Detective. It could be . . ."

"Do you mind if we look around, Miss Hene?"

"Certainly not, Detective."

Detective Charles Graham instructed his men to search the entire house and the yards for signs of fresh diggings. He surmised that if the body was not in the house, the Family might have tried to dispose of it during the night. In the meantime, the Detective questioned Miss Hene again. "Do you know where Leroy's body is?"

"Yes, Detective," replied Puncus St. John, trying to shield Miss Hene.

"Then show it to us," demanded Graham.

"Certainly. I locked it in the jail last night. Come with me; I will show you," Puncus said.

"Did you say you locked the dead body in the jail?"

"Yes, Detective."

"My God! You locked a dead body in jail?"

"Yes, Detective. Just after I bathed and prayed for it, Detective," Puncus said.

The Detective turned to Miss Hene and said: "I thought Congo told me he does not operate a jail here any more."

"He is right, Detective. It is not really a jail-jail."

"Then what is it?" asked the Detective.

"Purgatory!" said Puncus.

"If you say one more thing, St. John, I will have you arrested! I want you to know this is not a joke! It is a very serious investigation. There are two missing bodies to account for. Is that clear, St. John?"

"Very clear, Detective. Both were good friends of mine. I would surely love to meet them again!"

"I warned you, St John, not another word from you!"

"It's all right, Divine," Miss Hene said, rubbing his shoulder. "It's all right. I will show the Detective."

The group descended the poorly lit stairs and soon reached the door of the former jail.

"It's locked," said the Detective. "Where is the key?"

"Divine mistakenly left the key in the jail after he attended to the body last night, Detective," Miss Hene explained.

"Damn fool! Kick the bloody door in!" Graham ordered one of the officers.

The officer kicked the door in to find only an old, blood-soiled sheet on the cold, concrete floor and the keys on the table beside the bed where Puncus St. John had left them.

"Where is the body?" demanded the Detective.

"Good Heavens! He must have Walked early!" said Puncus somewhat absentmindedly.

"Walked, Puncus? You mean Stepped, don't you?" Miss Hene said.

"Stepped, Walked . . . where to?"

"To Heaven," Miss Hene replied.

"To Heaven. Is there a Heaven on . . ." the Detective was in the process of asking.

"No, Detective," said Divine. "That is another place. She said Heaven! He walked to Heaven. Heaven is in Fellowship. Do you understand?"

"Arrest him!" growled the Detective. "Arrest him! Shave his hair to the bone and lock him in that jail of his. Lock him up and throw away the key!"

Didn't Miss Hene give Uncle Puncus St. John fair warning about answering any questions? Apparently, he didn't learn. So they locked up the goodly Divine, the Pharisee of Providence, its first attempted Nazarite, in Barton House Jail until the Detective needed him for further questioning.

Walking

Heavy, steady, thundering drums announced Congo's arrival in Providence on the last day of Lent. He led the assembled Families from Fellowship and Galina to Providence. The group assembled on the level land above the pond.

Their first view was of the aged and massive cotton tree at the center of the meadow. It towered over everything, its robust trunk supporting wide arching branches. The shade brought respite to all those beneath its boughs. The enormous tree seemed to stand in the center of the place connecting earth and heaven.

Using Nweka's home as a staging post, Miss Hene, Ama, Congo, and their friends set out to feed the hungry.

With the eating done on that Holy Saturday, Dancing and singing followed. It continued until after sunset, at which time a bonfire on the far side of the pond flamed. A smoky aroma cascaded down the incline and across the water, reposing in silence. The scent filled the air with sweetness.

In the dark, a cool westward sea breeze brought more people out to Dance. The music got richer. Kumina drumming, led by the deep resonance of the bass thunder-drum, started. But it was not alone. Soon the repeater, the funde drum, and the syncopated, high-pitched akete drums joined. Everyone, young and old, moved. The earth shook, and the sky seemed ablaze, uniting the group and carrying their praise to glory— or so it appeared to Detective Graham. He had handcuffed Puncus to himself as he searched in the darkness for the proof he so desperately needed.

Even though Graham was absorbed in the newness and energy of the Walk, he never became distracted. He remained cold and objective, looking for proof, for truth. It was with some disbelief and disgust that he looked and saw the Monsignor, Ho, Laura, and even Watkins drawn into the ceremony. He wondered why he alone stood apart, stuck with Puncus, his interpreter.

Toward midnight trumpets wailed high above the sound of the drums, as if announcing the arrival of angels. Soon there was a parting of the crowd, and a procession led by the drummers marched across the incline, encircling the cotton tree. They seated themselves, as the drummers stooped, playing in a muted manner.

Following the drummers, Congo and Miss Hene escorted the saints from their temporary abode in Nweka's house into another circle beneath the sprawling boughs of the cotton tree. Congo's pure white robe flowed from his head, where it partly covered his face, down to his ankles. With both hands in front of him, he carried a black cross. It towered over his head.

Following closely behind Congo and Miss Hene was the entourage of saints paired to their attendants. The first duo was Lev and his escort, Ulu. Behind them were Esi and her companion, Charm. Bem and Kisi followed, then Vijay supported by Ama. Yoofi escorted Henry Isaac Love, while Laura walked with Aren Tyler. The last couple was Leroy with his arm across Patsy's shoulder. Their robes were similar; and the saints all walked alike, making them almost indistinguishable.

All were dressed in white except for Asa and Nweka; they wore jet-black silk gowns. They were the rear guard. All went barefoot.

As soon as the throng had descended the slopes, they formed a second, larger ring around the cotton tree. Congo and Miss Hene turned to face Asa and Nweka. Just then the thunder drums vibrated in deep resonance and Congo started to jump. Miss Hene joined him, as if electrified. Asa, Nweka and all the saints, from Lev to Leroy, and all their escorts started to Dance. The excitement raged and the earth rocked with Kumina spirit.

In the dim light, with bobbing shadows and crowds jostling for the front row, it was almost impossible to discern a face. The Detective pushed his way closer to the saints, dragging Puncus with him. He wanted to watch the entire spectacle. Never had he seen anything like it.

"Leroy! Leroy! Is that you, Leroy?" shouted the Detective, rushing the line to touch Leroy. Puncus pulled him back. He looked over his shoulder, seeing Patsy and Byah huddled with Ho.

"Hush, hush! Only the Messenger can speak," Puncus advised.

"Who? And who did I just see there, Divine?"

"Leroy, of course!"

"But . . . he is dead, Divine!"

"Yes. You could say that."

"And what would you say, Divine?"

"Resurrected!"

"So what is he doing here?"

"Can't you see, Detective? He is Walking!"

"Yes, Puncus . . . But can the dead Walk?"

"Yes, Detective. That's how they move. The dead Walk and the living Step; that's how Yoofi escaped you."

"You, Divine, you and all the rest, are demonic. Absolutely mad! After I clear up this mess, I never want to see you, Congo, or anyone from Providence again!"

"I understand. Some of this may be new to you, and there is a lot to grasp, Detective. But first we learn to Step, and then Walk."

The Detective looked back at Divine, puzzled, then at the procession. It continued to encircle the cotton tree, passing time and again before the crowds, until it had ringed the tree for the seventh time.

Just then a flame sprouted from within the earth and burned where Lev stood. To the astonished Detective, Zadie Blue grabbed the flame and, as she did, she danced and leaped, as if infected by madness. She soon fell on the ground beside Asa, where she foamed and convulsed. Finally, she lay relaxed. As her hands opened, the flame was gone and neither burns nor blisters marked her palms. Zadie ascended into the boughs of the cotton tree and seemingly vanished.

Graham moved impulsively, pointing at the tree and asking, "Zadie! Is that you, Zadie Blue?"

"Yoofi will lead you to Zadie, Detective," Puncus said. The Detective remained puzzled, preferring to untangle that one thread of the puzzle at once. He moved again, as if wanting to go after Zadie. St. John gently restrained him until the Detective became somewhat calmer.

Congo King looked at Lev and said, "The spirit is here, my Brother. Speak, Messenger. Tell us!"

"I am the spirit of Paul Bogle," the Messenger's deep voice resonated through Lev.

"First, I must thank you Father Asa, Mother Nweka, for this large Family you bring here. Thank you for inviting me, and for providing for my residence. I must thank you all for your patience and your endurance. I know this struggle. It is not easy. Lastly, I must thank my host, Lev, for this delicate, lovely body he possessed and the good care taken of it. For I must use it if I am to appear to you in person, now.

"Not too long ago or far from here, in St. Thomas, my body hanged from a tree like a thief's. So I was sent home. Now, from the great White Light, the All-Knowing One, I return to speak to you again. I am not here because you are special, but to give you a special message for those who could not be here. I want you to convey this message by living it out. One messenger is enough!

"Live as I shall show you, that you may avoid misery and confusion, and grow into wisdom."

"Speak, Brother Paul! Speak!" came the reply from the congregation.

Paul continued with his arms lifted and his eyes closed. "If you hadn't heard this message before, friends, I would stay here a long time preaching it to you. But it is the same message I brought years ago, in the flesh as Bogle, your Baptist Minister. I bring it here again. And, maybe, if I am so privileged to visit you at a future Walk, I will bring the same again: Love. But if I don't come again, then there will be others. Their message will be the same: Love.

"One such messenger may speak like a government. He will be misunderstood and destroyed, but his message is Love. And after him will come those who talk with music and poetry, with song and dance, but still the message is Love. And it does not matter if you are small or big, young or old, yellow, black, white or in between, the message is Love. If you seek fame and wealth, seek it with Love. If you seek Love, seek it with an open heart. Let it lead your life. When you wake and when you sleep, do so with Love. And when you leave tonight, leave with Love, and the joy of the Light will follow you.

"Some may ask: Preacher Bogle, how do I live with Love? To you, I say just remember this – what I lived for and how I died. It was always in the act of giving, doing something for someone else. That's how I lived and died. But that was only a part of it.

"You will remember that Governor Eyre and his council ruled with meanness. They thought they had something to lose. They believed that what I wanted you to have was to be taken from them. Quite the contrary!

"Eyre, like some here tonight, had limited eyesight. What they didn't see was how much more there was and could always be willed into being – more than their barns could hold. Much more.

"What they didn't know was that there is a larger land of abundance: a place without limit, where wealth lives. It was there that I wanted to take you. True wealth couldn't come from my superiors. They didn't have it. What they had was selfishness. So wealth couldn't be theirs to give. Bounty could only have come through your dreams and your labor, from that place of plenty.

"But those who have and are in fear of losing live in misery. They lack faith in the miracle of creating, for it means something coming from nothing: a pond where once there was none, forests filling deserts, wealth replacing poverty, you and me, my friends! It takes special eyes to see these miracles and to rejoice in them. But once you do, you become aware of abundance and you can share and let go. You can just let go and not hold!

"Those minds of my former life blighted our prosperity; they took my life. But here I am with you again. What a marvelous creation! Now, I thank the Governor for my death and you for my life! This thing called Love will make you do that.

"And to Love, you don't have to travel far or do anything great. Beside you, right now, there is someone wanting something. If you can, quench that need, do not question it. There is no reason to say that person is lazy or wasteful or wants something for nothing. Just consider. What did we give for our talents, our dreams: for ourselves?

"Do not question or condemn any need. Don't judge; just satisfy the want and be thankful it showed itself to you. Release everyone from misery, violence, or ignorance – the one closest to you. Comfort someone – the one nearest you. Remember: smiles bring hope and joy. So here is one of mine." He smiled.

"There is no reason to wait for service. You first provide, expecting naught. Love is not a business. It is not giving and expecting. It is knowing that you are the giver and the taker, the strong and the weak, the cursed and the blessed. For there is only one Light. And in it all things are unified, good and bad, up and down, right and wrong. In it there is only being, and no judgment: no hell or heaven, rich or poor. It is from that one Light that I come as your messenger.

"So, in the spirit of Kumina, knowing that there is no division – either in life or in death – go forth and Love."

His hands lowered as the bonfire threw cinders of light high in the night sky. The crowd grew silent, and the burru rhythm, as if toning from the depths of the earth, drummed a solemn, eternal beat. A slow incantation started from the singers. The crowds soon followed, as the saints marched back to Nweka's house, led by Congo King. Asa still stayed at the rear.

At the top of the hill, Congo looked down at the joyous throng. His eyes caught Graham, still hitched to his friend, Puncus. Congo wondered if St. John could steer Graham as he had guided him when Congo first came to Providence.

Detective Graham, weary and still bothered by what he had seen and heard, walked about in contemplation for a long time, taking the willing Puncus along with him. By then, the saints had been returned to Nweka's care. It was some time after that the Detective found his speech.

"Good heavens! What is this place, Divine?"

"You said it, Brother Charles. Did you find what you came for?"

"Yes . . . yes. I mean *no*! No, I mean, Divine. Leroy, the dead man is Walking, I still do not understand. And is that Yoofi I see going there?" He asked pointing at Hell House.

"He is tired, Detective. It is time for his rest," said Miss Hene, joining them along with a part of the Providence contingent.

"But, you should know, Detective," the Doctor said, "what we have seen is not for our understanding. This is for our enlightenment."

"Yes, a true religious experience," added Monsignor Silva.

"That's what the church is for . . . to teach religion. Clearly, Reverends, this is necromancy! It is a cult. It is illegal!" stated the Detective. "I hope you now understand why the authorities want to ban it. And that's what I intend to do!"

"You shouldn't, Detective," said Ho. "I go to church, too. And I get a doctrine, but never enlightenment. To be taken out of myself, transformed . . . this is religion!"

"This is just Kumina madness! Are you all forgetting your roots? We are Christians! Who will help me send the bunch of them to hell? Who?" asked the Detective. When time passed and the Detective was sure no one would respond, he asked, "What do they have that we don't? What do you get out of this crazed affair?"

"It's all in the drums, Detective," said the Monsignor. "There is a message in the drums for you and for me, Graham. We just need to follow it."

The Detective didn't seem to understand or care. He simply wanted to apprehend and question Yoofi. "I must be leaving," he said. "I am going after Yoofi. And he better lead me to Zadie, Divine!"

"You are such a man of the world, Detective," Monsignor Silva said.

"I have my duty. I am searching for the truth. Proof, Monsignor!"

"It does seem so, Graham."

"Let Ulu accompany you, Detective," Congo said.

The Detective released Puncus and walked with Ulu toward Nweka's guesthouse. He looked back and saw Shep following them.

"Whose dog is that, Ulu, and what is it doing here?"

"Why, Detective? This is Shep, our Family dog!" Ulu replied. "He must be looking for Yoofi."

Graham did not respond. As soon as the Detective entered Hell House, the weight of his long, disconcerting day took hold on his spent energy. An old, haunting aroma also greeted him. He searched the small house. He did not find Yoofi or the source of the perfume. But feeling tired, he sat.

"May I bring you refreshments, Detective?" asked Ulu.

"Yes, thank you, Ulu," replied Graham.

As Graham watched Ulu close the door, he saw an envelope there. He got up, took it, and saw it was addressed to him. He returned to his chair, opened it, and read:

Dear Detective Graham:

Now that my future is murky, I am looking to help my wife and my baby first of all.

The second thing I want is to tell you that I changed my name. I want you to know this, so you do not think I am hiding from you. The main thing I must do is to see that my family has their right name. The next thing is that I want to live so as to clear their name as well. And one last thing, Detective, I want you to know I really love myself and Aunt Ama and Uncle Congo and his name.

I must also tell you that when, as a toddler, my schooling was over, you took a chance on a simple Quashie and made something out of me. I hope you are not disappointed in me now, and I also wish to show you thanks.

But there is a bigger chance you must take on me and believe that I did not kill Leroy. I came from a safe place to tell you this. If you believe me, you can go in peace, knowing that your job in Providence is done, except for one thing. You didn't get to know my Family. Such a pity! But it is not too late, if you would only risk going to the Walk as a person and forget about being a Detective for a night or so.

But for that you would need a really good friend or a teacher.

I hope my Family will be of help to you. Now, please let me know if I should turn myself in to you as a criminal or just go back to work for Aunt Ulu on Monday. I will do whatever you want, but remember I did not kill Leroy.

I hope you find this note satisfactory.

Faithfully Yours,

Y. I. Love

More than anything else, Graham needed time to reflect. But most of all he wanted to rest. Ulu departed the building and, looking back over her shoulder, saw the Detective remove his hat, wipe his brow, and walk towards a comfortable seat in a dim corner of the room.

Ulu silently slipped out with Shep and Yoofi walking beside her.

Then Zadie Blue, his betrothed beauty, returned to the Detective. She came with glowing gray eyes and long, flowing blond hair. She stood before him. Rapt in amazement, the Detective followed as she took his hand and led him to her private chamber. They didn't talk. He didn't understand. The love of his youth had returned, and whatever he wished she obliged. She wanted to give what Charles had always yearned for, full understanding of herself. Charles would take it and then talk. She let him. And in the stillness of the candle-lit room, the lovers hugged, kissed and shared an eternity of bliss.

The pace of the music picked up and the drums talked until late the following afternoon, when the weary crowd slowly left Providence.

Detective Graham had no intention of parting from Zadie. They were late to rise. When they did, he turned to her and asked, "Is that really you, Zadie?"

Smiling, she looked at him. Graham could see the clear, shining pupils of her eyes as she replied, "Yes, Charles. It's all me."

"And where have you been all this time, Zadie?"

"Right here, Charles, or beneath the boughs of the old cotton tree."

"Hiding from me?"

"I'd rather say, in another space, looking out for you, Charles!"

"And why?"

"So, Charles, you could find me and get your promotion!"

"My promotion? I could work for that, Zadie!"

"You did, Charles."

"Ah! You must be right, Zadie. I feel perfect."

"Promoted," she said.

"We better find Congo."

"Yes, let's find him."

The couple left the house and walked down the incline toward Lev's table.

Taking Hell to Mass

Before dawn that Easter Sunday, Asa and his contingent had returned, all except Nweka. She stayed behind, tending to the saints who still remained in her house. Esi was again with her in Providence.

At the pond, the grounds were almost empty, except for the Family of Providence still huddled in conversation at Lev's table. Even Nweka had taken a break from her saintly duty to join the morning's conversation.

"I found Zadie!" Graham shouted as he approached.

"Zadie, my sister! Where have you been?" Patsy asked, leaning against Byah for support.

"Here. I have been here all this while," she said, looking up at the guesthouse.

"In Hell?" Reverend Watkins asked. "Were you in that place?"

Zadie laughed, but did not reply.

"That's the most comfortable place I know," Graham said.

"Was that the house that scared you, Watkins?" Monsignor Silva asked.

"Now, in hindsight, I wouldn't say scared. Let's just say . . . 'that was the house I didn't understand.'"

"With love comes understanding," Byah said.

Patsy looked at him with amazement. Puncus watched, amused.

"So you can talk! You can talk!" exclaimed Patsy, gently slapping Byah across his shoulder.

"If the dead can talk, why shouldn't I talk?" Byah asked, laughing.

"Well, just don't go hiding from me in Hell House," Patsy said.

"He can't, Patsy; it's now ours," Zadie said, pressing against the Detective.

"Quite so, and I will make it comfortable for you, Charles," Ulu said. "You and Zadie may have it. Don't you agree, Aunt Ama?" Ulu asked, sharing a full smile with her sister.

Ama, nodding, smiled graciously as she glanced at Congo.

"Thank you, Ulu," Zadie said, "but we like it just the way it is."

"You will have to revisit it, Watkins," Graham said.

"Yes, indeed," said Watkins. "Won't you join me, Monsignor?"

"Yes, of course. I rather look forward to visiting Hell with you."

After the laughter subsided, Ama asked, "So what do we do now?"

"We go home, Aunt Ama," replied Puncus.

"Not so fast," said Watkins. "What about Yoofi?"

"I am glad you asked, Watkins," Graham said. "There is something I must say. This has been a long journey for me, Reverend. And at the end I can say without a doubt: My search is over. I have my proof. Everything has been accounted for. Yoofi," he said, looking at the apprehensive young man, "you are innocent, sir, and free to go!"

"Not any more, Detective," Yoofi said. The Family looked astonished.

"First, Detective, I want you to know that I am very grateful for all you have given me."

"You are welcome, Yoofi."

"But I must say, Detective, I am not innocent. No, I am not innocent any longer, sir. But I am free!" Yoofi replied, looking at Charm. Her unrestrained smile turned into boisterous hilarity.

With the laughter ending, Watkins looked at Graham. "And Congo, Detective?"

"Well, Congo. I must congratulate you for giving me this journey," Graham said, shaking hands with Congo. "It brought new life to me, and a promotion as well," he said, sharing a smile with Zadie.

As the conversation stretched, not wanting to die, Ulu asked, "What happened to Princess? Where is she?"

"There," Miss Hene pointed. "She and the other children are playing in the pond with Shep."

"Oh, that pond! What a memory!" Laura said, glancing at Congo.

"I will take it to Mass," Monsignor Silva said, "and tell the world about it." He started to walk up the hill with Watkins following.

"Instead, Monsignor," Reverend Watkins said, "I'd just rather tell my congregation that Congo brought the world to Providence Pond!"

" . . . Bring the world to Providence Pond? Fancy you said that, Reverend!" Nweka remarked. "Those words are still ringing in my ear – the very thing Puncus said that Master Congo would do. Do you remember saying that, St John, at our very first meeting at this same pond? Do you remember? And fancy you would say that, Reverend."

"Ah!" Puncus exclaimed, sharing his laughter with Nweka, as he slid into one of his solitary Dances.

Ulu, with a sharp flash of her head, turned to face Congo. She grabbed him, pulling him to her, and buried her face against his heart. With a deep breath, she looked up at him and said, "You make me proud, Master Congo. You make Providence proud for building this wonderful Family."

Master Congo smiled, reflecting briefly on the hardships that brought them all together.

"Yes, and I must add, this is indeed a worthy sermon, Congo," Watkins said, trying to catch up with the Monsignor.

"And without any sacraments either, Reverend," Puncus said.

"What was that you said, Puncus?"

"A worthy sermon without the sacraments, Reverend!"

Watkins stopped. He did not move for a moment. Then suddenly he remembered what had transpired some forty years prior in that small school-office in Galina. In sharp memory he saw how he and Monsignor Silva had given their naive student, Puncus St. John, the ultimatum: partake of the holy sacraments – the only way – or leave the school! He finally said, "You know, I suppose you are right, Puncus . . . I suppose you are right. Love, really, is the only way!"

"That is good news, Reverend," Puncus said. "I will Dance to that!"

Congo and Miss Hene watched the men following the rugged, serpentine path up the hill. At once they shared the reassuring sentiment that the reverends had found their way home.

The group stood in solitude for a moment, contemplating the magnitude of what they had become.

High above, the celestial canopy glowed with embers of red and gold. Beneath, an easterly zephyr kissed the silent, silvery pond.

"Any Questions, anyone?" Puncus gently asked as he took Miss Hene's hand, preparing for their departure.

"Shut up, Puncus!" they all answered, laughing.

In solemn tears they all hugged, bidding adieu, and slowly walked up the hill.

Zadie and Charles were the last to leave. When everywhere was quiet, when all were gone, the lovers undressed and, holding hands, they walked into the pond.

Finally, they looked up at the hillside, still feeling the afterglow of the fire. The center of the hearth was still a quivering crimson. They wondered what would become of the fire . . . if it would ever die.

Family Ties

It was close to midnight that Sunday in her own house overlooking Providence Pond when Nweka started her rounds. She still cared for the bodies. Nweka had grown accustomed to them, liking each as her special, silent child. But it was Esi who still filled her life with joy.

Nweka, as Miss Hene had shown her, bathed and fed all the bodies and laid them again to rest. This time she saved Esi's, lying in her casket, Twilight, for later, for the very last. Nweka, her former wildness having been reshaped into thoughtfulness and speculative curiosity, now bathed herself. When all was at rest that night, when even the moon seemed to stand still over Providence Pond and the hills slumbered, when it was time, Nweka slowly sauntered down the path leading to the deep, crystal end of the pond. She was naked by then, clutching only a bundle of still-living cerace weed that she had coiled into a bathing pad. Fully submerged in her reverie, Nweka dipped beneath the warm, tingling water, scrubbing herself. Not once, not even twice. With her unbraided hair hanging lose, she scoured with the pad of fragrant, green herbs – still blossoming and fruited in gold – scenting herself, scrubbing, soaking clean . . . a bride before her wedding. Nweka, as if in a long parting gesture, dipped again and again, never counting, but mindful of closure. She finally arose, signaling the end.

Still trapped in thought and wonder of what lay ahead of her, Nweka finally walked from the now dead-looking water back up to her house.

Slowly, slowly, she opened the jar of black logwood honey textured with raw goat's milk and spiced with chopped herbs. Delicately she removed the small wooden spoon and tasted the nectar. That was her first taste. Nweka loved the forbidden food. She had more. With the same spoon, she fed Esi with the delicacy. They ate, she after Esi or Esi after her; Nweka could not tell.

Finally, Nweka cleaned Esi's body. She cleaned it and laid it to rest, in Twilight, but did not dress it as she had in the past. Nweka left her body bare, with Esi looking at nothing, or else, at eternity.

Overcome with an emotion she did not know, Nweka smiled at Esi as if to say *I will soon be back*. Nweka hurried to her bedroom and began a mad scramble in drawer after drawer of her old bureau until suddenly her face lit up. She found them! The very clothing that she and Esi shared in childhood still lay folded beneath her most intimate attire.

Without delay, Nweka – or more correctly, Afia, for so her parents named her – hastened back to her friend. Esi lay there, with her eyes fixed on her own toes, but inwardly seeing into the infinite. Afia went to the foot of the casket and, before disrobing, dangled the tiny blouse and skirt before Esi. Slowly, and as if drawn from glory, Esi's eyes strayed up at Afia.

"Do you remember?" Afia asked.

Without a word, Esi issued a faint, everlasting smile that filled the room with joy.

Afia, still naked and clutching their childhood garments, climbed into Twilight. It was a wide mahogany casket with red inlaid cedar. She lay with her head beside Esi's feet. Their eyes, as if seeing eternity, were fixed on each other.

Sharing yet another smile, Afia closed the casket.

All this time, Miss Hene and Puncus St. John had been watching Afia, first from Lev's perch and then as they silently followed the lonely sacrament from outside Afia's bedroom window. With the moonlight shining from high above, glinting on the mysterious Twilight, they looked on in silence, enamored by a sense of life and death, of cyclic continuity.

"Clean gone," St. John whispered with a wry smile.

"Yes! Gone clean in Love," Miss Hene replied.

"In Love?"

"Surely, the way to live . . . and to go."

"Quite so . . . quite so."

They whispered no more.

Puncus St. John and Miss Hene held hands as they watched. In that same solemn moment beneath the bright, golden moon, they kissed and blessed the space with Love.

Afterword

Jamaica: A Historical & Cultural Perspective
A Brief Overview

General Background

In 1655 when the British defeated the Spanish and captured Jamaica, they inherited an agricultural economy based on African slave labor. Sugar, introduced by the Spanish, became the dominant product. The established government was representative, giving British settlers the right of self-rule through an elected House of Assembly. At the dawn of the 18th century, Britain was given the monopoly of Caribbean slave trade in the Treaty of Utrecht. Jamaica, the largest and most prosperous British West Indian island, became the center of English Caribbean trading activity. Initially, slaves were imported mainly from the Gold Cost (Ghana) and Nigeria; later slaves came from the Congo (Kongo: Bantu areas of central Africa). In the 1800s contract workers were brought in from the Congo. The Ashanti (Ghana/Akan) left the most indelible mark on the Jamaican cultural landscape. As slaves, African Jamaicans were neither educated nor Christianized. Ironically, their first contact with the Bible came from black Baptist missionaries George Lisle and Moses Baker. Both had been freed from slavery in America during the 1790s. From as early as the 1800s the Baptists had strongly established themselves in the African Jamaican society. Their movement continually gained momentum until post-slavery, when it became a part of yet another movement, Revival.

A series of revolts between 1729 and 1831 brought about the end of slavery in 1834. Well-established groups led some, while individual slave leaders, most of Ghanaian origin, organized others. The following resulted:

1) Drastic decline in the work force, weakening the plantation economy.
2) Replacement labor from India and China, and later indentured workers from the Congo.
3) Increased land ownership and self-sufficiency by Africans.
4) African property owners given voting rights.

The British settlers, wanting to reverse the gains made by former slaves and their new political allies, passed a series of laws which decreased or prevented land ownership by African Jamaicans, thereby reducing franchise power. By losing land, many Africans were forced to choose between plantation work and severe hardship.

Paul Bogle: The Morant Bay Rebellion.

Paul Bogle (1820-1865) had George William Gordon, a powerful landowner and member of the House of Assembly, as an ally. Gordon was of mixed Scottish and African parentage. He was also a minister and had ordained the small-farmer Bogle as a Baptist deacon. They were neighbors in the parish of St. Thomas. Edward Eyre was the presiding Governor. Bogle made many attempts at getting Eyre to change the oppressive new laws which limited or denied voting privileges and land ownership to Africans or people of mixed heritage. In 1865, Bogle led a peaceful contingent to the courthouse at Morant Bay in support of two men who were on trial. One of the men, Robert Donaldson, was convicted for stealing a piece of sugarcane. His sentence was 60 days with hard labor. For robbing a certain length of rope, the other convict, Thomas Bower, was sentenced to ninety days hard labor. The men were from Bogle's district of Stony Gut in the parish of St. Thomas. A commotion in the courthouse – when a man called out, protesting the harsh punishment – would have led to yet another arrest. With Bogle and his supporters preventing the arrest, the suspect escaped to Stony Gut. The police pursued him there but were rebuffed by Bogle's supporters. Bogle returned to the Morant Bay courthouse. A fight ensued. Police and soldiers were forced into the courthouse, which was set on fire. This became known as the Morant Bay Rebellion. Governor Eyre responded by sending soldiers to destroy Stony Gut, where Bogle's chapel stood. Bogle and Gordon were captured and hanged for plotting the rebellion. Britain responded in 1866 by instituting a crown colony form of government with its Legislative Council appointed by Britain.

Kumina

With Africans culturally isolated from the British, many aspects of their old lifestyle remained vibrant, especially on the larger slave plantations. The Kumina religion and lifestyle was one such case. Kumina, as well as other African religious forms, existed intact throughout slavery. This happened because the African lifestyle was a plantation culture within, but separated from, the larger framework of English life. Of all African cultural forms, Kumina was the least adulterated by British influence. There is not general agreement on the origin of the word Kumina or its related form, Pocomania. Some sources trace Pocomania to the Spanish words "poco" and "mania", signifying a little madness. This, however, is void of deep insight. Other sources point to Kumina as having a Twi (Ghanaian) origin from "akom," to be possessed, and "ana," by an ancestor – hence: "ancestor possession." In Congo society, therefore, Kumina practice is based on the possession by the spirits of the deceased. The belief is that the spirit of the dead responds to certain drum-calls and, on leaving its abode beneath the earth, enters the body of the devotee through the feet, endowing the participant with an enlightened euphoria. Burru and Kumina drumming styles seem to have their roots in Congo (Bantu) traditions where burru, the more secular of the two, is used as bailo or entertainment. This points to the Congo (Kongo) as the most probable origin of Kumina, being refreshed by Bantu indentured, migrant workers.

It should be remembered, though, that cultural forms are not restricted to a specific location but move with people, and that African societies have always displayed some degree of mobility. If we accept this, then we may also agree that Kumina could have moved from the Congo to West Africa and, through the slave trade, to the Caribbean and specifically Jamaica.

The Jamaican plantation became the melting pot of various African cultures. Out of this grew the Jamaican version of Kumina. The practice, however, had its greatest roots in the parishes of Portland, St. Thomas, and St. Mary. A King (or Shepherd) and Queen (or Mother) typically head each Kumina community. Kumina belief is centered on the wholeness or circle of life, true and eternal existence: therefore, ancestral possession. On sacred meeting grounds, ancestral earth spirits called by Kumina drumming enter bodies that are in travail, i.e. are made ready. In this state of Mytal, or enlightenment, these selected entities prophesy for communal benefit. This more spiritual form of Kumina is called Kikongo. Elaborate costumes along with special drumming, a unique dance style, and abundant feasting are a part of the Kumina rite. Kumina ceremonies may be public in nature, such as at weddings, or for more private, sacred occasions. Kumina villages are self sufficient, based on collective participation akin to West African models. Farming and art are the basis of wealth. Of late, Kumina rhythms have been co-opted into modern Jamaican music while still retaining an authentic spiritual content. With extensive movement of agricultural workers from farming communities to cities, the country (Bantu) lifestyle – the old Kumina culture – is on the wane, except for sparse, well-established strongholds in the countryside and a few small, yet vibrant, city groups.

For further information please see:

http://www.moec.gov.jm/heroes/bogle.htm
http://www.anancybooks.com